To Dorothy

THE HARPIST OF MADRID

Best wishes,

Gordon Thomas

Gordon Thomas is now retired and lives with his wife in London, England. He began his career lecturing in physics at King's College, London. From there he went to the Home Office to work mainly as a scientist and also as an administrator. Latterly, his responsibilities were in police science and physical security. Since retiring he has become a keen writer and this is his debut novel.

THE HARPIST OF MADRID

Gordon Thomas

THE HARPIST OF MADRID

Olympia Publishers
London

www.olympiapublishers.com
OLYMPIA PAPERBACK EDITION

A CIP catalogue record for this title is
available from the British Library.

ISBN: 978-1-84897-154-7

Cover picture: The Death of Procris by Paolo Veronese,
Musée des Beaux-Arts, Strasbourg

First Published in 2011

Olympia Publishers
60 Cannon Street
London
EC4N 6NP

Printed in Great Britain

Acknowledgements

Many people have helped me by providing information, advice and encouragement in writing this book and I am deeply indebted to them all. I have relied heavily on material provided by the Biblioteca Naciónal, Madrid and by the Hispanic Society of America. I am grateful to Stacy Owens, Library Associate of the George Peabody College of Vanderbilt University, Nashville who gave me access to a 1968 PhD thesis by Ruth Landes Pitts. This thesis is about the life and work of Juan Hidalgo, the main character of my book. I am sure that had Dr Pitts not written her thesis, which was my major source of information and references, I would not have written this novel. So I owe Dr Pitts a special mention. I am also indebted to Professor Louise K Stein, of the University of Michigan School of Theatre, Music and Dance, whose book, *Songs of Mortals, Dialogues of the Gods: Music and Theatre in Seventeenth-Century Spain*, provided many useful insights, especially about Hidalgo's musical style.

I thank my son, Gregory, who was the first to read the manuscript in its entirety and who made a number of suggestions for amendment. Greg proposed ideas for enhancing not only the structure of the novel and the English but also for enriching the plot. I also thank my sisters-in-law, Karen Teuber and Kay Sinclair, Greg's fiancée, Susan Hartland, and Jane Greneker, a family friend, for spotting a number of errors and making other suggested improvements.

I also thank my daughter, Melanie, for her constant encouragement and, last but by no means least, my long suffering wife, Janet, who has patiently shared my life through the gestation and birth of this novel, as well as giving me a number of ideas.

Gordon Thomas, May 2011

Preface

This novel is based on the extraordinary life story of Juan Hidalgo, a 17th century composer and harpist who worked in the courts of King Philip IV and King Charles II of Spain. Juan Hidalgo became the most famous Spanish composer of his time and an outstanding harpist. He wrote the music for the first two operas to be written in Spanish.

While it focuses on a person who actually lived, this is a work of fiction. The era of Spanish history in which the story unfolds, the Golden Age, was turbulent, colourful and varied. Art and literature flourished as the Spanish battled in Europe. You, the reader, may believe that what is not verifiable fact must be fiction. But you should beware. The difference between history and mystery is not always clear, especially in such troubled times.

Glossary of Spanish words

azumbre	volume measure, about 4 pints
alguacil	constable, court official
calle	road, street
carcel	prison
cazuela	part of theatre auditorium, solely for women
chacona	dance
clavel	carnation
comedia	a play containing tragedy and comedy
corral	theatre
corregidor	magistrate
ducat	unit of currency: 1 *ducat* = 11 *reales*; 1 *real* = 34 *maravedís*; 1 *ducat* = 375 *maravedís*
familiar	honorary post in Spanish Inquisition
infanta	princess
infante	prince
libra	unit of weight, about 1 pound
legua	unit of distance, about 5km or 3.5 miles
loa	introduction to a *comedia*
madrileño	native of Madrid
maravedí	unit of currency (see *ducat*)
milla	unit of length, about a mile
notario	honorary post in Spanish Inquisition. More senior than *familiar*.
paso	unit of length, a step or about a yard

pie	unit of length, about a foot
plaza	a square or market square
plazuela	a small square
puerta	door
puente	bridge
pulgada	unit of length, about an inch
quemadero	place for burning at the stake
real	unit of currency (see *ducat*)
zarabanda	dance
tercio	Spanish infantryman
titulo	member of the landed gentry
tonelada	unit of weight, about a ton or metric tonne
vara	unit of length, about a yard
villancico	popular song, often sung in the vernacular
yugada	unit of area, about 80 acres or 32 hectares
zaguan	entrance hall or hallway
zarzuela	play in which more than half of the lines are sung

CHAPTER 1

No one dared to do it before, not in front of the King. But you never knew with Marfisa. The performance was rolling along sweetly. That is, until the scene in which Arethusa bathes in a river. Acting the part, Marfisa appeared on stage in a loose petticoat, carrying her bow and with her quiver slung across her shoulder. She placed her bow and arrows to one side and sat on the floor, as if to descend into the river. She moved her arms pretending to wash herself. Then Alpheus appeared. She rose from the floor and faced the audience. 'You have seen me bathing!' she shouted. As Alpheus stopped to reply, she eased her petticoat off her shoulders and let it drop delicately to the floor.

To the amazement of everyone, Marfisa stood totally naked. A shocked gasp filled the theatre: nakedness on stage is a criminal offence. Then the audience became a cacophony of loud and rapid talking. Those who had, and the few who had not, seen the bare Arethusa made urgent exchanges. 'Did you see that?' 'Did I see what?' The local people at the back burst into cheering and shouting. Joyous celebration erupted. Many of the men had never seen a completely naked woman before, not even their wives. The members of the royal household controlled their reactions. After all, the King, King Charles II, was present and none of them knew how he would respond if they were to celebrate, too. Marfisa had stunned the royal party into silence. Our sadly disabled King, sitting only ten feet away from her, looked dazed, as if he had been struck about the head by an invisible weapon. He stared at Marfisa's delicious form, transfixed by her pretty triangle of scant hair. The Archduke's wife blushed with embarrassment. She glanced at the Archduke, as if to say, 'If you think you can see me naked, you'd better think again'. The Archduke grinned with unconcealed delight. Then a nymph of Diana appeared and covered Marfisa's nakedness with a white bed sheet. The incident was over.

This shattering diversion took place ten minutes before the curtain could be drawn. Antonio de Escamilla, the manager of the company, walked to the front of the stage, still dressed as Momo, the wise buffoon, and appealed to the audience, 'Quiet, please. We want to carry on!' He quickly regained silence and the play concluded.

The audience appreciated our performance – for more than one reason – and, at the end, people cheered and applauded enthusiastically as the cast lined up on the stage. Antonio bent over towards the actors, an arm outstretched, to signal them to bow. The hand clapping ceased as the King and his entourage stood and left the theatre. Then the rest who attended dispersed, chatting and laughing among themselves.

***

We, the players and musicians, had previously agreed to meet afterwards in Bernalda de Molinas's tavern, which is in the Calle de Cantarranas, just around the corner from the Mentidero, a well known meeting point for actors, musicians and artists. We would meet at about seven o'clock in the evening, so I had time to go home first. I live in the Calle de la Madalena so it was not far for me to walk to the tavern. As I entered, the smell of the place hit me: an accidental blend of stale beer and urine. I could pick out about half a dozen or so of our group already sitting or standing at the back. Antonio and Manuela de Escamilla, his daughter, who had played the goddess Diana, had been the first to arrive and they and Simón Donoso, the guitarist, were arguing frantically.

'What the hell was she doing?' asked Manuela. 'That isn't in the script?'

'Well, yes, it is,' replied Antonio. 'At that point, Arethusa should be bathing naked in the river. It says that in the play.'

'She shocked me,' added Simón, 'especially when she stood facing the audience, showing all her charms.'

'So you dreamt up the idea, Antonio,' shouted Manuela.

'No, Manuela, dear. Not so.'

'Well, who did then?'

At that point, and as if to calm the discussion, Marfisa entered. She had heard Manuela's question and wanted to shift any blame away from Antonio. 'I thought it a good idea to appear naked, just as it says in the play. I know we hadn't rehearsed that but I did it on impulse. I hadn't intended to stand up naked until the last moment, when I thought – what a good idea.'

'You shameless tart,' said Manuela. 'Before we started, you told me you were afraid of the Archduke and then you decide to strip off in front of him.'

Marfisa burst into tears. 'I'm not a tart. I'm a professional actress and singer. I suddenly felt I had to do it so I did. If I've done anything wrong, I'm sorry,' she said softly and still weeping.

'Now, let's all calm down,' said Antonio. 'I'm more interested in what might happen than blaming Marfisa. You and I, Manuela, run a well known theatre company and it would be better to turn this around into something positive than to be fighting Marfisa or each other.'

'I admire Marfisa for trying to keep to Juan Bautista's plot,' said Juan de Roxas Carrión, one of the violinists. 'But we may not have heard the last of this. The company could be prosecuted by the courts or even by the Inquisition. Let's face it, it would not be the first time an artistic work had been taken up by them.'

Marfisa sobbed at the mention of the Inquisition. 'Oh God, what have I done?' she whimpered.

Perhaps Juan shouldn't have touched on this subject as it unsettled Marfisa again. 'Marfisa,' I said, 'you may have been misguided in what you did, but you did it for the best intentions and we will defend you.'

'I'm not so sure about that,' said Manuela. 'I don't see why the company should suffer just because Marfisa took it into her stupid head to strip naked for the audience.'

'That's not fair,' said Simón. 'It's better that we stick together than to openly blame Marfisa.'

'Well, what do we all think?' asked Antonio. 'What shall we do?'

'I agree with Simón,' said Luis de As, also a violinist. 'We all stick together and defend Marfisa, if we have to.'

'I agree,' I said.

'So do I,' said Juan.

'Thank you, Juan,' said Marfisa and, looking towards each of us in turn, said a separate 'Thank you' to us all.

'Who doesn't agree?' asked Antonio.

'Well, I suppose we all agree,' said Manuela, who then apologised to Marfisa for calling her a bad name.

'I love you, Manuela,' said Marfisa, smiling.

'Carried: we all stick together,' said Antonio, as if addressing a formal committee meeting, 'but what should we do to protect the company?'

'I suggest we do nothing for now,' I said. 'No one at the theatre wanted to pursue us or take us to court. There were several of the King's lawyers there and they said nothing. We just wait and see what happens.'

'That sounds right to me,' said Juan, 'but you, Juan Hidalgo, are a member of the Inquisition, so is there anything you can do to help us avoid any problem?'

'Maybe,' I said, 'but let's not cross any bridges until we reach them.'

Some of the other musicians and players arrived during our discussion and joined in. The unanimous conclusion remained that we all unite to defend Marfisa but do nothing for now. We agreed that I would think about an approach to the Inquisitor General but only if a case was made against the company. Antonio bought each of us a glass of wine or ale and we all drank to our future success.

***

By the time I arrived home it was late in the evening. I went to my music room and took out a pen and some paper. I had been thinking about this book for a long time. My excitement grew as I dipped my pen in the ink. I wrote the date at the top of the page: 19 January 1678. Then I began to write this, the first chapter of the story of my life. I had something interesting to say: there could not be many men who had been a composer, a spy and a member of the Inquisition; and even fewer who had lived long enough to tell their tale.

CHAPTER 2

It started early one morning. She shrieked out loud, frequently and fearsomely. 'My poor mother. Whatever is going on?' I asked myself, not knowing what was happening or why all this yelling was necessary. Her screams put my father and me in a state of numbing anxiety. Mother was passing through a kind of hell.

At about six o'clock in the evening, the horrendous noises stopped and I could hear the cries of a newborn baby from upstairs. 'It's a boy! It's a boy!' cried out my joyous father. 'Come and see!'

I ran up the stairs, almost falling over with excitement, and with some trepidation crept into the bedroom. My mother was holding my new brother to her breast. She looked pale and exhausted. 'Let me see! Let me see!' I demanded.

Mother was just about strong enough to hold him out to show me. 'Careful, Juan,' she whispered. He was tiny and pink and wrapped in a white shawl. I climbed up on the bed and kissed him gently on the cheek. That was my first act of brotherhood.

My mother was confined to her bed for well over a week after Francisco's birth and father told me many years later that she had nearly died that day. Remembering her obvious and prolonged pain, I was not surprised. Father took me to San Ginés church, the day after Francisco's birth, so that we could give thanks. I remember father kneeling and muttering away with his hands together. I couldn't really hear what he was saying and just sat next to him in the pew and watched. Since then, I have wondered many times what agonies mother must have gone through the day I was born, on 28 September 1614, almost six years before the frightening birth of Francisco.

***

We were a close family. I used to enjoy going with my parents to see my maternal grandparents, the Polancos. They also lived in Madrid, just off the Calle Mayor, opposite the San Felipe Convent. This was a short walk from where we lived in Lower San Ginés. I went holding my father's hand, or ran a few *pasos* ahead and, when Francisco was just a babe in arms, mother would carry him. The first landmark was the church of San Ginés, which we passed on the shady side. Along the dusty streets outside the church were fruit and vegetable stalls attended by women in long brown skirts and white, stained blouses, shouting out to advertise their wares, 'A *libra* of olives for six *maravedís*, the bargain of the day.' On the steps of the church, holding out their hands or bowls, there were often at least a dozen beggars. I imagine most were genuine but some were probably not.

We usually walked down the Calle de Arenal and past the Plazuela de Selenque where there was a daily market. This was the centre of activity in our little walk. Horses dragging carts were delivering produce to the fifty or so stalls. People were wandering around looking for bargains, adding to a constant hum of fast talking as the sellers explained their products to possible purchasers. You could buy a whole range of things at the market from jewellery, wine and fruit to meat, clothes and pottery. The colours of goods on sale contrasted with the various hues of the clothes the shoppers wore. The odour of horse dung and the stench of the human excrement, tipped from windows into the Plazuela at night, assaulted my nose. But you just had to accept these unpleasant smells. The Plazuela was just around the corner from my grandparents so it was a useful place for them to shop.

As we entered their house, we bathed in a happy exchange of greetings. Our grandmother was an excellent cook and quickly put a hearty meal on the table. She specialised in a tasty dish called 'rotten pot'. This is a pork and bean stew, cooked slowly in a clay pot which is placed over a fire. The name comes from *olla podrida*, which literally means 'putrid pot' but some say it is a contraction of *olla poderida* which means 'powerful dish'. As a child, I think I would have preferred the former interpretation. There is no dispute over its tastiness, especially as concocted by grandmother, with additional vegetables and sometimes with *chorizo*. We ate it with wheat and barley bread, amid lively conversation, often about our family friends and relatives but sometimes about politics and the men's work. They would drink ale as the rest of us would sip fruit juice.

My father worked as a musician and played the guitar and the violin. My grandfather was a professional guitarist. So I had the good fortune of being born into a richly musical family. At all of our visits, father and grandfather would entertain us with a duet: father on the violin and grandfather playing his guitar. When I was small, mother would bounce me up and down on her knee as grandmother sang to the music.

Like any child, I suppose, I loved the jolly, fast pieces in which everyone seemed happy but was less keen on the sadder, slower tunes. I played my first musical notes at one of these family gatherings. I must have been about three or four years old when grandfather put me on his knee while playing his guitar. He took hold of my tiny, right hand and gently strummed it across the strings as he picked out the chords. The sound we made was just like grandfather himself made but, of course, much quieter.

'You can play the guitar!' exclaimed my mother.

'That's brilliant!' said my father.

I felt quite proud of this early effort, despite knowing that grandfather was doing the work. Little did I realise where these first few notes would lead me.

I remember that, on one occasion, while sitting and eating a meal at my grandparents' house, we could hear a loud commotion outside. 'Whatever is that?' said grandfather.

'Let's go and see,' said father.

We opened the front door to witness a small but noisy gathering of people walking along the Calle Mayor from the direction of the Alcázar Palace. The town crier led the throng, clanging his bell and shouting repeatedly, 'The King is dead. Long live the King.' We eventually went back inside and my father explained it all to me. King Philip III had died, unexpectedly it seemed, and his young son would be King Philip IV. That fateful day was 31 March 1621.

***

By then, I had already been at the San Martín Convent School for more than eighteen months. This is located in the Plazuela de las Descalzas Reales, so only a short walk from where we lived. Like most children, I imagine, I was scared to death of starting school. I had seen all those nuns going in and out of the convent wearing those strange hats and dressed in black from neck to toe. I dreaded having much to do with them, let alone sitting in front of them as teachers. They looked so deadly serious and miserable. If this was what it was like to be married to God, I for one didn't want much to do with them, or Him, for that matter. I was well dressed for my first day, if not well prepared mentally. Mother took me to the school, probably to make sure I arrived there. We were met by one of the novices, Sister Ursula de Mendoza. I was not impressed, especially when she said to my mother, 'He obviously does not want to be here. You can go now and

I'll take him.' I'm not sure who was more upset, mother or me. At least I didn't cry and I followed Sister Ursula into the convent.

She took me to a classroom on the ground floor and opened the door for me. I walked in ahead of her. 'It's Juan,' I heard a girl say. Having walked along a dark corridor to the classroom, my eyes took a little time to adjust to the light pouring through the classroom window. Then I recognised Angela, one of the Suarez twins, who lived down the street from us, as the source of the voice.

'Yes, it's Juan,' said her sister, Andrea, who was sitting a few desks away. Sister Ursula led me to a desk a few rows from the front, presumably to keep an eye on me. It was a double desk and she sat me next to a boy who occupied the other half. It was Luis de As.

It became clear to me that the Sister had left the class at work while meeting me at the Convent School door. The twenty or so pupils were learning the alphabet by rote. Sister Ursula moved to the front and said, 'You may stop your work, children. Stand up, Juan Hidalgo.' I did. 'This is Juan Hidalgo whom, I gather, some of you already know. Now sit down.' And I did. She gave me a copy of the alphabet and told me to start learning it, along with the rest of the class. Fortunately, I already knew it because mother had taught me, but I kept that to myself.

Sister Ursula taught us for the whole time we were in the infants' school. I got to like her a lot. Beneath her apparent sternness lurked a jolly and humorous individual, who could lose her temper occasionally. She featured in a number of amusing classroom incidents. Or so we students thought, even if she did not. She constantly wore a string of rosary beads. One day, she leant over a boy's desk and her string of beads became caught in it, as the boy closed the lid. A girl at the back called out, 'Sister Ursula!' She turned around towards the girl. As she did so, the string broke and beads scattered all over the floor. She soon had us all on our hands and knees picking them up. I'm sure she thought this a minor conspiracy in which these two children tricked her into breaking the rosary string. So the whole class was punished with, 'No more play for today.'

Sister Ursula created the game of 'carts and bridges'. I remember playing it one afternoon. The easel of the blackboard was one bridge. The other was Sister Ursula who stood with her legs wide apart, with her white novice's habit pulled above her knees, so we could crawl between her legs. We children were the carts and each of us crawled under each of the bridges in turn and back around the loop again. I crawled from under the easel, across the floor and then between Sister Ursula's legs. When I reached

Sister Ursula, for about the third time, my inquisitiveness overcame me. I stopped between her legs and looked up towards her smooth, bare bottom. I traversed the loop again and stopped to look up once more. This time she noticed me. 'Get moving, Juan. Get moving.' So, disappointedly, my curiosity less than satisfied, I started crawling again.

Life during my years at the Convent School was a combination of play and learning, both at school and at home. At home, my mother helped me with my arithmetic and reading. My father taught me the basic techniques of playing the guitar and the violin. It took a lot of practice before I could play these instruments at all well. But father encouraged me and spent hours helping me. To begin with, he would show me how to play scales and very simple tunes. I would practise them day after day, sometimes with him, in a duet, and sometimes on my own. I am glad that I started playing these instruments when I was so young. I was privileged to have such a good teacher.

As a freelance professional musician, my father played at some time or another, with almost all of the music groups in and within easy reach of Madrid. He played for the theatre companies and for the Royal Chapel, as well as in a number of the festival bands. He made a good living from his music and this gave our family many benefits denied to those less fortunate than ourselves. Grandfather was a native of Retortillo, a tiny village near Salamanca, and moved with his family to Madrid when he was thirteen or fourteen years old. There he met grandmother who was originally from San Sebastián de los Reyes, a town about six *leguas* to the north east of Madrid. Grandfather learned to play the guitar in Madrid and soon became skilful enough to take up playing professionally. As did father, he played in many of the local groups and often travelled to towns around Madrid to play. My grandparents had two children, both of whom were daughters: my mother and Aunt Catalina. This meant that grandfather could not pass his profession on to a son. This is why, years before I was born, he encouraged my father to become a professional musician and, as it were, to take over the family business.

My mother was totally dedicated to our family. She did everything in the house except pay the bills and empty the chamber pots. She regarded both these tasks as 'men's work' and refused to do them. Not only did she care for father, Francisco and me, she visited her parents nearly every day to make sure they were all right, too. She did not want to be totally dependent on father's income so she decided that she would make purses out of pigskin. Father used to say that 'she could make a silk purse from a sow's ear.' It was a little business that she had developed solely by herself. She had organised a table at one side of the kitchen where she sat to do the sewing and a cupboard to store the pieces of pigskin, the needles and thread and the finished items. She sold them to a lady who ran a market stall in the Plazuela de Selenque. When she wanted to sell them at a slightly higher price she would embroider elaborate patterns on them. She also did special orders to embroider initials or personal messages. I was sure her income helped our family, especially when father was between jobs.

***

By the time I was ten years old, Francisco was coming up to five. This meant we could go out to play together. We regularly walked the streets, looking for interesting things to do. I have to admit to a degree of mischievousness, in particular, to stone throwing. Rocks of various shapes and sizes, many loosened by horses, littered the streets. I remember vividly a fight we had with some other children who lived in the Calle Hita, not far from our house. I started it by throwing a stone at one of a group of three. Little did I know that these children were similarly armed and we quickly became the victims of a fusillade of pebbles. We turned and ran. Unluckily, one of these stones hit Francisco on the back of the head and made him bleed badly. I took him straight home, with blood running down his neck. Mother was furious. I told her exactly what had happened. The outcome was that Francisco and I were banned for a week from going out together. In those days, that seemed a long time. It served me right, all the same.

More trouble was to come. Once we reached the end of our curfew period, we were out together again. We had known for some time that there was a derelict house in the Calle de los Peregrinos, which was just off the Plazuela de Selenque. Through an alleyway down the side, we found a way into the house which had been deserted since the owner, a retired wine merchant, had died, and we used it as a base. We called the house 'the Hideaway'.

We went there countless times, often just the two of us but mainly with friends such as the Suarez twins or Luis de As. Others who would occasionally come with us were Honofre and Teresa de Espinosa, who lived in the Puerta de Guadalajara, also nearby, and Balthasar Favales, who lived not far from us in the Plazuela de los Herradores. Honofre, Teresa and Balthasar were about the same age as me and Honofre was in my class at school. We would meet at the Hideaway for chats after school and discuss the events of the day, but our favourite time to meet there was weekends because there was no school after Saturday lunchtime. We were too young and lacking in judgement to realise that we were trespassing on the estate of the dead merchant.

We agreed to meet at the Hideaway one Sunday, after morning mass. There were five of us: Francisco and me, Honofre and Teresa Espinosa and Balthasar Favales. It was in the middle of winter and cold. So we decided to have a fire. We had no sulphur or flints so Honofre went to the market in the Plazuela de Selenque and bought some from a blind man. We found some old rags, some pieces of wood and some paper and, with the skill of an old gypsy, Honofre began to light the fire in the hearth of one of the downstairs rooms. He placed the sulphur in a small pile on some dry cloth and firmly stroked the flint with a knife he had found in a kitchen drawer. Within a minute or so, the sparks had set the sulphur alight, the cloth had burst into flames and we had a fire burning steadily. Everything seemed fine and we continued our chatting in the room while keeping a watchful eye on the fire. Suddenly, there was a muffled explosion in the hearth and bits of burning rag and paper flew out of the fireplace and landed on the floor in front of us. A shabby carpet covered the floor and within seconds it was alight and giving off clouds of smoke. We all stamped on the burning carpet to try to put out the fire, but to no avail.

'We must get out of here,' said Balthasar, by then gasping for air.

'We can't leave this fire burning,' replied Teresa, choking as she spoke.

'Yes we can,' I said, urgently. 'Let's go.'

I grabbed Francisco's hand and we all left the burning house. As we reached the end of the alleyway and turned on to the Calle de los Peregrinos, we looked round and could see smoke billowing out of the door, which we had left open, and seeping through the shuttered windows.

'What do we do now?' asked Teresa, by then quite frightened.

As she did so, we could see a tattered figure of a man emerging from the house. He ran towards us, coughing and spluttering. It was one of the beggars I had often seen on the steps of the San Ginés church. Not realising we were the culprits and sighing with relief, he said, 'Jesus, I was lucky. I've just escaped from a fire in that house.' We guessed he must have lived there. That explained the occasional noises from upstairs which Balthasar said was the ghost of the dead merchant.

'We must alert the fire watch,' I replied to Teresa, becoming anxious myself, 'or the whole street will go up in flames.'

Balthasar ran up the road and banged at a door. The watchman soon emerged and started frantically waving a large, noisy rattle above his head. 'Fire! Fire! Come and fight the fire!' he shouted, as Balthasar meekly followed him back. Within seconds, about twenty men and women, all carrying leather buckets, splashing full of water, dashed from their houses and formed a human chain leading into the merchant's house. Others carried fire beaters and ran straight inside. The warden manned a well pump in the road a few doors away, and the men and women ferried more water to the fire. Gradually, the smoke subsided and after about five minutes, which seemed an age, one of the men at the top of the chain, his face blackened by dust and smoke, came out and yelled, 'It's out! It's out! It's all over!' Our gang, who were watching and waiting, looked at each other in welcomed relief.

As we turned to go, we saw two of the parish constables walking towards us from the direction of the Plazuela de Selenque. One was large and looked quite menacing. 'Do you children know anything about this fire?' he asked, accusingly.

'We think it was one of the beggars who started it,' said Honofre, sounding surprisingly convincing.

'Did one of you buy some sulphur and flints from a blind man in the Plazuela?' asked the other.

'Now we are in trouble,' I thought.

Honofre then admitted to buying the flints and sulphur, which was just as well because one of the constables had seen him buy them. 'So it wasn't the beggar, it was you, then,' said the large one.

'Yes,' said Honofre, hanging his head in shame.

They asked for our names and addresses, said we would hear more about this and walked back towards the Plazuela. Francisco burst into tears. 'I'm afraid, Juan,' he said.

'Don't cry,' I said, gently trying to comfort him. 'We'll go home now and tell Mamá and Papá what has happened.'

'I suggest we all go now,' said Balthasar and we went our separate ways, feeling chastened and with our heads lowered.

When we arrived home, I related these events to our parents. They were surprised and angry. They were unhappy that we had not told them before about the Hideaway; shocked that we had been there so many times; furious because I had taken Francisco there; and incredulous that Honofre had lied to the constables. We were told never to go there again or to trespass onto any other property. Father said that if I did anything like this again he would flog me near to my death. Francisco and I were again banned from going out together, this time for a month, and I was given a range of tasks to complete every evening, before I could play my musical instruments.

The following day, a court official came to our house to report to our parents our involvement in the fire. Mother told Francisco and me to go upstairs while the man spoke to her and father. We were up there at least an hour before father called us down. 'You two, and especially you Juan, are very lucky,' he said. 'I told the official that you had already told me the full story and that you had already been punished.' The man had told father that normally there would be some recompense required to make good the fire damage to the house. However, because the property was an item in the dead merchant's estate, the damage, which was quite extensive, would be covered by an insurance bond taken out by the town hall, to which the estate owed death duties. Therefore we, who were responsible, would not have to pay and the authorities would take no further action. I did not understand much of this at the time, except 'not have to pay' and 'take no further action.' A good result.

Not many months later, I started at the grammar school.

CHAPTER 3

Imperial School stood out as the best in Madrid. The Jesuits founded it at the end of the previous century and a number of famous people had been educated there, including Lope de Vega and Francisco Quevedo. The school had a policy of engaging teaching staff from all over Europe, so it had a strong international flavour and Spanish was not the only language spoken or taught there. 'Imperial', as it was known, was in the Calle de Toledo and I could walk to school in less than ten minutes. My friends Honofre de Espinosa, Luis de As and Balthazar Favales, joined at the same time as I did, which was in the autumn.

Luis and I were the only ones in our class who played musical instruments, so we had individual tuition. At my first music lesson, which was during my first week there, my music teacher, Señor Vásquez, spent the whole time talking to me about my music and my future. He was a tall, thin man who had to bend over to speak to me. I said that I wanted to be a professional musician, like my father. He told me he would like me to play for him so I went home that evening and, with my father's help, chose a few pieces. The following day, I performed for him on each of my instruments.

'Good,' said Señor Vásquez, slowly nodding his head. 'That was very good. There is room for improvement and we can work on that.'

Relieved, I just said, 'Thank you, señor.'

'I recognise that second piece,' he said. 'It's by a composer called Antonio de Cabezón, a blind musician who lived in the last century.'

'I didn't know that,' I said.

'I didn't recognise those other pieces.'

'My father taught them to me and I think he made them up himself,' I said. He smiled.

'Now,' said Señor Vásquez, 'I have an idea for you. Do you prefer to play the guitar or the violin?'

'I like them both,' I replied, 'but I prefer playing the guitar.'

'So you would rather play directly with your hands rather than use a bow?'

'I suppose that is true,' I said, not knowing where this was leading.

'Well, my idea is that we teach you to play the harp.'

I was shocked and didn't know quite what to say. 'I can see that you are puzzled,' said the señor, 'but your hands move so well over the strings of your guitar that I can see you as a potentially excellent harpist. Another thing: there's a shortage of harpists in Madrid so you would earn a good living.'

My parents were paying enough for my place there and I didn't think that they would want to bear any more expense. 'I'm not sure my parents would want to buy a harp for me,' I said.

'That would not be a problem,' he replied. 'We have an excellent harp here that we could lend you. It would be yours until you left the school. Come over here.' I followed him to the corner of the room and could see a black sheet covering a large object behind a clavichord in the corner. He pulled back the sheet. 'There it is,' he said, smiling. 'Isn't it beautiful?' I agreed. It was an attractive and imposing instrument. He pulled up a stool and played a few short tunes on it. 'Do you like the sound it makes?'

It had a distinct character and was quite unlike the sound I could produce from my guitar. 'Yes. I like it. It is different. Would I be able to take it home for practice?'

'Yes,' he said. 'There's a special little cart for pulling it along the street.'

He asked me what I thought of this new idea. I said I liked it but that I would prefer to discuss it with my father before agreeing. He said that at my age it was a difficult decision to make and that he would not put me under any pressure. However, if I were to start playing the harp, the sooner I started the better. I thought about the idea in school, during the rest of the day. It would be good to play something different from the instruments which father and grandfather played. I liked the instrument's relaxed but vibrant sounds which resonated inside me. I felt stimulated and inspired by them. I liked the size and shape of the instrument. It was striking and graceful. I would try to convince father that this was the instrument for me.

I couldn't wait to get home that afternoon. I virtually ran all the way. In my excitement, I'd forgotten that my parents and Francisco had gone to see our grandparents. Eventually, they arrived back home. I told my parents and Francisco about the señor's idea and why I wanted to play the harp. 'It seems a shame, not to carry on with the guitar and the violin, but if that's what you want to do, Juan, I agree fully that you do it,' said my father.

'But it won't mean giving up the guitar and the violin,' I said. 'I enjoy playing them and would continue to do so. But I would specialise in playing the harp.'

'All right then,' said my father, in a resigned but encouraging tone. So, from that day forward, I was going to be a harpist.

***

I was fascinated by current affairs and history. The teacher was Señor Méndez, an odd-looking man, who wore a pince-nez with the thickest and smallest lenses I had ever seen. He wore, indoors and out, a pillbox-shaped purple hat, embroidered in red with a red tassel swinging from the top. He made his subject so entertaining he brought it to life. He had a brilliant way of developing discussion on historical events and encouraging us pupils to participate. It would prove an excellent technique for making us remember the pros and cons of an argument for later use in essays and examinations. One of the first of these discussions was about a comparatively recent event, the expulsion of the *moriscos* in 1609.

Señor Méndez gave us the background, which was that in the year 711, the Moors attacked us and took possession of the virtually the whole peninsula. After struggling against them for centuries, we gradually reclaimed our territory and in 1492 broke the last Moorish stronghold, which was in Granada. A *morisco* was any Moor, or a descendent of one, who converted to Catholicism after this reconquest. In 1609, King Philip III decided to expel all the *moriscos* and by 1614, the year of my birth, about a quarter of a million had been repatriated to North Africa. 'What we are going to discuss is, was the expulsion good or bad for Spain?' said Señor Méndez.

'Good,' said a boy called Christóbal de Agramontes. 'The *moriscos* would not mix with us Spaniards and wanted to cause us trouble.'

'I agree,' said Luis de As. 'They live in ghettos and have their own language and their own strange ways. They are the enemy within.'

'What rubbish,' said Balthasar Favales. 'You have both been listening too much to the rantings of the Archbishop of Valencia, who is so intolerant that he'd drown his grandmother if he found out she was a *morisca*!'

'Can we not use expressions like, "What rubbish"?' asked Señor Méndez. 'I don't really care about what you say about the archbishops but I won't have you being rude to each other.' The point was taken.

I related my father's view which was that the expulsions had been bad for Spain. 'The expulsions have caused havoc to the economies of Valencia and Aragon. The jobs they filled on the land have disappeared,' I said, 'and it will still take years for these regions to get back on their feet.'

'But the economies in these former kingdoms were being decimated anyway by the King's punitive tax policies, imposed because of the expense of war and the fall in income from the Americas,' said Señor Méndez, sounding very dignified but firmly injecting his views into the discussion.

So it continued, but it was a good way to understand history, even recent events. I was amazed how politically aware some of our eleven-year-olds were. No mention was made, however, of the Duke of Lerma, King

Phillip III's main advisor, who was supposed to have persuaded him to rid Spain of the *moriscos* or of the plight of the *moriscos* themselves who were even expected to pay for their passage to North Africa. It must have been agony for them to go to a country they had never experienced before and I doubted whether they were made particularly welcome there.

***

After the discussion with my father about my musical future, I returned to Señor Vásquez to tell him I had decided to take up playing the harp. He was delighted. In my first lesson, he demonstrated 'my harp' to me, showing me the various parts and what they were for. He explained that the lower arm to which the strings were attached was the sound box, and that the 's' shaped curved piece at the top was the neck. He showed me how to place the sound box on my shoulder with the harp tilted towards me. The heavy instrument balanced perfectly in this position and put virtually no weight on my shoulder. He showed me how to tune the strings. Then he began to show me how to play it. I found it quite difficult to use both of my hands to produce the notes. He warned me that my fingers would hurt but that the skin on my fingertips would gradually become harder and, once it had, I would be able to play for quite long periods at a time.

I wondered how I would, or whether I could, master this large, daunting instrument. But, with Señor Vásquez teaching me and a huge amount of practice and determination, I felt I would. I wanted to be the best harpist in Spain.

***

Life then was not all work. Spending time with my family was important to me and we did many things together. By the time I was fourteen, Francisco was eight and was therefore strong enough to travel. One day, my parents decided that we would visit my grandparents on my father's side, the Hidalgos, in Pedraza. We would go during a week in spring. My father visited his parents occasionally, mainly by calling in on his way back from playing at an event near where they lived, but Francisco and I had never met them before. Pedraza is about twenty *leguas* to the north of Madrid, about two to three days by road. A journey of this length needed serious planning. Father arranged to hire a covered wagon and two carthorses. He bought enough hay to feed the horses for a week, more than we should need but sufficient to cover any unexpected delays. Mother

31

prepared a range of food so we would not go hungry *en route* and packed clothes for our journey and the stay at our grandparents' house.

'Time to get up, everyone,' shouted father at dawn on the morning we were to go.

'We won't bother with breakfast now. We'll eat on the wagon,' said our mother, infectiously excited by the journey which faced us.

'Come on, Juan,' said father, as soon as I was dressed and ready. 'We'll fetch the wagon and horses.' There was an urgency in his voice which betrayed his eagerness to get on the road. The hiring stables were only a minute or two away and we were soon back to our house with father and me in the driving seats and father at the reins. The horses seemed to know that they had a long journey ahead of them and their heads were moving up and down and from side to side, in apparent anticipation.

Father and I loaded up the wagon. We put the hay and a bag with some other supplies at the back. Between us, we lifted four large earthenware pots of water on board, both for us and the horses, and secured them to the side of the wagon. We took some ropes in case we had to tow the wagon for any reason. We covered the remaining floor space with old clothes and blankets so we had something to sit on during the day and covers to sleep under at night. Father placed a large, torn-off piece of blanket by his booted feet, I assumed to keep them warm. As father and I were loading, mother held the horses by the reins and Francisco brought out the food and handed it up to us through the back of the wagon. Father and I sat up front and we set off. The speed of the horses dictated our progress, about a *legua* or so an hour.

We gingerly made our way to the Calle de los Angeles and from there through the Foncaral Gate, to the north of the town. We were then on the road to Alcobendas. The roads in Madrid were rough but outside the town they were rougher still. The wagon had no springs so it jolted from side to side as well as kicking up and down over the ruts and potholes. Mother shouted to father to slow down because she and Francisco were being tossed around inside the cart. Father pulled on the reins but did not want to ease back too much otherwise, as he said, we would never get to Pedraza. By just after midday, we were well past Alcobendas and had reached Santo Domingo where we made a short stop for refreshment and to feed and water the horses.

'The roads aren't going to be this bad all the way, are they?' asked mother, as she stepped down from the back of the wagon.

'Sorry love, but yes they are. I've travelled on this road a few times now. But it gets no worse!' replied my father.

'Try to drive the horses so that they miss the roughest bits,' mother said, with a hint of resignation, anticipating that the deep grooves and hidden holes could hardly be avoided.

We all climbed back into the wagon and moved off again, continuing our journey until nightfall but stopping occasionally to rest the horses and our weary bodies. Father said he knew of a place just off the road where we could stop for the night. This stopping area was just before the village of Cotos de Monterrey and we reached it as night was closing in. There were about ten other wagons stopped there and a quite luxurious-looking carriage. By the light of a candle, we located and ate some of the food which mother had prepared and washed it down with some of the water we had brought. Father tethered the horses and we settled down to sleep.

'What's that?' whispered mother, around midnight. None of us was sleeping very well so we all heard her. The sound of laughter and loud voices was coming from the direction of the luxury carriage. Father lifted the canvas at the back of the cart. We could see by the light of an oil lamp on the side of the carriage that a man was climbing out of it. The man was still laughing when a partially dressed woman also stepped out of the carriage, went up to the man and slapped him on the face.

'Don't you dare do that again,' she said. She stepped back in and locked the carriage door. 'You can damn well stay out there for the night.'

Despite hammering at the door, the man failed to get back into the carriage. 'You bitch. Open that fucking door,' he shouted.

'No!' the woman cried. He picked up a stone and threw it at the carriage window.

The sound of smashing glass was quickly followed by the woman shouting, 'I'm bleeding. I'm bleeding. Look what you've damn well done.' By then, nearly everybody in the parking area was awake and listening to, if not watching, this midnight dispute, and some were going to the aid of the woman.

'What should we do?' said mother.

'Nothing,' said father. 'We just look after the children.' We settled down again and did our best to sleep.

Awoken by the dawn sunlight, spearing through the gaps in the rear canvas door of the wagon, we got up, had some breakfast and were on our way. As we left the parking area, we saw the smashed window of the smart-looking carriage. There was no one inside. It was shiny and black with a small, red emblem painted on the door. We made good progress, made easier by the road which was less rutted and potholed than the one the previous day. There was less traffic and that was also a help. Having made a morning stop, we reached Buitrago before lunchtime. Again, we stopped for refreshment and to refresh and rest the horses. We set off again after about an hour.

Eventually, we turned off the main road towards Pedraza. The road became narrower and there was hardly any traffic. After we had been on this road for about ten minutes or so, we heard from behind the distant sound of horses galloping. The clatter of the hooves became louder as they approached us. Father pulled the wagon over to the right so that the horses and their riders could overtake. As they reached us, I looked towards the riders and was sure I recognised one of the two men as the one who, the night before, was ejected from the luxury carriage. They pulled up alongside and made us stop.

'Where are you going, señor?' asked the man with the familiar face.

'We're going to Pedraza,' said father.

'You are going nowhere,' said the other one, pulling out a gun and pointing it at father's head. 'What's in the back of the wagon?'

'My wife and son,' said father, keeping amazingly calm.

'Tell her to get out,' said the one we had seen the night before.

'Francisca, step down from the back,' shouted father. A frightened Francisco started to cry. I felt terrified and certain they would kill us. My heart thumped in my chest. Mother seemed surprisingly composed as she emerged from the cart.

'You're a tasty-looking wench,' said the man with the gun. 'Start undressing. I'm going to enjoy you.' Mother started to loosen her blouse. She did so with striking equanimity. The man handed his gun to his colleague and started to undo his breeches. As he did so, there were two loud explosions and the man who threatened mother fell to the ground clutching his chest in agony. The familiar one dropped the gun on the ground and collapsed with a torrent of blood streaming from his head. The horses reared up violently at the noise. Father was holding a smoking, double-barrelled, flintlock pistol which he had evidently concealed under the torn blanket by his feet.

'Get the rope, Juan,' said father. I jumped off the wagon and climbed quickly into the back. Mother went to comfort Francisco who thought we had all been shot. Father tied up the man writhing on the ground, who was bleeding badly. He had been hit in the upper chest by father's second bullet. His colleague, the familiar one, was dead.

'I've tied this one up so well, I think we are safe with him now,' said father.

The man was muttering, 'Help me! Help me!'

'Do you think you could stop the bleeding from his chest?' father asked.

'I'll try,' said mother. She went to the back of the wagon and brought out some sheeting which she tore into wide strips. She then eased off the man's shirt and tied the improvised bandages tightly around his chest. The bleeding was soon reduced to a trickle. As Francisco quietly watched, the rest of us bundled the man into the back of the wagon, tied some rag around his head to cover his mouth – we didn't want to put up with his noise for the rest of the journey – and knotted more rope around his legs for greater security.

'Phew. That was nasty,' said father, clearly relieved that we had prevailed over the highwaymen. His voice trembled as he spoke. He went over to mother and hugged her. She cried as she suddenly realised how close we had been to our deaths.

'I didn't know you had a gun,' I said.

'I did!' mother said, raising a wry smile, and wiping away her tears.

'That explains how you stayed so calm,' I replied, feeling much happier now that we were out of danger.

'We need to do something with that before we go,' father said, turning to me and nodding towards the motionless corpse on the ground. 'Let's drag him to that tree.' We left the highwayman's body propped up against an olive tree, about twenty *pasos* from the road. 'Now let's look for some landmarks so we can tell the constable in Pedraza where he is,' father said and we both looked around. 'There are two little peaks at the top of that hill. That will do,' he said. I took the dead man's gun and put it under the hay in the back of the wagon, along with his bloodstained bandana. Father reloaded his pistol and gave it to mother so she could use it on our captive, if necessary. We all clambered aboard the wagon and set off again.

We were still about four hours or so from Pedraza. 'We'll go straight to the constabulary,' said father, on the way. 'The sooner we get rid of him the better,' he said, pointing towards the back of the wagon. Mother agreed.

***

The local constable and two assistants helped us unload our unwanted cargo. The man was still alive but weak, having lost much blood. 'We'll throw him in the cells first and then get the doctor,' the constable said.

We tied up the horses and wagon and all went into the judicial office. Father related the whole story. He said that we recognised the man he had shot dead as the one being thrown out of the luxury carriage the night before and that the carriage was black and had a red emblem on the door.

'You are all lucky to be alive,' said the constable. 'These men have been terrorising travellers on the Madrid to Burgos road for weeks. Well done. You've well and truly stopped them now!' He was excited and grateful. 'That carriage sounds like the one stolen from around here a few days ago. You two: take a cart and get the body,' he said, instructing his assistants. 'I'll need you to sign statements,' he said to mother and father. 'I think that will be all for now,' said the constable, after the formalities had been completed. 'If we need to see you again, we can easily come round to the Hidalgos' house.'

The meeting with my grandparents in Pedraza was, not surprisingly, very emotional, especially as it was so soon after the terrifying encounter with the two highwaymen. As the wagon pulled up outside their house, grandmother peered out of the window. Both our grandparents came to greet us. Mother broke into tears and hugged grandmother. 'God, we have had a terrible time,' mother said.

'Come inside and tell us what happened,' said grandfather. Father untethered the horses and walked them to grandfather's stables at the back of the house as mother, Francisco and I unloaded the wagon. Father then related our story and mother joined in to elaborate. 'I think you are all very brave,' said grandfather. 'You must all be famished so let's have something to eat and drink.'

Grandfather was a farmer. His farm was about four *yugadas* in area, about two million square *varas*, so was quite substantial. He was the sole owner and grew grapes, cereals and olives. After we had had some refreshment, grandfather and father used one of grandfather's horse-drawn wagons to take Francisco and me on a tour of the farm. You had to see it to appreciate its size.

We started in the vineyards where we could see the farm labourers, men and women, cutting out the dead wood from the vines, which had been planted in straight rows about two *pasos* apart. This was to allow the labourers to drive their carts between the rows with the minimum loss of area for cultivation. The carts came into their own at harvest time when they were piled high with ripe grapes ready to be used for wine. This was early spring and the new shoots were just beginning to appear. Similarly, the olive trees were lined up like a parade of *tercios*, so as to make the farming processes as easy as possible. Among the olive trees there were about a dozen labourers, pulling out weeds close to the tree trunks and piling them onto carts. Yet more labourers were sowing the wheat seeds. They walked in rows, casting the seeds from wide baskets, singing like a church choir as they went.

'Let's go back. You've probably seen enough for now,' said grandfather, as we completed our tour. On the way back towards the house and the farm buildings, we approached a group of ten or so crudely built huts. Some were made of wood and others of mud. As we neared this cluster of tiny buildings, a slender, raven-haired woman emerged from one of the wooden huts, carrying a baby which was suckling at her left breast. Grandfather pulled up the horse and stopped. Completely oblivious to us, the woman lifted her skirt up to her waist, with the baby somehow balanced between her breast and knee, and coopied down with her white bottom towards us. She began to shit, right there in front of us. Her pushing produced a stream of pee. There was a pan of water next to where she crouched. When she finished, she dipped her hand into it and cleaned herself with the water. She then wiped her hand on the dry soil, dipped it into the water again and rinsed herself. She then took a dry cloth from the waist of her skirt and dried the area between her legs, wiping vigorously. She stood up, still balancing the baby, dropped her skirt back down and went back into the hut. She left her shit on the ground.

I was shocked by what I had seen and for a moment didn't know what to say. Then I asked, 'Who is she?'

'Ah, she's the wife of one of the farm labourers,' said grandfather. 'I wish they'd shit further out on the fields. It would be better for the crops if they did.'

'Really?' said father, in a descending voice, trying to disown what grandfather had said without actually disagreeing with him.

'Why can't you give them pots to use?' I asked.

'They wouldn't use them for that,' grandfather said. 'They'd use them for cooking, instead.'

'Can I see inside one of these huts?' I asked.

'Go into the woman's,' he said.

I climbed off the cart and approached the hut. There was no door to speak of, just a dirty curtain that didn't fully cover the opening. 'Can I come in?' I said, through the makeshift threshold.

'Who are you?' asked the woman. 'What do you want?'

'I am the farmer's grandson, Juan. I just wanted to meet you and speak to you.'

'Yes, come in,' said the woman, in a resigned tone, as if she had no choice but to let me inside. The crude, parchment windows in the hut were small and so high up the wall that only a small amount of light came in. There was just enough to be able to see the woman's features and what was inside. She was about twenty years old and had a delicately attractive face. Her baby was then feeding from her other breast. There was no furniture except a low table, towards the far end of the hut, and I could see the red embers of a fire in a basic, stone hearth.

'What's your name?' I asked.

'Barbola,' she replied, proudly.

'Do you live here?'

'Yes, with my husband and baby.'

'Where's the bedroom?' I asked.

'This is it,' she said. 'We sleep here on the floor.'

'Where's the kitchen?'

'This is the kitchen,' she said, pointing to the hearth. 'I cook on that fire.'

'You hardly have any furniture.'

'That's right,' said Barbola. 'We can hardly feed ourselves. We've no money for furniture.'

'I'll ask my grandfather if he can help you. Make you more comfortable.'

'Please, don't,' said Barbola, in a weak voice. 'I don't think that will help us at all.'

'Why not?'

'How well do you know your grandfather?' she asked.

I did not reply to her question but said, 'I won't say anything, Barbola.' Then, after a pause, 'I must go now.'

'Thank you, señor,' she said, with more than a hint of relief. 'Maybe I will see you again.'

'You never know,' I said. I walked towards the door, pulled the curtain to one side and went out. I was shocked and appalled by the poverty and deprivation I had just witnessed. I walked towards grandfather's cart and climbed aboard.

'What did you make of that?' said grandfather.

'I don't really know,' I said. 'I'm just getting over the shock.'

'Shock?' asked grandfather.

'Yes. What awful conditions to live in and bring up a child.'

'You have no experience of life,' said grandfather. 'According to the news sheets, there are two million people in Spain living like that. That's about one in four of the population.'

The wagon trundled along towards the house where we were met by mother and grandmother. 'What do you think of our farm?' asked grandmother.

'It's huge,' I said. 'And it's so well organised.' I did not mention Barbola.

That night, before we went to bed, father and grandfather discussed how well grandfather's farm business was operating. 'It's difficult,' said grandfather, 'mainly because of government taxes. They are crucifying me. It's lucky I own the land because if I had to rent it, as the peasant farmers do, I'd be barely able to survive. There is tax on all I buy, including the seed I sow, all the equipment I have to buy to run the farm and everything your mother buys to feed us. Then, of course I have to pay the farm labourers, all thirty of them.'

'Well, their wages won't cost you much, judging from the conditions they live in.' I realised straight away that I should not have said that, but it was true.

'Juan!' said mother. 'What do you know about it? You've never been here before.'

'I know,' I said, 'but I went into one of the labourer's huts and they live more like animals than people.'

'I am not an evil man,' said grandfather, attempting to defend himself. 'I'm trying to earn a living, just like the labourers on the farm. I pay them about the same as any of the other local farmers pay, about 150 *reales* a year. If I paid any more, I would soon be bankrupt. The problem is the King and his First Minister, that arrogant Count Duke Olivares. They both insist on fighting wars with everybody in Europe. That's why taxes are through the roof. And the poor pay is the reason these labourers are leaving the countryside to find jobs in the towns.'

'A hundred and fifty *reales*? That's about a *ducat* a month,' father said, making a statement rather than venturing an opinion.

'I know,' said grandmother. 'When you think that a loaf of bread costs three *maravedís,* that doesn't leave much for spending on clothing and other items for daily life.'

'It's time you and Francisco went to bed,' said father.

***

I'd stirred up a snake pit and grandfather was none too happy about it. He knew full well that the position a man occupies in Spanish society is generally determined by his inheritance, his income and the taxes he pays. There are distinct, if overlapping, levels in our social structure. At the bottom are the *jornaleros* or labourers on the land who possess no land themselves. Most are itinerant, looking for seasonal work where they can find it. Such was the family of Barbola. At the next level up are the peasant farmers or *labradores* who own their land or lease it. They comprise a range of levels of wealth from poor farmers, who barely have enough to pay for seed and their own labourers, to the significantly well off, such as grandfather Hidalgo, who owned a large farm from which he clearly made a profit, despite his protests.

Then there is the *hidalgo* class which is strongly resented by the *labradores* because, unlike the *labradores,* its members enjoy immunity from paying taxes. Grandfather Hidalgo was an Hidalgo in name only. He was not an *hidalgo,* even though he probably aspired to being one. Many *hidalgos* have sufficient of their own means, largely through inheritance, that they do not have to work. But many are poor, if not destitute, and work or beg for a living. Our family fitted between the *labradores* and the *hidalgos*: our father worked for a living and, while not wealthy, we enjoyed a comfortable existence.

Above the *hidalgos* are the *caballeros* and *titulos* in land. The *caballeros* are those with titles: the dukes, marquises, counts and viscounts. The *titulos* are the landed gentry and therefore the true nobility. The *caballeros* and *titulos* generally enjoy fabulous wealth, either by inheritance or from the large salaries they are paid by the state. Not only are they the beneficiaries of these massive stipends but they pay no taxes on them. Count Duke Olivares, though an industrious and dedicated servant of the state, was a case in point. His salary, at about 100,000 *ducats* a year, was about a hundred times that of reasonably successful peasant farmer, like my grandfather. But unlike my grandfather, he didn't pay tax.

So it is the common man, mainly the worker on the land, who bears the brunt of taxes imposed by the state and virtually nobody else. He pays the *alcabala,* a 10% sales tax imposed on the sale of goods, and the *milliones* a tax on basic foodstuffs. The *milliones* were originally taxes on wine, meat oil and vinegar but were extended to make more tax income for the state. The land worker also has to pay a 'tithe' to the church and to pay his rent. The nobility are not exempt from the *milliones.* However, they administer the tax system so contrive to pay as little as possible, if not to make a profit on their collection duties.

***

We prepared to leave my grandparents' house just after sunrise on the Saturday. We would have spent longer there but Francisco and I had to be back at school the following Monday. During the fond farewells, grandfather gave Francisco and me a silver *real* piece each. I could not resist asking, 'Please, Grandpapá, could you give that to Barbola from me?'

'Oh, if I must!' said grandfather, clearly irritated. Francisco thought for a second but said nothing, quietly putting his *real* in his pocket. We piled onto the wagon and off we went. The horses also seemed keen to get back.

Honofre Espinosa and Balthazar Favales were the first of my school friends to asked me about the holiday with my grandparents. I told them about the highwaymen who held us up. It was difficult to convince them that my father had killed one of our attackers and seriously injured the other. They thought I was fantasising. 'See that,' I said, taking a bloodstained square of fabric from my school bag. 'That's the dead man's bandana.' I think that persuaded them. I didn't tell them about our encounter with Barbola.

I repeated the tale several times in that first week back from the holidays. Señor Méndez heard about it and I had to relate the story of the highwaymen to the whole history class. I thought he was going to use it as the basis for a debate but, thankfully, he didn't.

***

As a family, we used to go to mass regularly and it seemed excessive to have to be taught religion at school. There was no escape from the classes so I simply had to go to them. A Jesuit priest called Father Sancho was the religious education teacher.

He was an intelligent and logical man and wanted to start at the beginning. This meant Genesis and the creation. Father Sancho opened up a huge Bible and started to paraphrase the opening verses. He explained that on the first day God said, 'Let there be light.' And there was light. He said that on the second day God made the firmament and divided the waters from under the firmament from the waters above and called the firmament heaven. He went on to say that on the third day, God created the dry land and called it earth. On the fourth day, God made the sun to shine on earth during the day and the moon and stars to shine at night. At this point Christóbal de Agramontes said, 'Please Father Sancho, may I ask a question?'

'Certainly,' said Father Sancho.

'Well,' said Christóbal. 'Where did the light come from on the first day if God didn't create the sun the moon and the stars until the fourth day?'

'Good question,' said Father Sancho. 'Does anyone know the answer?' No one replied.

'Well, it's very logical,' said Father Sancho. 'The sun, the moon and the stars must have been created from the light God created on the first day. It's obvious, isn't it?' We were all completely puzzled by his answer but said nothing because he was so convincing. How can anything be made of light other than light itself? Goodness knows.

Like Señor Méndez, Father Sancho was a liberal-minded individual who made his lessons interesting by introducing class discussion and delving deeply into the issues and questions. Was there a God? If so, what was the proof of His existence? Did Christ come back to life, after being crucified? Did the miracles actually happen? My position was and remains that I am a devout and practising Roman Catholic, but I have always had persistent doubts about these fundamental questions. I later found that I was in good company.

***

With the encouragement of Señor Vásquez, and my parents, I improved my harp playing so that by the time I was fifteen, I could play quite competently. I endlessly practised the techniques that Señor Vásquez had demonstrated to me. As the señor had predicted, my fingertips gradually became hardened and I could play continuously for a good hour at a time but that was about my limit. I became a familiar sight on the Calle de Toledo, tugging the harp cart home on a Friday night and back to school again on the following Monday morning. Even the beggars recognised me and teased me about the large object I was dragging along. Over the weekends, father and I would play duets to mother and Francisco, father on the violin and me on the harp. All of us enjoyed these sessions. Father would help if I went wrong, pointing out what notes I had missed or misplayed. I began to master playing tunes with individual notes, chords and *glissandi*. The more I played and the better I became, the more pleasure I gained from playing.

Señor Vásquez also taught me to read music. First, I regarded it as a chore. I soon realised, though, that being able to reproduce the exact notes on an instrument from symbols on a piece of paper would be a huge benefit to my career as a harpist. He taught me musical notation and how the various musical scales were related. With the ability to read music came the skill of writing it. I could set down any tunes that came into my head, or that I heard, so I would not forget them. It meant that I could become a composer of music.

As I was to become a professional musician, I needed to become used to playing in public. So I thought about performing in front of the whole school. This would at least be a start and I could use such a performance to test my nerves. I suggested to Luis de As that we perform as a trio with Juan de Roxas Carrión. He was a fellow musician who was a class ahead of us. Both Juan and Luis were accomplished violinists, especially for fifteen or sixteen year olds. We went to see Señor Vásquez about this. 'What a good idea. So you want to perform a recital?' said the señor, excitedly. 'Have you thought of having a singer, to give it more variety? I'm sure the San Isidro choir will provide us with one.' San Isidro was the recently built church, right next to the school. 'I'll ask the choirmaster, but only if you want me to.'

The three of us looked at each other in nodding agreement. We all thought it a good idea. We agreed that we four, including Señor Vásquez, would work together to make this musical event happen. He would find a girl singer, or maybe two, and we three boys would sort out some ideas for a programme, following the señor's advice of not performing for much over half an hour. He would talk to the headmaster about using the main school hall and we would arrange a date later. My father gave me great encouragement to do the concert and helped me select the music. 'The key to success is to have strongly contrasting pieces. To start with something jolly and quick and to finish in the same vein.' Sounded good to me.

Within a few days, we had put together an outline programme, which included a harp solo and a violin duet, both by Francisco de Cabézon, and some songs by Luis de Milán and by Juan de Encina. Señor Vásquez had succeeded in persuading two girls to sing with us, Bernarda Ramirez and Maria de Riquelme. Bernarda wanted to play her guitar with us, as well as to sing. The señor made a request, 'Now boys, I want to ask you a very special favour. My grandfather was a famous Spanish composer called Juan Vásquez. He wrote some beautiful songs and I would love you to include some in your programme.' I was pleasantly surprised that the señor was related to this brilliant composer. All three of us agreed to use some of his songs, not that we had much choice.

We timed our concert for the afternoon of the last day of the academic year, which was to be Juan de Roxas Carrión's last day at the school. The three of us boys met the girls at the church of San Isidro one Sunday, after mass. Maria was petite with long, blondish hair and Bernarda was taller and dark haired. I reckoned that each was a year or two older than me. They were accompanied by their mothers as chaperones. Although they said virtually nothing, it seemed to us boys that the girls' mothers were suspicious of how we intended to treat their daughters. We told the girls about our proposed programme which Juan de Roxas Carrión had neatly written in old Spanish text on a sheet of paper. We said that they could suggest any changes if they wished but both were happy with it. Maria said she already knew two of the songs, one by Vásquez and the other by Milán.

We agreed that our first rehearsal would be at Imperial, in the music room. Señor Vásquez wanted to attend and promised he would be helpful but not interfere. The girls arrived with Maria's father who left them in our care, having mumbled some kind of warning to the señor. Bernarda had brought her guitar and we boys already had our instruments at the school.

We nervously placed our music sheets on our stands. 'We'll start with you,' said Señor Vásquez, pointing at me.

'I'm not the first on the programme,' I said, timidly objecting.

'I know,' said the señor. 'But I want you to start off.'

I played the harp piece by Cabezón. 'You need to be more definite with your note making,' said the señor. 'You are merging one note into another.' I knew exactly what he meant. I think I was rushing the piece a bit. At his request, I played it again.

When it came to their turn, the girls sang well. Maria was a soprano and had the voice of a songbird while Bernarda was a contralto with such an intense and controlled vibrato that, at full intensity, it made the windows shake. The girls were accompanied by Luis and Juan de Roxas.

'I'd say we need one more rehearsal,' said Señor Vásquez. 'We'll meet again next Friday and then it will be the real thing!'

As he spoke, Maria's father came in. He snatched each girl by the hand and rushed them out. It was as if he had been listening outside.

We had advertised the concert by sticking posters on notice boards and school walls. Juan de Roxas wrote a dozen or so in beautiful script, similar to the one he had given our girl singers. They were certainly effective. Although attendance was optional, virtually every pupil and nearly all the teachers came to the concert. The San Isidro choirmaster was also there along with the girls' mothers.

We were all nervous before the performance, especially Luis and Bernarda. 'I'm not sure I can do this,' she said. 'I feel sick to my stomach.'

'I'm sure you will be brilliant,' said the señor. 'It's only natural to be nervous beforehand.'

'No. I can't do it,' said Bernarda, turning her back on us and moving as if to go.

'Bernarda, please stay,' said Juan de Roxas. 'Your name is on the programme.' It was as if merely being mentioned on the posters meant that she had to perform. Luis looked pale and said nothing.

'I'll do it,' said Bernarda. 'Let's start then.' Luis followed suit.

This little diversion had delayed us but by no more than a few minutes. We stayed in the wings of the hall stage as Señor Vásquez introduced the concert and our first piece which was one of the songs by his grandfather. The quick, boisterous music made the ideal start. All of us performed in it, Luis and Bernarda without a trace of nerves. Everyone enjoyed our little concert. The audience gave us five performers a standing ovation at the end, despite a few wrong notes and Juan de Roxas at one point dropping his bow.

Then came my final year at Imperial. I wanted to leave the school with good results in my exams and was prepared to work hard. I aimed to be the best harpist in Spain. So, however much effort I was to spend studying, I needed to make time, not only to play the harp but also to achieve a highly professional level of playing it. I also wanted to compose.

Three or four subjects seemed to be the norm for the final year's examinations so I chose music, history and politics, geography and mathematics. I discussed my future plans with my parents. I needed their help in deciding whether to go to university or find a job as a musician. There were arguments either way. If I went, I would doubtless have been qualified for a wide range of careers when I graduated. I would have a much improved education and understanding of the world and I would meet a range of intelligent people. On the other hand, I wanted to play the harp and compose music. That would be my career and I did not want unnecessarily to delay its start. As father said, I had always wanted to be a musician, ever since playing those first few guitar notes while sitting on grandfather's knee. We discussed the question at length and I decided that, when I left school at the end of the summer of 1630, I would find a job as a musician.

I had always enjoyed mathematics. The master was Señor Jean-Charles de la Faille. What an incredible man. He came to Imperial from a Jesuit College in Antwerp and was a well known mathematician, having published several advanced books on the subject. Neither he nor his family were poor and, in the summer vacation, the family commissioned Anthony van Dyck to paint his portrait. It is surprising how word gets around a school. In one of his lessons, one of the pupils, it may have been Honofre, asked, 'Is it true, señor, that you've had your portrait painted by some famous artist?'

The señor hesitated and blushed slightly then said, 'Yes, I have. By van Dyck.'

'Can we see it señor? Does it look like you?' asked another.

All this was quite embarrassing for him but he handled it well and, calling our bluff, said, 'I invite you all to my house to see it, after school tonight.'

So that night, five or six of us walked with him to his house in the Calle Mayor and, having explained to his wife why we were there, the señor showed us the portrait which was hung in an upstairs drawing room, among a number of other family pictures. It was a striking painting. The señor, seated at a table, wore his dark Jesuit gown which all but completely enveloped him. A sextant and a globe were placed on the table and the señor was holding an open compass in his right hand while his left was placed on his left thigh. His hands and his head formed an almost perfect isosceles triangle which gave the picture a calming symmetry. The background was sombre but the señor's hands and head were highlighted by the white of the paper, on which his right hand rested, his white cuffs and the collar of his white tunic. Van Dyck's genius showed in his depiction of the señor's face. He had not only captured his likeness but had reflected the gentleness and modesty of this exceptionally intelligent man.

The señor held some interesting political views. The ones about the *moriscos* influenced me most. He made the point that the Arabs made important developments in algebra, the science of medicine, astronomy and a host of other things. Why then had we thrown them out of Spain? Who knows?

I disliked our geography master, Señor Cerrada. His name, which means 'closed', reflected his attitude and personality. His knowledge was just about what it must have been when he himself left school. The world had changed since then. Literally. The Spanish Empire was changing, particularly in the Americas which were becoming more independent and self-reliant. Other European powers were also coming to the fore, such as England and the Dutch Republic. But all this had overtaken Señor Cerrada who was marooned in a world that existed at the turn of the century.

Señors Vásquez and Méndez continued to play major roles in my education in that final year. Señor Vásquez extended my repertoire in the harp and taught me the beginnings of musical composition. My father was quite amazed when I went home with two sheets of music paper with a sprightly little piece for the violin and harp written on it. 'Who wrote this?' he asked.

'I did.'

'We have to play it. It looks so jolly. When can you bring the harp home?'

'At the weekend.'

'That's good. We can play it to mother and Francisco. Then we'll ask them who wrote it!'

This was my very first composition and mother and Francisco gave us a hearty round of applause after father and I had played it. It soon became clear who had dreamt up the piece.

The history and current affairs lessons with the eccentric Señor Méndez took on the same pattern and flavour as before. Plenty of discussion and argument. The main lessons for the year were about the Spanish Empire and what it meant to the people of Spain. Current affairs covered the reign of our new King Philip IV, his triumphs and failures, his relationships with the Councils of State and with his First Minister, the merits or otherwise of his actions on the battlefields of Europe and his handling of our burgeoning national debt.

I did well in my end of year exams, except, not surprisingly, in geography. A few days after I had received the results, I was greeted by my father as I walked through the doorway of our house, 'Juan, I think I've found you a job.'

CHAPTER 4

'So you've found me a job. What is it then?'

'It is working for a theatre company.'

'A theatre company? I'm not an actor, Papá.'

'I know. I know, Juan, but you are a musician and you play the harp.'

'True.'

'Well, someone I have worked for many times, Manuel Vallejo, owns the company and he is working with Lope de Vega on a new play, a *comedia*. It will be called "Punishment without Revenge". He and Lope are putting together a cast for the *comedia* and they want a small troupe of musicians to play a musical accompaniment. Manuel asked me to play the violin. And he asked how you were getting on with the harp. I told him that you were doing well. And that you had left school with good results in your music exams. He asked me if you would be willing to play your harp in the *comedia*.

'That's fantastic, Papá. When can I start work?'

'Well, that's not the end of the story. He also wants someone to write the music. He and Lope want to use some well-known songs and tunes but they also want some new material. I said that you wanted to compose music. That composition was a subject you had studied. I also said that we had played some music you had composed and that it was good.'

'Papá, you exaggerate. I'm very unsure about writing the music.'

'No. I only said your music was good! Manuel can decide whether you are good enough. He asked if you'd want to be auditioned for a job in his company.'

'I'd love to do that, Papá. Love to.'

'I'll tell him, tomorrow,' said father, pleased with both himself and me.

I could hardly sleep that night, I was so excited. I felt as if I was in a dream. I could be working with the most famous playwright Spain had ever produced. I would have some money and be more independent of my family. Who else would be in the music troupe? Who would be acting in the *comedia*? I wondered whether it could be anyone I knew. Most important, when would I start?

The audition took place the following week and I was well prepared. I would show Señor Vallejo my piece for violin and harp that I had played at home about six months before. I thought it would be good to give it a name so I scribbled 'Pedraza', at the top of the manuscript to remind me of the young farmer's wife, Barbola. It would have been awkward to use her name directly. I did not want to be asked questions about her. I practised some quite difficult pieces for the harp that I had recently learnt, along with the piece by Cabezón that I had last played in the school concert.

I had to go to Señor Vallejo's house for the audition, which was in the Calle de la Lechuga, just off the Calle de Toledo near the Plaza Mayor. I dragged along the harp which, in effect, I still 'owned'. Life is full of little surprises and mine was to see Bernarda Ramirez and Maria de Riquelme also walking towards the señor's house.

'Where are you two going?' I asked.

'We are going to Señor Vallejo's,' said Bernarda.

'So am I! Where is the chaperone today?' I asked.

'We've got a day of freedom,' said Maria, laughing as the three of us walked along together. 'We are being auditioned for a new Lope *comedia* called, "Punishment without Revenge".'

'So am I! Is there singing in the *comedia*?'

'I don't know,' said Maria. 'We are being auditioned for acting parts. That is our main profession, not singing.'

I had not met the señor before. He welcomed each of us at his front door. 'Do you three already know each other?' he asked. We explained how we met a year or so before and performed at a concert at my school. He ushered us into a drawing room which he had arranged as a small theatre with six seats in two rows of three to one side of the room and an area that we had to think of as a stage at the opposite side. He invited us to sit down, went out of the room and shouted, 'Lope. They are here!'

Within a minute or so, the playwright appeared at the door. He shyly came in and modestly said, 'Hello. My name is Lope de Vega. I write poems and plays.' He appeared older than I had expected. He must have been about seventy but still had a straight, upright back. His hair was grey as was his pertly curved moustache and his tiny beard which did not reach the tip of his chin. One mistake with his razor and he would have lost it. He was dressed in black from head to toe, just like a priest. The cross of the Order of Saint John of Malta was emblazoned in white on his left sleeve. His eyes were brown and bright and, as he slowly walked across the room to introduce himself to us, his whole face lit up with a glowing smile.

'You are all so young,' he said. 'I so enjoy working with young people. It keeps me young, too.' He sat on one of the six chairs.

Señor Vallejo gave each of us, including Lope, a small bundle of papers which were a few pages of the first act of this new play. He said he thought we should all have a copy, even though it would only be the women who would be reading the parts.

I played the piece by Cabezón and the harp part in 'Pedraza'. The girls read from the pages of the script. Señor Vallejo and Lope de Vega looked at my manuscript score of 'Pedraza'. They seemed satisfied and Lope left straight away, saying he was looking forward to working with us. 'I want to discuss a contract with you first, Juan. Bernarda and Maria please wait here,' said Señor Vallejo. He led me into the room next door and sat on one side of a desk with me at the other.

'Read this,' he said, impassively. It was a draft contract. He would pay me eight *reales* a day for rehearsing and playing in the music troupe and, for writing the music, 200 *reales* for each act. He wanted continuous play for a troupe comprising two violins, a harp and a guitar and left me to choose what instruments should be playing at any one time, but wanted some popular tunes included. He called it incidental music. He explained that Lope had so far written only one act and he gave me a manuscript copy of it, saying that he, Señor Vallejo, would pass me copies of subsequent acts when they were ready. He said Lope was a fast writer and I could expect a further act in six weeks, allowing for the original to be copied. The contract, which was for one year and six months, expected delivery of the music within four weeks of my receiving each act.

I signed twice, one copy for Señor Vallejo and the other for me. We both stood up and shook hands. 'From this moment you are a member of my company. Congratulations. You can go now.'

I was excited and apprehensive about this new venture. It had all happened so quickly and what an abrupt conclusion: 'you can go now'. And what a strange collaboration this would be as I had been given so little guidance. I hadn't read one scene of the one act of Lope's *comedia*, that Manuel Vallejo had given me, let alone the whole act, so had no idea what it was about. There were a number of questions in my mind. Had I done the right thing? After all, this was the first job I had been offered. Should I have waited until there was another possibility so I had a choice? Did I know enough about musical composition to be able to keep my side of the contract? How many popular tunes should I include and what should be the balance between them and any original music which I would write?

By the time I reached home, dragging my harp behind me and clutching the contract, the act of the play I had been given and the manuscript of 'Pedraza', my mind had settled and I decided that I had been exceptionally lucky to land a job as good as this, working with Lope de Vega, and well paid into the bargain.

'How did you get on?' asked my parents, virtually in unison.

'I've got the job!' I said. 'I'm really delighted.' I told them about the contract, what Manuel Vallejo expected of me and how much I would be paid.

'Congratulations from both of us!' said my mother, excitedly.

'Did Manuel Vallejo tell you about the future performances of the play?' asked my father.

'He didn't say anything about performances or even where it will be performed.'

'Well, I can tell you. The plan is that the play is first performed later this year in the Corral del Príncipe and then in front of the King, at the Alcázar Palace, in the following January or February.' In front of the King – I could not believe my ears.

***

I had not been home for ten minutes when there was a knock at the front door. Francisco went to answer it and was greeted by the smiling faces of Maria de Riquelme and Bernarda Ramirez. 'Is Juan here?' asked Bernarda. They rushed in to greet me. 'You've got the job! So have we! So have we!' There were hugs and kisses all round as the girls boiled over with excitement.

After the initial euphoria, my parents left me with Maria and Bernarda. We sat down to discuss our respective roles in the play. Manuel Vallejo had told Bernarda that she would be playing 'Aurora' and Maria would play 'Casandra'.

'I have only written unaccompanied music before, that is, just music. I haven't written music for a single song, let alone for the spoken word,' I said.

'I'm sure we can work out the basic ideas,' said Maria. 'You will need to write the music to fit in with the length of the play.'

'How long is the first act?' I asked.

'About a thousand lines of verse,' said Bernarda.

'What!' I exclaimed. 'It's huge! It's going to take an age to write the music for one act and we haven't seen the other acts yet. I suppose there will be two more?' I was beginning to have doubts again about what I had taken on. Real doubts.

'There are several points to consider, Juan,' said Maria. 'Firstly, they've asked you to include some popular tunes. You only have to choose these, not compose them. Second, what you do compose can be repeated. For example, you may want a theme corresponding to a particular character and that could be repeated when he or she appears on the stage. You could have one for the mood at the time: a love theme; a jealousy theme; one for distain and so on.'

This was helpful. I was, with the aid of these young actresses, beginning to see a way through. 'Yes, I think I can do this,' I said, with renewed confidence.

'I knew you would,' said Bernarda. 'What about going up to the Mentidero, to celebrate? You know, where the actors and actresses meet.' Maria and I agreed that this was an excellent idea. I told my parents what we were doing and off we went, via the women's houses so we could tell their parents where we were going.

We went to a tavern in Calle de Cantarranas, just off the Calle de León. The main floor area was large and it was quite dark. I could just about identify individual people. About eighty young men and women were laughing and swilling pots of ale or drinking wine. It was so noisy that there could be a party underway. Maria and Bernarda wanted to introduce me to some of their colleagues and friends. I had not realised that they had each been actresses for over a year so they knew many others in the profession. I had not met any professional actresses before and did not know what to expect. As we made our way across the floor, Maria and Bernarda were mercilessly teased by a couple of drunken, rowdy women who may have been their colleagues but were clearly not their friends. 'Who's this young lad then, Maria? I suppose you're going to 'ave 'im tonight or 'ave you 'ad 'im already? If you don't, I damn well will!' 'Is 'e with you, Maria or with you, Bernarda or is 'e with both of ya? Christ alive, you could 'ave a threesome on yer 'ands!'

Neither Maria nor Bernarda responded verbally to these remarks but each gave the women a dismissive glare as we passed them and worked our way through to another group further back.

'Sorry about that Juan,' said Maria. 'We have some genuine friends here and want to introduce you to them. This is Geronima de Valcázar and Maria de Ceballos. They are already members of Manuel Vallejo's company and will probably have parts in Lope's new *comedia*.' Both Geronima and Maria de Ceballos seemed much older than me, probably in their early thirties.

'Good to meet you,' I said.

'So you are Juan Hidalgo,' said Geronima, smiling. 'Maria and Bernarda have already told us about you. You're the harpist and you compose music.' It was good to be known in advance.

'We are here to celebrate,' said Maria de Riquelme, telling Geronima and Maria de Ceballos about the new *comedia* and saying that the three of us would be involved in its performance.

'Congratulations! So are we,' said Geronima. 'Manuel Vallejo wants us to play in it, too.'

'Congratulations, to both of you, too,' said Bernarda.

'Has he given you the first act and have you read it?' asked Maria de Ceballos.

'Yes and no!' said Maria de Riquelme. 'We've got it but haven't read it yet.'

'Well, it looks like a spicy story,' said Maria de Ceballos. 'Let's buy you three a drink and I'll tell it to you.'

Three small jugs of ale arrived and Maria de Ceballos continued. 'It takes place in Ferrara, Italy and is about the Duke of Ferrara who has an illegitimate son, Federico. The Duke is a rampant lecher who goes out in disguise one day to find a woman he can indulge his passions with. He meets a woman called Cintia who is shocked when she recognises him and learns what he is after. He tells her that his fiancée, Casandra, is on her way from Mantua and he will forego these adventures as soon as he marries her. He wants Casandra to produce a legitimate son who can inherit the Duke's estate. While on the road to Ferrara, Casandra's carriage crashes into a river. Federico, who is charged with meeting Casandra, rescues her and the couple fall in love. The Marquis of Mantua, Casandra's escort, says how fortunate it was that Federico was able to rescue Casandra who protests that she would rather marry Federico than his father. The Duke realises that Federico is unhappy and suggests to Aurora, the Duke's niece, that she marries Federico. The act ends with Casandra marrying the Duke and Federico afraid of the dangerous feelings of desire he has towards Casandra, now his stepmother.'

'Then what happens?' asked Maria de Riquelme, without thinking.

'Who knows?' said Maria de Ceballos. 'That is the end of the first act!'

'Not a bad summary of about a thousand lines of verse,' said Geronima, who had apparently also read the manuscript.

'I see what you mean about a spicy plot!' said Bernarda.

'Do you know what parts you will be playing?'

'Yes,' said Maria de Ceballos. 'I will be "Cintia" and Geronima will be "Lucretia". But that's not all, Luis de As is now also in Manuel Vallejo's company. He will be playing the violin in the group of musicians, along with your father, Juan.'

'That's tremendous. Good for Luis,' I said. 'It will be great to have Luis in the team. We are already great friends and we can help each other. I already know my father is in it. It will be our first public performance together.' It seemed odd that these more senior actresses had apparently minor parts while Maria and Bernarda had principal roles in the play.

Discussion then turned to gossip. Bernarda Ramirez and Maria de Riquelme related the story of their being verbally attacked by the drunken actresses as we entered the inn and we all gave our views on our new employers. We all loved Lope de Vega. We were less sure about Manuel Vallejo who seemed to all of us to be abrupt and formal. Within another hour or so, we decided we had had enough of celebrating and went. To fulfil a promise I had made to their parents, I escorted Bernarda and Maria de Riquelme back to their respective houses before going home myself.

***

The following weeks were intensely active for me and my new colleagues. I knew a number of popular songs and I wrote down titles that corresponded to various moods or subjects. Most were songs from the previous century or even before. I read the manuscript of the first act several times and Maria de Riquelme and Bernarda Ramirez read the whole thing to me so I could time them and work out how much music I would need to accompany the text. Luis helped by playing all of the tunes I had composed and we were able to try out some of the duets I had written for the harp and the violin. I had used a separate tune to identify with each main character in the play. After about a month or so, I had completed the score. As I had been asked to produce 'incidental music', I kept the tunes simple and straightforward to play. It would be wrong to compose a range of virtuoso pieces that the players would use to show off their skills. This would overshadow Lope's text and I didn't want that at any price.

Lope was late writing the second and third acts. He had been unwell so we did not receive the second for nearly three months after our auditions and the third did not arrive until more than four months after that, in the May of 1631. Plans for performances of the *comedia* were coming together. The first would be in August, a second in October and then a performance on 3 February before the King. Yes, I would be performing my music on my harp for the King. What an unbelievable honour. It would be an honour for us all.

There was still a huge amount of work to do. Fortunately for our company, the second and third acts were about the same length as the other two. I began work on them as soon as they arrived and the first task was to read them. In act two, it becomes obvious that Casandra is desperately unhappy in the marriage. She tells Federico that she will not bear a son for the Duke. Federico reluctantly agrees to marry Aurora who wants Federico openly to declare his love for her to Casandra and the Duke. However, the Marquis of Mantua says he is in love with Aurora so she decides to marry the Marquis instead. Federico and Cassandra cannot resist the illicit love they share. The act ends with the Pope calling the Duke into battle.

At the beginning of the third act, the two lovers wonder what they will do when the Duke returns. The Duke receives an anonymous letter saying that Casandra and Federico are lovers. He is furious and devises a plan for punishing them without taking revenge. Casandra overhears the Duke's plan and is so shocked, she faints. The Duke ties her to a chair and gags her, so that she cannot cry out, and covers her with a silk cloth. The Duke then tells Federico that a noble of Ferrara has conspired against the Duke and that the noble is concealed beneath the cloth and tied to the chair. He instructs Federico to kill him. Federico strikes with his sword only to discover that the 'noble' is Casandra who is now dead. The Duke tells his soldiers that Federico has killed Casandra because she was to bear the Duke a legitimate son and, following the Duke's instructions, the soldiers kill Federico and that is the end of the play. What an incredible story, one which would hold the interest of any audience from the beginning to the end.

I could see from the two latest acts that I did not have to write any more tunes for new characters because there were none. Also, much of the popular music could be repeated from the first act. This made my task easier. The four of us who made up the troupe of musicians met several times to play some of the musical score together. The group comprised my father and Luis de As on the violins, me on harp and a new colleague, called Simón Donoso, a nervous young man who worked for the Royal Chapel, playing the guitar. Between them, they made several useful suggestions for improving the score, all of which I accepted. They also made me the lead player so I would have to conduct the music and play the harp.

***

I was still using 'my harp' from school and decided that I needed to buy a harp for myself. So I took the harp Señor Vásquez had lent me back on its cart to Imperial. 'Has anyone paid you for your work yet?' asked Señor Vásquez.

'Not yet, señor.'

'Then you may keep it until we need it or until you can comfortably afford to buy a new one for yourself. There is no one studying the harp at school at the moment.' So I thanked the señor profoundly and carried on using the harp. Had I bought a new one then, it would have left me virtually penniless.

***

The first full rehearsal took place in early August. Lope was there as was Manuel Vallejo who played the part of the Duke of Ferrara. The result was more changes to the score, the majority of which were suggested by Lope. We had one more rehearsal, two days before the first performance which was to be on 18 August. It was due to begin at two p.m.

I decided to go to the theatre early for the premiere. I arrived at about eleven a.m. with my harp and at the same time as Luis. By then there must have been at least 200 people in the auditorium. The theatre was in a courtyard between two houses, the backs of which faced each other. The stage was at one end of the courtyard. The rest of the courtyard was the main auditorium, which had standing room only, apart from four long benches at the front. The women were separated from the men and had to occupy the *cazuela* or 'stew pot' which was a gallery built into the back of the house on the right, as you faced the stage. Access for the women was through this house. The changing room for the actors was behind the stage which was covered, unlike the auditorium which, apart from the boxes and galleries, gave no protection from the sun or rain.

The first thing I noticed as I went in through the actors' entrance was the smell of urine. 'That's because if anyone needs a pee during the play, they just do it there and then!' said Luis. I found that difficult to believe. As we reached the front of the stage, by the benches, we were greeted by applause from the men who were already sitting there, quaffing ale and eating. 'Here's the band!' shouted one of them. 'They'd better be blinking good.'

'Thank you,' replied Luis as we sat in the orchestra pit, trying our best to be ignored.

As we sat chatting to each other, several women in long, light brown dresses and white bonnets were walking around the theatre selling apples, oranges, nuts, hard-boiled eggs, pies of dubious quality, strips of salted meat, cakes and a variety of drinks, including beer. People argued furiously about whether some of the men had paid to get in and about who should sit where. A man in the standing area had brought a guitar and, after we had been sitting in the pit for about half an hour, started playing a *zarabanda,* one of the most provocative dances known to mankind. A number of women in the *cazuela* stood up and started to dance. One of the women, facing the crowd below, pulled up her blouse to reveal her breasts which she swung from side to side in time with the music. The men whistled and shouted for more. Another woman also showed her breasts. Not to be outdone, the first woman, still moving in time with the music, lifted her skirt into the air to display her pubic hair. The men cheered even louder. Another woman threw a hand full of nutshells at the men below. They responded by swearing back at the women and throwing apple cores, banana skins and other rubbish into the *cazuela*. We were shocked into silence by this unruliness which rapidly escalated. Men and women began pelting each other with rubbish picked up from the floor, some of which had already been thrown at them by their antagonists. The resulting uproar prompted two *alguacils* to stir from their torpor. They had clearly been drinking heavily but were sober enough to shout, 'Order, order!' to the crowd. Eventually, the audience settled and the *alguacils* took the guitar from the man whose music had been the catalyst for this whole furore.

Having witnessed this kerfuffle, Luis and I took our instruments from the pit and secreted ourselves in the changing area behind the stage. Apart from anything else, we were afraid for the safety of the tools of our trade. Then, one by one, the other performers arrived and we explained to them what had just happened. 'That sort of lewd behaviour is fairly common at these events,' said Geronima, clearly speaking from experience. 'Let's see how they behave during the play.' About half an hour before we were due to start, Lope arrived with Manuel Vallejo. We new members of the company were naturally quite nervous. Lope told me, in jest, that I had more to worry about than anyone else. This was because I had assembled the music, was playing the harp and I was conducting. No one else had three functions in the play, not even him. He helped settle both Luis and Simón Donoso. My father also reassured the rest of us musicians.

Just before the performance started, Lope himself appeared on stage and waited for the babbling audience to settle down. In a brief speech, he gave the background to the play saying that this was its first performance and that it had originated from an idea an Italian playwright had produced over a century before. He said it was a story of love, honour and distain and he would not say how the plot would develop and definitely not how it would finish. He said it would captivate the audience and asked that they remain silent so that everybody there could hear the performance. 'Well, let us begin,' he concluded.

We in the 'band' started playing the music and the *comedia* started with the Duke and two of his servants appearing on stage. I had written a march tune to represent the Duke, played *pizzicato* on the violins, and a distinctive, brisk tune for Federico. For Casandra and Aurora, I had written slower tunes, more in the style of ballads, which I tried to give a feminine feel. I had tried to match the tone of the music with the action in the play, penning some dramatic discords, as Casandra's carriage overturned in the river. I had made abrupt tempo changes for major events, such as the Duke suggesting to Aurora that she marries Federico.

***

Towards the end of the first interval, we heard one of the women selling food and drinks scream out as a man in the stalls eased his hand up the inside of her dress. The *alguacils*, who had sobered up by then, dashed to the spot, grabbed the man and towed him by his ears to the back of the auditorium. The women in the *cazuela* cheered when he was being taken out and shouted even louder to the sound of the *aguacils* kicking and beating him as they meted out summary justice. The second interval passed without incident. No one else wanted to pay that sort of price for lewd or bad behaviour.

As Lope had requested, the audience listened, silently and in awe, to the unfolding plot. Here was a good story, well written and well acted. Maria de Riquelme showed her acting ability with a scintillating performance as Casandra. And Bernarda gave an equally mature and convincing performance as Aurora. I was pleased with the music. The high point for me was at the death of Casandra, for which I had written a simple two-note motif: a prolonged high note followed by a short low one, both played by all of us in unison. There were a few bad notes and a few stumblings over the script but we had overall produced a good result and this showed in the applause as the curtain closed.

I felt exhiliarated by my baptism as a public performer and composer. I have to say, looking back, that, while nervous to begin with, I enjoyed it more and more as we worked our way through the play. I was sure I was not the only one. We all adjourned to an inn afterwards where Lope bought us all a drink in celebration. He was delighted, if not overwhelmed, saying that if that was how we performed at the palace then we would probably not be executed!

***

In the morning, two days later, there was a knock on the door of my parents' house. A surprise was in store: I had been summoned to an audience with the King. At first I was terrified: what had I done? How did he know of me? Was this some form of punishment? The royal messenger explained that one of the King's *corregidors* was in the royal box at the theatre and had reported to the King that he was impressed with my harp playing. As a result, the King had said he wanted me to be considered for a post in the Royal Chapel. I was to be at the palace in three days time at eleven a.m. My parents and I were astonished. What an honour, to work in the palace. But I already had a job with Manuel Vallejo.

58

***

After the royal messenger had left and the initial shock and excitement had passed, my father said that he felt that there was another aspect of my education that needed attention. He said that he was going to take me that afternoon to meet someone he knew, who would discuss various topics with me, which were sure to be to my advantage. He said he would prefer not to elaborate further and that he would appreciate my going along with him. This, to say the least, puzzled me but I agreed and, just after lunch, we left our house together to go to this enigmatic meeting. He said we were heading for a pretty house in the Calle de Santa Clara, overlooking the Plazuela de Santiago. When we reached the house, my father knocked on the door and a well-dressed lady answered. 'Good afternoon, señora. This is my son, Juan Hidalgo.'

'Pleased to meet you, Juan,' she said, cheerfully. 'I am Esmeralda Pechada de Burgos. Do come in.'

I was about to enter when my father said, 'Well, I'll leave you here, Juan.' So he left me alone with the lady and, hesitatingly, I said goodbye to him.

The señora showed me in through the hall. There was an antique side table against the left-hand wall with a large gilt-framed mirror suspended above it. The polished wooden floor had a long, purple carpet covering its centre and there were some pictures of scenes from Greek mythology hanging on the right-hand wall. She took me into a drawing room, the large window of which overlooked the street below. It was well furnished with beautifully upholstered armchairs and several, elaborately woven Turkish carpets scattered randomly on the gleaming wooden floors. There were several paintings on the walls including an oil of the señora herself, painted when she was younger, probably in her forties. The señora appeared to be about fifty to fifty-five years old and had a friendly, welcoming manner. She had an attractive, oval face with bright, greenish eyes. Her cheeks and forehead were just a little wrinkled. She wore a slight blush of rouge on her face and had reddened her lips. Her long, brown hair, with the odd grey thread, fell over her shoulders. She wore a green and blue, swirl-patterned skirt which came midway down her calves and a white blouse with a daringly plunging neckline which revealed a *pulgada* or two of cleavage. Apart from her slightly lowered breasts, she had the figure of a woman of thirtyish and was obviously proud of her appearance. She was highly attractive.

As I looked around the room, she invited me to sit down on one of her sumptuous armchairs. I did so and she sat down in a matching chair facing me. As she did, she tucked her left leg underneath her right thigh, revealing her knees and an expanse of upper leg as she lifted her skirt slightly to complete the manoeuvre.

'So you are Don Juan Hidalgo de Polanco,' she said, smiling broadly.

'Yes, señora, indeed I am.'

'You left school recently?' she asked. 'And you already have a job?'

'Yes, I'm working in a theatre company,' I said. 'She's interviewing me,' I thought. 'What is this about? Is it something to do with etiquette, how I should treat the King? Yes, that's it. She teaches etiquette!'

'And you are a musician?' she said.

'Yes, I play the harp, the guitar and the violin but I am best at the harp. I also compose music.'

'Ah,' she said with a puzzled look. 'So you compose music and play it?'

'Yes,' I said. 'So far my most difficult piece was the score for a Lope de Vega *comedia*.'

'Yes, "Punishment without Revenge", I think,' she said. 'Are you going to concentrate on the composing?'

'Yes, she knows I'm seeing the King,' I thought. 'I really hope so,' I replied, 'especially if I am commissioned to do more. I also want to continue playing the harp.'

'I do like your house,' I said. I wished I hadn't because her immediate response was, 'Come with me. I'll show you around,' thus delaying my discovery of why I was there.

She stood and invited me to follow her. We walked around, room by room, starting on the first floor where there were four bedrooms and a large drawing room, overlooking a cobbled courtyard in the centre of which was a small, raised pond with a working fountain at its centre.

'I am very proud of this drawing room,' she said, 'these paintings in particular.' She pointed her delicate right hand to several more scenes from Greek mythology but, in contrast to those which were hung in the hall, these were much larger pictures. They burst with colour and action.

'Do you like this bedroom?' she asked, opening the door to an extravagant boudoir. The theme of the room was pink with a pink, patterned carpet and drapes in various shades of pink at the windows. The bedspread and other bed linen was also pink as was the floral pattered paper on the walls. The huge, four-poster bed had a canopy suspended over it, like an Arab tent.

I stayed by the door and said, 'Well, yes. It's beautiful.'

She showed me the other upstairs rooms and then took me downstairs to show me the ground floor area. In the spacious kitchen, there was a large stove by the wall opposite the door. There were cooking utensils hung from a rack suspended from the high ceiling and a solid oak table in the middle of the floor with matching oak chairs surrounding it. Opening into the kitchen was a pantry, in which there were shelves of fresh fruit and vegetables, jars of tea and coffee, various preserves, boxes of dried fruits and nuts and earthenware jars on the floor, presumably containing water and juices of different sorts.

She took me into the dining room which had a mahogany table along its length. The table was encircled by a set of smooth, polished mahogany chairs with red and white striped seats. She then showed me into a second, larger drawing room on the ground floor which she said was used for parties and receptions. The furnishings, drapes and carpets in the house showed a degree of opulence and quality that I had never seen before.

'Do you live alone?' I asked.

'Yes,' she said, adding, 'I have a man friend but he comes here only by invitation. His next visit is the day after tomorrow.

'Would you like to sit down again?' she asked, as we entered the smaller drawing room into which she had first invited me. I sat in the chair I occupied at my earlier visit to the room and she assumed the same position in the same chair again. It is strange that people seem comfortable when they return to a room only if they each reoccupy the chair they sat on before they left it.

'Do you know why you are here?' asked the señora, still smiling.

'Not really,' I said. 'Is it something to do with etiquette perhaps?'

She then stood up and walked the few paces to the window and looked out. 'You have a wonderful father,' she said.

'Yes,' I said. 'He has been a great help to me, especially with my music.'

'Well, your father has asked me to help you with your education and etiquette is not far from the mark.'

'What exactly does my father want you to do?'

Then she came out with it. 'I am a whore,' she said, firmly and solemnly, with a degree of pride. 'To be more exact, a retired whore.'

'Really?' I asked, trying to conceal my absolute surprise and astonishment.

'Yes,' she replied, resuming her friendly countenance. 'I am going to teach you how to make love.'

I simply could not believe what I was hearing. Suddenly, everything seemed to fall into place. My father had left me here without saying anything because he did not want to give me the opportunity to refuse to stay. She had wanted to delay the moment of explanation until she had found out more about me. She had showed me around and been friendly towards me simply to make me feel relaxed. She had explained that she was not meeting her lover until later in the week. Presumably, that had been to let me know that we would not be interrupted. I felt like getting up and running but that could be difficult to explain to my father. I was trapped. I had to go through with this. I decided to stay, that is, if I had a choice.

***

'Come and sit next to me on this sofa,' she said, quietly and invitingly, 'on my right-hand side.'

'Have you ever touched a woman's breasts?' she asked. Her casual tone was as if she was asking me about the weather, rather than about my past experience with such exquisite parts of the female body.

'Never,' I said, still somewhat in shock.

She unbuttoned her blouse beginning with the button nearest the top, just below her exposed cleavage. She undid almost all of them down to her waist and opened her blouse to reveal her full, pendulous, smooth, white breasts which emerged as if by their own accord into the daylight. Her nipples were lightly rouged and stood just above the profile of the surrounding breast area.

'Touch them; fondle them,' she said, making it clear, in an enchanting way, that this was an instruction. I obeyed, stroking them in turn with my right hand for a full couple of minutes as neither of us said a word. New to this form of pleasure, I lifted them slightly and felt the warm fold under her breasts where they joined her chest. Then I touched her nipples.

'Very good,' she said. 'You see, they are really standing up now because of the pleasure of your stimulating them. That was lovely and just how lovemaking can start. Has that put you in the mood to continue?'

A little unsure but still curious, I just said, 'Yes.'

'In which case, we will continue in the pink bedroom,' she said, smiling enticingly and looking me directly in the eye.

She grabbed my left arm and loped, like a frisky gazelle, up the stairs, whisking me to her boudoir. She kicked off her shoes, jumped on to the huge bed and pulled me onto it beside her. She was still wearing her blue and green skirt and her unbuttoned blouse provided scant cover, mainly for her back. 'Let's get rid of this,' she said, pulling at her top. 'You can take it off.' I did so, gently pushing it off her left shoulder, so that it fell down her left arm, and moving it down her right arm so that it dropped away completely. She rocked her naked shoulders from side to side, showing me her moving bosoms. 'Aren't they gorgeous?' she said, chuckling over her question.

'Beautiful,' I said, now entering a little more into the spirit of this extraordinary event.

'Carry on fondling them and stiffen up my nipples again,' she said and sitting to her right side I did so, feeling a stirring in my breeches which I found quite enjoyable.

'Take your breeches off,' she instructed. So I did, exposing to her my half erect manhood. 'We'll work on that later,' she said.

'Now for the next stage.' She then undid the buttons on the side of her skirt and pulled it off over her feet, along with a creamy white petticoat, and threw both garments to the floor. 'I want you to kneel between my legs,' she directed, as she raised her knees and opened her legs wide. She was then completely naked, save for a light gold chain around her neck and an emerald ring on the middle finger of her left hand.

'Have you seen anything like this before?' she asked.

Remembering my view of Sister Ursula's lower body when I was only five, I said, 'Not in this detail.'

'I'll explain it all to you.' Then, showing not the least trace of inhibition and clearly relishing the task, she proceeded to conduct the most intimate of demonstrations. 'This is called the vulva,' she said, moving her hand across her genital area. 'You can see at the top here a raised narrow, rounded strip of flesh that sticks out further from my body as you go down about a *pulgada* or two from the top. Just under the crescent-shaped curve at the end is a little round button and I'll tell you about that in a minute. Lower down, this part that emerges from below the little button, is my labia and it is quite sensitive.' She touched it gently and moved it around. 'It is made up of two lips that are joined together at the moment but they open up and you can just see where they join down the middle. You can touch the labia, if you like, to get a feel for it.'

I touched this magical piece of her body. It was soft and pliable and its shape changed as I moved it from side to side. It would fold, bend and stretch. It was about two or three *pulgadas* long and protruded one or two *pulgadas* from the crease in the skin on each side of it. 'Now wet your finger and rub it on this little round button, just above my labia.'

I wet my finger with saliva and let her guide it to the spot. 'Oh!' she yelped. 'That is lovely. Keep doing it. This is my clitoris and it is so, so sensitive. The rubbing gives me great pleasure.'

'Now,' she said, 'I will open my labia and let you explore inside.' She parted her labia and held the lips wide apart with her thumbs and forefingers. Separated and symmetrical, the labia looked like a butterfly with wings that were a caramel colour at the wrinkled edges, gradually becoming a pinkish red towards the centre where they met. I could see her clitoris much more clearly now, above the labia and within the round cover which tightly enclosed it. Between and at the centre of her labia was a narrow, pink ridge that led down to a tiny opening in a small raised area which looked like a tiny red volcano. 'That's my pee hole,' she said softly, guiding the index finger of my left hand to touch it.

She opened her legs a little wider and gently, with her hands, opened up the area right at the bottom of her labia. 'This is my vagina,' she said. 'In a minute or two we'll put your organ in here. Look inside.' She put the index and forefinger of each hand into her vagina and used them to open it up. The room was well lit from the large window, facing the street, and I could see right inside this fascinating, pinkish red aperture as she opened it even wider. 'Can you see right in?' she asked. 'There is an opening at the top, through which your fluid goes before it finds its way to the womb. Fortunately, I am too old now to bear children, so you cannot make me pregnant!' she said, laughing.

Her vulva was a beautiful, intricate structure and the señora was a skilful guide in helping me to explore it. I was still kneeling between her legs. 'Cross your index finger and forefinger of your right hand and put them into my vagina and move them in and out. Now make bigger strokes and, when you move them out, bring them up to touch my clitoris, before you put them back in again. Do it again. And again! That's lovely! Oh! Oh!' she said, as I continued repeating the movements. Suddenly, her whole body shook and she looked up at the ceiling as if passing out. 'Oooooh!' she shrieked. 'That was a climax. It was fantastic. You did that!' she said, excitedly praising me for my modest success. 'I want you inside me now. That is the next step.' She stroked my manhood for a few seconds as I looked at her open labia and vagina which had become wet as I manipulated it. 'You are ready now. Put it into my vagina.' Again, I did as I was told and slid it in gently, leaning over her and taking my full weight on my hands and arms. It seemed natural to move it in and out and I did so. On about the fourth stroke, my fluid burst into her and I went into an ecstatic spasm. She laughed and said, 'What did you think of that?'

'That was just wonderful, señora. Thank you so much,' I said, withdrawing myself from her. She turned to take a pink towel from on top of the bedside table and wiped herself gently with it, removing my fluid which had leaked out as I withdrew and was beginning to flow down to her bottom and onto the bedclothes.

'Don't thank me. Thank your father. He paid me well for this,' she said, still lying on her side and using the towel.

'May I ask how much?'

'That is between me and my client which in this case is your father. We've plenty of time for you to make love to me again, if you want to.'

'Can we?' I asked. I was really enjoying this now and, apparently, so was she.

'I would like you to do it again, starting with my breasts, as we did before.' We moved to the centre of the bed again and I soon had a good stiffness in my manhood. 'Now get on top,' she said.

It all lasted much longer that time and I felt I had done a better job.

'You could be good at this, with a little practice! Did you enjoy that?'

'I certainly did,' I said and thanked her again.

'Well, that's it,' she said, wiping herself with the towel once more. 'Let's get dressed.' We slid off the bed. As she did so her back was towards me for a moment and I noticed a small tattoo, just below her right shoulder. I was sure I recognised it as the Habsburg royal coat of arms. We put our clothes back on and she then sat in front of a mirror and combed her hair. 'That's better,' she observed as I watched. She then rang a bell that was standing on her dressing table. A young woman entered the room and stood just inside the door. So there had been someone in the house while I was having this 'lesson'. 'Juan, I wish you every success for the future and, who knows, I may see you playing your harp in public before long. It was good to meet you. Would you escort Señor Hidalgo to the front door, please?'

I thanked her yet again, said goodbye and walked towards the maid standing by the door. The girl's face seemed vaguely familiar and then it dawned on me. It was Barbola. I said nothing until we were walking towards the stairs.

'You are Barbola, aren't you?'

'Yes, señor, I recognise you, too. Thank you for the silver *real*!'

'I'd forgotten about that.'

'I hadn't. It was such an act of kindness from a young man.'

'Why are you here?'

'It's a long story, Señor Hidalgo. My husband was killed on the farm, about a week after I met you. He was in a fight with another farm hand who threw a pitchfork at him. One of the prongs went straight into his heart and he died instantly. I was devastated and could not stay at the farm. I decided to come to Madrid to find a job. And this is it. I am maid to Esmeralda Pechada de Burgos.'

'I am so sorry to hear about your husband. Where is your baby?'

'She's with my mother who lives at the northern end of the Calle de los Preciados. I am living with my mother.'

'Do you do any other work?' I asked.

'No, I am just the maid here. I do the housework which mainly means keeping the house clean. I could manage to do some other work as well. So if you know of anybody who needs some housework done, could you please let me know?'

'Of course. Does the señora have many guests like me?'

'No. She is retired now but does still give the occasional lesson to young lads. They are all about your age.'

I pulled my purse from the pocket in my breeches and took out a silver *real* which I gave her as I said goodbye.

'Thank you, Señor Hidalgo. That is so kind of you. Good to see you again.'

As I left the house, my mind was in a state of turmoil. What would I say to my father when I reached home? Would I thank him? Would I simply say nothing? How would he know whether I had stayed with Esmeralda and had the 'lesson'? Was my mother involved? Would I mention Barbola? I needed some time to work out what to say when I arrived. For certain, I had had the most amazing experience for which I would be forever grateful to my father and to Esmeralda.

My father greeted me as I walked in. 'How was that?' he asked, in a respectfully neutral tone.

'Fine. Many thanks, Papá. That certainly improved the state of my education!' I said, smiling.

CHAPTER 5

I was walking to the palace. I was nervous and tense. I wanted to impress. I had to be on form. I had to fill that vacancy.

I arrived about fifteen minutes early, so I walked around the Plaza del Palacio for about five minutes. I observed the action by the entrance to the palace. This made me relax. I just watched. It was obviously a busy day. There were people going in and others coming out. There were footmen restraining horses. Some bewigged coachmen were preparing a carriage for a royal visit. I walked in at the main palace entrance. There were guards there, one at each side, standing stationary and looking directly ahead with staring eyes, as if in a trance. Just inside there were two attendants, a man and a woman sitting at desks. I went up to the man and said, 'I am Juan Hildago. I have an audience with the King.'

'What is your full name?' asked the man.

'Don Juan Hidalgo de Polanco.'

'Follow me,' said the woman.

She led me into the main part of the palace. We turned left towards the west wing where the King had his quarters. The corridors bustled with activity as dignitaries, notaries, clergy, lawyers, messengers, guards, flunkies, secretaries and every other rank of palace official, were going to and fro. My escort showed me into a small anteroom and asked me to sit on one of the chairs. I did so and she went out, leaving me alone. I seemed to be there an age but it was probably no more than five minutes when a man with a waistcoat and tails appeared. 'Who is Don Juan Hidalgo de Polanco?' he asked, as if the room was full of people.

'I am,' I replied.

'Come with me,' he said, coldly and frowning.

I followed him into a larger, more ornately furnished room and he directed me to sit in front of a plain oak desk. On its opposite side there were two vacant chairs.

'Sit there, please,' he said. He left and closed the door behind him.

Within a minute or so the door opened and two men walked in. One of them came up to me, smiled and asked, 'Are you Juan Hildago?'

I stood and replied, 'Yes, I am.'

'Good. We want to speak to you about a post as harpist in the Royal Chapel,' he said, in an encouraging tone. 'Please sit down.'

The two men sat at the far side of the desk. The one who had spoken introduced himself as Mateo Romero, Maestro of the Royal Chapel. He did not introduce the other, bearded and stern-looking man by name but simply said that he was a colleague. The friendly, smiling Maestro said that one of the King's *corregidors* had seen me and heard me playing the harp at the premiere of Lope de Vega's 'Punishment without Revenge'. The *corregidor* had been impressed with what he had heard, the more so because he was told that I had assembled the musical score and that I had composed much of the music. He said that the *corregidor* had reported back to the Maestro and that that was why I was being considered for a post as harpist in the Royal Chapel.

He questioned me about my family and my origins, asking if all the members of my family were of pure Spanish blood. I assured him that they were. He asked about my music, including how long I had been playing musical instruments, which ones I played and liked playing most, to what standard I had been examined, how much music I had composed, from whom I had learnt to compose, whether I would be willing to take further lessons in composing and in playing the harp, how I liked my job with Manuel Vallejo, for how long I was contracted to work for him and whether I would be prepared to negotiate a termination of the contract if I were to be offered a post in the Royal Chapel. He asked about Spanish composers and whether I liked the music of any in particular and whether there were any I particularly disliked.

At the end of the interview, the men showed me into another room nearby where there was a harp and a chair. 'We would like you to play us some music,' said Señor Romero. 'I apologise for not advising you in advance, but we want to see how you approach this without warning. You can start by playing anything you want.' The harp was in perfect tune. I played 'Pedraza' and then the piece that I knew by Cabezón. I then played some pieces which were new to me. I had to read the music straight from printed sheets which the señor placed on a stand in front of me. I thought I did quite well, despite my nervousness which I hoped was not too obvious. We returned to the room in which I was interviewed and all sat around the desk.

'Do you have any questions?' asked the señor. I said I had none which I thought was the safest response. The two men stood and I then stood. 'We will let you know within a week whether you are being offered a post,' said the cheery Maestro. The other man broke into a smile and said, 'Thank you Señor Hidalgo. My name is Philip the Fourth. I am the King of Spain.'

'Your Majesty,' I said and bowed deeply as both the King and the Maestro left the room. I sat down again, astonished by this whole experience but mostly by the revelation that the Maestro's 'colleague' was the King.

Within a week, I received a letter offering me a job as harpist in the Royal Chapel, under Mateo Romero. I was so elated I jumped into the air and cheered aloud. There was a draft contract for me to sign and return. I had to provide my own harp. I would have to be available ten hours a day to play music to the King or Queen. I would have to be smartly dressed at all times while in the palace and 'appropriately attired to appear and play before their Royal Highnesses and their guests and to renounce all other contractual commitments, save any previously agreed by Their Majesties' Court'. The annual salary would be 5000 *reales* plus expenses of eighty-five *reales* that is, about 450 *ducats* and my costs. A fortune.

I spoke to Manuel Vallejo and we agreed that he would release me from the contract but he wanted me to play in the second public performance of the Lope *comedia*, which would be on 4 October, and in the one for the King on 3 February. I signed the contract and took it to the palace with a covering letter about the points Señor Vallejo had made. Within a further few days, I received a printed copy of the contract and a letter telling me to report to the office of Maestro Mateo Romero on 28 September. That was my birthday and I would be seventeen.

The day I signed the contract, I went to the music shop in the Calle de San Juan Miguel, which is just off the Platería, hoping to buy a new harp. My excitement grew as I entered. I cast my eye around the shop and my heart dropped: I just could not see one there. I walked slowly towards the back of the shop and there it stood, obscured by the wing of a grey curtain: an instrument of dazzling beauty. Its polished, wooden body shone, reflecting the light from outside. I sat on a stool, and shuffled myself into a position to play a few chords. The crisp, clear tone totally captivated me. Its full and vibrant sound made my neck hairs tingle. I fell immediately in love with this glorious harp and felt compelled to own it. The shopkeeper came over as I played. 'Do you like it, señor? She's yours for seventy-five *ducats*.' A shock. I had earned little more than this in my whole time working for Señor Vallejo. I did not argue and bought her there and then. So I became the proud owner of this spectacular instrument. It would be a major part of my life.

I took 'my harp' back to Señor Vásquez and thanked him for letting me use it for so many years. I could detect his disappointment but he wished me well with my new one and good luck in my new job. The look on his face triggered an idea. 'Señor Vásquez, I have been playing the school harp for six years now. I am bringing it back battered and worn. I want to take it to the music shop off the Platería and have it cleaned, serviced and refinished. I will pay.'

'Yes, please, Juan. That is so generous of you,' he said, smiling anew. I took the harp away again and within a week returned it in sparkling condition to a grateful Señor Vásquez.

My family basked in my success in winning the job at the palace. My father paid for a celebration drink for me, my friends and work colleagues at a tavern in the Mentidero. It would be at the inn to which Lope took us on 18 August, after the premiere of 'Punishment without Revenge'. Nearly the whole cast came. Maria de Riquelme and Bernarda Ramirez were escorted by Maria's mother and, once again, I agreed to see them home. Luis de As and some of my other friends from school were there, including Balthazar Favales, Christóbal de Agramontes and Honofre Espinosa with his sister, Teresa. Apart from being a chance to celebrate my luck, it was an opportunity to catch up with school friends who were by then in jobs. It struck me as amusing that Honofre, who had lied to the constable about the fire at the 'Hideaway', was applying for a post in the Inquisition. Christóbal, who had questioned Father Sancho about the creation, was being trained for the priesthood. Balthasar had a job as sales agent, working for a building company.

'Why work for the Inquisition?' I asked Honofre.

'I am a patriotic person and I want Spain protected against outsiders. And those who are against us Catholics.'

'Maybe, but do you have to do the dirty work?' asked Bernarda.

'You will meet all sorts of people in the palace,' said Geronima, changing the subject. 'I have performed there in Manuel's company.'

'Yes,' said Manuel, 'you will have such an interesting time but you will be busy. The King is very demanding. You will be working for his ministers, as well the royal family.'

'I hope you will be well paid,' said Balthasar. 'I don't want to have to buy the drinks every time we meet.'

'You won't have to worry about that,' said Maria de Riquelme, leaving me puzzled about how she could know about my salary, if indeed she did.

'You may not be paid at all,' Honofre said. 'There is such a shortage of cash in the Treasury that many of the staff are paid months in arrears. Especially at the end of the year when the money runs out. At least, that's what I've heard.'

'I hope that isn't a problem in my case,' I replied.

We all left the tavern at about eleven p.m. My father went home alone. Honofre and Balthasar left together and Teresa, who lived with her family in the Puerta de Guadalajara, quite near my house, decided to join me,

Maria de Riquelme and Bernarda Ramirez, both of whom I was escorting home. We all chatted as we walked down the Mentidero, down to the Calle de las Huertas, towards the Calle de Príncipe where Maria and Bernarda lived. Teresa and I kissed Maria and Bernarda as we bid them goodnight. Maria and Bernarda wished me good luck in my new job.

That left just me and Teresa who, after the others had left us, placed her right hand in my left. We walked hand in hand up the Calle de Príncipe, turned left at the top towards the Puerta del Sol and straight on to the Puerta de Guadalajara. As usual, the streets were busy with beggars on most corners and ladies of the night showing themselves off as they sought custom. The air was permeated by the smell of human excrement which the occupiers of houses were dumping in the streets through their front doors.

Apart from my mother's, which I often clasped as a small child, I had never held a woman's hand before. At first, I felt awkward but enjoyed the warm, wanted feeling more and more as our night walk continued. I started a conversation by asking Teresa her age and what her interests were. She said she was sixteen and still at school. She loved to work with linen and especially enjoyed embroidery. 'I do like you, Juan, and that is why I wanted to walk home with you, Maria and Bernarda,' she said, softly but with a note of passion in her voice.

'That is kind of you, Teresa,' I replied, clumsily but wanting to show my feelings towards her. 'I like you, too.' I wondered if she could be my first girlfriend. She was certainly intelligent and had really grown up since our little gang used to meet in the 'Hideaway'. She was good looking, as tall as me and trimly built. She held her head high and had the look of the self-assured.

Our conversation became more relaxed as we talked about music, my new job and Honofre's wish to join the Inquisition. I said that I still didn't understand why he wanted to do that but, like the job of a jailer, someone had to do it. I asked her if she was interested in drama and told her about the Lope *comedia*. She said she'd like to see it and I outlined the story to her but not how it finished.

'Go on! Tell me! I want to know!' she laughingly demanded.

'No! You may see it sometime and it will spoil it if you know the ending!'

'I'll hit you if you don't tell me!'

I let go of her hand and ran ahead, pretending to be scared.

'Stop, stop, I'm only fooling!' she said.

I relented and we carried on hand in hand. As we approached her house in the Puerta de Guadalajara, she stopped and said, 'I want to kiss you, but not outside my house. Come here.' She gently eased me into a passageway between the Puerta de Guadalajara and the empty Plazuela de los Herradores and pushed my back up against the wall of one of the buildings. She held my shoulders and kissed me full on the lips, rotating her head to and fro like the pendulum of a clock. It was beautiful and we joined in an embrace. 'That's it,' she said, pulling away after about half a minute of what to me was perfect pleasure. 'We must see each other again.'

'For sure,' I said, as we turned towards the Puerta de Guadalajara to walk the rest of the way to her house.

***

On my first day at the palace, an escort took me, dragging my new harp on its cart, to Señor Romero's office on the ground floor of the west wing. Once again, the palace was bubbling with activity, with officials rushing around as if there was some crisis to deal with. My escort knocked on the señor's door but there was no reply so we waited. About five minutes later, the Maestro arrived, apologising for his absence but greeting me with his familiar smile and outstretched arms. 'Welcome to the Royal Chapel, Juan. I hope you will be happy here.'

He sat me at his desk and we had an introductory chat. He said that he would be my boss but that the King's Office would also deal with me direct. I would be expected to play virtually every day, sometimes as a solo player and sometimes in a group with guitarists, violinists and singers. The Maestro was responsible for assembling the music programme for the week ahead and at the end of each week would tell me what it was. There would often be unexpected changes. I would play for the King or the Queen or both. The Maestro would introduce me to a number of colleagues in the Royal Chapel, nearly all of whom were instrumentalists. There were no other composers at the court other than the Maestro himself. He said, laughing all over his face, that he was known in the palace as 'El Maestro Capitán' because he served in the Flemish army before he joined the Chapel. He was sure we would get on very well together and I readily agreed.

He then showed me to my office, which was small and which I would share with two other musicians, both of whom were violinists. It was located in the west wing of the palace near the Golden Tower and overlooking the King's Courtyard. We went in. There were three wooden chairs, a wooden, sloping topped desk, several old-looking, wooden cabinets scattered around the walls, a wardrobe and a hat stand. The walls were bare stone and the floor was laid in grey stone slabs which were so uneven that the chairs and desk stood with only three out of four legs on the stone. A folded piece of paper had been placed under the airborne leg of the desk to give it some transient stability. The room was bare, dark and unwelcoming.

'Well this is it!' said the Maestro, still cheerful and smiling.

'Where are the colleagues with whom I will be sharing?'

'They are upstairs.'

'Upstairs?'

The Maestro explained that 'upstairs' meant in the royal apartments and suites which occupied the whole of the first and second floors of the palace. I would soon see that there was a huge range of rooms used by their Majesties: kitchens, storage rooms, offices, drawing rooms, dining rooms, meeting rooms, lounges, studies, libraries, music rooms and, of course, bedrooms. He said that the King occupied the west wing and the Queen the east wing and that the Royal Chapel was based in the west wing because we were the King's Chapel.

I went to the window. There was a busy market in the courtyard outside. People were wandering around from stall to stall, bargaining and buying from hawkers and traders. Some were walking on the grass and some were standing in groups talking. It bustled out there, just as it did at the market in the Plazuela de Selenque. The Maestro explained that I was lucky to have a room overlooking the courtyard. The King's councils occupied most with the view but not this one. He could not resist telling me about these councils which were the King's most important sources of advice. He said that the most important was the Council of State which considered major issues of policy. The Council of War reported to this council which was chaired by the King. He explained that the other councils were the Councils of Finance, of Castile, of the Indies, of Aragon, of the Inquisition, of Italy, of Flanders, of Portugal and that there was one for State Security. I had heard of all of these before, except for the mysterious last.

He said that the offices on the outer side of the wings were occupied by a range of government and royal staff from the Chief Minister and his Private Office, the Inquisitor General, the Archbishop of Toledo, the Keeper of the Palace and the Director of Building and Works, through to the royal portrait painters, the staff of the Royal Archives, the palace messengers and escorts and, not least, the Royal Paymaster, by whom we were paid our salaries. Off the main building were the Royal Stables and the Royal Mews. He explained that the palace was originally a fortress so designed to be occupied by soldiers. This is why it was uncomfortable, draughty and dark. But it was all we had and we had to make the best of it.

I asked him what music the King and Queen liked best. He told me that most of what we played to Their Majesties was in the form of songbooks and sheet music, kept in the wooden cabinets against the walls of the office. He said that Their Majesties loved fairly modern music, much of which was in the Songbook of Sablonara. This contained songs written by himself, his friend Juan Blas de Castro who, sadly, had died blind and ill only a few weeks before then, and several other composers who had written recently for the Court. He said he was very proud of this song collection and delighted that Their Majesties liked these songs so much. They also enjoyed popular songs, and often just the tunes, from the Palace Songbook which contained many older songs, some by Juan de Encina, Juan de Anchieta and others who wrote their music towards the end of the fifteenth century and the beginning of the sixteenth. They also enjoyed the music of Cabezón and the songs of Milán.

I told him that I was keen on many of these composers, especially Cabezón and Encina and that I had played some of their works. I knew Cabezón's plaintive piece 'The Lady Pleas to Him' for solo harp, which I had played in 'public' at the school recital and, of course, to him and the King at my interview. I also enjoyed several violin duets he had written. I said I knew a good many songs by Encina, most from the Palace Songbook, and I especially enjoyed the touching songs of Juan Vásquez. I also told him that the grandson of Vásquez was my music teacher at Imperial and that that was how I came to know about his music.

'You will love working here,' he said, giving me the comfortable feeling that he and the King had made the right choice in selecting me for the job. 'You will fit in so well and be in your element. You already know a number of the pieces which are favourites of Their Majesties and that will be a good start. You will be free to write music yourself, apart from being commissioned to compose for special occasions.' I immediately took to Mateo Romero and could see that he would make a good mentor and colleague.

The door of the office burst open and two boisterous, laughing figures carrying violin cases appeared. 'We did a good job there. Well done, Juan,' said one to the other.

'Juan! It's you. I didn't know you worked here!' I said to a startled Juan Roxas de Carrión.

'Yes, I've been here for over a year now, working for the Maestro. I'm enjoying it. Congratulations, Juan. It's great that you've got a job here, too. This is my colleague Francisco de Guypúzcoa. He also plays the violin and shares this office with me. We'll be sharing it with you now! That'll be such good fun. We've just got back from playing for His Majesty. He applauded after our little session so he liked it!'

Francisco de Guypúzcoa shook my hand heartily. 'Good to meet you, Juan. I'm looking forward to working with you. Welcome to our tiny home!'

The Maestro told me he had nothing else to say to me for then except that I would be playing for the King the following morning at eleven o'clock. He did not want to put me under too much pressure, playing for His Majesty for the first time, and said I would be the accompanying harpist in pieces for two violins and a harp. There would also be a singer. He suggested I play 'The Lady Pleas to Him'. He said I should play it right at the end of the half hour recital in which Juan de Roxas and Francisco de Guypúzcoa would also be playing.

I spent the next few hours talking to Juan and Francisco. They had some interesting views about working at the palace. They confirmed my first impression that Mateo Romero was an excellent Maestro and ideal person to work for. They said that the sad thing was that he would be retiring in a few years and they had no idea who would be replacing him. He was, nevertheless, a hard taskmaster and expected high standards from his performers. They said that, as long as I practised the pieces we were to play for the King, and became very good at playing them, I would be fine.

I asked how many of us there were working in the Royal Chapel. Strangely, they said that they did not really know. A number of quite well known performers had been made honorary members of the Chapel and there was a large number of part-time performers whom they saw only occasionally. They reckoned about fifty in all, but that excluded a large number of singers who were drafted in for choral works.

They said I would love His Majesty the King. He was still a young king at twenty-six years of age. He was gentle, courteous and kind. He was a musician in his own right and played both the violin and the cello. He often played with members of the Royal Chapel and played with his brothers Ferdinand, the Cardinal Infante and, the older of the two, the Infante Don Carlos, each of whom played the violin. The King could compose music, write poetry and spoke several languages. They said I would also like the King's two colourful brothers.

They mentioned the King's amorous adventures with women, particularly actresses, such as the famous Maria Calderón. She was one of many of the King's mistresses and was the mother of his illegitimate son, Don Juan, who was then two years old. They said that the King was an accomplished horse rider and that he enjoyed hunting in the forests around Madrid.

They also spoke of the Chief Minister, the Count Duke Olivares, to whom the King had virtually abdicated his powers. The domineering

Olivares distracted the King from his duties and encouraged him in his pursuit of pleasure, even procuring women for him. Olivares was not a diplomat and had to manipulate and bully to achieve his ends. They said that, in common with many others in the palace, I would not like him. We could only wait and see. The palace, they said, seethed with gossip, scandal and rumour and this alone made it a fascinating place in which to work.

I said that we needed to discuss what we would be playing for the King the following day. Juan de Roxas said it was only a short programme which was to be played for his Majesty and the Inquisitor General who was coming to see His Royal Highness. 'Not about indulging himself with all these women!' said Francisco de Guypúzcoa, laughing raucously.

Juan said that we would play a few popular songs by Encina and Milán but they would be religious, pastoral or humorous so as to avoid offending the Inquisitor General: apparently some of the Encina songs were quite ribald. We spent an hour or so practising the chosen material, but not with the singer. I practised my piece by Cabezón.

When I arrived home, I was subjected to a full interrogation by my parents and Francisco. I told them how much I liked the cheerful Mateo Romero and about my wild, new colleagues Francisco de Guypúzcoa and Juan de Roxas Carrión. I was excited but apprehensive about having to play for the King and the Inquisitor General. My father was reassuring and said that I could now play the Cabezón piece wearing a blindfold. I said I had also learnt about the layout of the palace and who occupied the main areas. I also said that the Maestro had mentioned a council I had not heard of before, the Council for State Security.

'If I were you, I would forget about that one,' said my father, abruptly and with a hint of mystery. 'Some odd things have happened to people investigated by them. My advice to you, Juan, is not to speak about it.' That was advice I would follow, at least for the time being.

The following day, I arrived at my office at nine o'clock and started practising for the session with the King and the Inquisitor General. I had that slight, healthy nervousness that a passably competent performer has before playing. I was glad that Juan and Francisco de Guypúzcoa had the same feelings. I was surprised when they told me that, for the performance, I had to change into a cream-coloured shirt with maroon pantaloons. This was standard dress, apparently. I tried several of each from the wardrobe in my office and found a combination that fitted. It was freshly laundered.

At about ten o'clock, a palace escort took us, along with the singer, a tenor called Alonso Arias de Soria, to the drawing room in the King's apartments where we were to perform. We were to use an area in a corner of the room. I set up my harp opposite a chair and the violinists placed their violins on the chairs they would be occupying. We set up our music stands. We were then escorted back to our room where we, including Alonso Arias, waited to be escorted back for our eleven o'clock performance.

Twenty minutes before we were due to start, the Maestro appeared at the door of our office. 'Don't forget, the King is not going to get involved with you. So just go in, prepare yourselves and start playing when you see the signal from the Assistant Private Secretary. This will probably be just after eleven. You will be able to tell the time by the clock above the door at the far end of the room. You, Juan de Roxas, will be the lead player so you will direct.'

Not long after, the escort took us back and we prepared ourselves for the recital. I sat nervously with my harp resting on my shoulder and the other three were also sitting but looking quite relaxed. At just after eleven o'clock, four men appeared through the entrance at the far end of the room. I recognised the King. His Majesty sat about thirty *pies* from us on an ornate, gilded chair. The man whom I imagined to be the Inquisitor General then sat, half facing the King but only a few *pies* from him. The other two sat about five or six *pies* away from the King and the Inquisitor General. A discussion started with the Inquisitor putting some points, rather bluntly I thought, to His Majesty. The only words I heard clearly were spoken by the King who asked one of the other men, who was writing notes, whether he had recorded a particular point. This discussion continued for a full ten minutes and I was beginning to wonder whether we were going to perform after all. Then one of the men, wearing an extravagantly embroidered jacket almost down to his knees, came towards us and signalled us to start. He was the Assistant Private Secretary. He was looking at Juan so presumably he knew that he was the leader.

The King and his party concluded their discussion and turned to face us. We started our recital. The first piece was a song by Encina which was played by Juan de Roxas and Francisco de Guypúzcoa. Alonso Arias de Soria sang. The second and third were ballads by Milán and the fourth a song I had not heard before for a solo singer. It was about a peasant farmer who had fallen in love with a milkmaid. The others played a few other short pieces and then, finally, I performed the solo harp piece by Cabezón.

The King stood as soon as we finished and applauded enthusiastically. The other three in his party immediately followed. His Majesty then came towards us, clapping until he reached us, followed by the Inquisitor General who had stopped applauding by then. We all stood and bowed. 'Well done, gentlemen. That was excellent.'

Then, turning to me, he said, 'I recognised that harp solo. It was delightful. Are you the young man we interviewed the other day? Is this the first time you have since played for me?'

'Yes, Your Majesty. You did interview me. This is the first time I've played for you since I joined the Royal Chapel.'

'Good. You are a skilled harpist. Welcome to the palace. I hope you enjoy working here and I'm sure we will hear you playing again soon,' he said, with not more than a trace of a smile.

'Thank you, Your Majesty.'

The King turned and walked back to sit in his ornate chair, followed by the Inquisitor. The Assistant Private Secretary waved his hand towards the door and we left.

As we arrived back at our office we were greeted by the Maestro asking us whether the King was happy with our performance. 'He liked it,' said Juan de Roxas Carrión. 'Juan was great on the harp and the King praised him.'

'What do you think, Juan?' he said, looking at me.

'I agree with Juan de Roxas. I could not have played so well without Juan and Francisco. I think we all did well and Alonso, too.'

'Well, here is the programme for next week,' said the Maestro.

So, my first experience of playing in front of His Majesty seemed to go well. Apart from my initial nervousness, I enjoyed it and the King made me feel good when he complimented me at the end. Juan and Francisco de Guypúzcoa were right. It was impossible not to like the King. I gained confidence from that first performance for His Majesty but knew that I could play still better. I realised that I needed to work more, not only to improve my skills as a harpist, but also to familiarise myself with the hundreds of pieces that I would have to play to Their Majesties. I spent many hours practising, reading and playing various songs and instrumental pieces. My jolly, new roommates were a great help and much of the practising was with them making up a threesome. During this time, I met many new colleagues in the Royal Chapel. I renewed my acquaintance with Simón Donoso, the edgy guitarist, who played with us in 'Punishment without Revenge'. I got to know Hernando de Eslava, a cello player, Gabriel Cortes and Esteban Marques, both of whom were violinists and Vitoria de Cuenca, a soprano.

CHAPTER 6

One morning, I arrived at the palace much earlier than usual to practise a difficult piece which was new to me. I was playing with the door of the rehearsal room open. This room was near to the office and had a door onto the main corridor of the west wing. I had been playing for about twenty minutes or so when a man appeared at the door. 'That's a lovely piece,' he said. 'You play well!'

'You're very kind.'

'I haven't seen you before,' said the stranger. 'You're new?'

'Yes. Been here about three months,' I laughed. I didn't feel new at all. 'And you, señor?'

'I paint portraits.'

'Of whom?' I could imagine well enough.

'You can guess,' he said, amused at our banter

'How long have you been working here?'

'Since 6 September '23. I remember the day as vividly as yesterday.'

The painter was substantially older than me, about thirty, I thought. He was a tall, proud looking man with sharp brown eyes and a wide mop of dark hair, cut to the level of his mouth. The tips of his striking moustache curved towards his eyes. He said he had painted quite a number of portraits of the King, the Queen, the *infantes* and *infantas* as well as a number of palace staff.

'Have you painted one of us yet?' I asked.

'No. Not yet,' he chuckled, 'but I know some of you better than I know the King. What a group of characters you are!'

'I'd love to see some of your paintings. Could I?'

'Of course,' said the painter. 'You must come along to my studio. It's on the other side of this wing. Come along now if you want.'

'Thank you. I will, but only if it's convenient.'

'Yes. Let's go.' We walked along the corridor. At that time of the morning, there was nowhere near the bustle and hubbub that there would inevitably be, later in the day.

'Here it is. Come in.'

The studio was much larger that our tiny little office. It was about thirty *pies* long by about twenty wide and completely dominated by an unfinished picture. The painting reached almost to the ceiling and was wider than my height. It was colossal. It portrayed a military figure, wearing a large, tasselled hat, dressed in black armour and sat on a magnificent horse, which was rearing up, its front feet a good three *pies* from the ground. The face of the rider was unfinished, as was his uniform and much of the background, but the horse was completely finished, or was to my untrained eye. The sheer size of the painting and the life-size image of the horse and its rider gave it a startling but exhilarating presence.

'Goodness me,' I said, still recovering from the impact of this amazing though unfinished work. 'Who's that?'

'The Count Duke Olivares. As you can see, I am having trouble with it. It's nowhere near finished. I just can't tie him down to a sitting. So I can't finish his face.'

'Why are you painting him? He's not a general is he?'

'You are right, of course. He's definitely not a general and holds no military rank. Said he'd look good as a field marshal. How I came to paint him is an interesting story and I won't bore you with the detail. Each of us came from Seville and he encouraged me to work in the palace. So he and I know each other well. But it was the King who asked me to paint his portrait, when I came back from Italy.'

'From Italy? Why did you go to Italy?'

The painter explained more of the story. He visited Italy with General Spínola on a mission to buy some works by Italian masters for the King's collection. He was away for eighteen months. 'I bought about twenty paintings. Came back about a year ago. It was then that the King asked me to paint a portrait of the Count Duke but I couldn't start it until I had completed some other jobs.'

'Why did General Spínola go?' I asked.

'Hmm. Tricky question,' the painter replied, hesitatingly, as if not wishing to answer. 'The General was on a separate mission. Supposed to report to the Council for State Security when he returned. He died in Italy so never made it.'

I remembered my father's advice not to ask questions about that council so I didn't. The painter showed me some other work he had started and a finished picture of a dwarf who worked in the palace.

'I think I should be going back,' I said. 'I have taken enough of your time.'

'I'm sure we'll see each other again,' he said. 'What is your name?'

'Juan Hidalgo. What's yours?'

'Diego, Diego Velázquez.'

***

Not many days after I met Diego, Mateo Romero called me into his office. By then, I had played dozens of times for His Majesty and three or four times for the King and Queen together so I was beginning to feel well settled into the job. Mateo asked me how I felt I was progressing and I confidently told him just that. He was pleased, too. He asked me if I would be prepared to have some further lessons in composition and that he already had a teacher in mind. It was Carlos Patiño, a young composer whom he thought to be good. I said I would be pleased to have further lessons. I was hungry for knowledge.

'That's good, Juan. The cost of your lessons will be borne by the palace and I have already made arrangements for that. You must not take this as a criticism. You are already a very good harpist. You drive yourself mercilessly in learning new pieces and practising them. Now I want you to become a first rate composer. The King wants a highly skilled composer working here and that should be you.'

'But what about you, Mateo? You are the resident composer.'

'Yes, for now, maybe. But I won't be here for ever.'

Just before my first Christmas at the palace, I had my first lesson with Carlos Patiño. The Maestro had already told me that Señor Patiño was more experienced in writing church music than the kind of music I had previously composed. The largest piece of work I had written up to then was the incidental music for 'Punishment without Revenge', which was about as distant as it was possible to be from a piece to be played in a church. However, if I was to be a major force in composing for the Royal Chapel, I would have to master composing liturgical music.

Señor Patiño asked me what I hoped to achieve by these lessons. I told him that I wanted to be a competent composer of a wide range of music. He asked me what I had composed already. I had taken along the score of 'Pedraza' and the music for the Lope *comedia* and showed him both. 'Is that all you have written?' he asked, sounding quite disappointed.

'I've written a few other practice pieces. But that's about all I've kept.'

He looked through what I had brought. 'Not too bad, but we need to do quite a lot of work if you really want to achieve your aim. You have only composed for a narrow range of instruments. We need to extend that. I want you to learn to write for the full range of stringed instruments. Not just guitars and violins. You need to know how to deal with wind instruments, including trumpets and flutes. And also percussion. You have not written for a choir, let alone for more than one choir singing at the same time. We need to teach you to compose for solo singers, for two, three, four voices and so on. And you need to write for keyboard instruments such as the organ and clavichord. You also need to know more about counterpoint and using harmony as well as constructing melodies. You have written some nice tunes but it would be good to be more versatile in generating them. We need to get you to use a wider range of rhythms. And managing the players. You must not be afraid to stretch them. Right to the full limit of their abilities.'

Señor Patiño breathed new life into my composing. He was setting the agenda for a fairly extensive course of lessons and I was happy with that, provided it did not interfere with my performing at the palace.

***

Then came 3 February and the performance of 'Punishment without Revenge' in front of the King and Queen. We had exactly the same performers as we had had previously for the August and October performances. It was good to work with Manuel Vallejo again, despite his coolness. For the first time in my life, I had to reassure my father about playing for the King. For an accomplished and experienced musician he was surprisingly nervous.

The King had invited several guests to the performance: Lope and his mistress Doña Marta who looked unwell; the Cardinal Infante; the Inquisitor General; the Count Duke; and about a dozen other senior officials and dignitaries who served the King. The performance was more polished than the one we had given in the Corral de Príncipe. Maria de Riquelme and Bernarda Ramirez were outstanding. I was proud of my father who dispelled his nerves and gave a virtuoso rendition on his violin. Listening to and playing in my compositions for the incidental music, I could understand what Señor Patiño saw as lacking in my experience and skill as a composer.

At the end of the performance, the King came over to congratulate us and brought Lope with him. The King made a huge fuss of Maria de Ceballos, a mature but attractive woman, in a serious attempt to seduce her. Maria slid around to the back of the group of us to avoid him. It was lucky for Maria that the Queen was there, too. That seemed to inhibit the King in persisting with his advances. Sadly, Doña Marta died a month after this performance and poor Lope was totally distraught.

***

A few days before the performance of the *comedia,* while on my way home, I met Teresa in the street. After briefly chatting, we agreed that we would meet on the afternoon after the performance and go for a walk together. That day, I walked straight to Teresa's house. I knocked on the door and was greeted by her mother who was clearly disappointed to see me and to know about our meeting. She told me that Teresa was out and to go away. Fortunately, Teresa overheard her. She came to the door and admonished her mother for telling fibs.

'If you are worried, why not come out with us?' she shrieked. 'We are only going up to the river to walk by the bank for a chat.'

'I want you back by dusk,' she said, grudgingly.

That gave us at least a couple of hours together. We strolled down the Puerta de Guadalajara through the Platería, through the Puerta de la Vegva towards the Puente de Segoviana and turned there to cross the 'Tela' to reach the banks of the Manzanares. It was about fifteen hundred or so *varas* from her home. We were chatting all the way, mainly about little things: how Teresa was getting on at school, what her brother Honofre was up to and how his application to the Inquisition was progressing and why her mother was not keen on her going out with young men. She was, apparently, afraid that Teresa would lose her 'purity' before she got married.

'What do you think of that?' I asked.

'I can understand. I want to keep my virginity until I'm married,' she said.

'I'd be the same... but... umm... well... I've already lost mine.' It came out eventually.

She looked at me in amazement. 'I thought you'd have been totally pure,' she said.

'It's... well it's like this,' I said and told her about my experience with Señora Esmeralda Pechada de Burgos.

'So your father was behind the whole thing?' she asked.

'Yes, and I felt I had no choice but to go through with it.'

'Well, if I married you, you'd at least know what you were doing!'

We reached the riverbank to find that the area was completely deserted. We sat down and I told her about my new job at the palace.

'I didn't know Juan de Roxas was working there. Kept that to himself,' she said.

'I was surprised, too.'

I told her that Señor Romero had told me about the inner workings of the palace and where the councils, senior officials and the members of the royal family were located. I asked her if she was aware of the Council for State Security.

'Yes, Juan. That's the one that checks up on people. To see if they are plotting to overthrow the state.'

'How do you know that?'

'I can't remember who told me. But stay out of the way of that one, Juan. They have a rule: if in doubt, dispose. And dispose means kill.'

'Do you fancy a swim?' she asked, suddenly changing the subject.

'Only if you're willing,' I said.

'Right, we will then but I don't want you to see me naked. You look the other way. I'll get undressed and get into the water. When I shout "ready", I'll look the other way and you take your clothes off and follow me in. We'll try to keep our heads above the water to keep our hair dry.'

'What about drying off when we get out?' I asked.

'I'll get out first and dry myself with my skirt, behind those bushes,' she said, pointing to a little thicket. 'Then, as I'm drying myself and dressing, you can get out and dry yourself with your breeches. They'll soon dry out while we're walking home.'

'Let's do that,' I said.

'Ready!'

I peeled my clothes off and slid down the bank into the water. 'I'm in, too,' I said.

'Not too close!' she shouted. She was up to her shoulders in the river which obscured all but her head. She had knotted her hair and was laughing at our naughtiness. She splashed the water, trying to wet my hair.

'I'll do the same to you,' I said.

'Race you to the other bank and back,' she said. She was a good swimmer and just slid through the water, hardly making a ripple. I was well behind her but caught her up as she turned round near the far bank, in water deep enough to ensure she was covered up to her neck. She just beat me back to the point we had started from.

'Well done,' I said, reaching over to kiss her.

'No! Not too close.'

'All right! I just got carried away a bit.'

'That was good. Let's get dressed then. Turn away as I get out and head for the bushes. I'll shout when I get there.'

I turned to face the opposite bank as she got out of the water.

'Ready!' she shouted. I turned to discover that she had shouted about two seconds early so glimpsed her naked, pearl white rear as she dropped down behind the thicket.

I then climbed out, dried myself down and put my clothes back on. She was dressed a little before me. 'Ready?' she asked.

'Just a second, Teresa,' I said, as I pulled on my breeches. 'Yes, I'm decent now!'

'It's going to start getting dark in a moment or so,' I added. 'We'd better start walking back'. And off we went to Teresa's house the same way as we came.

'We'll have to do that again, Juan. It was lovely.'

'Yes. We will. But don't shout so early next time you get out. I looked round to see your bum disappearing behind the bushes!'

'Too bad,' she said. 'It could have been worse.' As before, we parted with a kiss, if a little less passionate than the previous one, maybe because we were right outside of her house. We arranged to meet again, a few days later and I turned to go home.

'Don't forget: don't go near the Council for State Security,' she said.

I was astonished that Teresa, who was not that sophisticated, knew of this mysterious council. I wondered if she had learnt about it from her brother, Honofre, and whether there was a connection with the Inquisition. The whole subject triggered my curiosity.

***

Within a week or so, Maestro Romero asked to see me when I arrived at my office. 'The King is having a music session tonight with his brothers, Cardinal Infante Ferdinand and the Infante Don Carlos,' he said. 'He wants you to play the harp for them. They will play their own instruments and sing and probably have a few jugs of wine and a few ales. Who knows exactly? They want to play some *villancicos* and ballads from the Palace Songbook. That's all I know, Juan. They want only you to play with them, no one else.'

The Maestro sent me home early that day because the music session was to start at eight p.m. and he wanted me to be awake and fresh to play, and possibly sing, until whatever time the King decided he had had enough. This could, as he said, be any time between midnight and four in the morning. I duly presented myself to the King's Assistant Private Secretary at about twenty minutes before we were due to start our little private recital. He helped me set up my harp and music stand in a small room, upstairs in the west wing. I asked him what I could be expected to play but he had no more of an idea than I had. As usual, I was dressed in the cream shirt and maroon breeches. I sat near to the door on a gilded chair, ready to play at a moment's notice.

The King and his brothers entered, the King clumsily wielding his cello and his brothers carrying their violins under their arms. They were laughing and joking to each other and clearly looking forward to the session.

'I want to introduce you to my brothers... er?'

'Juan,' I said, as the King had apparently forgotten my name. 'Juan Hidalgo.'

'Yes, Juan. I'm sorry; a momentary lapse of memory! This is my brother Ferdinand, the Cardinal Infante and Archbishop of Toledo. He spends half his time fighting wars for me and the other half carrying out his duties as Cardinal. He's never been ordained as a priest but he's paid a massive salary all the same. He will soon be taking over from his Aunt Isabel as our Governor of the Netherlands but he has to get there yet and that will be his next major challenge.'

I bowed towards the Cardinal Infante and said, 'Delighted to meet you, Your Royal Highness.'

'And this is my other brother, the Infante Don Carlos. He spends some of his time helping me and my Chief Minister, the Count Duke, to run the affairs of state and empire. I don't know what he does with the rest of his time!'

Likewise, I bowed to acknowledge Don Carlos.

'Right, Juan. We now stop all this formal nonsense and you become part of our music group. You are one of us now and we are four men having fun.' Brilliant. I was a temporary member of the royal family.

'We usually start these sessions, Juan, with some instrumental pieces. I know you won't have rehearsed anything but I want you to join in and improvise your part. Right boys, off we go with a piece for three violins by Ortego Diez. I'll make up a cello part and you come in when you like with the harp, Juan'.

We did as the King had instructed and created a quite acceptable sound. Fortunately, there was a fair bit of repetition in the piece and I was able quickly to pick out a line I could play. We then did some solo pieces, starting with the King, then the Cardinal Infante, then Don Carlos and, of course, finishing with me. 'Play the music you played at your first recital for me,' instructed the King. I glowed with confidence at playing this familiar piece again.

We then moved to less familiar territory, at least for me, and played some of the music of Guerrero and Salinas. The King and the Infantes were good players and mocked the culprit mercilessly when one of them hit a wrong note. We carried on playing and generally enjoying ourselves for about two hours or so before we stopped for half an hour to enjoy a drink or two and some friendly banter. I did not initiate any comments but joined in the jollity and frequent laughter, even though I drank only the fruit cordials.

'Right,' said the King. 'We'll give the instruments a break now. We'll sing some songs. Is that a good idea, Juan?'

'Sounds good to me!' I said, for the first time omitting the 'Your Majesty'.

We sang well into the night and picked up our instruments and played them when our voices had had enough. Again, just like some of the instrumental pieces we had played, many of the songs were new to me. Some were religious, some about love, others about victorious battles, others about friendship and some, towards the end of the session were downright ribald.

One especially violent song was about a woman who is killed because her husband catches her in bed with a lover. The lover escapes and the husband threatens to hammer him to death if he catches him. Another was the famous ditty by Encina:

> *Coo-coo, coo-coo!*
> *Make sure the coo-coo is not you.*
> *Chum you must know,*
> *that the best of women,*
> *is always mad to screw,*
> *satisfy yours well.*
> *Chum you must make sure,*
> *you are not cuckolded,*
> *if your wife goes out to pee,*
> *you go out with her, too.*
> *Coo-coo, coo-coo!*

It was revealing that the King and the Infantes enjoyed these indecent songs but what group of men, who sing together after a few drinks, stick to the purest songs they know? I must admit that I enjoyed them, too, and the spirit of camaraderie in which we all sang them.

'When are we going hunting again, Philip?' asked the Cardinal Infante. 'It's time we went out to catch a boar or two.'

'Great idea,' said Don Carlos.

'Have you ever been hunting, Juan?'

'No, Your Majesty, I haven't.'

'Then you will come, too.'

CHAPTER 7

The injunction from the King that 'you will come, too' had to be obeyed. I could ride well, but had never hunted in my life so I would have to learn. Although I could not see it myself, Mateo Romero believed that there was something underlying the King's command that I join the hunt, something that implied that the King would make me a new offer or request.

'Juan, I do not know what the King wants of you. But I have a feeling he expects you to help him in some way which is not to do with music. I haven't had this feeling before about one of my new recruits and it is clear to me that you have impressed His Majesty in some way that is different. We'll have to wait and see. You'll need to see the Head Groom who will, I'm sure, help you to learn. First though, I'll take you to see the Royal Master Huntsman, Don Juan Mateos.'

The King's head huntsman had his own office in the west wing of the palace. It was not large but it was at least an office, similar to ones I had seen for middle-ranking civil servants. We knocked on the closed door.

'Come in,' was the gloomy, gruff response.

We entered to see a large man standing next to an open fronted cupboard, just inside the door.

'Are you the Royal Master Huntsman?' asked Mateo Romero.

'Yes, that's me,' he said. The Master was a bluff, stern-looking individual with brown upraised eyebrows, a curled moustache and a small ginger beard on the end of his chin. He was wearing a black tunic over black riding breeches, all of which seemed to be designed to cover a substantial, paunchy stomach.

'He's big to be riding a horse,' I thought. 'Poor horse!'

'What do you two want?' he asked.

The Maestro was slightly unnerved by this unwelcoming question, but recovered well. 'This is Juan Hidalgo, one of my staff in the Royal Chapel. His Majesty has told him that he must join a boar hunt so I thought it would be a good idea to introduce him to you.'

'That's the first I've heard of it,' replied the Master, haughtily.

'That is a fact,' said the Maestro, now a little angry. 'I am telling you what the King said to Juan here. That's right isn't it, Juan?'

'Yes,' I said. 'Last night at a music session I had with His Majesty and the Infantes.'

'Well, I suppose we'd better do something about it. I take it you've been hunting before?' he asked.

'No. Never. Don't know a thing about it.'

The Master Huntsman erupted into laughter. 'You've never been on a hunt and you are coming hunting with the King. How stupid! How ridiculous!'

'I think not,' said Mateo Romero, barely keeping his anger in check. 'He'll just have to learn. It can't be that difficult.'

'Take him to the stables and get someone to teach him,' said the Master. 'Then come back to me, son, and we'll sort something out. If you are any good on a horse, you can pick it up in a month or so. But you'll have to work hard.'

'That wasn't very helpful, was it?' said the Maestro as we walked back towards his office. 'I wasn't much help there either, Juan. You go to the stables and ask the Head Groom if he can teach you. Start today if you can. This must take priority for now.' The Maestro was such an understanding boss. I found the Head Groom in his office and told him what I needed and why.

'No problem,' said the Head Groom. 'I'll ask one of the stable maids to teach you. 'When can you start?'

'Now, if possible?' I said, hopefully.

'Let's go!'

This is the response I wanted: friendly and helpful. The Head Groom took me right into the depths of the Royal Stables. We must have passed two dozen stalls and horses' heads were looking out in all directions over the half gates. We saw several busy stable maids, to each of whom he gave a nodding, 'Hello' and, eventually, we reached the one whom he wanted to teach me.

'Juan, this is Lucia Nelleda. Lucia, this is Juan Hidalgo, one of the new musicians in the Royal Chapel. He needs to learn to hunt. He'll tell you why. Can you start him off now?'

'I can do that,' said Lucia.

The Head Groom left me in the hands of Lucia who led me towards one of the stable buildings.

'Let me tell you something, Juan,' she said as we walked in. 'Today, I'm going to tell you about the hunt. Tomorrow we'll ride to hounds and I'll teach you some of the techniques and niceties. I'll show you boar spearing from the saddle. You'll hear the horn calls and you'll have to learn them. I'll teach you the etiquette of the hunt. First, though, we'll pick out a horse for you. You won't ride her today but at least you'll see your mount for tomorrow. Come with me.'

She walked past several stalls and stopped where a beautiful chestnut mare was flicking her head to and fro over the gate. 'This horse is a great hunter. She's big, strong and reliable. Just what you want. She's called Clara.'

My heart leapt at seeing this stunning creature and I could feel my excitement rise as I contemplated riding her.

'Hunting is so different from just plain riding,' she said, patting Clara on the neck. 'You will have to be disciplined. You cannot hunt without boarhounds. They are the key to success. They will corner the boar. Never get ahead of them. Stay back and follow them. Don't follow a hound that breaks from the pack. He could lead you away. Keep an eye on the leader, the one in front. He will take you to your quarry.'

She placed a heavy spear in my hand. 'This is a boar spear. You will need it at the kill. You will become skilled in using it. And I will show you how. See these wings behind the blade. They stop the boar from driving it too far into its body. You'd never get it out without them!'

There seemed so much I'd have to do and learn but I felt confident I would become a good hunter, especially with the aid of this amenable, self-assured young stable maid. I returned to Mateo Romero and told him how I had progressed. 'A healthy start, Juan. Good luck tomorrow!'

***

The next day came and I eagerly went to see Lucia. She saddled up Clara for me, chose herself a horse and off we rode out of the palace gates, down through the Puerta de la Vegva towards the Tela outside.

'Where are the hounds, Lucia? You said you cannot hunt without them.'

'We are meeting one of the royal huntsmen and he'll have a kennelman with a pack of eight. That'll be enough for now. He'll bring a horn and some boar spears.'

It wasn't long before I realised that there was more to boar hunting than simply being told what to do and doing it, even if your instructors were highly experienced professionals, like these, and more than willing to show you. Lucia and her colleagues, especially the young kennelman, delighted in watching and encouraging me as I began to familiarise myself with the finer points of hunting and, dare I say, master them. It all took time. My instructors insisted that I return to the Tela with them to practice my technique, especially in using the boar spear which was so cumbersome and awkward. They even made an artificial boar which they dragged behind a horse. I would spear it as the horse came charging by. 'Now you're getting it!' shouted the kennelman, as I jousted the rolling sack and just managed to pull out the spear.

Thanks to Lucia, and many such visits to the Tela, I was after about six weeks able to return to the Maestro and tell him that I felt confident enough to go boar hunting. 'That's excellent, Juan. I think you should go to the Master Huntsman and let him know, too. Why not now?' The Maestro was as pleased as I was.

I knocked on the Master Huntsman's door and he called me in. 'I have had my tuition and can hunt now, so I can join His Majesty and you on a boar hunt at any time.'

'You think so, do you? Well, we'll see. I want you to show me what you can do,' he said, challengingly. 'When are you available?'

'The day after tomorrow,' I said.

'That's fine. I'll see you at the Head Groom's office at nine o'clock in the morning, the day after tomorrow. Off you go.'

* * *

During these weeks, Carlos Patiño had given me some lessons and showed me some examples of composition in counterpoint. He loved teaching and reminded me of Señor Vásquez, my school music teacher. 'Just be patient with yourself. You'll soon get the hang of it!' he said, as I was beginning to sound frustrated.

He left me with some basic tunes and a request to write them down as an example in this technique. I could use any rhythm I wanted and he insisted on some variations on these tunes as well. So this was a period of intense learning for me: boar hunting and composing music. Could two subjects be more different?

* * *

The following day, I met with the Royal Master Huntsman at the Head Groom's office. Lucia was with the Head Groom who asked her to saddle up a horse for me. We gave no clues to the Master that she was one of my teachers and saddled up Clara. The Master rode his own horse, a large grey. 'We'll go to the Tela. You are coming too!' he said, staring straight at Lucia. She saddled up and off the three of us went.

'I'm going to get you to gallop fast. I'll go first and you can chase after me. You, too, young lady. Be careful because I shall turn and swerve the horse as if we are riding to hounds.'

So off he went at full stretch, with Lucia and me not far behind him. He turned his horse and galloped it at full tilt. I could not see how he could be testing me as I was behind him with Lucia most of the time, both of us in chase. He shouted and whistled at the horse which obeyed his every move. He suddenly shouted back at us. 'Now we are going over that wall!' Lucia and I turned and she and the Master charged at the same low point. Lucia jumped first and as she did so, the Master's horse crashed into the wall and threw him headlong over it. He landed in a pathetic heap on the other side.

'Are you hurt?' I said.

'Are you all right?' asked Lucia, returning to the wall. I could not help thinking to myself that there was some cold justice here somewhere.

'No. I'm damned well not. The accursed horse threw me,' he replied, furious and still on the ground and rubbing his elbow.

'Unlucky,' I said, coolly. 'Let's give you a hand.' I climbed over the wall and Lucia and I helped him to his feet. He staggered as if his legs were reluctant to take his weight and we eased him back over the wall.

'I think I'll be all right. I'd like to go back now.'

'I'll help you up on to the horse,' I said, and eased his right leg around so that he could sit in the saddle. He was obviously quite sore. The three of us rode the horses at a walk back to the stables and not a word was exchanged between us.

'I'll let you know about the next hunt and you can join us,' he said as we arrived. Just what I wanted.

'That was his fault,' said Lucia, as the Master limped off towards the main part of the palace. 'The rule is that he should give way to the woman. So it just about serves him right, the ignorant pig.'

***

I went straight back to Mateo Romero to tell him what had happened to the Master in front of Lucia and me. 'I can't say I am glad, Juan, but he has not willingly cooperated with either of us. After the treatment he gave you and me when we first met him, I can't help thinking that he deserved that.'

'Me too,' I said.

'Tomorrow you have a major job to do. The Queen is entertaining the wives of the Solicitor General and the Inquisitor General at a luncheon in her quarters at the palace and has asked for a small group of musicians to play for them. I want you on the harp, Juan de Roxas, Francisco de Guypúzcoa, Gabriel Cortes and Esteban Marques, on violins, Simón Donoso, on the guitar, and Hernando de Eslava on the cello. I have already told the others. This is going to be a very formal occasion so I want you to play some music from the Palace Songbook and some of Encina's music for them. This has been requested at short notice and I will prepare a programme this afternoon and let you see it before you go tonight. I'll make sure we play pieces for which I already have sufficient sheet music for you all to use.'

As usual, we appeared in our cream shirts and maroon pantaloons and sat with our instruments until Her Royal Highness and her guests arrived. I was amazed at the Queen's serene beauty. She looked stunning in a full-length grey and white patterned dress with long sleeves and a heavy cape, slung from her shoulders. Her face was round and her sharp features reflected her French origins as daughter of Henry IV. It was no surprise that she was so popular with the people of Spain.

At the nod of her Private Secretary, our short recital began. Once again, Juan de Roxas played the lead part and we played to our select audience, who sat in chairs facing us, for about half an hour. At the end of the concert the Queen stood. We all followed and bowed. She complimented us on our performance and we left, the job done, at least to the Queen's satisfaction.

As we arrived back at our offices in the west wing, the Maestro was there to greet us. We told him that the Queen seemed pleased with the recital and we were just going towards our offices when the Maestro called after me. 'Juan, I have a note for you from the Royal Master Huntsman,' he said, handing me an envelope. I opened it, unfolded the note within and read it aloud:

'Don Juan Hidalgo, You are invited to join His Majesty and others in a boar hunt tomorrow. We are to meet at the Head Groom's Office at 7.30a.m.
Signed, Don Juan Mateos, Royal Master Huntsman.'

'You didn't have to wait long for that, Juan. Well done! You'll meet some interesting people on the hunt. It will be quite an experience.'

I arrived at the Head Groom's office at seven o'clock the following morning. I felt I needed to go early to select and saddle up a horse. I also felt nervous to be going to one of these events for the first time and thought that arriving early would settle me down. I was greeted by a smiling Lucia who said she was always an early starter and wondered if I would be invited to this hunt. I asked her about a horse and she suggested I should ride Clara again, mainly because I had already ridden on her and that she knew me, but also because she was a good chaser and would easily keep up with the hunt.

'I'll saddle her up and make sure that your riding boots are clean,' Lucia said as we left to go to the stables.

I waited in the Head Groom's office for the other members of the hunt to arrive. I was relieved that the Head Groom was the first. 'Hello, Señor Hidalgo. Welcome to your first boar hunt. I hope it goes well for you. Have you seen Lucia?'

'Yes, we were just talking here and then she went to the stables.'

'She's working out the allocation of horses. She'll be back in a moment.'

One by one, other riders arrived at the Head Groom's office. 'Have you met Diego Velázquez, Juan? He is a painter here.'

'Yes, we've met. Good morning, Diego. I didn't know you were a huntsman.'

'Yes, I regularly hunt with the King. I didn't expect to see you.'

'I'm here only because the King invited me to the hunt.'

'That's interesting,' said Diego, as if there was something more to this than simply my presence there.

I felt flattered to meet a number of other senior people from the palace. The Head Groom introduced me to the Count Duke Olivares, to the Head of Buildings and Works, to the Keeper of the Palace, to the Inquisitor General, Antonio de Sotomayor, to the Paymaster General and to several of the council chairmen. I was delighted that I was not the only one there from the Royal Chapel: the Maestro himself had been invited and so had Simón Donoso. A number of other palace staff had been invited, including several from the private offices and the Royal Physician, presumably in case of any accidents.

We all assembled at the main stable gate and, a few minutes later, the King arrived on horseback. He was dressed in a brown, soft leather tunic, breeches of the same material and a dark brown, wide-brimmed hat. He wore elbow length gloves of a lighter brown and had a single barrelled flintlock musket slung over his right shoulder. He was flanked by Cardinal Infante Ferdinand and Infante Don Carlos who also had long muskets hung across their backs. There were two dozen mounted, palace guards in three rows of four to the front and to the rear of the royal party. Each guard was armed with a long stave and had a sword at his side. The royal party and guards stopped outside of the stable entrance in the Plaza del Palacio. The Royal Master Huntsman appeared from the stables on the same horse that had thrown him a few days before. He rode to the front of the first group of palace guards to lead the hunt. A covered horse-drawn wagon, with a uniformed driver, followed him. The Master waved a musket in the air and shouted, 'Forward, after me,' and the royal party, with the guards to the front and rear, trotted after him and the wagon along the Plaza towards the Puerta de la Vegva. The rest of us tagged along, in rank order, behind the formation of guards. The junior ranks, including us three musicians, brought up the rear. A large crowd of people in the Plaza watched the hunt procession and cheered and shouted, or merely looked on, as we passed.

The Master led us through the Puerta de la Vegva on to the Puente Segoviana, across the River Manzanares and on to the Camino de Mostoles. At about 1000 *varas* down the road the Master brought the procession to a halt, alongside a pack of about thirty hounds.

I heard a voice I immediately recognised. 'Good morning, señor. I wish you good luck.' I smiled back at the kennelman who helped teach me to hunt.

'That's strange,' said the Maestro. 'Some of those dogs are greyhounds. I wonder why they've brought them.'

The Master shouted his instructions: 'As soon as I sound my horn to signify the off, the kennelman will unleash the dogs. We then ride to hounds. There are several packs so just keep with one of them. As soon as your pack has cornered a boar, one of the huntsmen will sound his horn for quarry in sight. We all immediately head in the direction of the horn call. We then go in for the kill.' He then sounded the off.

Unlike many in this varied group of hunters, I made sure I rode a good distance from the hounds. The Maestro, Simón Donoso and I stayed together, along with a couple of the private secretaries. The King and his brothers, while protected by his guards, rode confidently and, like us, were enjoying the run of the hunt. The horses' hooves drummed loudly on the firm ground. We crossed low-lying scrub, passed through woods and jumped over ditches in this torrent of man, horse and dog.

Suddenly, a horn sounded to our east. We galloped over towards it and soon we could see a pair of wild boar, right out in the open. Totally oblivious to any danger they could be in, they launched at us in attack. The Master shouted. 'Don't fire yet! Use the boar spears!'

The huge animals, almost the size of our horses, charged around madly in large circles, trying to gore the horses and scare the dogs. We could soon see why. The greyhounds had disturbed some sows and their piglets. They were barking at the sows and frightening their young.

'This has all gone wrong,' shouted the Maestro to me and Simón. 'They should never have released those hounds. The boarhounds wouldn't have disturbed the sows. Now there's no chance of trapping these brutes! We could all be in trouble.'

As one of the large boars came raging towards me, I aimed my spear towards it but missed. It then turned and chased one of the private secretaries and his mount. He tried to spear it but he missed, too. The boar turned and dug its tusks into the rump of his horse. It bolted with the man on its back, clinging on to save his life. One of the hunters managed to spear the other large boar which threw itself around, shrieking in agony. The hunter heaved but could not free his spear and, while holding it in defiance, fell to the ground. He yelled out as the boar turned and gored him in the leg. He tried to staunch the blood. The Royal Physician came up, jumped off his horse and sped to help him.

Within seconds, the first large boar attacked the Inquisitor General's horse. As it dug its tusks in the animal's underbelly, the horse twisted round to shake off the boar, only to let it dig its tusks in deeper. Eventually, the injured horse broke free but immediately fell to the ground. The Inquisitor fell off and his right leg became stuck under his writhing mount. 'Someone help me! Quick!' he cried.

'I'm on my way!' I shouted.

I jumped off Clara and pulled him from under his horse. As I did so, one of the sows came to attack me so I kicked it hard in the head. I helped the Inquisitor General on to my horse, grabbed my boar spear, which I had dropped in the melee, kicked the approaching boar again, climbed up behind the Inquisitor and took the reins. The horses, which were our only escape, were in imminent danger. Some had already fled. The two large boars, by then both injured, were attacking us with every muscle in their bodies. 'Use your guns!' shouted the Master Huntsman. 'But shoot downwards, and away from the rest of us.'

A fusillade of musket shots cracked at our ears. The King and Diego had each shot a boar but only wounded them. They were alive but bleeding and vicious. The violent animals became even angrier. They hurtled towards us and, even though injured, launched another attack. More horses and riders took fright and ran for the road. Blood spurted everywhere as, with still fewer men, the fight continued.

'Enough is enough. Let's go!' yelled the Royal Master Huntsman. He put his horn to his lips and blew for home. We were losing the battle. We were tiring and relieved at his decision. He had to be right. We all galloped our retreat towards the road. I turned to the anxious call of a huntsman. It was Simón Donoso whose horse was lame and motionless.

'Help me. Help me. I'm stuck!' he called out.

Still with the Inquisitor General in front on Clara, I could do nothing to help my colleague in peril. 'Go to Simón!' I shouted to Mateo Romero. At that moment, the King, who had reloaded his rifle, let fire at a boar which was about to maul Simón. It dropped stone dead to the ground. Mateo went over to Simón and heaved him up onto his horse. With his passenger hanging on, he galloped towards the road. I followed with the Inquisitor General on board and with the King at my side.

Consumed by exhaustion, sweating and panting, we met at the roadside with the royal guards. We looked around to see boars running back to the woods. We paid a high price for this exploit: three dead horses and ten injured huntsmen. Three boars lay dead on the ground.

'Should we take the dead boars?' asked one of us, desperate to recover something positive from this debacle.

'No,' said the Royal Master Huntsman, firmly. 'We have to accept defeat and to retrieve those dead boars would be like robbing a grave. Leave them to the vultures.'

'Here! Here!' piped up a number of the hunters, including the King.

'We now reassemble in our procession and go back to the palace,' said the Master.

The return ride to the palace was an anti-climax. The Inquisitor General rode back next to the driver on the covered wagon, into which we had disgorged our weaponry, and Simón sat in the back. We all felt miserable at our failure and must have appeared so.

The hunting procession returned to the Plaza del Palacio in the same orderly way in which it had left, but without the trophy of a hunted boar. In the Plaza there was a large crowd, much bigger than when we left, waiting to greet us. These folk could have had little idea of when we were likely to return and I imagine many had been there whiling their time away, chatting and joking to each other, the whole two hours or so that we had been gone, but waiting in expectation that they would see at least one dead, wild boar, tied to a stake and suspended between two of the horses.

'Where are the boars?' a man with a walking stick shouted.

'Didn't you catch anything?' shouted a dishevelled-looking woman.

'We didn't catch one,' replied one of the hunters.

'Lot of damned use you lot are if you can't bring back a boar!'

After the King and guards had passed the crowd, a man in a tricorne hat shouted, 'Let them have it!' Needing no more prompting, a large section of the crowd became a mob and threw at us all manner of rubbish from over-ripe tomatoes and melons to eggs and rotten cabbages. It was as if they had pre-armed themselves with these messy missiles, in case the hunt had failed. Some of these objects hit their targets but most missed and spattered on the ground. Some of the horses were shaken and reared up into the air. Many of us yelled back in protest.

'Leave us alone. Who do you think you are?'

Hearing us shouting and the general commotion, the rear group of a dozen guards turned back to come to our aid. Still carrying their lances, the guards rode their horses towards the main offenders. By then, three or four of the protesting women, who had run out of ammunition, had their skirts up to their chests and were standing with their legs apart, urinating on the ground as a further insult. The mounted guards entered the crowd and jostled the offenders with their horses. Some of the onlookers fell and many cursed the guards and told them to, 'bugger off and mind their own business.' By their prompt action, the guards had successfully distracted the crowd from us beleaguered hunters so we sped towards the stables and rode inside, away from the bellowing mob.

***

A few days later, an injunction was issued by the King instructing all those who had attended the hunt to a meeting that afternoon in the palace. The meeting would be chaired by the Royal Master Huntsman. We assembled at four o'clock. With the exception of the royal guards, nearly everyone who was at the hunt attended. The King was there, as was the Cardinal Infante, but not the Infante Don Carlos. The Master was formal and impassive as he started the meeting. He said that His Majesty the King had convened it to discuss what had happened at the hunt and afterwards, so we could learn from the experience.

The King interrupted and said, 'Before we get the meeting underway, I would like to praise the heroism shown by our musicians from the Royal Chapel. Mateo Romero, the Maestro, could well have saved the life of his guitarist, Simón Donoso, by rescuing him from the onslaught of the boars. Likewise, Juan Hidalgo saved the Inquisitor General when his injured horse fell and trapped him. Well done you two. You deserve to be recognised as the heroes of the day.'

Someone said, 'Here, here' and there was a round of applause. The Maestro and I looked at each other, savouring our brief moment of praise.

The Master then took over and the discussion centred on the failure of the hunt to subdue the boars. There was an element of surprise: the hunters had not expected to disturb the sows and their young. The boars had been warned by the barking dogs so couldn't be cornered.

'You need more hunters,' said someone.

'No. You need boarhounds,' said another.

'We had boarhounds,' said yet another.

'Yes but there were greyhounds as well. They barked and frightened the sows,' said the Maestro.

'Someone fired a rifle, just as the boarhounds were reaching the boars,' said someone else.

'I didn't hear it,' replied another.

The discussion continued for at least an hour and reached a number of conclusions. First, in future, there would be only boarhounds in the pack. Second, no one would be allowed to carry a rifle. Only muskets would be allowed. Third, the King's guards would take a more active role in the hunt. Fourth, there would be a dozen guards at the back of the procession so that those hunters in the rear would be less vulnerable to attack by onlookers.

The meeting then disbanded. As it did so, the King approached me and said he wanted a private word. 'I have been impressed by you, Juan, since I first met you at your interview with Maestro Mateo Romero. I think that the way you have taken to working here is exemplary. I was struck by the way you integrated with my brothers and me in our night of music. You became one of us. Not only that, you were so brave and showed outstanding courage on the hunt. You astonished me. You had never hunted before! In short, I have come to trust you. So I want you to help me on a special mission. Your main job is to be a musician in the Royal Chapel, and that will always be so, but there are forces working in this palace, this town and in our country which plot to overthrow me. I want you to help me in neutralising them. Keep a watchful eye and ear on what is going on around you. Inform the Council for State Security if you suspect anything is happening which could usurp my position as King. Are you willing to help in this way? If so you will soon discover that others have the same mission and who they are.'

'Your Majesty,' I said, 'I will do anything in my power to help you.'

'Thank you. That is all I wanted to know,' said the King, smiling gratefully as he turned towards the door. It burst open in front of him and a wide-eyed, anxious Private Secretary faced him and blurted out, 'Your Majesty, I have terrible news. The Infante Don Carlos is dead.'

'That cannot be so: I saw him only this morning. He said he did not feel well but surely he cannot be dead. He is only twenty-four years old.'

'Your Majesty, I would not tell you if it were not true,' said the Private Secretary, his eyes full of tears.

'My brother is dead,' said the King. 'That is terrible, terrible, so sad.' The King immediately broke down and began sobbing to himself.

I could not believe that The Infante had died. I was laughing and joking with him and his brothers only a month or two before. 'I am so sorry, Your Majesty,' I said. 'Is there anything I can do?'

'I want to see him. That is the only way I will be convinced that he is dead.'

'His body is laid out in his room in the royal apartments,' said the Private Secretary. 'He was given the last rites an hour ago.'

'I will go there now,' said the King and he left the room with the Private Secretary. It was 30 July 1632.

I went to see Mateo Romero to tell him what had happened. 'I thought the King wanted you to do something special for him, but let me give you some advice. Be careful who you tell about this. In effect, you are now a spy, acting on behalf of the King.'

'But I have no terms of reference and no formal description of what I have to do.'

'Yes, you do,' he said. 'You had formal terms of reference as soon as the King told you that you had a special mission. To report any suspicious activity to the Council for State Security. When you go home, write down what you agreed with the King. Put the piece of paper in a safe place for future reference.

'Like you, I am saddened by the death of Don Carlos. I cannot believe that a man so young and healthy has died. Do you think he has been murdered? Nothing surprises me anymore in this world. I know that Olivares detests him. I wonder if he was involved. We now have a funeral to attend to.'

***

Later that week, I was summoned to a meeting with the Chief Clerk of the Council for State Security. He said he understood that I had agreed to act as a special agent of His Majesty the King – agent, not spy – and gave me a short memorandum explaining this. Basically, it was that I was to report any suspicion of subversive activity to the Council. That is, I would report it to the Chief Clerk who would put it to the Ministerial Head of the Council for his consideration. The Clerk told me that I should tell no other individual that I was a special agent. I said that I had already told my boss the Maestro.

'That is not a problem,' said the Chief Clerk. 'As you will see from the relevant paragraph in this memorandum, your manager will be officially informed of your status as an agent.'

He also showed me a list of others I already knew in the palace, who were also special agents, and some others I knew outside. On that list were the names of Mateo Romero, my father, Antonio Hidalgo, and Diego Velázquez.

'There are just three other things,' said the Clerk. 'First you must sign this document, swearing your allegiance to the King and that you will tell nobody of your new status.

'Second, I must give you this key which will enable you to enter the outer office of the Council for State Security. The room number is on the key fob. You should go there about once a month to see, but not to remove, any briefing that has been issued.

'Third, you should go to the tattooist in the Platería, where the symbol of your position will be tattooed on your body. It is a small Habsburg coat of arms which will be put on your right shoulder.' I remembered seeing such a tattoo on the shoulder of Esmeralda Pechada de Burgos. Interesting.

'What if I don't sign the oath of allegiance?' I asked.

'Then you will not become a special agent. You will never be asked again and you will have to swear another document to the effect that you will never tell anyone you have been asked to become an agent,' he said.

'Before I do sign, I need to know one other thing. Can I discuss matters relating to my new status with any other special agents?'

'Yes, you may, but use great discretion.'

'Then I will sign,' I said and did so.

'Thank you. You will be paid a nominal four *ducats* a month for being a special agent of His Majesty the King.'

I decided that, for the time being, I would not discuss the fact that I had accepted this new responsibility with anyone, except my father. But what a surprise that he was one, too. Obviously, he could not have told me before. This could also explain how he knew Esmeralda Pechada de Burgos.

My father had very little to say about being an agent. 'Yes, Juan, I have been a special agent for many years. Please do not ask me what work I have done as an agent because I won't tell you. I simply can't. Be very discreet about your new function. You may well be asked, as I have, to do things that are in conflict with your principles. But you can trust me. I can help with any issues that confront you in this role.'

CHAPTER 8

I began to crave more independence. So, near the time of my twentieth birthday, I rented a family-sized, furnished house in the Puerta Cerrada, just off the Calle de Toledo and close to the palace. It belonged to Don Juan Pardo Moncón who charged me four *ducats* a month, exactly what I earned as a special agent.

The day I moved out of the family home was upsetting for my mother but my father and Francisco, who was coming up to fourteen years old, were more philosophical.

'Mamá, I shall only be moving about 500 *varas,* down San Ginés across the Plaza Mayor and down the Calle de Toledo. I'm not even moving to the other side of our town!'

'I suppose I can a come round and cook you a meal or do your washing,' said mother, sadly but resigned to the fact.

'It will be great, Juan. I can come to stay with you. We'll have fun!' said Francisco.

I soon settled into a routine and could fend for myself quite well, as my mother had shown me the rudiments of cooking. I decided to engage a lady to do the housework and asked Barbola, whom I had seen at Esmeralda Pechada's house. I vaguely remembered her saying she would like more work. Luckily, she was available and would do my cleaning for three *reales* a week and some cooking, if I wanted her to do so.

I decided to have a party at the house soon after I moved in. I invited colleagues from the palace and friends. I did not invite my parents. In fact, I told them I only wanted my colleagues and friends there and they understood, but I did decide to ask Francisco. Barbola and Teresa prepared the food and Honofre and I brought in some wine, ale and fruit juices. My idea in inviting Honofre was to make it easy for Teresa to come as well. I still liked her and needed some means of attracting her there without a chaperone. We held the party in the evening in candlelight. My palace colleagues seemed to like my friends. Diego Velázquez was interested in the work of Bernarda Ramirez and Maria de Riquelme. In fact, he said he was at the first performance of Lope's 'Punishment without Revenge' that we had staged in the Príncipe some three years before. He remembered the outrageous behaviour provoked by the guitarist in the audience when he started playing the *zarabanda*. Diego invited the two actresses to come to the palace to see some of his paintings.

Maestro Mateo Romero spent some time talking to Francisco, who had just started to learn the harp at school. He told the Maestro that he wanted to follow in my footsteps as a harpist to the King. The Maestro encouraged him to practise and improve his playing. Luis de As, whom I had not seen for many months, had by then been working in Manuel Vallejo's theatre company for about three years. He said his relationship with Vallejo was deteriorating, that he had just about had enough of the man's abruptness and was actively looking for another job.

The Maestro said he knew of a vacancy in the group of musicians in the Royal Chapel who played for Her Majesty the Queen. Luis spoke to Juan de Roxas Carrión whom he already knew from school, Francisco de Guypúzcoa, Simón Donoso, Vitoria de Cuenca and Hernando de Eslava. They all told him how good it was to be working in the Royal Chapel. Within a month, Luis was also working at the palace. He was then one of us.

A party is not a party without some music and dancing. Luis and Francisco de Guypúzcoa had brought their violins, I had my harp at home and Simón Donoso had his guitar with him. We had a band. 'Let's dance,' I shouted and we played a lively *chacona.* We had cleared an area in the drawing room for dancing, sufficient for about twenty people. Just about everyone took to the floor. It was a great occasion and we all let our hair down and swirled around to the riotous music.

One of the private secretaries arrived late. 'Have you heard the news?' he said. 'We have beaten the Swedes and Saxons at Nördlingen! We routed them!' This was probably our greatest moment of triumph in the War in Europe.

Spain was deeply involved in this war. It started in May, 1618 when Ferdinand, the new Habsburg King of Bohemia, who, a year later, was to be crowned Ferdinand II, Holy Roman Emperor, sent two royal councillors to Prague, the capital, to impose Catholicism on the mainly Protestant Bohemia. Bohemian rebels threw the two councillors out of a window of the capital's Hradčany Castle. They fell about fifty *pies* but, luckily, landed in a large pile of horse dung which saved their lives. Bohemia went quickly into revolt. Ferdinand needed help so he called in the support of Maximilian I of Bavaria. In November 1620 the joint forces, supported by our King, retook Bohemia in the Battle of the White Mountain, near Prague.

The Battle of Nördlingen was provoked by the Protestants. Earlier in 1634, a joint Swedish-Saxon Protestant army had attacked Bohemia in an attempt to dethrone the Habsburgs. Ferdinand, soon to become Ferdinand

III, the subsequent Catholic King of Bohemia and Hungary, decided to attack the German states in the south to distract the Protestant army from its fighting in Bohemia. Each of the rival armies knew that an army led by the Cardinal Infante Ferdinand was on its way north from Italy to the Spanish Netherlands. As the King had explained to me at the music session with the two Infantes, the Cardinal Infante was on his way take up the post of Governor of the Netherlands. The two cousins, Ferdinand and the Cardinal Infante Ferdinand, joined forces and prepared for battle. The joint army was huge. It had 42,000 men, about 8,000 more than the Protestants, and was based on the highly professional Spanish infantry, the old *tercios*, which had not before fought the Swedes.

Nördlingen was surrounded by prominent hills. The Spaniards captured one of them and repulsed over a dozen Swedish assaults upon it. A face-to-face confrontation did not take place until late in the battle but by then the Swedes and Saxons had been desperately weakened and quickly collapsed. The Catholic armies closed off any possible escape routes and the two Ferdinands and Spain celebrated a famous victory.

It was hard to analyse at that time what this triumph would mean for our country and its empire. Various opinions were exchanged at the party. Some, including Juan de Roxas, believed that this victory would frighten the Protestants into submission. Others, including Diego and the Maestro, thought the opposite would happen and that the victory would catalyse the slumbering French into activity and renew their determination to weaken the Spanish position in northern Europe. We would have to wait and see.

Vitoria de Cuenca was much less enthusiastic about the battle. 'It's all very well but my uncle is one of the old *tercios*. He went to Italy with the Cardinal Infante's army. I just hope that he didn't get hurt.'

It brought it home to all of us that our brothers and cousins, husbands and lovers, and fathers and sons were fighting courageously for our country. We could only hope that there was a minimum number of casualties on the Spanish side, and the Protestant side for that matter. But there were sure to be some.

'I propose a toast to our victorious army. And to all our soldiers,' said Honofre and we all raised our glasses.

'I propose one to His Majesty the King,' said Luis and we all refilled our glasses and raised them again.

By the time we had toasted the Virgin Mary, Jesus Christ, the Angel Gabriel, the Pope and, of course the Cardinal Infante, we had all had about enough to drink and the serious conversation evaporated into the air. Discussion then turned to gossip and bawdy humour.

Infante Don Carlos had been dead for about two years by then but there were still the last embers of a rumour about his early death. 'I'm sure that the Count Duke murdered him,' said one of the private secretaries in a seriously unguarded moment.

'Yes, it was an untraceable poison,' said Christóbal de Agramontes who should have known better.

'I don't think so,' said Diego Velázquez, bringing the discussion back to reality. 'We all know the Count Duke disliked Don Carlos but, if his feelings were that strong, he would have sent him off to some sinecure in Italy or Portugal, not taken the risk of killing him and being found out.'

Even in the candlelight, we could not fail to notice that Christóbal was making a serious play for Vitoria, who did little to resist his advances. Both Christóbal and Vitoria had had plenty to drink and were beginning to enjoy each other's company as some of us looked on. After intimately whispering to each other, they began to embrace. It was quite a sight with Christóbal in his priest's black surplice, tied around his waist by a heavy cord with a crucifix suspended from it, and Vitoria in a red skirt with a white, open-necked blouse. Many of us tried to ignore them as Christóbal manoeuvred her against the wall in the drawing room. She seemed only too willing to comply. The kissing gradually became more intense as Christóbal moved his hand towards Vitoria's upper thigh.

I was beginning to wonder whether I wanted this behaviour in my house when Luis came up to me and asked the same question. 'Isn't it difficult to throw out a priest?' I asked.

'We don't throw him out. We ask him to stop trying to have his way with Vitoria. She's too drunk to know what she's doing anyway.'

'I'll ask him,' I said.

I moved towards the pair of them whose embracing had become even more passionate and fevered. 'Christóbal, I want you to stop that. Vitoria is half drunk? If she was sober she wouldn't want you pawing all over her. The last thing she wants is to give birth to a priest's bastard.'

'Hang on. We are just enjoying an embrace. Aren't we, Vitoria?' said Christóbal. Vitoria let out an incomprehensible murmur. It was neither a yes nor a no.

'In that case, would you mind getting out of my house? I have my reputation…'

'It's best that we stop,' said Christóbal. What a relief. They decoupled and continued just chatting in the drawing room.

With this little incident hopefully over, I asked Honofre how he was getting on with the Inquisition. 'I have submitted all the papers. What a job. I had to find a dozen references. Luckily, my father helped by using a number of his contacts. I won't have an interview until they are satisfied with the replies.'

'What will you actually be doing, then?' I asked.

'I don't know for sure. It will be a minor position, that of *familiar*. I will be assisting the tribunal. Dealing with those who are summoned to it. I won't be a member of the tribunal itself.'

'I still don't understand why you want to join. Wouldn't you feel better having an ordinary job, like the rest of us?'

'Well, Juan, that is where you have misunderstood the situation. I have a job with Manuel de Foronda, the wool merchant. I buy wool from the farmers and sell it on. That is my paid employment. My job for the Inquisition is an honorary post and I will not receive a *maravedí* for it.'

'Then it is even less clear why you want to work for them. I'm even more puzzled now.'

'There is a certain amount of perceived status which the position of *familiar* provides. But it is not that which I'm interested in. The main issue, from my point of view, is that I want to serve my country. I am a patriot. I believe in Spain. The purity of the Catholic faith and its maintenance. And if you succeed in becoming a *familiar* you are recognised as having the purity of blood, which is necessary to be a true Spanish Catholic.'

'So you are doing it for the status then?'

'Not at all. I just want to do something for my country, as well as have a normal job.'

I still did not know what to think of what Honofre was doing. Would I want a position like this myself? It would certainly fit well with my position as special agent for the King. I would think further about it.

Just before midnight, we started up the band for the last time and danced until we almost dropped. By then, the food and drinks had run out and we had all had enough. The party finished, we said our goodbyes and, in dribs and drabs, my guests drifted away. That is, all except Teresa who wanted to stay for longer.

'What excuse am I going to give your mother when I go home without you?' asked Honofre.

'They will be in bed by now and I will be home soon, certainly by the time they wake up. Juan will take me home won't you Juan.'

'Yes, of course, Teresa,' I said. 'Probably within an hour.'

Honofre was satisfied with that and went home.

Teresa and I sat together on the sofa in the drawing room and chatted. 'What a good party, Juan. Whose idea was it? Yours?'

'Yes, I just thought I'd like to do something to mark the move into my new house. And that it would be a great opportunity for my colleagues to meet my friends. I'm pleased it went so well.'

'I am angry that you did not introduce me to any of your colleagues.'

She was right. What an omission, especially as she was my girlfriend, more or less. 'I'm so sorry, Teresa. I saw Honofre introducing you so I left it at that. But I should have introduced you to them myself. I hope I haven't hurt you.'

'I don't think so, Juan, and I feel better now that you have explained yourself.'

'What did you think of my new colleagues?'

'I loved the older ones, Diego and Mateo. Is Mateo your boss? It must be wonderful to work for a man as nice as that. And Diego. What a modest man. I am sure he was the painter of a portrait of the King I once saw exhibited in the Plaza Mayor. Your musician colleagues, Francisco de Guypúzcoa and Simón Donoso, know how to get a party to swing!'

'I'm glad you like them,' I said, as I moved just a little closer to her on the sofa.

'But I was surprised at Vitoria. Didn't she make a play for Christóbal? What a little hussy. I thought she was going to eat him!'

'She was drunk and he took advantage. I really thought they were going to go the whole way. Right there in my drawing room.'

'You did the right thing, breaking them up.'

The candles were beginning to flicker. Teresa moved closer to me and I put my left arm around her shoulder to embrace her.

'That is nice Juan,' she whispered as she brought her face closer to mine. Our lips met and we kissed. 'Juan, that was lovely. Let's do it again. And make it last longer this time.' We kissed again and I could feel her tongue trying gently to penetrate my lips. I placed my right hand over her left breast and stroked it until I could feel the nipple stiffen inside her blouse. Then I began to work gently on the right breast as she sighed with enjoyment.

'Where did you learn to do that?' she said.

'You know full well. I told you about my love lessons.'

'What else did she teach you?'

'Let me try this,' I said, gradually lifting her skirt up from her ankles and sliding my right hand up slowly on the inside of her naked thigh. I stopped just below the top and slid my hand down again and up and down about a dozen times. I could feel the warmth of her body and hear her breathing more intensely. I slid my hand up just a little higher and stopped. We had never gone this far before and I could feel myself responding.

'I want to touch you, Juan, before you go any further.'

I undid the belt on my breeches and slid them down a little. She put her hand in and felt me. She let out a little yelp. 'Goodness, Juan, it is ready now. What are we to do?'

'We just fondle each other. We mustn't go the whole way. We must not do that. Do you remember what your mother said? You told me that you wanted to be a virgin when you got married.'

'Can't we go all the way, Juan? I won't say anything. My parents will never find out. I want to do it.'

'No, Teresa. It would be wrong. We must go no further than fondling.'

'I know, Juan, but this feels so good,' she said opening her legs wider and putting her left leg up over the arm of the sofa. 'Juan, touch me inside, please.' I crossed my fingers, just as Esmeralda had instructed, and gently applied them to Teresa.

'Juan, that is so nice, I could let you do this all night!' Then after about five minutes of me touching her in this way, still with her hand on me, she shuddered uncontrollably. 'Juan, Juan, Juan... more, more, what have you done to me?'

'I have just brought you to a climax. Was it nice?'

'It was stupendous. It was the nicest feeling ever and it went through my whole body. I thought I was passing out!'

'Now I want to taste you,' I said. 'I'll lie on the floor and you lay on top of me face down so that your bottom is over my face.'

'I can take you into my mouth at the same time.'

'Only if you want to, but be careful because I may lose control.'

'Don't worry about that, Juan.'

We moved into our new positions and I opened her legs wider. The taste of her juices was like nectar, especially after the wine we had drunk that night. Suddenly, her fluid began to taste horrible and metallic. The volume of it increased. It smelt unpleasant and felt sticky, like congealing blood. I took a candlestick from the table and by its flickering light I could see blood flowing from her, down on to my shirt. She still had me in her mouth.

'Teresa,' I said, 'I think you are having your monthly bleed.'

'Oh, God! Juan, I'm sorry.'

'Don't worry. It's just an accident. You were not to know. I must have worked on you too much and made it start early,' I said, taking the blame and hoping this would make her feel better. 'I think we've got some cleaning up to do!'

We washed ourselves with some hot water and had a drink of grape juice before sitting back down on the sofa to rest a little. Teresa had by then torn a piece off an old towel and gently eased it inside herself to staunch the flow.

'Maybe it's time to go,' I suggested. 'I'll walk you home.' It was past one o'clock in the morning. She let herself into her house with a key that Honofre had left her.

'See you soon,' she said and planted a kiss on my lips.

It worried me that, having criticised Vitoria about her exploits with Christóbal, Teresa wanted to go the whole way in our lovemaking. If she had become pregnant that would have had the most awkward consequences.

***

Moving into my rented house marked the beginning of a new era for me. I intended to enjoy my new freedom and way of life. My relationship with Teresa tested and preoccupied me. I felt I was falling in love with her but this was tainted by an uncomfortable feeling of uncertainty. She said she liked me and I liked her but she never expressed her love. It seemed her parents had someone else in mind and were using me as a plaything. I did not know what to think. But, if anyone asked me if I had a girlfriend, I would say it was Teresa.

Early that year, Maestro Mateo Romero came to tell us, one by one, about his imminent retirement. That came as no surprise to me, especially as he had begun to groom me as the main composer in the Royal Chapel. Other than my father, I admired Mateo Romero more than any other man. He miraculously combined being a boss, a colleague and a friend. I would never forget his first words on my first day at the Royal Chapel: 'You will fit in so well and be in your element.' We were astonished to hear that, Carlos Patiño was appointed to replace him. Obviously, my relationship with Carlos would change but I respected him as a musician and composer and that would be a good start.

News of Lope's death spread across Madrid like darkness on a summer's night. He presented me with my first professional challenge as a composer so deserved my lasting gratitude. The last few years of his life were shrouded in misery. Not only did he lose to illness one of his favourite mistresses, the beloved Doña Marta, his son Lopito from another affair was lost, presumed drowned at sea, and his daughter Antonia, defying the will of her father, eloped with a member of the court. The year 1635 bore heavily on him and in the August, at the age of seventy-three, he succumbed to scarlet fever.

At Carlos's request I wrote a march for Lope's funeral. I scored this modest, highly repetitive piece for a side drum, two trumpets and two

109

tambourines. A group at the front of the procession performed it. A boy soldier played the side drum and Lope would have delighted in that. The people of Madrid thronged the streets that day, mainly ordinary people who loved the storylines Lope wrote with their twists and turns and sudden surprises. Dukes, marquises and other civil dignitaries lined the route. At some points the procession had to stop so the *alguacils* could move people out of the way. The procession slowly snaked its way from his house in the Calle de Francos, down the Calle de San Josefe, past the Convent of the Barefoot Trinitarians, and from there to the Calle de las Huertas where it turned west towards the San Sebastian Church in which he was interred. Lope planned this circuitous route himself and instructed that his cortege should pass the convent so that his daughter, Sor Marcela, who was a nun there, could see the procession as it passed.

I watched the procession with Teresa and Simón Donoso at a point along the Calle de las Huertas. I was sure the two of them were holding hands and released their clasp as soon as they saw me. The King had declared a state of mourning for nine days; such was the reputation of this great Spanish playwright. The one disappointment was that a number of Lope's literary contemporaries failed to sign the book of condolence. The playwright, Calderón de la Barca, and the poet and satirist, Francisco de Quevedo, were among them. All this was to do with petty jealousies of those who winced at the public acclamation enjoyed by Lope.

Calderón de la Barca was, almost immediately after Lope's death, appointed as the King's playwright and I met him soon afterwards at the palace. He was completely different in character to Lope and at first I could not see a way in which I could work with him. He seemed fussy, petulant and conceited. I also met Francisco de Quevedo who had, thanks to some help from the Count Duke, manoeuvred himself into the position of the King's Principal Private Secretary. Much as I tried to like Quevedo, I failed. His arrogance and rudeness could not be surpassed.

CHAPTER 9

Carlos Patiño comfortably adopted the mantle of Mateo Romero and soon had us at his command. He was a little more formal than Maestro Romero but had an underlying warmth of personality. For several years, and given the opportunity, he continued giving me lessons in composition. Although he encouraged me to write what he called 'practice pieces', he gave priority to music for which the Royal Chapel had been commissioned. He would promulgate the fact that he had two composers in the Chapel, himself and me, and that we were both available for work.

Carlos did not detach himself from his staff in the Royal Chapel. Far from it. He spoke to most of us each day about something or other. He brought us comments from Their Majesties about our performances in their presence and suggestions that they had made for changing the programmes we prepared for them. One of his best attributes was his ability to deal with senior officials and royalty. During his early years as Maestro, he developed a network of contacts in the palace, to which he could refer for advice or for solutions to problems. Some of the issues he dealt with were minor but important to those of us involved.

I remember that, at the end of a particular month, none of us in the Chapel were paid our salaries. He went to the Office of the Paymaster General to discuss the issue with the Paymaster, himself. Within a few days, sure enough, we were all paid. He was widely respected for this. He also had the ear of the King, something that Mateo had not fully succeeded in achieving. Mateo seemed almost frightened of the King and obsequious towards him. Carlos Patiño would drop into the King's Private Office and ask Private Secretary Quevedo if the King could spare a few minutes to discuss a matter with the Maestro Patiño.

'It's a matter to do with His Majesty's Chapel and his musicians,' he would say, with unabashed authority.

More often than not, the King would give the Maestro a few minutes. The one thing His Majesty appreciated was someone, like Carlos, who had the knack of making his point in few words, awaiting a reply, perhaps engaging in a few moments consequential discussion and then concluding with, 'Will that be all, Your Majesty?'

I recall very well an occasion when Carlos came back from one of these self-invited audiences.

'Juan, Juan, come into my office. I've something big to tell you!'

I could not wait to hear.

'His Majesty wants you to write some songs!'

'Me? Some songs? How did you manage that?'

'I went to tell him that some of the material in the Songbook of Sablonara and in the Palace Songbook was old and too often repeated. I suggested that we compose say twenty or so new songs that we could play to him and the Queen in the form of actual songs or just as tunes without the words.'

'What did he think of that?'

'Well, he first said he was happy with what we played from the existing material. Then I said there was nothing new he hadn't heard before. So I said we would willingly write some new songs. We could do this in our spare time.'

'And what did he say to that?'

'He said, "You seem determined to write some new material so go away and get your harpist, composer colleague, Hidalgo, to write some new songs. And I don't want religious songs!"'

'So when do I start? When do you want them?' I asked, more than a little perplexed because I had never written a song before.

'We start as soon as we can and return to the King once we have a reasonable number for him and the Queen to listen to.'

'That also means I'll have to write some verses,' I said.

'Yes, that is so. But as you are a musician, the rhythm of the word will come easily to you. Go away and compose something!'

So this is why I started to write some songs! With the new Maestro's blunt, but encouraging words, I became excited and enthused by this new, unexpected commission. My immediate thoughts were to write, say, four to six hugely contrasting songs. We would play these to the King and Queen and hopefully they would want us to write some more. We could have a love song; a sad song; something amusing; mainly solos and a couple of duets. We would have a variety of orchestration from a small group to a solo instrument and male and female singers. I told Carlos Patiño my thoughts and he just said, 'Fine. Go and get on with it!'

***

I decided to celebrate this new commission by taking Teresa to a performance of a *comedia*, 'The Three Greatest Wonders', by Calderón de la Barca, at the new Buen Retiro Palace. The Buen Retiro was one of the most spectacular and expensive projects ever conceived in Madrid. The whole site was colossal. There were ornate gardens divided geometrically into plots containing flowers of many contrasting colours. There was an artificial lake fed by an artificial river. Scenes from plays could be enacted on the lake. There was lighting that could be controlled remotely, an amazing innovation for its day. The whole concept was dreamt up by the Count Duke Olivares, some say to distract the King from the work of government.

The *comedia* took place in the main theatre. There were three acts, each played by a different cast on a separate stage, with the three casts combining for the final scene. It was based on three separate stories, the first on Jason and the Golden Fleece, the second on Theseus and the Minotaur, and the third on Hercules and his wife Deianira. Deianira provided the link between the three acts. The centaur had kidnapped her and the characters in each act had been looking for her.

We chatted about the *comedia* while walking back from the theatre. We had both enjoyed it and thought that the play was unique in its presentation. I said that it could benefit from some music, if only incidental music, of the kind I had written for Lope in 'Punishment without Revenge'. Teresa was less sure, saying that music could overpower the acting. We stopped for a drink at one of our favourite taverns near the Mentidero and, disappointed that there was no one there that we knew, continued back to my house in the Puerta Cerrada.

We resumed a familiar courting position on the sofa in the drawing room and began to kiss each other. I won't repeat the detail here, but it was not unlike our previous episode of mutual physical enjoyment.

'I wish I knew where this relationship was going, Teresa,' I said afterwards, hoping that she might have some better idea than me. 'I am twenty-three now and you are twenty-two. Where do you want our relationship to go?'

'I don't really know, Juan. I like both sides of it: the physical and the friendship we mutually enjoy. I appreciate your presence and your generosity. Thank you for taking me to the Buen Retiro today. It must have cost you a fortune,' she said, attempting to change the subject.

'That's fine. But I really think we should work out what we want for the future. This is not a proposal of marriage. But would you consider me as a possible husband?'

'I need notice of questions like that, Juan,' she replied, just before planting a kiss on my lips, as if to quieten me. 'I don't know what my parents would think of my getting married. I'm still quite young and so are you.'

So it looked as if she was happy to muddle along with me as a male companion until someone else appeared in her vision. Oh well.

'Let me take you back to your house,' I said, disappointedly, detecting that she had had enough of this encounter.

***

It was not long before I had written a number of songs for the King. I decided not to write my own words for the first one but chose a piece by the poet Luis de Góngora called 'The Flowers of Rosemary'. I wrote it for a tenor voice, a harp and a guitar. I wrote the words for all the others. The second song was called 'The Victor Marches On' for a tenor and solo guitar, and a third was called 'I am Going on a Journey' which I scored for a soprano and two violins. I wrote a duet called 'Watching the Stars Above' for a tenor and soprano, accompanied by a guitar, and a lament for a soprano and harp called 'The End of Love'.

The Maestro Patiño was pleased with my efforts which I delivered to his office about a month or so after the King had made the request. Surprisingly, he made no changes to the pieces themselves but did change the titles slightly. I was not sure why. He wrote a short note for the King about each of the songs. It attributed the words of the first piece to Góngora, and credited me with the words and the music for all of the others. He took this note along to the King's Private Office.

He came back smiling wryly like a naughty child caught stealing cakes. 'Quevedo was furious,' he said, gleefully.

'Why was that?'

'We acknowledged his sworn enemy, Luis de Góngora.'

'But Góngora died about ten years ago.'

'I know but Quevedo is still smarting. He wanted me to remove "all reference to that ghastly, evil man". I said we couldn't pretend to the King that you had written all the songs when you hadn't. And I refused to delete one of them just because Quevedo wasn't happy. We had quite a row!'

'What was the conclusion?'

'We agreed not to mention Góngora and not to give any credits for the words. He did agree that, if we ever published the songs or made them available outside the palace, we would have to acknowledge Góngora. Whether he liked it or not.'

I agreed with Maestro Carlos that we would have to wait for the King's reaction before we performed them for Their Majesties or composed any more.

***

That night, while Barbola was cooking my evening meal, there was a knock on the front door. It was Teresa.

'Come in, Teresa. Good to see you.'

She seemed unhappy and shied away from me as I attempted to kiss her cheek. There was something badly wrong. She walked in front of me towards the sofa in the drawing room and I followed.

'I have some news for you, Juan. I'm not sure how to put this and I don't want to hurt you. I want to stop seeing you.'

I was shocked but not totally surprised. 'Why is that?' I said, without a trace of reaction.

'I am seeing someone else, Simón Donoso.' That was not a total surprise either. I saw them together about a year or so before, when they joined me to watch Lope's funeral procession. I suspected then that they may be friends. 'Only, after our discussion the night after the theatre, I thought I should tell you, before our relationship went any further.'

'She's been going out with both of us,' I thought. 'The two timing hussie! He can have her.'

'Good of you to tell me. Is that all?' I said, as unemotionally as I could.

'I'll go then,' she said and turned towards the door.

'Good luck with Simón,' I said.

I felt rejected, sorry for myself, angry and horrible, all at the same time. I needed to think about what she had said. My thoughts were random and confused but they had an ironic logic. I could not be jealous of Simón. I had enjoyed several aspects of the relationship with Teresa but I could not see where it was going. All was clear now: it was finished. What had I done, I wondered, to provoke this? I had asked her where the relationship was heading. That simple, little question made her feel bad about seeing me and Simón at the same time. She was the guilty one. My honour was preserved intact. Had I been wasting my time with Teresa; had I wasted those years? No, was my conclusion. It was all experience. Neither of us was committed to the other and neither made any expression of love for the other. I poured myself a glass of wine. She was his now and he was welcomed to her.

Failure can often be the spur for success and the loss of Teresa, if I could call it that, stimulated me to think hard about my future and where my life was going. I would not rush into a new relationship. I was twenty-two, coming up to twenty-three so there was plenty of time ahead of me. I would not hop straight from one woman to the next.

I also decided that I would go through with something I had been thinking about for some time: apply for membership of the Spanish

115

Inquisition. I would become a *familiar,* the same position as that for which Honofre had applied. This decision was helped by the fact that Lope, whom I had always admired, had also been a *familiar.* Like Honofre, I felt strongly about the security of Spain and that was partly why I had become an agent of the Council for State Security.

I had no idea how difficult it was to achieve the position of *familiar.* I would, as Honofre had said before, need at least a dozen references. After reflecting for a week or so, I went to Honofre's house to ask him about applying. Teresa answered the door.

'Hello, Juan. How are you?'

I was sure she thought I had gone there to see her to discuss reconciliation. If so, she was wrong. 'Hello, Teresa. Is Honofre in? I was hoping to speak to him.'

'Yes. Come in,' she said, still bewildered by my presence there.

Honofre explained how I should apply. First, I needed to seek general approval from the Inquisitor's Office; then I needed to solicit for references. The Inquisitor's Office would itself send out the necessary papers to my supporters. Honofre would provide one for me as he was already a *familiar* and had known me for a long time, upwards of ten or eleven years.

The Inquisitor's Office made enquires of our family and friends in Pedraza, San Sebastián de los Reyes, Retortillo and Madrid. Most people hate dealing with official documents and my friends, colleagues and contacts were no exception. In the end, I managed to extract references from: Juan de Roxas Carrión, Francisco de Guypúzcoa, Simón Donoso, despite his friendship with Teresa, Honofre of course, Christóbal de Agramontes, Luis de As, Balthazar Favales and Vitoria de Cuenca. This was not enough but my father came to my aid and managed to obtain another ten more to make it up to eighteen. We expected the Inquisitor's Office to take months to come to a decision, so I just had to wait.

***

Months drifted by before we received a response from the King's Private Office to the Maestro's note about our new songs. We were beginning to think the papers had been lost or that Maestro Carlos had upset Quevedo so much that he had filed them away somewhere for posterity. Then, just as Carlos had decided to make some enquiries himself, we had a reply in the form of a memorandum from an assistant private secretary, tellingly not from Quevedo. It said that His Majesty was 'content' with the note and wanted to hear some of the songs, in particular, 'The Flowers of Rosemary' and 'Watching the Stars Above'. He wanted them to be presented in a short recital along with some contrasting songs from the Palace Songbook or elsewhere. The note said that he wanted to hear these two new songs before we presented any more new ones to him or wrote any more.

Carlos Patiño assembled the programme for the recital. It included one of his own songs 'Nothing Much Costs Little' and 'Flowery Romerico', a song by Mateo Romero, which I always thought could have been an allusion to his own love life. He put in this song of Mateo's because of the rosemary theme which contrasted nicely with the rosemary of the Góngora poem. There was also a song by Encina called 'He That Has Such a Lady', an anonymous song called 'In Comes May and Out Goes April' and three other songs Carlos thought the King would like to hear again. The Private Office fixed the date for the recital and that gave us a month to prepare.

The usual group of us was selected to perform: Juan de Roxas Carrión, Francisco de Guypúzcoa, Simón Donoso, myself, Hernando de Eslava, Vitoria de Cuenca and the tenor, Alonso Arias de Soria. This was quite an ambitious programme so there was much practising and rehearsing to do, especially of the two new songs that I had written.

***

Much of our practising was carried out on an individual basis and, as before, I came to the palace early for at least a week before the final rehearsals to familiarise myself with the harp parts and to make sure I could play them well. One morning, I was practising by about eight o'clock in the morning, quite oblivious to the presence of two figures who had surreptitiously sneaked into the practice room. I was playing the Góngora piece. As I reached the end of it, the two interlopers applauded.

'Bravo. Bravo!'

It was Diego, the artist, accompanied by a beautiful but austere, worried-looking young woman. She was wearing a dark dress and a black shawl, that came down well past her shoulders, and white, silk gloves that reached halfway up her forearms. She was dark haired, about twenty years old and had the most striking brown eyes. Her sombre, burnt umber dress was cut low at the front to reveal a modest amount of cleavage, which was framed by the pretty edging of a white slip that just peeped out from the line of her dress. It was an unusual assemblage of clothing to be wearing so early in the day.

'Hello, Juan. We couldn't fail to hear you. I thought it would be you,' said Diego.

I wondered what he would be doing with this stunning woman at that time of the morning.

'This is Señorita Francisca Paula de Abaunza who is sitting for me today. Francisca, this is my friend and colleague, Juan Hidalgo. Juan is, as you have already heard, a harpist in the Royal Chapel. He is also a composer and is writing some new songs for His Majesty.'

'Delighted to meet you, Señorita Abaunza. I hope Diego is looking after you well.'

'He is a wonderful painter and the complete gentleman,' she said, dispelling immediately the startled look I first saw in her eyes. 'I love sitting for him. The only problem is that he talks too much. So takes longer painting than he really should!' she said, smiling and looking at Diego.

'Now you're teasing me,' he said.

'I haven't seen you in the palace before, señorita,' I said. 'Do you work here?'

'Goodness, no,' said the young lady. 'I am a friend of Diego's wife. She told me that the King had asked him to paint some pictures of the people of Madrid, ordinary people like me. Anyway, I volunteered myself to be painted by Diego and here I am.'

'That's right,' said Diego, as if the expression on my face was one of quiet disbelief. 'We know the Abaunza family because they are neighbours of ours in the Calle de Concepción. Over the years we have become close friends.'

'Interesting way for a painting to be commissioned,' I said. 'How are you getting on with it?'

'I have only just started. So we'll be seeing quite a bit of Francisca, for a week or two...maybe even longer.'

'You live close to my house, Señorita Abaunza. I live in the Puerta Cerrada, just across the Calle de Toledo from you. So, if you want an escort to or from the palace, anytime... Well, anytime Diego is not available, please let me know or ask Diego to tell me.'

'That is very kind of you, Señor Hidalgo. I may take you up on that. The streets are so full of vagabonds and ruffians these days, you cannot be too careful.'

The two of them said their goodbyes and left. I felt an immediate attraction for the woman. I was breathless and quite faint. My heart was pounding. Was this love at first sight? It was a warm, tingling feeling. I liked her and felt I wanted to be her partner and protect her. Then I began to recover my thoughts. Was she already committed to someone else? If she lives with her family she may not be. I had never felt like this before. I certainly did not get this intensity of feeling with Teresa, even though the relationship with her was quite physical. Would I have broken off with Teresa if I had felt like this about someone else? Not at this stage but, if the relationship went anywhere, I would have had to tell Teresa. So, unknowingly, she might have saved me from doing to her what she did to me. So, I could have been lucky.

I remember thinking to myself, the day Teresa said she no longer wanted to be my girlfriend, that I would not rush into a relationship with another woman and here I was doing just that. Well, at least thinking of a new relationship, if not exactly rushing into one. It was then four months since Teresa's departure. I needed to move slowly, carefully so as not to hurt anyone, either this young woman or myself. I had to find out more about her but I would not rush. I would let things happen.

***

I resumed my practice session but my mind was in a state of turmoil and it took several minutes before I could concentrate enough to play well. Then I had another visitor. It was the Maestro Patiño to tell me about the first full rehearsal of the song recital for the King.

'I have an idea, Juan, and I want to know what you think about it. I don't want to rehearse the recital here at the palace, especially as it would mean playing your new songs here. Others would inevitably hear them before the King did and we don't want that. What do you think of rehearsing in a private house? I know Antonio de Prado, the playwright and theatre company manager, quite well and he has several times offered me the use of his house for rehearsing. He lives in the Calle de Infante, just off the Mentidero.'

'The only drawback I can see,' I said, 'is that we would have to take our instruments there. But that would not be a real problem. The only other one is that we might be quite loud and be heard from the street.'

'De Prado has wooden covers on the walls in his rehearsal room. So we shouldn't disturb the neighbours or people walking by.'

'Then, let's do it, Carlos.'

The Maestro arranged to use Antonio de Prado's house for three days. There was then a free day before the actual recital in the palace. Carlos played a major role in directing the rehearsals. He was determined to produce a first-class recital for the King. His attention to detail was phenomenal, even down to exactly where we should position ourselves during the recital and to where we should move after each song had been sung. Despite his efforts, the first rehearsal was a disaster. The problem centred on one of the two new songs, the Góngora poem, and Carlos began to despair.

'Alonso Arias de Soria is doing his best but you, Juan, and Simón are simply not playing well. You are totally out of time with each other. What's going on?'

There was a problem and I thought it could be due to our relationships with Teresa. Neither of us had broached the issue with the other. I felt awkward in Simón's presence and I assumed he felt uncomfortable with me.

'Can I have a private word with Simón?' I asked Carlos.

'If you think that might help, then, yes. Please don't take long. We have work to do.'

Simón and I left the rehearsal room and I closed the door behind us.

'What is the matter, Simón? Is it something to do with Teresa?' I asked.

'Yes,' said Simón, 'I feel so bad that she has rejected you, Juan, in favour of me. It is influencing my guitar playing. What can I do?'

'Simple. Don't worry about it. I still regard you as a friend and I think we need to remain friends. So we can play well together. As far as I am concerned, Teresa is yours now and I have absolutely no problem with that. I am not the least bit jealous and wish you both a happy future.'

'You are a good man, Juan, and I am grateful to you. Let's go back to rehearse.'

We returned and both told the Maestro that everything would be fine and, sure enough, it was. The rehearsal finished with the Maestro suggesting a few minor changes to my songs, which we incorporated into the following rehearsal. We used the final one to smooth out and perfect our overall performance of all the works in the programme.

The King had decided to make a major event of the recital and, as well as the Queen, had invited a number of senior people from the various councils and committees including the Count Duke and his wife, the Inquisitor General and his wife, Francisco de Quevedo and Diego Velázquez and his wife. He also invited some of the less senior people in the palace, including the dwarfs, Don Diego de Acedo, known as 'the Cousin', and Sebastian de Morra. The recital started well with Carlos directing our group of musicians. The first song performed was 'Flowery Romerico', followed by two of the additional songs Carlos had chosen.

Then came 'Nothing Much Costs Little.' Carlos had scored this version for the soprano, Vitoria de Cuenca, the tenor, Alonso Arias de Soria, a single violin, in this case Francisco de Guypúzcoa, and a guitar, played by Simón Donoso. Suddenly, Simón was completely overcome by an attack of nerves and played a number of obviously wrong notes. This put Vitoria off balance and she too made a number of mistakes. The piece started so badly that Carlos tapped his baton on the top of his music stand.

'Stop! Stop!' he said. 'We cannot continue like this. Is there a problem, Simón?'

'I don't feel right. It's not Vitoria's fault. My bad play is putting her off.'

'Let's start this one again. Just pretend there is no one here. No audience at all.'

The King was superb. 'Yes, we are not here,' he said. 'Just relax and enjoy playing!'

We did as the King had said and this piece and the rest of the recital were fine. I'm not sure whether it was the King or the Maestro who saved the day but there was something there to be learned by all of us: make sure you know the pieces so well you can play them through your nerves and don't be put off by someone else's errors.

***

On the 26 November 1638, at the age of twenty-four, I was sworn in as a *familiar* of the Holy Office of the Inquisition of Toledo, thus satisfying all the requirements of purity of blood and of reputation.

CHAPTER 10

Not many weeks after the recital, Diego Velázquez called into the office I shared with Juan de Roxas Carrión and Francisco de Guypúzcoa.

'Juan, can you help me? It is late in the afternoon and I have just been asked to see Private Secretary Quevedo. I promised I would take Francisca de Abaunza home and I just haven't the time before the meeting. You volunteered to escort her, if I could not take her. Could you take her home, please?'

This was what I hoped would happen. 'Of course, Diego. I'd be delighted to.'

'I'll bring her to you in, say, five minutes. All right?'

'I'm more or less ready to leave. What if I come round to your studio now?'

I followed Diego to the studio where the young woman was looking at some of Diego's work, some finished and some hardly sketched out.

'Here's your escort, Francisca!' said Diego.

'It's Señor Hidalgo, the harpist,' she said. 'Thank you for helping out, Señor Hidalgo.'

'I'm at your service, Señorita Abaunza. Before we go, I would like you to show me how much progress Diego has made with your portrait. Is that all right?'

'I'd rather Diego show you. I'm a bit embarrassed by it!' she said, modestly.

'Here it is,' said Diego, pulling back a cloth which was covering the incomplete work. 'There's still a lot to do but you can see where it's going.'

The painting was going to be an excellent likeness of the young woman. She was half facing out of the picture and those large brown eyes, twin pools of rapture, were looking straight out of the portrait. Her clothes were exactly what she had been wearing when we first met: the black shawl over a regal, dark umber dress; the modest revelation of cleavage, cosseted in the white edging of her slip; and the long, white gloves. She was wearing something totally different and more relaxed that day: a white blouse with a ruffled collar and a black, long skirt. It was as if Diego did not need her to pose in the deep umber dress because he could remember every crease and fold in it. He had almost finished her face and upper body but there was still much of the portrait which was incomplete.

'Goodness!' was my reaction. 'What an incredible likeness. It's as if there are two of you in this room, señorita, the real you and the portrait. It is so beautiful. Even moving. Diego, you are a genius!' Diego had even captured that slightly nervous, austere look on the woman's face that I had noticed when I first met her. It was almost as if she was frightened of something.

'Are you ready to go, Señorita Abaunza?'

'Yes, Señor Hidalgo, I am,' she said, sounding anxious to leave.

'I'll see you at your house the day after tomorrow,' said Diego.

The young lady and I left and began to walk to her house. After about five minutes of silence, during which she failed to look at me directly, I decided to start a conversation. 'I am intrigued by how you came to sit for Diego,' I said.

Her initial quietness gradually evaporated and she soon became quite forthcoming. 'Well, I know his wife because we are close neighbours and she told me that he always wanted to paint me. The King had said he wanted to see some pictures of the people of Madrid. So this gave Diego an immediate excuse to paint my portrait, if he needed one. We have been friends with Diego's family for quite a number of years now. We have mutual friends in Madrid, especially around the Calle de la Concepción. Unfortunately, my mother died only a few years ago and Diego's wife has been like a mother to me ever since. So now I live just with my father.' So she was obviously single.

'I am sorry to hear about your mother. What a sad loss for you. She must have been very young when she died.'

'It makes me sad to talk about it, Señor Hidalgo, but she was only forty-one. It was a mystery illness that killed her. None of the doctors could work out what it was. Anyway, what about you? Tell me about yourself. How long have you been working at the palace? Do you do any composing?'

'I've been there about seven years now. Most of my work is playing the harp to Their Majesties in concerts and recitals. I also play in the chapel at the palace on more sombre occasions. It's only in the last few years that I've started composing seriously. I've just written five songs for the King, at his request. Carlos Patiño, the Maestro of the Royal Chapel, persuaded the King that he should commission more works from his composers. So this is a new initiative for us. Carlos and I are the only composers in the Royal Chapel.'

'I love music, Señor Hidalgo. Can I hear you play something?'

'Of course,' I said. 'I have a harp at home and I could play you some music tonight. Some I've composed and some other pieces, if you would like to come round to my house. But I can't sing, so there will be no songs.'

'That's a good idea, Señor Hidalgo. But I need to tell my father what I'll be doing. Then we will be fine. Would you please escort me home after our little concert?'

'Yes, I'd be delighted.'

We walked down the Calle de Santa Maria to the Plazuela de Cordon and then along to the Puerta Cerrada. I showed her where I lived. 'I should tell you that I live alone and that we will be alone in my house. Unless you want to invite your father along to our little concert as well.'

'It's good of you to tell me that,' said the young woman, 'but I already know you live alone. I think Diego must have told me. There is no need to invite my father along. He's not that keen on music anyway. Diego assures me that you're a nice man and that I can trust you. Do you agree that we forego the formalities and call each other by our first names?'

I agreed to this welcomed request. It was refreshing to speak to a woman whom I hardly knew in familiar, friendly terms. We became more relaxed with each other as we passed my house and turned towards hers. We passed out of the south corner of the Puerta Cerrada and crossed the Calle de Toledo straight into the Calle de la Concepción. She lived on the south side of the road almost opposite the Velázquez family.

'Come in,' she said, as she opened the heavy front door. She led me into the kitchen where her father was sitting at a table reading some papers.

'Papa, this is Señor Juan Hidalgo, a harpist and composer at the palace. He is a friend of Diego and agreed to escort me back home. He has asked me if I want to have dinner with him tonight and to listen to some of his music. Is that all right? He will bring me back afterwards.' I invited her to dinner as well? I didn't remember saying that!

'Yes, Francisca. That will be fine. You are old enough now to know what you want. Anyway, I am pleased to meet you, Señor Hidalgo,' he said, firmly shaking my hand. 'Look after her won't you? She's all I've got!'

We then walked back to my house. 'I'm sorry about the invitation to dinner,' she said, 'but it sounded a better reason for going back with you than just to listen to some music. And my father would understand that better. But it is not necessary to cook a meal for me, really.'

'Don't worry, Francisca,' I said, venturing to use her first name. 'I'd be delighted if you stayed for something to eat. I have to prepare a meal for myself and it is just as easy to do a meal for two as it is for just one.'

'That's kind of you, Juan,' she reciprocated. 'Then I accept your invitation to dinner!'

I opened my front door and showed her in. 'What a large property, Juan,' she said, as I took her around. 'It's more of a family house than a house for one person.'

'You are probably right. I wanted a large house so I could entertain and so that I could practise my music without disturbing people. I rent it and I have a cleaning lady, Barbola, who comes in a few times a week for three *reales*. She cooks for me, too.'

'You are well organised, Juan.'

'Thank you. We can eat first or play some music, whatever you prefer. The choice is yours, Francisca.'

'What if we play some music first? Is there anything we can do now to prepare vegetables or put something on to cook, while you are playing?'

'I was thinking of having a casserole of some beef, left from yesterday, and some green beans. How does that sound?'

'Fine to me.'

'Let's prepare the vegetables and get the casserole started.'

Within a few minutes, we had the dish on the stove and the beans ready for cooking. I showed Francisca into the drawing room and I sat by my harp.

'I haven't seen a harp this close up before. Isn't it big? Do you own it?'

'Yes, it is a cumbersome instrument and the street beggars ribbed me mercilessly when I used to drag it on its cart to and from the palace but I've now bought this one which I keep at home. I also own the one at the palace which you have heard me play. I thought I'd start with two pieces by Cabezón, one straight after the other.' She applauded when I reached the end.

'That was lovely, Juan. I think I have heard of Cabezón. Wasn't he blind?'

'Yes, he was,' I said, impressed that she knew. I then played the harp line in my version of the Góngora poem, 'The Flowers of Rosemary'.

'That was wonderful, Juan. I really enjoyed that. I don't know anything about composing music but it sounds to me as if you are a very good composer.'

'That is kind of you, Francisca. I'm glad you enjoyed it. I can play some more after dinner, if you want.'

'Let's see.'

The casserole of beef was all but ready when we returned to the kitchen. Within ten minutes, we had finished preparing the meal, which I served on the kitchen table.

'This is really tasty, Juan. You are a good cook, too.'

'My mother showed me the basics of cooking before I moved here. I have one cooked meal a day, usually in the evening. Then I can relax and read or go for a walk, maybe to see my parents or my brother, Francisco.'

'Do they live near here? Tell me about them.'

'Yes, in the Lower San Ginés, not 500 *varas* from here on the other side of the Plaza Mayor. My mother is also called Francisca. And my father's name is Antonio. They are so proud that I now work in the palace,' I said. 'Would you like a glass of wine, Francisca?'

'Yes please, just a small one.'

'What about your family? You say they came from the north.'

'Yes. Both of my parents are from Durango in Viscaya. They married in Durango in 1614 and I was born there, three years later. Father was a land merchant but his business collapsed in the depression of '27. This was because much of the land he sold was bought by construction companies and banks. When the government declared itself bankrupt, they defaulted on payments to my father. We sold up and moved to Madrid ten years ago when I was eleven. We rented a house at first but then, as my father's new business grew, we bought the house in the Calle de la Concepción. He now rents and sells property so is in a business similar to the one which folded.'

There were many reasons for our country's bankruptcy. We had a burgeoning, freeloading aristocracy, the members of which paid no taxes. There were the opulent palaces, not least the Alcázar Palace and the Buen Retiro. There were the extravagant new churches and cathedrals and, of course, the Spanish armies and the navy. These presented a colossal financial burden on the state. There were then about 300,000 infantrymen and cavalrymen on the payroll and 500,000 armed soldiers in the militia. We had 130 warships. Alongside, was our massive commitment to the War in Europe. Often there were battles on several fronts simultaneously, each of which implied the need for provisions, transport and weaponry. We also had to maintain a supply route, via Italy and the Habsburg City State of Besançon, to Brussels, the capital of the Spanish Netherlands. Then there was the parasitic, self-interested civil service which constantly expanded itself. The costs of these commitments could not be met by income and the diminishing number of silver shipments coming from the Americas. Despite numerous devices, including devaluations of the currency and the introduction of copper coinage – the *vellon* – our finances collapsed. We simply could not service our debts.

'What about you, Francisca? What are your interests? Some more bread?'

'Yes, please. Thank you. My main interest is in the Convent of the Shod Carmen. In the Calle de la Carmena. I run a soup kitchen there, which opens daily. I have a number of women helpers and I go there nearly every day with one who lives near me. You see the raw end of life at the soup kitchen, I can tell you. I am also interested in music and plays. I have seen some of Lope de Vega's *comedias* and Corpus Christi plays. And I have been to several concerts in the Buen Retiro. I also read *comedias* if I can find a script!'

'We clearly have some shared interests. You have probably seen and read more plays than I have. I admire you for working with the poor. Not many people would want to do that.'

Our conversation continued through dinner and we became more and more relaxed in each other's company. We told each other more about our lives so far, about our grandparents, where we had been and who we knew. Then she asked me an interesting question.

'Juan, do you have a girlfriend?'

'No, not at present.'

'Have you had any girlfriends?'

Where was this going? 'Yes, I had a girlfriend for a number of years but we split up about six months or so ago. I've not had a girlfriend since then.'

'I have an idea, Juan. I like you a lot and we have so much in common. Would you like me to be your next girlfriend?' she said, with a beaming smile.

'Can I tell you something, Francisca? The first time I saw you, in the practice room, I nearly fainted. I asked myself if this was love at first sight. You completely enthralled me. I could not concentrate after you left and it took ages for me to recover. Yes. I would love you to be my girlfriend. That would be wonderful for me and, hopefully, for both of us.'

She rose from her chair and came over to my side. She then planted a soft kiss on my right cheek. I stood, too, and we kissed each other on the lips. I felt a magical glow, even after we had stopped.

'That seals it, then,' I said, after moment's pause.

'I feel as if I am in love, Juan. I am so happy.'

'Me, too. I feel I want to look after you for the rest of my life. That is what love is.'

'We have to meet again soon,' she said.

'What about after your next sitting with Diego? We can go somewhere together, maybe a walk down by the river.'

'The day after tomorrow, then!'

I asked her if she would like me to play some more music for her but, after this amazing conversation, I really did not feel like it. I think she detected my lack of enthusiasm and said she felt she ought to go home. So I took her home. We held hands all the way to her front door.

'Until the day after tomorrow then, Juan,' she said, again kissing me on the cheek.

I walked home in a daze. Was I really in love? She was a lovely person. Was she the one? We had so much in common. Could I live with her?

Marriage? Slow down. Step by step. Don't rush. You hardly know her. I felt as if I had known her all my life. What was happening in her head? What did she really think of me? Was I that interesting to her?

I could hardly sleep that night and got up early. My mind was still in a spin. I was sitting at the kitchen table, having some bread, olive oil and some tomatoes for breakfast, when there was a loud knock on the door. There were two men, in tricorne hats and long, brown coats, standing there.

'Are you Don Juan Hildalgo de Polanco?'

'Yes, I am the same.'

'We are *notarios* from the Holy Office of The Inquisition. We have a document for you. It sets out some duties the Holy Office expects you to perform. These functions must take precedence over all other matters,' said one of them, sternly.

'Sign here,' said the other, handing me a receipt already dated that day. I signed, and the first one handed me a scrolled document tied with a red ribbon and sealed in red wax with the coat of arms of the Inquisition. They turned and walked away. I went inside, broke the seal and unrolled the scroll. It read:

'Notice is hereby given to Don Juan Hidalgo de Polanco, familiar of the Holy Office of the Inquisition of Toledo, to carry out the following functions:

On 21 January 1639, to accompany familiar Honofre de Espinosa in charging Don Manuel Mergildo de Andrada, of the Calle de los Angeles, with the offence, under Ecclesiastical law, of common heresy. He is accused of promoting the books of Moses and translating them into Spanish.

On 20 February 1639, to attend, with Honofre de Espinosa, the auto de fe and, along with the said Señor Espinosa, to accompany a released person, later to be named, to his execution.'

Good God. What have I done in joining this organisation? They want to try someone on the grounds that he is a practising Jew and want me to walk some poor wretch to his own funeral. And they don't know who he is yet. I had to see Honofre. I had only four days before making the arrest so I'd better move quickly. I rolled up the scroll and took it straight to Honofre, on my way to the palace.

'You're early,' he said, opening the door in his dressing gown.

'Have you received a notice like this?'

He took it from me and read it. 'Yes, five minutes ago: for your name read mine.'

'What do we do?'

'Just as it says, no more and no less. At the arrest of Señor Andrada, we will be helped by two sergeants. We will have to accompany him to the secret prison where he will have to await his tribunal. He could be there for months.'

'Is that a walk away from his house?'

'Yes, it's the Carcel de Villa, in the Plazuela de la Villa.'

'What if we meet at your house before we go to charge Señor Andrada?' I said, still feeling as if this was all very new.

'That will be fine, Juan. Let's meet at eight o'clock in the morning and I'll get the sergeants to meet us here as well.'

'Until Monday, then,' I said. 'When the instruction says, "accompany a released person, later to be named, to his execution" presumably "release" has some other meaning than to set free?'

'Yes, it means to release from the jurisdiction of the Inquisition to that of the civil authorities for execution. Don't worry, Juan. We don't know if there will be an execution yet. But there probably will be.'

I walked straight to the palace after this rather formal encounter with Honofre. Had I upset him or something? Maybe Teresa had said something. I could not worry. I had other things to think about.

***

Shortly after I had arrived in the office and was tuning my harp, Carlos appeared. 'The King's comments on our song recital for him were favourable, despite our messing up the piece I wrote. He enjoyed the two new songs we played to him. He wants us to write some more.'

'Good news, Carlos. We already have three others written.'

'I know. I didn't mention those. We can learn them before he knows we have written them. That'll give us some breathing space.'

'Did he make any comments about the piece that went wrong?'

'Yes, he did. He was not happy about it. He said that everyone makes mistakes, but asked us to spend more time rehearsing. I thought that was fair and we will do just that. He also said he wanted to attend a rehearsal. He said he would let me know when.'

'That's an interesting idea!'

'I agree. I can't see a problem. In effect, he is our supreme customer and he should have a say in what we are delivering.'

'I'll think about some more songs, Carlos. Do you have any specific ideas?'

'I would like you to write some dramatic pieces, songs you might hear in a *comedia*. Maybe, portraying some specific characters. See what you can come up with.'

***

The following day, and as we had agreed, Francisca knocked on my office door just after she had finished a session with Diego.

'Hello, Juan,' she said, excitedly. 'I've finished my session and Diego has to go now. I told him we were meeting and that you were taking me home. You look busy. Shall I come back later?'

'No, Francisca. I was just roughing out some ideas for some new songs. It's time to go now anyway.'

We decided to go for a walk, down by the river, as we had suggested when we had dinner two days before. We walked to the Manzanares via the Puerta de la Vegva. 'I have been dying to see you again, Juan. I keep thinking of you. I think I am in love with you.'

'Francisca, that is wonderful. I feel the same about you.'

'What are we going to do about it, Juan?' she said, as if this was a totally new experience and she did not know how she should cope with it.

'For the time being, I think we should go on seeing each other. Spend as much time as we can with each other and see how things develop. We both believe we are in love. Let's be totally honest with each other. Neither of us is certain. We both need more time.'

'Juan, that is so mature of you. Let's see how things go before we make a final commitment.'

'Francisca, there are things we need to know about each other. For example, there is one thing I have to tell you.'

'What is that, Juan?' she asked, looking as if her world was about to collapse.

'Well… it's… it's not much really, for a man of twenty-four.' Then, after a little hesitation, I told her about Esmeralda Pechada de Burgos. I said that it was nothing more than a lesson in making love.

'Did you enjoy her body, Juan? Did she make you feel good? Were you gentle with her and did you respect her?'

'I am ashamed to admit it, but "yes" to both of your first two questions. But equally, I am pleased to say "yes" in answer to your second two questions.'

I wondered what her reaction would be. She was silent and looked quizzical for what seemed an age. 'Juan, you have nothing to be ashamed of. Your father saw this as part of your education. Hundreds of fathers do the same for their sons. I am glad you have had this experience because it will help us in the early stages of our own physical relationship.

'Juan, I have also had a sexual experience which I think I should tell you about.' She began to sob so I put my arm around her.

'If it helps, you need not tell me, Francisca.'

'No. I must tell you, Juan, however painful it is for me to relate. I cannot say I am a virgin. Just after my mother died, we had several visits by a particular priest. I won't tell you his name because you would kill him if you knew. Anyway, he has moved to Seville. This priest said that, because I was so upset, I needed some professional counselling and he took me to his office in a church to the north of the town. The first time I went he was kind and helpful. I felt confident with him.

'The second time I went to see him, he was completely different, as if something had taken possession of him. He closed his office door behind me. I heard him lock it and remove the key. I was terrified. He told me he wanted to give me some therapy which involved him making love to me and that it would make me relax. He told me to lie on the table with my skirt up and my legs apart. I said I would not but he told me to do so "in the name of God" or he would kill me. I did what he said and within seconds he was trying to push his member into me.

'It was painful and I screamed and yelled. He was standing at the end of the table so I pushed myself back, away from him, grabbed his member and his testicles and squeezed it all as hard as I possibly could. I really hurt him by twisting it all around. He had only just penetrated me and I managed to get him out. I slid off the table. He shouted at me and told me to get back on or he would kill me. I said I would and, as I was about to, I grabbed a heavy, brass candelabrum and smashed it over his bald head with as much strength as I could muster. He collapsed unconscious to the ground. His head was bleeding badly. I thought I'd killed him. I screamed out for help.

'Within a few seconds, I could hear someone trying to open the door. There was a man's voice from outside shouting, "What's going on in there?"

'I shouted back. "Help! I've been raped. Help!"

'I heard a key turn in the lock and a man came in. "What's the matter, love. I'm the churchwarden."

'I said, "This priest raped me. I think I've killed him".

'"Let's hope you have," the churchwarden said. "He's a nasty piece of work, this one. Any excuse and he's trying to stick it in some poor woman."

'Anyway, that's the gist of the story. My father reported the case to the bishop and to the judiciary but they didn't really want to know. The church officials closed ranks and he got away with it. The good thing was that they sent him to a parish in one of the roughest areas of Seville. That just about served him right. If they'd left him in Madrid, my father would have killed him.'

Francisca was sobbing quietly or near to tears the whole of the time she related this awful tale. I just held her hand and kept an arm round her shoulder.

'I feel much better now I have told you this, Juan. But it has made me afraid of men. That is, I was afraid until I met you. But I do not want to rush into a full physical relationship before I get married. I'd like to preserve what little virginity I've got left.'

'As we said, Francisca, we just take things gently and I'm sure everything will be fine,' I said, as reassuringly as I knew how.

We eventually arrived at the river bank. It was the exact spot where Teresa and I had stripped off naked and swam in the river. That seemed like a century ago. This was not the situation, even to suggest anything as adventurous as that. So we sat there hand in hand for half an hour, not really saying much at all. I thought I would tell Francisca about one more thing.

'Francisca, there is something else I think you should know about me. But a bit less shocking, I hope. I have recently been appointed to the post of *familiar* to the Inquisition. My first assignment is on Monday.'

'But, Juan you are not twenty-five yet and still single. You don't qualify!'

'You are right, but they made an exception in my case. I was sworn in on 26 November.'

'This is a great honour for you, Juan. I am delighted for you. Well done. What's your first assignment?'

'I have to go with another *familiar*, Honofre de Espinosa, who has been a friend of mine for many years, to charge a man with the offence of common heresy.'

'What has he done?'

'He is a practising Jew and has translated the works of Moses into Spanish.'

'What do you think about the crime?'

'I am not so sure. On the one hand, there is a crime. He should be a practising convert. He should respect the law of Catholicism. Not pushing another religion. On the other hand, I do wonder what harm he's doing. I shall follow his case, and see what harm he's done. If he's guilty, he'll be executed.'

'But that's the law, Juan, and it has to be obeyed. There is no choice. Are you a believer?'

'It's interesting that you ask that. I attend mass and pray and I am a Catholic. But sometimes I have my doubts. I am not sure about the existence of God. While I am fairly certain that Jesus existed, I am less sure that he was from a virgin birth. Or that he was resurrected from the dead. I just don't see the evidence. And I have a problem with the miracles. But, believe me, Francisca, I will never be a heretic. I just have these doubts that nag at me.'

'I suppose I'm lucky, Juan. I believe strongly in all those things that you doubt. It is a matter of faith. I have the faith not to doubt them. But you shouldn't worry. I am sure I'll love you all the same! Jesus loved the non-believers!'

'Yes, and we want to execute them! The one thing I am sure of, Francisca, is that I won't change the system. I can only go along with it but I'm not totally convinced that the ways of the Inquisition are the right way forward. I'd be surprised if it still exists in, say, a hundred years' time. Not that we will be there to see! What I am really dreading is my first *auto de fe*. That will probably take place next month and, if so, I will have to escort a man to his execution.'

'I don't envy you that, Juan, but I support what you are doing. That man will at least have a decent person escorting him.'

CHAPTER 11

The two sergeants were already waiting at the front door of Honofre's house, as if they were too nervous to knock. One was a stocky, red-faced individual who looked as if he had been drinking half the night. The other was thin, pallid and sober as a cardinal. I wished them good day and knocked on the door.

'Hello, Juan. You are spot on time. Good morning gentlemen. You must be the sergeants. Coming with Señor Hildalgo and me to arrest Señor Andrada.'

'Yes, señor. We are.'

'Let's go.'

We followed the sergeants up the Calle de las Fuentes, through the Plazuela de Santa Catalina to the Calle de los Angeles. There were quite a few people on the streets for that time of the morning and I could hear the mutterings of some: '*Familiars* going to do an arrest', 'Look. *Familiars* and the sergeants. Let's follow them.'

One of the sergeants turned around and took out his baton. 'Just you go away or you'll get a taste of this.' The followers retreated. Even so, when we arrived at Señor Andrada's house, there were still a few curious souls following at a distance and four or five stopped on the far side of the street to watch what was about to happen.

The stocky sergeant resolutely directed Honofre, 'It's your job to knock on the door, mate.' He knocked firmly, three times. Nothing happened. After about a minute, he knocked three times again. A short, plump woman answered the door and stood expressionlessly on the threshold.

'Is this the house of Don Manuel Mergildo de Andrada?' asked Honofre.

'Yes,' said the woman, glimpsing at each of the four of us in turn. 'What do you want?'

'In the name of the Holy Inquisition, we have come to charge Don Manuel Mergildo de Andrada with the offence of common heresy.'

'Señor Manuel, it's the Inquisition.'

A man's voice from inside shouted, 'Get out of the way!'

The woman ran back in the house and a man appeared with a flintlock pistol. Honofre saw the gun and jumped quickly to one side. As he did so, a shot rang out and the stocky sergeant fell to the floor clutching his right knee.

'The bastard's shot me! Get him!' he shouted. With that the door of the house slammed shut.

There was laughter and shouting from the onlookers on the other side of the road. 'Damned hard luck!' 'What a bunch of ninnies.' 'What happened?' 'These idiots tried to arrest someone and he shot one of them. What a joke!' 'I'm a doctor. Let me attend to the man who has been shot,' said another.

The thin, pallid sergeant blew his whistle to summon reinforcements and within seconds about a dozen constables appeared. He explained to them what had happened and a senior looking one knocked on the door, shouting, 'Open up in the name of the law!'

The short, plump woman answered again and all the officers, except the injured one, burst in, leaving the woman pinned against the wall behind the open door. Honofre and I, both shocked rigid by Señor Andrada's surprise use of the pistol, stood silently outside with the sergeant who had been hit in the knee.

'You'll be fine,' said the doctor. 'It could have been much worse. Luckily, the bullet glanced off the kneecap. I'll just tidy you up,' he said, taking some white linen bandages from his medical bag.

After about a quarter of an hour, the officers who had entered the house arrived back in the road outside. The senior-looking one said, 'Well, he's not there now. We've turned the place upside-down. He must have run for it. Out the back of the house.'

'He can't have gone far,' I said, having recovered from the unexpected gunshot. 'Are you going to look for him?'

'We're on our way now, señor. He must be around here somewhere.'

'This is a terrace of houses so he could be in the attic space over another house,' I said.

All attempts to find Señor Andrada failed and, by midmorning, the local search had been abandoned. Honofre asked the officers if they would continue to search for Señor Andrada.

The senior-looking one said, 'Of course, señor. He has committed a serious crime in discharging that firearm at one of my officers. If he wasn't in trouble before, he is now.' He made his anger and frustration clear to both of us.

'I'll report to the Inquisitor's Office that he resisted arrest. Could you please send in your report?' Honofre said to the uninjured sergeant.

'Yes, señor, fine,' he said, in a tone that blamed Honofre for the trouble.

The whole group of constables dispersed and the thin sergeant helped his plump colleague away.

***

That evening, I told Francisca about the events of the morning. She thought the attempted arrest was an incompetent bungle and I agreed.

'I hate to say this, but your friend Honofre could be in trouble for this. As far as I know, the words, "In the name of the Inquisition" should only be addressed directly to the person charged. In this case, he said them to the woman who answered the door. Doing that gave the man chance to arm himself and decide what to do. I hope the Office of Inquisition takes a lenient view.'

'I hadn't thought of that,' I confessed to Francisca.

My relationship with Francisca went from strength to strength and we continued seeing each other regularly. We did many things together. I took her to a performance of the 'Three Greatest Wonders' at the Buen Retiro. I hired a box so that we could see it together and so she would not be herded into the *cazuela*.

Francisca took me to the Shod Carmen soup kitchen. It opened every day at midday and was outside the main door of the convent. A canvas awning protected it from the weather. The women served the soup from large urns which were placed on a heavy, wooden table. I could only admire the way Francisca dealt with her customers, who ranged from vagabonds of all kinds, beggars and street pedlars to low-class prostitutes and the destitute. I choked on the overpowering smell of these poor unfortunates. It was a combination of urine and stale sweat. Several were insane. A bearded man, dressed in tatters, stood nodding his head to and fro muttering something so unintelligible it was as if he had invented his own language. I felt threatened by his loudness and jabbing eyes. A woman shouted and swore at everyone near her but failed to provoke a reaction.

'Stay in the queue,' Francisca would say, as one or two were tempted to jump up the line a few spaces.

'Just one bowl each. You can always go round again. No. I'm sorry. All the bread has gone.'

It made me feel proud to see her putting her stamp on the operation. It was, of course, a job for charity and she was paid nothing for it.

We would often end up at my house after an evening's stroll. Like me, she enjoyed the atmosphere of the street markets and we frequently went to one to buy some items for a meal. I always escorted her back, after she had spent an evening or a weekend afternoon at my house. She said she loved it there because she felt she could relax. I was happy with Francisca's decision not to go the whole way in making love before she got married. She said she found the experience with the priest so traumatic that she wasn't looking forward to it, anyway.

I eventually suggested that she might just want to take gradual approach to the physical side of our relationship, starting with kissing and going on to slightly more intimate contact. I felt that my lessons with Esmeralda Pechada de Burgos could be put to good use in helping Francisca overcome her fears. One night, after we had had dinner, we put some of these ideas into practice. Francisca sat on the sofa in my drawing room and I sat next to her, on her right. We were both shy to begin with and started awkwardly. I brushed my hand on her cheek and wondered at the softness of her skin. She smiled as she touched my lips. I let my fingers drop to her neck where I could feel her quickening pulse. She responded by lightly kissing my lips. I then touched the soft mounds of her breasts which rose and fell with her breathing. Then our lips met again, more firmly and with compulsion. I slid my right hand up on the inside of her right thigh, but on the outside of her dress. I could feel my member arousing itself and suggested she touch it through my breeches.

'Goodness, Juan, is that yours?'

'Yes, señorita, it's all mine. You'll gradually get used to it, I'm sure.'

'Can I see it, Juan?'

'Let's do some showing next time we have dinner here, say, tomorrow!'

Neither of us could wait the passing of the following day. I arrived at her house at about six o'clock. She was ready and, having said our goodbyes to her father, we dashed to my house. I unlocked the door and we went in. She then took off all of her clothes and stood stark naked in the hall.

'Now you do the same, Juan,' she said and I did. 'Let's sit on the sofa,' she said.

We sat and embraced, as we had the night before, and kissed each other on the lips. Each of us wanted urgent contact with the other.

'I want to touch you, Juan. I have been waiting all day for this.'

My manhood was already enlarged and became even more so, as she began to fondle it with her left hand, while I gently stroked her youthful, firm breasts.

'Do you want to touch me further down?' she asked, opening her legs a little.

'I think we should stop there for now and maybe go a little further next time we have dinner,' I said, breathless and still excited.

'I'm not free tomorrow, Juan. I have promised my father that I will accompany him to a dinner of the Land and Property Agents' Guild. Is that all right?'

'Of course, Francisca,' I said. 'Maybe, we can meet the evening after.'

***

The following day, I received a letter from the Office of the Inquisition. My heart leapt in fear as I broke its wax seal. It was about the *auto de fe*. The man that Honofre and I were to accompany to his execution was French. His name was Maurice Mireaux. He was guilty of heresy. I was to report to the gatekeeper at the Carcel de Villa at seven a.m. on 20 February to be allocated my position in the *auto de fe* procession which would leave the prison at seven thirty for the Plaza Mayor where the main ceremony would be held. Those condemned to death would then be escorted to a place outside the Puerta de Foncaral, to the north of Madrid, where the death sentence would be carried out by burning at the stake.

I felt very apprehensive and was wondering again why I had offered my services as a *familiar*. 'Was it a mistake?' I asked myself. All the same, the job had to be done and I should not shirk from doing it. At least I had a week to prepare myself mentally for the task.

I saw Francisca again on the evening of the following day.

'Guess what, Juan? Diego has completely finished my portrait. He wants you to see it. He needs to keep it in his studio for two weeks so that the paint completely dries and so he can make any last minute changes. Then he presents it to the King.'

'I must see it,' I said. 'What do you think of it?'

'It feels strange to look at it. I appear to be a shy, sombre woman which I don't think I am now I have met you. But it is a beautiful work of art. The care he has taken and the detail in it are incredible. I like it and I think you will, too.'

'I loved it before it was finished. I just hope I don't love your portrait more than I love you! I also have some news, Francisca. Not good, I'm afraid. I have to attend the *auto de fe* on 20 February and accompany a man to his death by burning at the stake. I feel terrible about it.'

'Juan, as I said before, at least he will be accompanied by a decent person. Someone has to do it.'

'You are stronger than me, Francisca.'

'It's easy for me to say because I won't be doing what you will be doing. I can come if that will help.'

'You are a courageous woman. Let's think about that idea, first.'

'Do you know anything about the man?'

'His name is Maurice Mireaux and he is French. He has been found guilty of heresy. It seems odd that we are going to execute a Frenchman but that is the outcome of the tribunal which must be obeyed.'

'I have never heard anything like it before, Juan. This is the sort of thing that starts wars. Are you sure he is French?'

'Just a minute. I'll get the letter.'

Moments later I came back with it. 'Yes. It says, "a Frenchman, named Maurice Mireaux".'

'Let's assume the Inquisition know what they are doing.'

'I suppose he could be of French origin but he is probably settled in Spain, and therefore comes under the jurisdiction of our Inquisition.'

Francisca was keen to carry on where we left off on the sofa, two nights before. It was colder than that night and I had made a fire in the hearth. She sat down and held her arms out for me to sit next to her. Hardly a word was exchanged as we touched each other through our clothes and kissed each other eagerly on the lips. Her head moved rapidly to and fro. I felt the energy of her body and pushed mine towards hers.

'Let's take our clothes off,' she said. 'You can undress me and I will undress you.'

It was not long before we were both completely naked except for her hoop-patterned white and purple stockings which came halfway up her thighs and were tied with fine white ribbons.

'You look absolutely gorgeous,' I said. 'I could eat you.'

'Let me play with you again,' she said as she took my manhood in her hand.

'God. It's really stiff tonight. What are we going to do with it?'

'Don't stroke it too much. It might explode!' I said. 'I'd love to kiss you lower down. Is that all right?'

'Do it, Juan. Go there and enjoy it.'

I did as invited and relished the taste and musky aroma of her womanhood. After a few minutes, I stopped, mainly to look at this wonderful piece of nature's engineering.

'Juan, keep going. That is wonderful. Let me take you into my mouth at the same time.'

We slid off the seat and I laid on my back, on the floor in front of the fire. She placed herself, face down, on top of me.

'Let's find something to catch my fluid, Francisca.'

'No, Juan. That is not necessary!'

We took to this form of contact like a starving man takes to freshly picked grapes. Within about ten or fifteen minutes, she let out a piercing yell. 'Juan, Juan I am passing out!' she shouted, as her body straightened up and shuddered.

'Oh, that was fantastic,' she said just about coming back to reality. 'That has never happened to me before.' She took me back into her mouth.

'I'm about to burst, too!' I said, giving her a moment to prepare to take mine. She stroked and helped it. Afterwards, all I could say was, 'Great! That was fabulous.'

She fell off me onto the floor and turned to look me in the eye. 'Things are getting even better between us, Juan. I think you have helped rid me of all my lovemaking inhibitions. I feel ecstatic that you have done that. Meeting you was the best thing I ever did. I love you. There is no doubt in my mind.'

'Let's get dressed, Francisca. There is something I must do,' I said. We put our clothes back on. I felt satisfied, exhausted and warm with my love for her.

'Sit on the sofa, please,' I said. She sat with her hands outstretched, wondering what I was going to do. I got down on bended knee.

'Francisca. I love you. I want to live with you and look after you for the rest of my life. I want to have a family with you. Will you marry me?'

'Yes, Juan, if my father agrees.'

'I have already asked him. And he agreed that I could take your hand in marriage.'

'Then, definitely, I will marry you,' she said with tears rolling down her face.

'I think we both deserve a drink,' I said. 'I'll get some wine and some glasses.'

'Well,' she said. 'Let's drink to our future happiness!'

'I'll drink to that!'

'The next big thing is to plan the wedding. That will be fun,' said Francisca.

'I don't know how we'll fit it in. What with your work at the convent and mine at the palace, but we'll just have to manage.'

'It's easy. We set the date. We choose the church. We chose the venue for the celebration. We decide on the menu. I chose my dress. I embroider a shirt for you. We send out the invitations and we're nearly there! I only wish my mother could be there,' and she started to sob again.

'Oh, poor Francisca. She will be there in spirit, looking down on us and giving us her blessing. Never fear.'

'You are right, Juan. Life has to go on.'

'But you are right about the preparations. They can all be done. The next step is to tell your father that we are now betrothed, and then for me to tell my family.'

We told our respective families, Francisca's father that night. He was thrilled, if not too surprised. He shook my hand so hard I thought my arm would fall off. My poor mother immediately burst into tears and was comforted by father who was delighted and kissed Francisca on both cheeks. Francisco, who was coming up to twenty years old by then, joked that I badly needed someone to look after me.

We started the detailed planning. In the order of Francisca's list, we set a provisional date of Saturday, 21 September 1639. We decided to get married in the San Justo church, just off the Calle de San Miguel and within an easy walk of each of our houses. Within a week of our decision to marry, we had seen the priest and booked the church for a traditional evening service. We reserved the Royal Weights and Measures House, just off the Plaza Mayor, for the wedding party. So we had made a good start.

***

The day I was dreading most was arriving inexorably: the day of the *auto de fe*. Francisca and I walked up to the Platería to see the solemn procession of the Green Cross, which always takes place the night before the *auto*. We stood with an assortment of other citizens who also grimly watched. At the head of the display, a rambling crowd of *familiars* and *notarios* carried lighted candles. None wanted to lead this parade of misery. Some of the older ones were on mules but most walked in a large, disorganised group. One of the younger ones, mounted on a white horse, carried the Standard of the Inquisition, which gleamed in the flickering light. Behind him walked a Dominican prior, carrying the Green Cross itself. The cross bearer's outrageous giggling and laughing at his friars, who all carried torches, unsettled us onlookers. Francisca put her hand to her mouth in shock. 'Look at him, Juan. How can anyone act so badly when doing a job as serious as that?'

'He's a disgrace,' I said. 'A churchman behaving like that. An utter disgrace.'

A senior, grey-faced official of the local judiciary followed, bearing the White Cross of the Inquisition. Then there were the bearers of the crosses of the various religious orders, including that of the parish of San Justo which was the parish where the *auto* was to take place. Although we stayed in the Platería to observe the ceremony and to sample the atmosphere of the impending *auto de fe,* we knew only too well that the White Cross would be carried that night all the way to the Puerta de Foncaral where the executions were to take place the following day. As the bearer of this symbol of death passed us, I looked at Francisca's gloomy face. It seemed that she felt as I did. 'This is a funeral cortège but with no dead body. I didn't expect it to be so dismal,' I said.

'Could they make this a worse experience?' she asked. I simply nodded to agree with her question.

At twenty past six in the morning of the *auto*, Honofre met me for breakfast at my house. Neither of us said much to each other as we ate: Honofre was as apprehensive about being part of this gruesome event as I was. We then went to meet the gatekeeper at the prison. We walked there past San Justo's, where Francisca and I were to be married, and through the Plazuela del Cordon. Church bells rang out from every quarter of the town to announce this, the day of death, as if we didn't know. We could see that the Plazuela de la Villa, on to which the main gate of the prison faced, was crammed with people. There were hundreds there, from bystanders to priests to beggars, hoping to make a *maravedí* or two, to peddlars selling green crosses and cheap rosaries. A few enterprising street traders had erected stands and were selling hot drinks, fruit and buns.

'How do we get through this lot?' Honofre asked.

'I suppose we just work our way to the prison gates.'

We pushed our way through, trying not to be separated. Evidently, many others also had an appointment there.

Eventually, we faced the prison gates which were closed and were patrolled by guards outside. The gatekeeper peered out at us through a metal grid.

'We are *familiars*,' said Honofre. 'Can we come in?'

'What is your function?'

'We accompany a released person, Maurice Mireaux.'

'Just a minute. Yes, here he is,' he said, looking at a list. 'What are your names?'

'I am Honofre de Espinosa and this is Juan Hidalgo.'

'Come in.'

We entered the prison yard only to confront a swirling pool of human misery and chaos. There were men and women sobbing. There were people being sick. Some were tucking into food, handed out by prison guards from a stand, as if it was their last meal, as in some cases it was. Others, both men and women, were relieving themselves, taking advantage of any wall or corner. The stench was enough to make a dead dog heave. I took out my handkerchief to put it to my nose but changed my mind when I saw that others were simply bearing the smell unaided.

We made our way over to where a motley line of the guilty was being assembled, ready for them to join the procession to the Plaza Mayor where the solemn ceremony of the *auto de fe* would take place. The prison guards and Inquisition officials were arguing frantically about where these poor souls should be in the queue. Most of the guilty ones looked thoroughly dejected and a number were already in tears. I felt sorry for them as I cast a glance from one of these poor wretches to another. They wore bright yellow tunics – the *sanbenito* – which bore the cross of Saint Andrew at the front. Many had their prospective punishment indicated by a sign at the rear: flames over a fire for burning at the stake. Some were donning, or were already wearing, long pointed caps – the *coroza* – as a further token of humiliation.

'Which one is Maurice Mireaux?' I asked one of the guards.

'That's me!' shouted a short, cheerful looking, round faced man with his hair tied in a pony tail. 'Are you my *familiars*?'

'Yes. We are,' I said, surprised at the man's smiling and cheerful bearing.

'I'm pleased to meet you, gentleman. I'm not sure where we join this queue but somewhere at the back, I presume. Spaces there are for those to be executed and I am one of five, I think. We'll just have to be patient while they are sorting out the people at the front. Have you come very far to be my *familiars*? It's good to have a couple of strong looking young men for the job.'

This was extraordinary. The tone of his voice and general demeanour indicated to me that he did not to care a bent *maravedi* that within twelve hours he would be nothing more than a pile of smouldering ash and bone.

'No. We both live very near here, four or five hundred *varas*,' I said, still puzzled by his easy-going countenance.

'Have you been *familiars* for very long?'

'No,' I said. 'Only since last November.'

'I've been one for about a year or so longer,' said Honofre.

'We are going to spend the whole of the day together, at least until you escort me to the stake, so we may as well be on first name turns. As you know, my name is Maurice. What are yours?'

'Juan, Juan Hildago. You can call me Juan.'

'Honofre. Honofre de Espinosa.'

A scruffy-looking priest came up to us. His surplice was filthy and he smelt like something vile. He asked to speak to Señor Mireaux. He said if he wanted to confess to his crime he could be strangled before being burned. That way he would avoid the pain of being burned alive. 'Thank you, but no,' said Señor Mireaux. The priest shrugged his shoulders and drifted off to one of the other poor unfortunates. 'Didn't he stink,' said Señor Mireaux, pretending to squeeze the end of his nose. 'What do you gentlemen do for your main occupations?' he asked.

'I am a harpist and composer for the King.'

'I work for a wool merchant.'

A prison guard directed Señor Mireaux to put on his *sanbenito* and his *coroza* and told the three of us to move into our positions in the queue to join the procession. There was a shout from one of the guards, 'Lead off from the front!'

Those at the head of the queue began to move. Eventually, Señor Mireaux and the two of us followed, just ahead of three other released persons and their *familiars*. The other one was in front of us. Two of the others were in tears and screaming to the skies for mercy. The other two looked grey and mournful, evidently accepting their fate.

'You will have to put up with the noise from these other poor souls,' said Señor Mireaux. 'I don't feel bad about any of this. Maybe the reality hasn't hit me yet.' His *coroza* slipped to one side and he lifted his hands to straighten it. 'What a stupid thing to have to wear,' he said.

As we reached the Fuente de San Francisco, a prison guard raised his hand in front of the man in front of us, stopping the five to be released, us *familiars* and the accompanying priests. From another building in the Plazuela, a ghostly addition joined the procession, immediately in front of us. This was the parade of the bones and ashes of those guilty souls who had died before the *auto de fe* and the effigies of those who had escaped or who were too ill to endure their own execution. The tragic and ridiculous picture of the effigies was reinforced by their wearing of the *coroza* and the *sanbenito*, suitably emblazoned with the sign of the relevant misdemeanour. The released and those of us escorting them followed behind this grim adjunct.

'That's a bit rich, isn't it, putting the already dead in front of us?' said a still cheerful Señor Mireaux. The significance of his words struck me like a whip lash. A dryness in my throat prevented me replying.

As we arrived in the Plaza Mayor, we could see a huge theatre had been constructed for this bizarre spectacle. We passed a huge bank of seating to our left as we entered the square. A covered, vacant throne topped this enormous construction. The soldiers of the Zarza, who were leading the parade, divided ranks as they entered the Plaza. They showed the guilty ones to their places on the benches facing the throne. They put Señor Mireaux and his four companions in death on an upper tier, above those who were to be sent to prison or the galleys. Honofre and I sat on his right and left.

'That wasn't much of a walk, was it?' said Señor Mireaux, still in an incredibly nonchalant mood, given that he was within hours of an excruciating death.

'No. The Plaza Mayor is only a stone's throw from the prison,' said Honofre.

'I wonder how long we will be sitting here?' he said.

'We have to hear all the charges and punishments of all the guilty ones before we go anywhere,' I said.

'Well, don't wake me up if I fall asleep,' said Señor Mireaux. 'Only if I start snoring. I don't want to embarrass you two.'

The Standard of the Inquisition followed us, borne on high by the same young *familiar* we had seen the night before. He carried it to its place in front of the throne. The same Dominican friar, more sober than the night before, placed the Green Cross in a stand near the altar. Then, sombre faced inquisitors and tribunal members paraded in and sat in the bank of seats opposite us, along with officials and dignitaries from the courts and the palace. The Count Duke Olivares arrived. Finally, and with due ceremony, the Inquisitor General himself, Antonio de Sotomayor, appeared, the man I had rescued at the boar hunt. He climbed the steps and, with a swirl of his cape, sat on the throne.

Then the ceremony of the *auto de fe* began. The Inquisitor, at the very top of his voice, swore the Oath of Allegiance to the Catholic Faith and to the Holy Office of the Inquisition. A priest then went to the rostrum by the altar and pleaded for the guilty to repent. A bishop gave a sermon. At the end of his tedious, sleep inducing monologue, the *notarios* read the charges and sentences for each of the 300 or so guilty ones, saving the released until last.

'I suppose that's it then,' said Señor Mireaux, as he sat down after his death sentence was pronounced. 'I hope the fire's not too hot.'

I failed to see how this man could cope so well with his inevitable fate. There was nothing that any mortal could do to prevent the implementation of the ineluctable laws of the Inquisition. Or was there?

I felt a rising sense of disgust at my part in this ritual and sorrow for Señor Mireaux as Honofre and I joined the final stage of this macabre exercise: the procession to the *quemadero*, the place of execution. We helped the señor to climb on a mule and tied his hands behind his back and to a small green cross, while he muttered his objections. The parade then left the Plaza. Hundreds of onlookers lined the route. Their jibing and throwing of objects at the condemned was as merciless as it was pointless. I felt frightened and vulnerable as some of the debris they threw landed at my feet, missing me by *pulgadas*.

'These are not nice people, are they?' said Señor Mireaux as we went at a crawl up the Calle de las Fuentes, one of the narrowest roads on the route. 'I wonder how some of us would behave towards them if they were about to die?' I detected a note of quivering uncertainty in his voice, as if even he was beginning to feel the inevitability of his death.

'Hard to say,' said Honofre. 'I guess we'll never know.'

'How often do you play your harp for the King?' asked Señor Mireaux, seeming relaxed again. 'You must be good to play for such an illustrious audience.'

'At least twice a week,' I replied. 'I can play well enough to keep the King entertained.'

'Bravo, Bravo,' said Señor Mireaux but in a quiet, slightly tense voice, once again a little less oblivious to his fate. Then he smiled and easing himself again, asked Honofre about his job with the wool merchant.

Progress was slow. The mules were not as cooperative as horses and the noisy crowds almost completely blocked the roads at some of these narrower stretches. It was beginning to get dark. We continued our chatting with Señor Mireaux and, as we did so, I saw Señor Mireaux glance anxiously to his right, then to his left, almost as if he was looking for somebody in the crowd, maybe someone he knew. Eventually, we reached the crossroads where the Calle de los Convalecientes de San Barnardo meets the Calle de Flor and the Calle de Flor Alta. The road was wide at that point and the number of people in the crowd by the side of the road had decreased. Suddenly, to our left, from the direction of the Calle de Flor, we could hear explosive discharges, like guns being fired, and the sound of horses galloping.

'What's that?' asked Señor Mireaux, smiling mischievously.

'Guns,' said Honofre, looking anxiously across at me. 'Let's try to stay back a little.'

The whole procession stopped in its tracks and some fifty mounted horsemen charged towards us from the Calle de Flor. The lower halves of their faces were covered by black bandanas. We halted in fear and watched. People following the procession ran for cover. The clergy accompanying the condemned scrambled off. The soldiers of the Zarza were taken completely by surprise and could only defend us on foot with their pikestaffs. They were no match for the galloping horsemen and their guns. Our attackers fired into the air and rode into the parade. One of our assailants shot at a Zarza soldier who was about to impale him on a pikestaff. A few of the soldiers were brave enough to stay to try to fight off our attackers. The rest retreated to the sides of the road to stand and gape.

Three horsemen came up to Señor Mireaux. The first jumped off his mount, took a knife from his belt and cut the rope securing Señor Mireaux's hands and the green cross. Meanwhile, the second dismounted and grabbed the reins of the first man's horse. The first man helped Señor Mireaux on to the horse of the third, shouting, 'Put your arms around the rider. We're going now.'

The second remounted and the three horsemen galloped off, with Señor Mireaux as passenger. He shouted, 'Goodbye, goodbye!' as he turned around, laughed and waved to us. I waved a clenched fist at him, albeit a useless gesture.

Other horsemen freed the rest of the condemned. Instead of going back west up the Calle de Flor, they charged east, along the Calle de Flor Alta.

The whole audacious exercise was over in a matter of a few minutes and left everyone, including the bystanders, in stunned silence.

'He knew all along he was going to be rescued,' I said. 'That explains his almost total obliviousness to what was happening, contempt even.'

'Incredible,' said Honofre. 'This has never happened before. Who are these people? Where are they taking the condemned?'

'I think they will somehow remove Señor Mireaux to France. From the crying and wailing we heard from the other four, they had no idea what was going to happen,' I said. I felt aghast and a wave of guilt as if, somehow, I should have prevented his escape.

'I agree,' said Honofre. 'They are probably heading to the Puerta de Santa Barbara and will head north, towards the border with France.'

'What will they do with the other four?' I said.

'We can only guess. I cannot imagine the French authorities will want them. They will probably drop them off on the way, in a town. Or desert them by the roadside to fend for themselves.'

'Can I tell you something, Honofre?' I said.

'What's that?'

'I recognised the voice of the man who got off his horse to untie Señor Mireaux. And I recognised his eyes. It was Pedro Ibáñez who works in the Council of the Indies, at the palace.'

'How do you know that?'

'He has a strange accent as if he's from Viscaya. I could just make him out in the fading light. One of his eyes is brown and the other is blue. I'm sure it's him.'

'Do you know? I thought it was an odd accent,' said Honofre. 'You could be right.'

The soldiers gradually reassembled in a smaller procession. There were still the bones in their boxes and the effigies which had to be burnt at the *quemadero*. The captain of the Zarza troop dismissed the *familiars* attending the escaped condemned. He spent a few minutes briefing a group of armed, mounted constables which then galloped in the direction of the gunmen. The procession then set off again to the Puerta de Foncaral. Honofre and I then rode back to the Plaza Mayor.

'What are you going to do about Pedro Ibáñez?' asked Honofre. 'Shouldn't you have mentioned him to the constables, back at the crossroads?'

'Don't worry. I'll sort that out at the palace, tomorrow.' I didn't want to tell Honofre I was one of the King's special agents. My intention was to report my suspicions about Pedro Ibáñez to the Clerk of the Council for State Security. Honofre had no reason to know. This was to be the first time I would use my position as an agent.

'I still cannot believe what happened back there,' said Honofre. 'The penalty for abducting or rescuing condemned men from a procession to the *quemadero* must be the death sentence.'

'It has to be,' I said.

We arrived back at the Plaza at about eight o'clock and dropped off the mules. I then headed to Francisca's house where she was waiting anxiously to know what had happened.

'Let's go to your house, Juan, and I can cook you a meal.'

Francisca was equally amazed and shocked. 'This must be the first time in the hundred and sixty years of the Inquisition that anything like this has happened. It will be all over the news sheets tomorrow.'

'I'm certain that it was only Señor Mireaux who knew about the plot. Even he was anxious towards the end. The other four were so distraught before being rescued. They could not have known what would happen.'

I told her about my suspicions over Pedro Ibáñez and of my intention to report him to the palace the following day. I explained how guilty I felt at Señor Mireaux's escape.

'Juan, you must not feel like that. There was nothing you could do to stop them. Nothing. Those men were armed. They could have killed you. They will be in real trouble if they are caught. Do you think they will be?' she asked.

'I hope so,' I said. 'There's sure to be a big effort put into catching them. You can be sure that about half of them are still in the town. They won't all have gone as escorts.'

We both enjoyed a meal she cooked for the two of us. We then relaxed on the sofa together for a time.

'Juan, I can't tell you how happy I am.'

'I am totally happy, too, Francisca. How could I be anything else?'

It was about midnight when I walked Francisca home. I was still numbed by what had happened at the *auto de fe* and haunted by a sense of guilt and shame.

CHAPTER 12

The following day, I went straight to the office of the Chief Clerk of the Council for State Security.

'I am Juan Hidalgo. I need to speak urgently to the Chief Clerk,' I said to the Private Secretary in the outer office.

'May I ask what it is about?'

'It is to report an individual for an attempt to undermine state security. If I have identified the individual correctly, he may be at large and the subject of an investigation.'

'Sit down Señor Hidalgo. I will just see if the Chief Clerk is available.'

Moments later, the Private Secretary emerged. 'Yes. He will see you immediately. Follow me.'

The two of us went in. This was a different, somewhat friendlier, Chief Clerk from the one who had sworn me in as a special agent, more than six years before. He stood up from behind his desk and held out his hand. 'Good morning, Señor Hidalgo. I am Alvaro Gutierro de Marchena. I am pleased to meet you. I understand you are one of the King's special agents and you wish to report something to me. I hope you don't mind the presence of my Private Secretary who will take a note.'

'Not at all Señor Gutierro. Likewise, I am pleased to meet you. Yes, I have something important to report to you. Are you aware of the ambush of the procession of the condemned yesterday, which took place on the road to the Puerta de Foncaral?'

'Yes, only too well, Señor Hidalgo. I am writing a report about it, this morning, for presentation to the King at two o'clock this afternoon.'

'Getting straight to my point, Señor Gutierro, I was one of the *familiars* escorting the condemned and I think I recognised one of the assailants.'

'Who was he, do you think?'

'I believe he is Pedro Ibáñez who is a clerk for the Council of the Indies. He works on the far side of the west wing.'

'How do you know it is him?'

'He has a Viscaya accent and has eyes of two different colours, one blue and the other brown.'

'How can you be sure it's him?'

'I can't but I am almost certain.'

'Do you have any other witnesses we could call upon?'

'Yes, Honofre de Espinosa, also a *familiar*. He recognised the Viscaya accent but he had never seen Ibáñez before.'

The Chief Clerk instructed the Private Secretary to go quickly to the Palace Constable's office, which was along the same corridor, and arrange an urgent meeting with him. 'We will stay here until he comes back.'

The Constable was immediately available and the three of us hastily walked to his office. He sat and listened in awe to what I said. He then instructed one of his officers to go urgently to Pedro Ibáñez's office and, if he was there, to arrest him on suspicion and to take him to the judicial office in the Plaza del Palacio for interview. 'We may need you and Honofre de Espinosa as witnesses which, in the first instance, may mean giving statements. We will let you know in due course. Thank you for your help, Señor Hidalgo.'

I dashed to my office, only to be greeted by the Maestro.

'You are late this morning, Juan. Are you all right?' he said, with genuine concern in his voice.

I explained the whole sequence of events to the Maestro, right up to my meeting with the Palace Constable.

'This is almost unbelievable, Juan. I have never heard of anything like it. You did the right thing in going to the Chief Clerk to the Council. I saw this morning in a news sheet that the procession to the *quemadero* had been attacked and the condemned taken away. The main thing is that you are fine. I want to talk to you about something else, Juan, the new songs for His Majesty. We haven't spoken about them for some time, and I wondered how they were going.'

'I have not yet finished them,' I said. 'I am planning on five new songs and have roughed out some ideas. I am finding it very difficult. I don't have a problem with the music. But I am having terrible trouble with the words!'

The Maestro was not impressed. 'I am relying on you, Juan, to write these songs. You must complete them within a week. The King has a right to them. It will look bad for both of us if he has to wait any longer.'

I told him I would, even though I had tried but failed many times to write a passable song. This was the first time in my career that I had been reprimanded for any reason at all and I felt bad about it.

Just about everything seemed an anticlimax after the events of the day before. I settled down at my desk and read through the following week's programme for the King and Queen, which the Maestro had left for me.

Then, after spending the rest of the morning practising, I remembered that Francisca had told me that Diego had completed her portrait. I just had to see it so I went around to Diego's studio.

'Congratulations,' he said. 'So you are now betrothed to my neighbour. You lucky man! I am sure you will be happy for ever!'

'Thank you, Diego. I hope so! I have come to see her completed portrait. Is that possible?'

'Yes. Come over here.'

He removed a dust sheet from a frame set on an easel. 'There it is,' he said, modestly.

I could feel my pulse quicken as I gazed at this absolute masterpiece. In some way, only known to an artist, Diego had produced a softness of edge around her face and neck which made it appear as if she blended with the air, as if her body had taken control of the part of the universe it occupied, as if she had condensed from the firmament. She was the owner of her own destiny, endowed with the presence of a goddess. She was, in this portrait, the human manifestation of a divine power, one that occupied another world.

Everything else in the portrait was subservient to her face and its vaporous perimeter. The incidental was in sharp, composed focus. Her veil and hair was in a mist, as if enveloped by the softness of her face which had a serene and at the same time that apprehensive look. The whiteness in her clothing was clear and emphatic. There were the white gloves, the rosary with a complex bow tied to it, the crucifix which recognised a separate, distinct but earlier divinity and the fan, half in a forbidding shade, which posed its own questions.

'Are you all right?' asked Diego, breaking me out of the reverie of examining this overwhelming accomplishment.

'Honestly, I am fine, Diego. You are a rare craftsman to produce a portrait like this. You have captured Francisca like a lion captures an antelope. You have given her a place in eternity. This work will last for ever.'

'Thank you, Juan. I am pleased that you like it so much. I'm going to ask the King if I can paint your portrait. Time I painted someone from the Royal Chapel. And I'd like that someone to be you.'

'What an honour, Diego,' I said with due humility. But my immediate priority was to complete the five songs that the Maestro wanted.

***

Francisca and I met again that night for dinner and I explained to her my problem over the new songs for the King.

'But you have been so busy, Juan. You've had the failed arrest of Manuel Mergildo de Andrada, the *auto de fe*, the issue over Pedro Ibáñez and you've still been expected to play the harp at the drop of a hat.'

'Yes, but I really must complete the songs. Not only complete them but make a really good job of them.'

'I have an idea,' said Francisca. 'What if I help you? I used to love writing poetry at school. I'm sure I can still write in verse. If you tell me what you want then I could write the words and you could write the music.'

'That is all very well, Francisca, but we would have to acknowledge your contribution and I would feel awkward about having to admit that the songs were not all my own work.'

'Nonsense, Juan. You would know and I would know. But no one else need know. It would be our secret. Let's give it a try and see how the songs turn out!' A little reluctantly, I agreed.

Within a few days, Francisca had written the first two of the songs I needed. They were brilliant, subtle and sensitive and showed a dimension of Francisca that I could never have known without her offering to write for me. She clearly had a special talent for composing verse and showed a background in literature and the classics that I had not appreciated before. The first song she gave me was about the sleeping Cupid who should not be disturbed and the second was about the effect of dawn on the stars and flowers. While I set the words to music she wrote two other songs, one about the Greek goddess, Phyllis, and another about the sweet prison of love. The one I liked best was the last of the five which was a song about our mutual love:

You birds wake up the sun
From his cradle of carnation
Love and know of me
That I love until not to know
That I love well
Him who loves me
Not to let him know
That I love well.
I love well that lad
Whom I permit not
To be of my eyes

When hero of my eyes he is
That I love well
Him who loves me
Not to let him know
That I love well.

I was nearly moved to tears when I read this love poem written by the woman who was clearly overwhelmed by my love for her and her love for me. These simple but poignant verses had a telling effect on me which I hoped I would convey in the music. Francisca and I laboured into the night to write down the five completed songs in the form that the Maestro wanted. I took them into the palace the following morning and, after saying he was delighted with them, he took them to Señor Quevedo, without changing as much as a punctuation mark.

'You have redeemed yourself, Juan. Just in time,' he said. I was not sure what the 'just in time' meant but was not inclined to ask.

Two days later, the Maestro came into my office to say that the King was pleased with the songs and wanted to have them performed, in about a month's time, in front of a small audience of senior palace officials and foreign dignitaries. Quevedo would let us know the chosen date. The King wanted to be present at the final rehearsal.

That evening, Francisca and I had dinner together and she was thrilled at the King's reaction. I told her that I felt immensely proud of her work and that I truly recognised her talent as a songwriter. She was relieved that our combined efforts meant that we had met the deadline set by Maestro Carlos Patiño. Like me, she could not understand what he meant by 'just in time' but we both interpreted it as a mild threat. I'd learnt my lesson. Whenever I had been commissioned to compose, I should seek the early setting of a deadline and make sure I met it with a few days to spare, just in case the Maestro wanted me to make any changes.

'We must celebrate our achievement, Juan,' she said, undoing the buttons on her blouse. 'Let's play on the floor.' We had the most passionate session of love, our naked bodies merging into one but avoiding somehow the final step which we were determined to save until after the wedding.

Within a few further days, the Maestro heard from Private Secretary Quevedo that the song recital was to be on a Friday afternoon in a month's time. The King had said that there should be a rehearsal on the Wednesday before at the venue which would be the palace of the Buen Retiro. This would be the first time that the Royal Chapel musicians had played there so it would be a major event for us. The invitation list was huge with over 400 people to be invited. So much for playing to a select group that the King wanted to impress! Quevedo wanted a programme with a short summary of each of the songs. There would be ten altogether, the five new ones that Francisca had written and the five we had submitted to the King before. There was a huge amount of work to complete before the concert, the urgent job being to give the singers, Vitoria de Cuenca and Alonso Arias de Soria, the texts of the eight songs the King had not heard before so that they could learn them by heart.

Carlos brought together the usual band of players: Juan de Roxas Carrión, Francisco de Guypúzcoa, Simón Donoso, who was still going out with Teresa, and me. Along with our usual daily programme of playing for the King and meeting the insatiable demands of his court, we memorised and practised these ten songs until our hands and brains were numb. Carlos sought nothing but perfection. He admitted that he felt his job was at risk and that he was under the same pressure as the rest of us to do well. The King was a generous and thoroughly reasonable man but this was his court and he had the inalienable right to expect the highest standards in the land from his players.

After two weeks from the setting of the date for the recital, Carlos made us rehearse all the pieces. He made several changes to my scoring. He wanted a slightly bigger orchestra to give the music more body and depth. So he engaged Hernando de Eslava, the cello player, and my friend Luis de As, who still played mainly for the Queen. I felt sceptical about the changes but, the first time I listened to the result of his amendments, I realised that the experienced Maestro was right.

***

Meanwhile, Francisca and I were working our way along the road towards our marriage. Poor Francisca. She shed so many tears over the bitter fact that her mother was not there to help her chose the dress. This is where Diego's wife, Juana, came to our aid. She was a homely, intelligent and entertaining character who managed to find a humorous side to most situations. So Francisca's tears of sadness were often swamped by tears of laughter. Juana took Francisca to a dress shop in the Calle de Pardo. The shop specialised in making dresses for the actresses at the Príncipe, which was close by, and the other theatres, and made wedding dresses only as a sideline. The shop bell made a resounding ping as they both entered this treasure trove of exotic fabrics. There was damask, silk, taffeta, cotton and finely woven wool in a myriad of shades and patterns. The materials were wound on large rolls, lined up like a series of multicoloured waves. A plump lady, wearing a drab blue dress and a white, floppy, cloth hat appeared from the back of the store and gradually made her way toward them, walking with the gait of an overfed alligator.

'Can I 'elp you, señoras?'

'We want to buy a wedding dress,' said Juana.

'Which one of you is it for?' said the plump woman. Not a totally unreasonable question as Juana was still not yet forty.

'Guess,' said Juana.

'Guessing ain't my job,' said the woman, not showing much humour.

'Well, you can only be out by one, whichever one of us you pick,' said Juana.

'Right. You're older so it's not you,' said the woman.

'Dead right,' said Juana. 'It's for my friend Francisca here.'

'Got anything in mind?' asked the woman.

'Yes, a traditional black silk dress,' Francisca said, speaking for the first time.

'I've got a number here that you could try.' The plump woman brought out three different dresses all of about average size and spread them, like huge slumbering bats, on some adjacent fabric rolls. 'Want to try some on?'

'Yes,' said Juana. 'Have you a changing room?'

'Over there,' said the woman, pointing to an area behind a heavy purple curtain suspended from a bent wooden pole.

They went into the changing area and Juana suggested, partly out of devilment, that she, Juana, try on the dresses so as to confuse the plump woman. 'The good thing is that you will be able to see what the dresses look like on me before you choose one. We're more or less the same size.'

'That will be fun,' said Francisca, her eyes alight with naughtiness.

Juana emerged from the changing room, draped in one of the black silk gowns. She looked beautiful. 'What do you think?' she said to Francisca and the plump shop assistant.

'I'm getting confused,' said the woman. 'Which one of you is getting married?'

'Me,' said Francisca.

'Well, why are you trying on the dress?' asked the woman, her hands on her hips, and glaring at Juana.

'I've come here as one of Francisca's pet animals. I'm her clothes horse!'

Francisca laughed and so did Juana. Seeing Juana laughing, Francisca laughed even more and Juana laughed more, too. They both ended up in tears of laughter and, like a couple of little girls, could not stop their giggling.

'Are you two serious about a dress or not?' said the plump woman, angrily.

'Of course we're serious,' said Juana. 'But we can have a laugh, can't we?'

Juana tried on all three dresses and Francisca tried the two she liked best, choosing the one with a neckline similar to the dress in Diego's portrait. 'I've just got to have this one,' she said still wearing it. 'Mamá would have loved this one.' Then the tears of laughter broke again into tears of sadness.

Juana put her arms around Francisca to comfort her and wiped the tears from her cheeks with a white silk handkerchief. 'Don't worry, my love. I understand.' Then, on the verge of tears herself, 'You have a little whimper. It will make you feel better.'

They both composed themselves, dressed back into their own clothes and the woman measured up Francisca for the dress she had chosen. They left a deposit of five *ducats*, agreeing to come back in two weeks for the first fitting.

***

The King wanted a full rehearsal of the recital in the palace of the Buen Retiro. Maestro Carlos was none too happy at having to arrange it but had no choice but to agree. 'If that's what he wants, that's what he gets,' he was resigned to say. We struggled to move everything we wanted to the Buen Retiro but, in going there for the rehearsal, at least we were able to be sure that we had all we would eventually need for the concert. It also became clear that Carlos had to organise the actual event, from getting the programmes printed to providing the interval refreshments and even to instructing the management there on how he wanted the chairs put out for the audience. He displayed stoic calm but muttered a few curses in Quevedo's direction for failing to tell him himself.

The King told us he was overjoyed at what we had achieved in practising the new material. He was visibly delighted by the new songs and said he would introduce the recital in person to his audience. He asked Carlos to draft him a little speech just for that and to include all our names so he could make his speech personal. He wanted the draft at least two days before the recital so he could write it in his own handwriting. 'I don't want them to think you wrote it,' he said jokingly to Carlos. His enthusiastic reception was good for our morale and we all wanted to make the recital a success. Philip IV was, for all his faults, an inspiration and a totally loveable man. He talked to the Maestro for a short time afterwards but was so pleased with what he had listened to that he did not want anything changed. As a result, our confidence was lifted. 'Do it as you did today,' he said, waving a 'thumbs up' as he swept out of the room with his Assistant Private Secretary in tow, like a dog on an invisible lead.

***

Francisca was so pleased with the wedding gown that she and Juana had chosen. She could not wait to describe it to me when we had dinner, the evening after they had been to the dressmakers. 'Juana was so funny,' she said, 'and the little plump lady in the shop was so serious.' We needed to work out the next steps towards the wedding and decided that that would be to settle on the arrangements for the wedding reception which would be held in the evening of the great day. Francisca said she wanted to continue to involve Juana in the wedding plans and I was only too pleased that she had someone experienced to help.

I told Francisca about the rehearsal in front of the King, reiterating that any success we might have would be largely due to her efforts as a songwriter. After our dinner, which she cooked – 'I need to get used to where things are in this house!' – we settled down to a session of kissing and caressing. We both stripped off and played on the floor of the drawing room. It was a hot, oppressive evening so we took turns in flicking water over each other's squirming, naked bodies.

***

The following morning, the Maestro told me to report immediately to the Chief Clerk of the Council for State Security who wanted to see me urgently. I sat and waited nervously in his outer office, looking around at the well-worn furniture, the grey, blotchy ceiling and then out of the window at the bustling market in the courtyard below. After a full five minutes, he called me in and asked me to sit at his desk opposite him.

'I have some news... some news for you, Señor Hidalgo,' he said, hesitating as he spoke. 'I'll get to the point. Early this morning, Pedro Ibáñez committed suicide. He hanged himself in the detention cell.'

I immediately broke down in tears. 'That was my fault. What have I done? If it hadn't been for me, he'd still be alive. I've as good as killed him.'

The Chief Clerk came around the desk to comfort me. 'No. That was not your fault, Señor Hidalgo. You are to be admired for doing your duty to report him. We are confident that he was guilty. Two other people, employed at the palace, named him as a suspect. Señor Ibáñez fell off his horse, not far from where he rescued Maurice Mireaux. A witness removed his bandana and Ibáñez ran off. But both witnesses were able to identify him, quite unambiguously. So don't worry, Señor Hidalgo. Señor Ibáñez knew that the punishment for his offence would be execution. And he took the coward's way out.

'We have also arrested nine other suspects. I felt I had to let you know what happened. I was afraid you might find out by some other means. But that is the whole story, if somewhat summarised. Thank you for all you did.'

'Thank you for informing me,' I said, having more or less regained my composure.

What a shock. I was simply not prepared for that. It was not the only surprise that day. Luis de As came to my office later that morning to tell me that Honofre de Espinosa had been sacked from the Holy Office of the Inquisition. This was because he had knowingly uttered the statement of arrest to the wrong person and therefore had misused the words, 'In the name of the Holy Inquisition.' Honofre was unfortunate but this is just what Francisca had suspected.

Bad things often happen in threes and, while Francisca and I were enjoying dinner at my house that evening, there was a knock on the door. It was my father who looked pale and was shaking. I asked him into the kitchen where we were eating.

'Whatever is the matter, Papá?' I asked, thinking something had happened to mother or Francisco.

'Grandfather Polanco has died. He died three days ago. We've just received a letter from grandmother. She is obviously in a terrible state and I must go to see her.'

'I'm so sorry, Papá. I really am. He was a great fellow. We all loved him.'

'I am going to Pedraza in the morning. I'll hire a horse. It will take a few days to get there but I will be as quick as I can.'

'Is there anything I can do?'

'No, Juan. I want you to stay here. I want you to keep an eye on your mother. She'll be fine, I'm sure, but knowing you're around will comfort her. I could be away for a week or so.'

'Be careful, Papá. You know what to take to protect yourself,' I said, hinting that he should take the flintlock pistol he had used to such brilliant effect when the highwayman was about to rape mother, all those years ago.

'Yes, Juan, I'll take the gun. I must leave you now. I have a lot to do before I go.'

He hugged me and Francisca and left. Francisca expressed soft, well meant condolences. I told her that, although he was my grandfather and that I had a deep respect for him and the way he looked after grandmother, I never really liked him. I told her how I had met Barbola and the squalid place she and her husband existed in on grandfather's farm. I told her how I had remarked about the appalling conditions and about grandfather's defensive, unconvincing justification. She nodded as I spoke but said nothing.

***

The recital of our songs at the Buen Retiro, which was attended by both the King and Queen, was a huge success, thanks, in my view, to the inspiring remarks made by the King at the rehearsal. None of us was sure how much of the King's introductory speech followed the draft by Maestro Carlos, but that was elevating, too. There was, however, an incident at the interval which could have unsettled us but didn't. The Duke of Guadalajara attended with a woman who was not his wife, as did the Count of Montevedra. Both men were in their court finery, sporting swords in scabbards, ornate gold braided jackets, short pantaloons and white stockings. The ladies accompanying them were also dressed for a major royal occasion in extravagant, full length gowns. Carlos had arranged for wine, some local cheeses and cakes and pastries to be available, which was to be served from tables along the back of a side room, adjacent to the main concert hall. At the interval, members of the audience, led by the King and

Queen, made their way to the refreshment area, talking to each other and clearly pleased with what they had heard so far.

This languid tranquillity was shattered by an outburst from the Duke of Guadalajara. 'What the hell do you think you are doing with her?' he shouted to the Count of Montevedra.

'That's none of your business,' retorted the Count. 'And who is that tart at your hand?'

A violent row started and the Duke unsheathed his sword. So did the Count and, within a few seconds, the Duke's right ear was hanging from his face and the Count's left cheek had been pierced by the Duke's sword. Blood splattered the floor. Gentlemen dignitaries grabbed and struggled with each of the combatants and held them back from each other. By then, the King's guards had escorted the King and his entourage to another room, out of the fray. Some of the ladies present helped clean up the two men. The King's surgeon barber bandaged them. It was fortunate that the surgeon was there and the Duke didn't lose his ear. We thought there was something wrong when the King and Queen returned to their seats unescorted with the King anxiously looking over his shoulder, as if he thought he and the Queen could be in danger.

The applause at the end of the recital was overwhelming. There were shouts of 'Bravo!' and 'Encore!' from around the hall. The King and Queen stood as did everyone else in a long, standing ovation. The Maestro, in a typical act of generosity, took each of us to the front of the stage in turn so the audience could applaud us individually. The loudest applause was for Vitoria de Cuenca who had sung the love song written by Francisca, 'You Birds Wake up the Sun' which I had scored for a soprano, a harp and two violins. So, to a delighted audience, we played it again, and again for a third time. The King stood once more and we enjoyed another rapturous burst of applause. The King and Queen came on the stage and shook our hands. He planted an unforgettable kiss, right on Vitoria's lips. The incident between the Duke and Count had been all but forgotten.

We had trouble believing the account that Carlos gave us of the sword fight, when he called us all together the following day, but happen it did. Carlos was the only one of us invited to the interval refreshments so he witnessed the angry dispute. Carlos soon dismissed that unfortunate event and, with tears in his eyes and choking on his words, told us how proud he was of our performance. 'It was perfect, flawless. You were a troupe of angels. You were the musicians of Apollo. Magic. I love you all,' he said. It was the largest audience we had performed to for several years. 'The more there are to play for, the better you perform!'

***

Juana and Francisca departed for the Royal Weights and Measures House to organise the meal for the wedding reception. They were greeted by a hand-wringing assistant who failed to find anything in his records about a booking and soon gave up looking for it.

'Just you get the manager,' said an angry Juana. 'We want someone in authority to speak to.' He quivered off to a back room and a tall, narrow-faced woman appeared, wearing a clean white blouse and a black skirt down to her ankles. She had a look of competence and precision about her. There was a large gold, hoop-shaped earring suspended from each of her earlobes in a vain attempt to make her head look wider.

'The manager's not available. Can I help you?'

She looked through the same records and found our booking straightaway.

'What a relief,' said Juana.

There was to be an outside catering company that would provide the food, drink, glasses, cutlery, tablecloths, napkins and table decorations and the narrow-faced woman had a handwritten catalogue, setting out everything they could deliver. She spread it out over a desk and all three, the woman, Juana and Francisca, leant over the desk to discuss the various items. They said what they needed and selected the food and the wine. They were just settling on the type of wine glasses they would choose when the narrow-faced lady broke wind.

'What was that?' asked Juana, choosing not to ignore it. 'Did you hear anything?'

'Yes,' said Francisca.

'All right then, I farted. I apologise.'

With that all three burst out laughing. Trust Juana to make an amusing incident from a little gust of wind!

***

The wedding arrived with an inevitable certainty.

Francisca's father came around to my house the night before to make sure I did not see Francisca again until we met in the church. He brought a couple of jars of wine and, between us, we drank it all. He took up my suggestion of staying the night.

'I hope you will look after Francisca,' he said, 'especially now her mother has passed away.'

'Don't worry, Señor Abaunza,' I said. 'I love your daughter and I want to look after her for ever.'

We chatted about his business and my work at the palace until the small hours and then went to bed. I woke up with a slight hangover but felt it would go off before the wedding ceremony which was not until the early evening. After a late breakfast, Señor Abaunza escorted me to my parents' house. It was the job of my mother to escort me to the church and she gave us the welcome I expected when we arrived.

'Where have you been, Juan? It's lunchtime and you have only just appeared.'

'Sorry, Mamá, we had some business to transact so are later than we meant to be. I have been kept away from Francisca. So Señor Abaunza has performed his duties well.'

With that, Señor Abaunza left. My grandmother on my father's side then appeared by the door and greeted me with a hug and tears. This was the first time I had seen her for three years and the death of grandfather was still fresh. She looked tired and her skin was more wrinkled and pallid than ever but she had a sparkle about her and was clearly determined to enjoy the wedding.

'I'm sorry, Juan. I was just overcome for a moment. I have been looking forward to your wedding ever since we heard about it. I'm longing to meet the bride.'

'You will love her, Grandmamá. She is a lovely person.'

It was not long before I had washed and shaved and changed into the shirt that, according to tradition, Francisca had to embroider for me to wear on the day. My mother had bought me a new pair of black pantaloons and some new patent leather shoes. Father had hired a sparkling, black coach to take grandmother and my grandparent's on my mother's side to the church. He would go with them and Francisco would walk there with me and mother.

The service in the San Justo church was to take place at seven p.m. It was still light when we all left the house. We planned to be settled in the church before Francisca and her father entered. Mother, Francisco and I left in good time to walk to the church and father left in the carriage, just a little later. Mother looked beautiful in a deep red silk dress, bedecked by swirls of sequins. She wore a similar coloured bonnet, tied under her chin with a black lace ribbon. Her nerves had evaporated and it was a jolly walk to the church. She held my hand all the way. A number of memories of her flashed across my mind: the birth of Francisco when she nearly died; her forgiveness of Francisco and me after our feckless, childhood pranks; the time she was nearly raped on the road to Pedraza; the look of pride on her smiling face when I was offered the job at the palace; her sadness when I left home.

Francisco was his usual joking self. 'It's time he got a wife. He's hopeless at looking after himself. A part-time housekeeper just isn't enough,' he said, making a clear if tangential reference to Barbola's other job with the amazing Esmeralda.

It was obvious from mother's dress, Francisco's well ordered clothes and my outfit, that we were a wedding party and all manner of folk, traders, beggars, even the street prostitutes and parish constables who saw us on the road, applauded and wished us luck.

San Justo was a mass of flowers. Their mingling perfumes filled the air with freshness and a feeling of expectation. As mother and I walked down the aisle, we were greeted again with applause. To my astonishment, my colleagues at the palace had arranged themselves at the side of the church, near the organ, so that they became the orchestra. Mother looked at me knowingly and Antonio seemed aware of this, too. Father and the grandparents were already seated on their pews when we arrived and looked around as we approached. The three of us sat in our designated places on the right of the altar to a rise in the intensity of quiet which was sustained, all but for the usual whispered chatting that happens in churches.

Suddenly, the organ and orchestra burst forth in unison, as Francisca and her father entered. As they came in, a spontaneous wave of applause started at the back of the church and moved to the front as they walked down the aisle and took up their places at the left-hand side of the altar. Francisca looked beautiful in her black silk dress with a black, embroidered lace veil covering her face. The dress so reminded me of the deep umber one she had worn when Diego painted her portrait. A feeling of pride and admiration for this woman, soon to be my wife, poured into me.

Tied to her waistband was a little maroon bag containing the thirteen silver *reales* I had given her as symbol of both my eternal love for her and my vow to support her. With her head held high and carrying a bouquet of orange blossoms, Francisca was a picture of serenity and composure. It was as if our marriage was simply the fulfilment her destiny. Juana, Francisca's

Matron of Honour, held the train of the dress and, helped by her daughter, Francisca de Silva y Velázquez, the only bridesmaid, placed it neatly behind the bride as she stopped in front of the altar. By then, I was standing before the priest who was ready to conduct the ceremony.

Father Pletes somehow knew so much about us. He spoke of Francisca's work for the Convent of the Shod Carmen and her knowledge of the theatre as well as the brilliant education she had received. He mentioned my work as a harpist and composer in the Royal Chapel and my interest in modern Spanish history and current affairs. Most important, though, was his praise for the strength and love of our families, as well as the support we could expect from them in our married lives. Then there were the vows. My mother could stand no more at this point and flooded with tears so father comforted her. I could not help think that this was supposed to be a happy occasion. Then I, too, was almost overcome as Francisca placed a gold ring on the ring finger of my right hand and I placed one on hers. Then the priest blessed us. During his prayer, Francisca and I stood together as Juana and my mother wrapped a rosary around us, a further if temporary symbol of our eternal togetherness. We signed the register and from then on we were married.

We were married! We kissed and made our way down the aisle arm-in-arm and climbed into the coach my father had hired. Grandmother Hidalgo joined us, and all three of us went to the Royal Weights and Measures House to greet our guests, as they arrived from the church for the wedding reception. These are wonderful occasions at which something unexpected usually happens which lingers in the memory long after the event, if not for ever. Francisca had invited a number of her friends, Beatrix de Santander who worked with her at the Shod Carmen soup kitchen, Marina de Riviera and Antonia Rodríguez, her friends from school and Susana Muñoz who was a friend of Francisca at the college she attended in Madrid after she had left school.

Many of Francisca's friends and relatives lived in Durango, Viscaya and they just could not, it seems, justify the arduous journey to attend the wedding. They had all sent their congratulations and best wishes by letter. We had also invited just about all my friends, all of whom lived in Madrid. We invited all my colleagues at the Royal Chapel, all of my school friends and all those I had worked with in Manuel Vallejo's company when we had performed Lope's 'Punishment without Revenge'.

Francisca and I, my mother and father and Francisca's father joyously greeted each of our guests at the imposing front door of the Royal Weights and Measures House. By then, it was dark and the building was lit by enormous candle-laden chandeliers and oil lamps attached to the walls. Francisca gave each of the women a pin with a symbolic, red heart joined to it. She attached the pin upside-down on the dresses of the unmarried women. Eventually, everybody arrived and had a glass of wine or beer to commence the celebrations. The huge dining room, which was usually a public meeting hall, had been arranged with three rows of tables and chairs for the guests and a 'top table' with Francisca and myself at the centre, her father and his lady friend on her side, and my mother and father sitting next to me.

Francisca's father, quite without prompting, and seemingly unprepared, gave a short speech, in which he wished us good fortune in our marriage and thanked me for taking his daughter off his hands. He said he was hoping for grandchildren in the near future. Not to be outdone, my father gave a reply, thanking Francisca's father, who had paid for everything, including the fees at the church, for giving his daughter what promised to be an excellent reception and, similarly, thanking Francisca for marrying me, and giving me a good home. It was all good humoured, well appreciated banter.

A team of waitresses in long cream dresses served the tables. There were five courses, the first, a light fruit cocktail, based mainly on oranges, then a cold soup followed by ham and melon and then the main course which was a classic, Madrid paella. This was served from huge pans, which the waitresses wheeled around the dining hall on little carts. The last course was a small plate of wedding biscuits, flavoured with almonds and spices. Each course was washed down with a liberal serving of wine or beer or both. The dining hall became noisier as we and our guests consumed more and more of the drink. Towards the end of the meal, I presented each of the men with a Cuban cigar.

Francisca and I then cut the magnificent cake and the party really began with the Chapel orchestra becoming a dance band. The atmosphere we created was wonderful with people who had never met before willingly dancing with each other and enjoying themselves. Francisca and I were the first to the floor, quickly followed by Juan de Roxas Carrión and Francisca's friend Beatrix de Santander. They danced in a frenzy, as if they had the energy of a pair of wild horses. Others quickly joined in. My father and mother danced, as did Francisca's father and his lady friend. Then my father danced with my Aunt Catalina who delighted us in showing off her dancing skills as she moved energetically and with abandon around the dance floor. The priest, Christóbal de Agramontes, who had made such a fool of himself at my house warming party, took the hand of Marina de Riviera and spun her round the dance floor with his hands around her waist. Luis de As danced with Angela, one of the Suarez twins, who was Luis's new girlfriend and Balthasar Favales, danced with her sister, Andrea. We loved to see it all.

When Luis and his dance partner passed me on the dance floor, he whispered to me, 'I wonder if Christóbal will cause us any embarrassment this time?' It was, of course, Luis who helped me to deal with him the last time he was misbehaving.

All I could say was, 'We'll see!'

It is interesting how these parties reveal hidden veins of jealousy, especially where, as in this one, the drink flows freely. From happily having a beer and chatting with some friends, Honofre, who was Andrea Suarez's boyfriend, straightened his jacket and with his head held back walked straight across the dance floor to Balthasar Favales and spoke to him sharply.

'Do you mind not dancing with my girlfriend?' He moved as if to take her away from Balthasar.

Balthasar was completely taken by surprise, 'I'm sorry, Honofre, I didn't realise that Andrea was your girlfriend. I thought we were all friends here. By all means we will stop dancing together if that makes you happier.'

I thought Honofre was still feeling bruised after being sacked by the Office of the Inquisition but his behaviour was unnecessarily aggressive. That was all soon forgotten and Balthasar quickly found another willing dance partner: Vitoria de Cuenca.

The Royal Weights and Measures House was a classic style Spanish house with the rooms on the inner side facing a courtyard. Two small tents had been erected in the courtyard, respectively for the relief of the women and the men. During a short interlude in the dancing, I realised that my father was missing from the main dancing area which was also the room used for the wedding meal. I found him in a corner of a corridor in a slightly awkward situation with Aunt Catalina. As soon as I appeared, they hastily separated and Aunt Catalina made off towards the door for the ladies' tent outside.

'Trust me, Juan,' he said, surprised to see me. 'There was nothing in that. Aunt Catalina came up to me and said that we had not had a proper embrace for many years. So that was just one for old time's sake. Nothing more.'

'I'll believe you, Papá, but some wouldn't!' I said, leaving him just a little perplexed and wondering what I was thinking.

I walked further round the corridor and could hear sounds coming from one of the offices. There would be no Weights and Measures staff there then. It was about midnight. The door was partially open so I walked in. It was Christóbal de Agramontes having his way with Marina de Riviera. They were completely oblivious to my presence. Each was exposed from the waist down and she was lying on a desk with him on top, energetically thrusting at her. 'What are you up to now?' I asked, clearly directing my question at Christóbal.

'Nothing serious,' said Christóbal.

'Are you sure Marina wants you to do that?' I asked.

'Totally.'

'Marina can speak for herself. Marina, do you know what is happening to you?'

'Yes, Christóbal, is giving me great pleasure,' she said.

'Do you realise he's a priest?'

'Yes, but I don't see what difference that makes.'

'I hope you don't end up pregnant,' I replied. I could not see the point in further intervention, so I left and returned to the party.

It was still in full swing. The Royal Chapel band was still playing lively music and the dancers revelled in it. I thought Honofre, in his jealous outburst, had far from hindered Balthasar who was having a tremendous time dancing with Vitoria. She could really dance and showed us her daring movements in the *chacona* and the *zarabanda*. Balthasar and Vitoria spent most of the rest of the party in each other's company. What an unlikely combination: a soprano and a sales agent for a building company. They say opposites attract! They attracted each other to the point of being inseparable: from our reception they became a couple. Nor were they the only ones. The tenor Alonso Arias de Soria hitched up with Francisca's friend Antonia Rodríguez, another interesting match. Of the pins, which Francisca had attached upside down to the unmarried women's dresses, Vitoria's fell to the floor first. So Vitoria, according to ancient lore, should be the first of the single women there to be married. Francisca and I were delighted that four of our friends had become two couples at our wedding reception. Goodness knows what their parents would think, especially in those days of pre-arranged marriages.

By three o'clock in the morning, our wedding party was all but over. All of us, except my mother and grandmothers, who had only one celebratory glass of wine, had had enough to drink. Francisca and I bid farewell to our guests, my parents and Antonio and Francisca's father and his lady. We were the last to leave and walked arm-in-arm back to my house. Thanks to Francisca and Juana, everything worked smoothly and well. They had planned the wedding to be as traditional as it could be. Although a day of sustained emotion, it was one of the best in my life. And we were married!

CHAPTER 13

By the year of our wedding, Francisco was nineteen years old and working as a freelance harpist in Madrid or wherever else he could find work. He had followed closely in my footsteps. He had gone to the San Martín Convent School in the Plazuela de las Descalzas Reales and from there to the Imperial School in the Calle de Toledo. There he started to play the harp, desperately wanting to be as good as he imagined I was, and often quoting to me and my parents the encouraging words that Maestro Mateo Romero had said to him when he attended my house warming party. His teacher was the dedicated and talented Señor Vásquez who had taught me. Francisco became a brilliant harpist in his own right. He learnt to play on 'my harp' which I returned to the school before I went to work at the palace. Little did I know that he would be the first to use the instrument, after I had had it serviced and refinished. He even dragged it to and from the school, as I did, and was teased by the same street beggars as he went.

Francisco and I were not only brothers but were always the best of friends. He would often stay the night at my house and we would play duets together. We would discuss the state of Spain and have a drink or two, often staying up until the early hours. He knew of every scrap of gossip in our town: who was having an affair with whom and who were the fathers of the unwanted offspring. He knew about the odd peccadilloes of some of our judges and about the excesses of the dukes and marquises in the town. He was aware of the complicated relationships between the actors and actresses, some of whom had so many lovers that even Francisco lost count of them. I marvelled about how he discovered these little gems of information.

Francisco was a well built young man who had an interesting and rare physical attribute. While it was about the same length as that of most other men, his manhood had an exceptionally large girth, more than twice the normal. The penis of a rampant and ready stallion was certainly no wider. Needless to say, the object in question was inevitably noticed by his school friends but first seriously acknowledged by our Aunt Catalina, who was single and lived with two women friends in a rented house in the Calle de San Eugenio, which is to the far east of the town. Aunt Catalina used to visit us frequently and, when she did so and stayed the night, shared Francisco's bedroom. According to Francisco, Aunt Catalina, who at that time was in her mid-forties, was extremely discreet in dressing and undressing herself in Francisco's room and either did so in Francisco's absence or when she was sure he was asleep. Sometimes, of course, he was just pretending to be asleep and enjoyed casting a squinting eye over her well proportioned nakedness. However, Francisco, although still a virgin, was somewhat less discreet in Aunt Catalina's presence. One morning while she was in bed and talking to him, he stimulated his member to its full size, climbed naked out of bed and continued the conversation, standing facing her.

'My goodness,' she said. 'What an incredible appliance.'

Francisco and Aunt Catalina spent the next twenty minutes or so trying to engage the said appliance with her private opening. They tried every conceivable position. Aunt Catalina lay on the bed with Francisco on top; he lay on the bed with her on top; they tried it lying on the floor; then they tried it sitting on the floor; they tried it standing up against the wall; he tried lifting her and using her weight to impale her on it. Every attempt ended in frustrating failure.

'It's too big,' said Aunt Catalina.

'It is beginning to hurt,' said Francisco.

At that moment our mother appeared at the door. Fortunately, Aunt Catalina had pulled her nightdress back down by then but Francisco was still standing naked by his bed with his member in full readiness.

'Put that thing away,' said mother.

'What thing?' said Francisco. 'Oh that. I hadn't noticed it was like that. Sorry, Aunty.'

Mother retreated and a major embarrassment was avoided. Nonetheless, Aunt Catalina was determined to achieve what she wanted from Francisco and, at breakfast that day, asked him if he would go around to her house after school to help her move a wardrobe. Francisco duly agreed, realising her actual intention, but said that it would have to be after he had completed some homework he knew he would be set that afternoon. He did his homework and arrived at Aunt Catalina's house later than he expected. She said that they needed to move quickly because her two housemates, who were both nurses at the General Hospital, would be arriving home in about an hour. She led him off to her bedroom, carrying a small white jug of clear, greenish yellow fluid. They each took off their clothes and lay on the bed.

'What's that in the jug?' asked Francisco.

'It's olive oil,' said Aunt Catalina. 'I want you to work some into me and put some on your appliance before you put it inside me.'

Francisco lubricated her with the olive oil. He would surely be able to penetrate her now and sure enough he did. It still took quite a push but, as she lay on the bed with him on top, his member went right home. Aunt

Catalina was delighted and wanted Francisco to last as long as he could. Surprisingly, for a virgin fourteen-year-old, he held on well so that by the time he had released his rhythmic gush of fluid, Aunt Catalina was writhing between agony and ecstasy.

'That was majestic, Francisco. You were brilliant. Now you are a man.'

***

So that was Francisco's first sexual encounter but it was far from the last, even while still at school. Some of Francisco's skill and achievements as a harpist were due to the additional lessons he had received from a private tutor. Imperial School introduced a scheme under which pupils who demonstrated exceptional talent in a particular subject could apply for additional scholarships for which the school paid. With my parents' encouragement, Francisco applied successfully for a scholarship in playing the harp. The result was that, twice a week, he had additional lessons and supervised practice at the hands of a recognised and qualified harpist. In Francisco's case, his outside tutor was Señora Floriana Cerrada, the wife of my geography teacher who still taught at Imperial. The lessons were at her house in the Calle del Barrio Nuevo, which was quite close to the school. Francisco said that, from the very first lesson, she wanted to be on first name terms, quite unlike the practice at Imperial, and insisted that he call her 'Flori'.

For the first three or four lessons 'Flori' did nothing but teach. She was an excellent harpist and certainly improved Francisco's technique. She also taught him some useful ways of quickly recognising chords from a written score which he passed on to me. These lessons were usually after school but some took place in the afternoon siesta period. Sometimes, Señor Cerrada was in the house and other times he was not. Francisco detected, even during the earlier lessons, that Flori did not seem to mind exposing quite extensive areas of her flesh, especially while demonstrating some technique by playing the harp herself. He noticed that these exposures of her body occurred mainly while her husband was not in the house. For example, while settling down to play the harp, she would raise her skirt in an exaggerated fashion showing the upper regions of her thighs or while bending over would show an excessive amount of cleavage.

One day, about halfway through his fourth or fifth lesson, which took place in a siesta period, Francisco said he needed to relieve himself so Flori brought him a chamber pot. Francisco took the pot and went to leave the room.

'Don't worry about that,' she said. 'Just do it here.'

Francisco dropped his trousers to the ground, thus showing his almighty manhood. Flori could not contain herself and immediately commented on its size. In a spontaneous onset of passion and anxious to make the most of this opportunity, she asked Francisco if he would like to make love to her, there and then. There was still time before her husband came in from school. He just could not resist and within moments they were both naked and she was fondling him and he was touching her. As with his experience with Aunt Catalina, Francisco could not insert himself into Flori but he knew the solution.

'What can we do, Francisco? It's too wide for me. It won't go in.'

'Get some olive oil, Flori. We'll try that.'

It worked and everything was perfect. Flori was in tears of ecstasy and screamed out at the height of her pleasure. When they finished she kissed him passionately and seemed to want to go on kissing him until she realised she would have to stop before her husband came in. They threw their clothes back on and, continuing the break in the lesson, she told Francisco that she was beginning to loathe her husband who was lazy, selfish and took her for granted. Francisco, attempting to show a degree of loyalty to the hardly competent señor, explained that Señor Cerrada was his geography teacher. The harp lesson finished and Francisco went home, slightly in a daze over what had happened.

They made love during each of the next four lessons, inevitably with the aid of the olive oil. During the fourth, Flori came up with an incredible idea.

'Francisco, I am fed up with my husband and I have decided to leave him. I love you more than I can tell and I want you to come away with me. My mother died three years ago and left me a small fortune, about three thousand *ducats*. My plan is that we elope to Toledo and rent a house there. You can carry on playing the harp and, of course, I will continue to teach you. My money and what you earn from playing will keep us for many years. I will try to do some teaching in Toledo, maybe in a school.'

Francisco was dumbfounded. He thought all she wanted was to be satisfied by his unusual manhood but it seemed there was more to it than that. At first he did not know what to do and asked her for some time to think about this extraordinary proposal. At that time, he was still only fifteen so still had a year or more of attending school. While he had many friends at school, he did not want to tell any of them for fear that they might inform his family. He racked his brain to work out whom he might tell and from whom to seek advice.

Francisco decided to ask Aunt Catalina and went round to see her one evening after school, on the pretext that she had asked him to help her with some indeterminate task. She was not helpful. All she said was that he should follow his feelings and go with Flori – he did not say where – only if he loved her. Poor Francisco didn't know whether he loved her or not. He did not know what love was. He could see several potential problems. He was fifteen and she was about thirty-five. That was a huge age difference. Her husband would kill him if he caught them. Our father would probably kill him, if Señor Cerrada didn't extinguish him first. His school work would suffer, perhaps irretrievably.

So it was obvious what he should do: he would elope to Toledo with Flori. What an adventure! What tremendous fun! So the following day, he went to see Flori to tell her what he had decided. She was totally overcome and burst into tears as he told her. After another love session, aided again by the olive oil, they sat down and calmly worked out their plans to go to Toledo. She would pack her things and arrange for a carriage to take them there the next day. She would buy some food to eat on the way. Most importantly, she would pack her harp and take along some music. Francisco would pack some clothing and a few odds and ends and leave a note for his parents saying he was going away to live with Flori. She would leave a note for Señor Cerrada. They would use different names in Toledo. She would be Señora Floriana Suero de Montoya and he would be her young brother Francisco Suero. They would say, if they had to, that their parents had died of the plague.

The following morning, just before leaving home, supposedly for school, Francisco left the note under the pillow in his room and made his way to Flori's. There was a black, horse-drawn carriage waiting outside, already loaded with several cases of her belongings. A brown, harp-shaped package was secured to a rack on the roof. It was not long before the two of them were in each other's arms, sitting in the back seat of the carriage. They drew the curtains so that they could not be seen and consequently had no idea of the route the carriage took. They stopped at a roadside tavern for the night before continuing the trip to Toledo the following morning, arriving in the middle of the afternoon. They booked into a small inn near the centre of the town close to the cathedral. Within a matter of a few days, they had found a small furnished house on the outskirts of the town which they rented and set up as their home.

Francisco had to admit that he was happy, basking in the constant attention of Flori. She bought him a harp and they spent many hours playing duets together. He could, like father, play the guitar and she bought him a guitar as well. She was an excellent cook and she indulged him with her passion for good quality food. They both loved to read so she bought them books and journals. He liked to do jobs around the house so, with the owner's enthusiastic approval, he started to paint the outside, the walls a blinding white and the windows and doors an incandescent blue. They spent days exploring Toledo.

Most of all they were committed lovers and made love sometimes four or five times a day. They hated the days when they should not do it but even then occasionally succumbed. Her delicate undercarriage gradually accustomed itself to being penetrated by Francisco's stump of flesh so they were gradually able to dispense with the olive oil. They did it joyfully, in every room of the house, out in the yard and, in one dark and daring night, outside in the road against the newly painted wall.

Francisco's departure nearly killed our mother. She discovered his pathetic little note as she was making his bed. She was in tears for days wondering where he had gone with Flori, who was mentioned in the note. Who was 'Flori'? She had raging pangs of guilt wondering what she and father had done to upset him. She did not eat for days and her hands shook constantly with the worry.

Father was furious. 'We've spent all that money on his education. I've spent so much time teaching him the violin and the guitar. Now see how he rewards us.'

Although both Flori and Francisco had mentioned each other in their notes, neither had given a surname of the other. This meant that neither family knew who their loved one's new partner was. Francisco had told us he was having lessons from Señora Cerrada but had not previously mentioned that he called her 'Flori'. We had no idea that they were lovers and Aunt Catalina had kept her word up to then and said nothing, not that she knew anything useful anyway. The first to find any of the facts was Señor Cerrada who worked out that Francisco was one of his wife's scholarship students. He discovered from a list held by the Imperial School administrator that his wife taught only one Francisco: Francisco Hidalgo. Señor Cerrada lost no time in going to our family's house in the Lower San Ginés to speak to my parents about what had happened.

'You've got to be joking,' said my father. 'Do you mean to say Francisco has gone off with a woman old enough to be his mother?'

'I'm afraid so,' said the shy, embarrassed Señor Cerrada. 'What should we do to get them back?'

Having recovered from the initial shock and anger, my parents sat down at the kitchen table with Señor Cerrada to work out what to do. They rapidly concluded that they should do everything to make the lovers return. They had no idea where they might have gone but quickly ruled out the slight chance that they had secreted themselves in Madrid because they were most likely to be seen there. They could therefore be in any town or village outside Madrid. There were endless possibilities: Cuenca, Valladolid, Salamanca, Segovia, Toledo, Guadalajara, Ávila, Aranjuez and even places as far away as Córdoba or Seville. Should they involve the constables of the crown or friends and relatives?

That night they all met up again and included me and Señor Cerrada's brother Pedro in the meeting. It was not long before we had a plan and decided that a two-pronged approach was necessary. First, we would report Floriana and Francisco to the crown constables as missing persons. The evidence would be the notes they had left as well as the fact that they were an unlikely pairing: a woman of about thirty-five and her lover, a schoolboy of fifteen. Second, we would write to all our friends and relatives who lived outside Madrid and tell them that the two had gone missing and ask them to help look for them. Whenever any of us was out of the town, we would do our best to check with people we knew whether they had been seen. We would also keep a look out in Madrid, just in case they were still here. There was nothing else we could think of doing.

The constables alerted their colleagues in neighbouring towns and put Floriana's and Francisco's names on the missing persons list. They asked their colleagues outside Madrid to check the inns in their towns and villages to ask if the unlikely couple had stayed in any of them. They asked us to give detailed descriptions of the two and asked about any distinguishing features. My mother saw no point in mentioning anything Francisco kept in his trousers.

Mother was the one who was most upset by Francisco's departure and transferred the blame from herself and my father to Floriana whom she came to regard as an evil, sex-mad bitch. At one point, mother was all for going to some of these towns and villages to search them herself. Father discouraged her and while still very angry also transferred the blame to Floriana. He had a different approach: his view was that wherever they were, Francisco would soon become bored with the woman and he would then find his way home. The sooner he was bored with her, the better: he did not want Francisco to produce him a grandson, not in these circumstances anyway. I strongly favoured that view and was just as anxious about him.

The days, weeks and months passed by and nothing was heard of the lovers and no one reported seeing them. My father went to the crown constables and asked them what they were doing and what progress they had made. This reawakened their interest and a clever young sergeant then came up with an idea that, in retrospect, we should all have thought of earlier. The constables would check all the carriage and wagon hire companies in Madrid to find out if any of them had taken the unlikely couple out of the town on the day they had disappeared. Wherever they had gone, they surely had to hire a horse-drawn vehicle. They certainly would not have bought one, driven it to wherever they went and sold it when they arrived. Nor would any friend have taken them, without eventually saying; and Floriana had taken so many of her possessions, including her harp, that they could definitely not have waved down a passing vehicle to ask for a lift. A few days after the constables gave light to this idea, a carriage company told the young sergeant that they had taken a couple that matched their descriptions to Toledo on that very day. At last, something to go on.

Within a few more days, the local constabulary had traced an inn near the cathedral in Toledo that the odd couple, assuming it was them, had stayed for about a week, apparently while looking for a house to rent. Fortunately, there was only a relatively small number of property agents in Toledo and the officers soon had the likely address of the house the couple had rented. The game was up. At first they did not want to come back to Madrid but, when the constables threatened to arrest Floriana for abducting a minor, they agreed to return, Floriana to her husband and Francisco to our house in Lower San Ginés.

My parents were so pleased to get Francisco back, they hadn't the heart to reprimand him, at least not too seriously, and they did not ask too many questions about his relationship with Floriana. We were all anxious for a month or so to hear whether Floriana had missed her bleed but heard nothing. However, almost exactly nine months after Francisco returned, Floriana gave birth to a baby daughter. We never did know whether Francisco was the father or whether Floriana and her husband had celebrated her return in reawakened conjugal bliss.

***

Francisco left school at sixteen and soon found work as a freelance harp player. He had kept up his guitar and violin playing and his versatility paid off. The events with 'Flori' were never completely forgotten but they soon found their way into the most dormant parts of our memories. Much to my surprise, my father told Francisco one day, not long after he had started work, that there was a certain aspect of his education that may need attention and that father wanted to introduce him to someone who would give him some information that would be to his advantage. That person was the ageing but still beautiful, Esmeralda Pechada de Burgos. I suppose my father wanted to treat us the same and, for all he knew, Francisco's relationship with 'Flori' had been purely platonic.

From what Francisco told me about his meeting with Esmeralda Pechada, it started along similar lines to my extraordinary meeting with her. Downstairs in her beautiful drawing room, she encouraged him to fondle her substantial, mobile breasts. She then took him to the pink room upstairs and allowed him to take off her blouse and again stimulate her wobbling bosoms. She then invited him to take off his breeches to reveal his manhood. She was staggered by its enormous girth even though it was, by then, only partially ready.

'Goodness gracious, Francisco. I have made love to over forty thousand men and that must be the widest piece of manhood I've ever seen. Have you ever put it inside a woman?'

Francisco told her the story of Flori and their going away together and that they had stayed in a house in Toledo where they made love two or three times or more a day.

'How did you manage to put that inside of your Flori?' she asked.

He explained his attempts at penetrating Aunt Catalina and her suggestion about using the olive oil and of his need to use it on Flori.

'I'm not at all surprised that you needed some form of lubrication to insert that,' she said. 'I'm just dying for you to put it inside me. Before that though, I'll show you around my parts and how to stimulate a woman before making love. You may find that, once you have mastered the techniques I will show you, you may not need olive oil. The woman's body will provide you with all the wetness you will need.'

She then gave him the identical lesson to the one she gave me, six years before, showing him, without a hint of embarrassment or self-consciousness, the complex, fascinating structure between her legs with all its internal ravines, crevasses, folds, unexpected twists and turnings and the specific points of pleasure and the apertures which were part of it. Then, as she had instructed him, he inserted two fingers into her vagina and moved them in and out so as to stimulate it and her clitoris, which for some odd reason, she referred to as her 'gatekeeper', and to bring her to a climax. By then his manhood was as solid as ever it could be and she begged him to insert it into her. She was right. It slid in without the need for any olive oil and, with Francisco's natural ability to control his emissions, he kept it moving inside her for a good fifteen minutes, by which time she had almost lost control of her shuddering body.

'Come! Come!' she screamed at him. 'I can't take any more of this pain. Speed up and come for Christ's sake!' Francisco pumped faster and faster and eventually managed to finish.

'That was excellent,' she said, breathlessly. 'That was just wonderful. One of the best lovemaking experiences I have had in years.' They both got off the bed and dressed and Esmeralda Pechada rang a small bell on the dressing table. A maid then appeared at the door and escorted Francisco to the front door.

'I know you, don't I?' said Francisco.

***

The most extraordinary, if not unbelievable, of Francisco's adventures occurred at the palace. As I said, he was a harpist of amazing talent and became well known in and around Madrid. He played for a number of the well known theatre companies, including that of Manuel Vallejo and Pedro de la Rosa. So he knew many of the actors and actresses that I had met and worked with before I started at the palace. He worked with Maria de Riquelme and Bernarda Ramirez, both of whom I had kept in touch with while at the palace, and Geronima de Valcázar and Maria de Ceballos who also played in Lope's 'Punishment without Revenge'. As well as these very respectable actresses he also came across many of lesser morals who soon found out that he was blessed with an exceptional manhood. I suppose word gets around. Anyway, he was constantly the house guest of many of these ladies whom he pleasured with alacrity. Within a year or two of him starting work, his reputation as a quite remarkable lover spread around Madrid and even found its way back to my family. None of us could see that he had done anything to be ashamed of: he hadn't committed any crime. Indeed, in these troubled and fearsome times, he had given a lot of women more pleasure than they could have expected. He never charged for any of his services as a lover but, naturally, was more than willing to accept a gift, especially in the form of cash.

One cold, dark morning when we were all suffering from one of Madrid's coldest winters, Francisco was summoned by letter to the palace. It was, I think, the year before Francisca and I were married so he would have been about eighteen then. None of us could guess what this was about and Francisco duly arrived at the palace with the letter in the afternoon of the day he received it. Without much ceremony, he was escorted to the Queen's apartments and was met by her Head Lady-in-Waiting. The woman pointed out, rightly, that Francisco would have no idea why he had been summoned. She said that the Queen had heard of his reputation as a lover and wanted to experience his extraordinary manhood herself, in fact that afternoon.

Francisco had little choice but to obey but wanted some matters clarified before confirming his agreement. He knew about the King's reputation as a prolific lover, particularly of actresses, and also knew that many of his conquests had ended up in convents where they would spend the rest of their days in penury. He was not willing, as a result of this single encounter, to be sent to a monastery or worse for the rest of his days. The Head Lady-in-Waiting said that this would not happen. She did, however, say that on no account should he tell a single soul about what was going to happen that afternoon. He would have to swear his agreement to that, on pain of death. Francisco said that that would be difficult because he had told his family and others that he had been summoned to see the Queen.

The Head Lady-in-Waiting said that he would have to tell a 'little white lie' about the events of the day. It was that he had been invited to consider a post as harpist in the Brussels court of the Governor of the Spanish Netherlands, working mostly for the Queen's brother-in-law, Ferdinand, the Cardinal Infante. Of course, there was no such post and after 'consideration' Francisco would reply that he would 'reluctantly decline'. Francisco was happy with the story but also said that he wanted the 'pain of death' clause changed to 'deportation to the Americas' and that his silence would hold only until he was fifty years old or until the Queen had been dead for ten years, whatever occurred first.

'I can't ask Her Majesty to change anything,' she said.

'Well, I'm leaving. Would you mind getting the escort?'

'I'll ask her.'

The Head Lady-in-Waiting changed two copies of the document and initialled the modifications. Francisco signed both documents.

Francisco was then taken to the Queen's bedchamber where he met the Head Lady of the Bedchamber. She was a large, older woman who took him into the anteroom and introduced him to three of her pretty, young assistants, none of whom was much older than Francisco. All three wore masks over their eyes and full, expensive-looking dresses. One had a black mask and the others' masks were red. The Head Lady of the Bedchamber explained that she would leave Francisco in the care of these three masked assistants and said that the lady in the black mask would be in charge. The atmosphere became much lighter when the large, older lady left.

'We are so glad you could help us,' said the lady in the black mask. 'My name is Rosita and this is Mylita and Dimita.' Names of convenience, Francisco presumed.

'The Queen is ready now but there are a number of royal protocols that we need to follow. She will not speak to you or touch you. You may not touch any part of her body with your hands. She may not touch the area between her legs. That is our job. This is what is going to happen. We will take you into the Queen's bedchamber where you will strip off your clothes and sit on the bed. We will follow you and take off all of our clothes. We will play with you on the bed, and you will play with us until you are fully stimulated and prepared to make love to the Queen. We will signal to the Queen that you are ready and we will all get off the bed. She will appear from the other side of the bed wearing a nightgown. We will draw the curtains around the bed so that you cannot see her intimate parts and you will climb onto the bed between the Queen's legs. Mylita and Dimita will make the Queen's body ready to receive you. I will put you inside the Queen. You then start to make love to her for as long as you can maintain yourself.

'Once the Queen has had enough she will say, "Sufficient" and that will give you about two minutes to finish. You anyway withdraw after that time and say, "Thank you, Your Majesty." You then get off the bed on the side you get onto it and the Queen will get off on the opposite side, go out of the curtains and walk out of the room. We will come back in and help you to dress and give you a drink.'

This is exactly what happened with one slight variation. Francisco was still firmly erect when the three assistants came back into the room, chuckling and giggling amongst themselves, still completely naked but for their masks One of those in a red mask pulled back the curtains around the royal bed, so that they could all see what was about to happen.

'We would all like you to make love to us,' said Rosita. 'We've all had the olive oil treatment.' The other two let out a high-pitched laugh. 'We've put some in each other,' said Mylita. 'And we've brought some in,' said Dimita. They had lightly covered themselves in perfume, too, giving off the delicate aroma of distilled rose petals, musk and orange blossom. The smell was intoxicating. Not one to miss such an opportunity, Francisco gratefully accepted this challenge. They all four piled onto the enormous bed and Francisco made love to each of them in turn. The two not making love continued treating each other with the olive oil, before and even after making love. They did this with pleasurable vigour and shrieked and laughed while doing so. He was sure he saw tiny hands disappearing into the inner reaches of their nymph-like youthful bodies. Saving his fluid for Rosita, he enjoyed her with the greatest intensity and afterwards fell off her onto the bed.

Francisco came home astounded. He could not believe what had happened. He had to be the only man in the whole of Spain, other than the King himself, who had made love to the Queen. What an honour and something he would treasure as long as he lived. However, he needed to calm himself so that he could tell the 'little white lie' dreamt up by the Head Lady-in-Waiting. Each of our parents and I agreed that he should not go to the Spanish Netherlands but what a privilege to have been made such an offer. Sadly, the Queen died not many years after on 6 October 1644.

On that same day in 1654, Francisco told me the story of his lovemaking with the Queen. To back up his account he showed me the copy of the note that he and the Head Lady-in-Waiting had signed. He was in a state of great emotion, having had to keep this secret for all but fifteen years. We discussed what we would do with this information and decided that the best course was to preserve the honour of Her Majesty by saying nothing. The story did eventually become public but not because we had made it so. Francisco made an interesting response when asked about the events. He admitted to making love with a lady in the palace but denied that it was the Queen. He said he never saw the woman's face or heard her speak so she could have been any woman there!

CHAPTER 14

Francisca and I soon settled into an idyllic existence in my rented house in the Puerta Cerrada. Fortunately, the house was large enough to accommodate all of Francisca's things without it seeming cluttered. We reorganised the place. The room I called my music room, downstairs, which was designed as a small drawing room, became a study and we used the larger downstairs drawing room as a music room and lounge. This was because Francisca loved to listen to me playing the harp, even if it was repetitive practice, and she could relax and have more space to do so under the new arrangements. We changed the third reception room downstairs to a dining room so that we did not always have to eat in the kitchen.

The largest move by far was to change the bedrooms around. I had been sleeping in a double bed in the bedroom overlooking the street. The windows were low and Francisca thought that she had 'too much on display' while dressing and undressing in that room. We therefore dismantled the bed and rebuilt it in the second bedroom around the back of the house where the windows were higher up from the floor. The room had the additional advantage of not being in the direct view of any other houses.

'We can walk around in here naked if we want to, Juan, and no one will see us, even if we have an oil lamp on.'

Francisca insisted on doing nearly all of the house work herself. 'Do we need to keep Barbola?' she asked, seeming to want to be rid of her.

'I would like to keep her, at least for the time being,' I said. 'After all, you are a busy woman. You work at the Shod Carmen's soup kitchen nearly every day and Barbola keeps the place clean for only three *reales* a week. And cooks the occasional meal.'

'It's difficult to have two women running a house!' she said, half in jest.

'But you are the lady of the house, so you will be able to instruct her. You can correct her if she has not been working to your standard. You can take over from me in being in charge of her.'

'Agreed!' said Francisca. 'We'll see how that goes.'

Francisca made the beds, bought the consumables, did all the washing, did most of the cooking and was still able to spend some time in the back garden growing vegetables. Very reluctantly, she agreed that I could prepare a meal once a week, 'just to keep your hand in, in case I'm ill.' It was just as well that she liked my cooking and enjoyed being waited upon, otherwise I would not have won that concession, either.

My only worry was about the financial side. I know they say that two can live as cheaply as one. That is true, of course, but only if you share meals and drinks and just about everything else between the 'two' that the 'one' would have had on their own. It was a real struggle but we managed to get by, even if we had to forego some of life's little luxuries. However, about six months after our wedding, Maestro Carlos Patiño called me into his office, smiling all over his face.

'Juan, I have some good news for you. Somehow the King has discovered that you are married and he wants to give you a pay rise. According to Quevedo, the King feels bad that you have been composing for him for several years now and for no additional payment. So he wants to increase your salary by 300 *ducats* to 750 *ducats* a year. And increase your expenses to 150 *reales* a year.' You could have knocked me over with a goose feather! That was a fortune. Much more than we needed to live on.

Francisca was delighted at this incredible news. 'We can do anything we want with that sort of money, Juan. That's marvellous. Any ideas?'

'I can't think of anything we need. The house is in good order. We don't need to buy our own house, not yet anyway... I know! What about buying ourselves a horse each? We could take up horse riding!'

'I can't ride a horse, Juan. Can you?'

'Yes, quite well.'

'What a brilliant idea, Juan. Shall we buy one each? We'll have to start saving.'

'Yes, we'll have our own horses. We can do some long distance riding. And that will give us the freedom to go just about anywhere we like. We'll find some stables nearby that will keep them for us.'

One of the great achievements of our relatively short engagement was that we had actually managed not to go the whole way in our lovemaking. We both agreed that this had been an excellent policy. It meant that when we were married there was something wonderful and new we could enjoy with each other that we had not experienced before. So with that restriction lifted, we went the whole way as often as we both wanted. On the days we were not working we would spent whole days totally naked together, kissing and cuddling and doing it. We would get up naked, wash naked, cook naked, eat naked, drink naked, do the chores naked, even sneak out into the garden naked. We were in love and we didn't really care. We did it in every room of the house, on the floor, against the wall, in the garden at night when no one could see us, in the bed, on the bed, sometimes four times a day. We would put the bath in the middle of the kitchen floor and bathe and dry each other, powder each other, perfume each other and then do it. We were always gentle with each other and vigorous only when it suited both of us. We would go to bed exhausted and sometimes sore but it was bliss. Francisca's experience with the priest, who had all but stolen her virginity, found its way into one of those inaccessible vaults of the memory and was never mentioned again.

***

My work at the palace continued, mainly through entertaining the King. Every day that he was there, the 'Royal Chapel band' would play for him and if he was away we would play for his senior officials and their guests. I spent so many hours playing my harps – I had one at home and one at the palace, both of which I had bought myself – that they became shabby and difficult to keep in tune. I went to see Maestro Carlos about this and asked what I could do. I didn't really want the expense of replacing them, despite my increase in salary.

'Write to the King and ask him to pay to replace them,' he instructed. So one night, after Francisca and I had had dinner, we both sat down in the study and composed a letter to the King. It took us fifteen drafts but we ended up with a very simple letter which, if I was His Majesty, I would not be displeased to receive. So I sent it to the King and never had a reply. My ageing, decaying harps were dying and no one wanted to help. This was one of the few times in my career when I was disappointed by His Majesty. So I carried on playing with my decrepit harps, doing my best to repair them and retune them when necessary.

***

We spent the first months of our marriage totally wrapped up in each other, pleasing each other and loving each other. It was wonderful. But, in doing so, we had neglected our friends and family so decided we must come out of this shell and invest more time in others. We invited my parents and Francisca's father and his lady friend around to our house – it was no longer my house – for dinner. This was not only a good opportunity for us to see them all again and, in particular, to show my mother how well Francisca was looking after me, but a useful occasion for my parents to get to know Francisca's father and his lady. They got on famously with each other and by the end of the evening, my father had invited Francisca's father and his lady to attend a concert he and a band of players were putting on at one of the theatres in our town.

We also threw some dinner parties for our friends. It was good to be able to entertain the two couples, Balthasar Favales and Vitoria de Cuenca, and Alonso Arias de Soria and Antonia Rodríguez, especially as they had come together as couples at our wedding reception. We invited them and Luis de As and Angela Suarez. By then Balthasar and Vitoria were engaged. 'I knew! I knew!' said Francisca, 'You were the first of the unmarried women to lose her pin at our wedding. You will be the next one to be married.'

'I'm not so sure,' said Balthasar, teasingly. 'I'm only a poor property merchant and we won't be able to afford a wedding for a long time.'

Balthasar was an interesting character. I had known him from when we were playmates in the area where we lived. His parents had been killed when a carriage they were all travelling in, to see his grandparents in Ávila, veered off the road and crashed down a ravine. Balthasar was rescued and almost died but a surgeon, who was also travelling on that road, saved him by applying a tourniquet to his leg to stop him from bleeding to death. He was brought up by an aunt in Madrid and won his place at Imperial by passing a scholarship reserved for orphans. He was very good at mathematics and languages and became very interested in architecture and old buildings. He went straight from school to a college for building engineers and he qualified with honours. Then he found a job working as a sales agent for a building company.

About a year after he joined, he was sacked from the company for forgetting to lock up an expensive house in the Calle de Santa Cruz after showing a client around. Nothing would have happened except that the house became occupied by a horde of beggars, tramps, vagabonds, thieves and prostitutes who transformed the house from an elegant gentleman's property into a disgusting hell hole. It was a hard winter that year and to heat the property they burnt just about every stick of furniture and piece of carpet in the place. They did not trouble to remove their own body waste from the house so it stank like an open sewer. Eventually, the bailiffs ejected all twenty-three of these misguided souls. It took three months to cleanse the property and to restore it to its former splendour.

His sacking from the building company was a blessing in disguise. He took out a loan from a bank and set up a company, buying, selling and renting domestic property. He had been exceptionally lucky to rent a shop on the Calle Mayor, the day after it had become vacant because the previous tenant was in arrears to the tune of 108 *ducats* with his rent. He engaged two sales agents and a receptionist and decided he could save a whole salary by doing all the surveying himself. He specialised in expensive, luxury properties because he could make much more money by selling one of these houses than five of the cheaper ones. He was shrewd enough to notice that most of the better properties were near the centre of the town so almost all his portfolio of property was within a short walk from his offices. People in Madrid were always moving house and in his first year of business he sold thirty one houses and rented out fifteen more. His profit for that year was more than 2,500 *ducats*, most of which he reinvested in the business.

All eight of us were able to sit at our table in the rearranged dining room. At first, the conversation was slow and each of us seemed to be struggling for something to talk about. We started chatting about the food for the meal. With help from Barbola, Francisca had prepared four courses with a simple fruit cocktail starter followed by chicken soup and a lamb casserole for a main course. Everyone liked Francisca's cooking and even the simple starter prompted favourable comment. The men drank beer to start with and then went on to wine. The women kept to water and fruit juices. Antonia touched on an interesting topic when she spoke about events at our wedding.

'I just couldn't believe the behaviour of that priest fellow with Marina. He was all over her. I know we'd all had a few drinks but you don't expect a priest to behave like that do you?' She paused and then said, with concern in her voice, 'You know that Marina is pregnant do you?'

'I had no idea,' said Francisca, totally taken by surprise. 'When did she find out?'

'She missed her period after the wedding and hasn't done it with anyone else. So she's convinced it's the priest. He denies it. He says he only danced with her and her story about making love to her is a lie. She is distraught. She doesn't know what to do.'

'I know differently,' I said, emphatically. 'I saw him on top of her in one of the rooms off the hallway. When I went out for some fresh air. They had their clothes on but in disarray. So it was obvious what they were doing. When I told her he was a priest, I remember her saying that he was giving her a lot of pleasure and didn't want him to stop.'

'What can we do, Juan? Can we help Marina in any way?'

'Yes, I will have a word with Christóbal. That is the least I can do. I'll repeat to him what I saw. I'll get him to help Marina with the baby.'

'I remember the priest,' said Vitoria. 'I made myself look a fool with him at your house warming party, Juan. Do you remember? I was half drunk and he made a play for me. If you hadn't interfered then, Juan, I think I could have been raped. I hardly knew what I was doing.'

'Yes, I do remember. You could be an independent witness against him, if he still denies penetrating Marina,' I said.

We changed the subject but still stayed in the realm of romance.

'We are so pleased with you two, Alonso and Antonia and you, too, Balthasar and Vitoria. Meeting at our wedding. We must be the original unintended match makers,' said Francisca.

'I'm so pleased,' said Antonia. 'Alonso is my first boyfriend and it is wonderful when he sings to me. I wish I could sing, too, and then we could be a duet.'

'You can sing well,' said Alonso. 'We have discovered that we have so much in common. My father and Antonia's mother and father all came from Seville. This came out when we introduced them to each other. Our fathers vaguely thought they recognised each other and they could name people they both knew in Seville. They lived only a few streets away from each other!'

'It turns out that both our fathers are "men of letters",' said Antonia. 'My father prints news sheets and books and Alonso's father sells books from a shop in the Calle Mayor, opposite San Felipe.'

'I know the shop,' said Balthasar. 'It is only a few doors away from my property agents. I often buy books in there.'

'I think the fact that our parents had so much in common helped our relationship because Antonia's mother had another man lined up to be her betrothed,' said Alonso. 'She seems to have forgotten him now!'

'Do you live at home, Antonia?' asked Luis. 'What do you do with your time?'

'I am very lucky,' said Antonia. 'I live at home and make jewellery in a workshop at the back of the house.'

'Tell us more!' I said.

'Well, I design it and then I make it. It is very intricate work and I love it. It's so satisfying. I make a lot of pieces for the shops in the Platería. They gold plate it for me and sell it. I make bracelets, rings and brooches, sometimes out of gold and usually under commission. But I have a little line in small items which I sell in the Platería and to other jewellers in the town.

'I hope you don't keep the gold at home,' said Balthasar.

'No. I just keep enough for the piece I am working on or maybe just a little more,' said Antonia.

'What is the biggest piece you have made?' asked Luis.

'I recently made an emerald pendant that a lady wanted to match to an emerald ring. The ring had been given to her by a special person to commemorate her name. I had to buy a large emerald and make a complicated gold clasp to retain it. I cannot tell you much about the lady except that she said that she had retired about fifteen years ago. From being a lady of pleasure, would you believe?'

'That was Esmeralda Pechada de Burgos,' I thought but said only, 'How interesting.'

'Could you make me a small pendant?' asked Vitoria. 'I know the King likes me to sing to him in low cut dresses. And a long shaped gold pendant on a gold chain would be ideal. It would show off my cleavage better. The King would love my voice even more then!'

We all burst into laughter.

'Yes, but you'd end up having to sing to him more often!' I said.

'Of course I can,' said Antonia. 'You may like one of several that I've already made.' They arranged to meet to sort out a pendant for Vitoria.

'What about you, Vitoria, where does your family originate from?' asked Angela Suarez.

'Well, my mother was a singer before me. Where do a lot of famous singers come from? Italy. We are originally from Genoa. We left there in '26 when I was ten and moved to Barcelona. Mother was an opera singer but did not like singing in the new Italian style. There are a number of theatres in Barcelona and they thought that she would do better there. Father is a lawyer so felt he could get a job anywhere. So we all moved to Barcelona but hated it there. We were made unwelcome by the Catalans and neither of my parents could find permanent work. Father did some odd bits of work, witnessing wills and oaths, and mother sang in some of the low-class drinking dens. It was horrible. The men were always propositioning her and touching her up. The behaviour in these places was appalling. So we gave up on Barcelona and moved to Madrid. Mother does a little work for the theatre companies now but my father is the main breadwinner. He has his own law practice and is a legislator for the government. He specialises in drafting criminal law.'

'It is interesting that you mention Barcelona. Have you heard the latest news about what is going on there?' I said.

'The Catalan workers are in revolt and there have been a number of deaths,' said Luis, knowingly. 'The whole place is a mess. The Viceroy from Madrid, Santa Coloma, was killed trying to escape by boat. The farm workers are in open revolt and plundering the countryside, setting fire to the houses of the farmers and anyone who has property and money. In the towns judges and noblemen are being openly fought on the streets. There have been many deaths and no one can see an end to the hostilities. There is a civil war going on there. It's anarchy.'

Luis was right. Catalonia had been all but independent of Castile for many years. Under the authority of Philip IV, Count Duke Olivares had tried in vain to compel the Catalans to pay more taxes to support the War in Europe and to provide troops for the Spanish armies. Then, in '39 he hit on what he thought was a brilliant idea. The French had joined the War in 1635, on the advice of Cardinal Richelieu. Olivares decided to fight the French at the Catalan border so as to encourage the Catalans to contribute to the war effort. The campaign degenerated to a catastrophe. There was weakness in leadership, bickering and resentment, not helped by the failure of Castile to pay the newly recruited Catalan troops. The situation was exacerbated by the presence of an army of 9,000 of the King's troops which overwintered near Barcelona. The troops raped, pillaged and generally ran amuck to the extent that the Catalans turned to hating them and the King. Their anger erupted into revolt. The peasants attacked the army, the *tercios*, and by May, with the aid of the *segadores*, the casual labourers, had the whole city of Barcelona at their mercy. Royal judges were humiliated on the streets. It was a rebellion of the 'have nots' against the 'haves' and the former were clearly in the ascendency. It was total anarchy and there was no solution in sight. Olivares had made a huge mistake.

'My uncle is a *tercio* in the King's army in Catalonia,' said Vitoria. 'My mother had a letter from him about two weeks ago. He said the conditions for the troops were abominable. They were begging from the locals for food and some of them were starving. Luckily, my uncle had found a Catalan family which had helped him and some of his friends. They were doing well but were in a minority.'

'At least he is still fine.' I said. 'That must be a great comfort for your family.'

'He is a lovely man,' said Vitoria. 'He wouldn't hurt anyone unless he had to.'

'I don't doubt you, Vitoria,' said Francisca. 'The problem is not the troops on the ground. It is that the government wants to fight on too many fronts at the same time. The fracas in Catalonia has given the Portuguese the chance to revolt. And they are now ready for independence. I'll wager that they will be a separate state before the year is out. And Richelieu will help them. Just wait and see!'

So we were in breach of the first rule of a successful party: never discuss politics or religion. In fact we had had a great party, had got to know each other a lot better and Francisca and I had returned to the company of our friends after quite a few months simply caring for each other. We all parted better friends still and vowed to have another 'political debate' at another party later.

Francisca and I settled into bed at about three a.m. 'That was an amazing story Antonia told about the emerald pendant, Juan. You seemed very intent on listening. Do you think the retired prostitute was the lady who gave you those wonderful lessons in lovemaking?'

'I think so, Francisca. In fact I'm more or less certain. The emerald ring she was wearing was very noticeable, especially as she was wearing nothing else!'

'You will speak to Christóbal Agramontes about Marina, won't you?'

'Of course, but I'll have to find him first.'

***

It wasn't long before I had tracked down the errant priest. He was based at the church in the old monastery of San Geronimo el Real in the Calle del Pardo. I arranged to see him, after work one evening.

'Hello, Juan. To what do I owe you the pleasure?' he said, quite welcomingly.

'I have come to see you to discuss a very sensitive matter, Christóbal.'

'Well, tell me, Juan.'

'It's about a friend of Francisca's and mine called Marina de Riviera.'

'That tart,' said Christóbal, angrily. 'She's accusing me of being the father of her baby.'

'Are you denying it?'

'Of course I am. Wouldn't you?'

'That's not the point, Christóbal. I haven't made love to her so that's a purely hypothetical question.'

'What makes you think I have?'

'I saw you. It was at our wedding reception.'

'I did not make love to her there. Definitely not. We were just fooling about.'

'Christóbal, I saw you. You know I did. I came in while you were doing it. I reminded her that you are a priest. Don't you remember?'

'I don't remember a thing.'

'Christóbal, you have various responsibilities as a priest and as a human being. You made love to Marina and she is now pregnant. What are you going to do about it?

'Nothing. How do I know it is my baby?'

'So you don't deny making love to her, then?'

'All right, I made love to her. It was at your wedding reception. But how does anyone know I am the father?'

'She knows you are the father because she did not make love to any other man before she missed her next period. She hasn't had a period since before seeing you. And is obviously pregnant. The baby is due soon. It is an inescapable fact that you are the father.'

'All right. What has it got to do with you? If you weren't an old friend I'd tell you to clear off and mind your own business.'

'It's like this, Christóbal. Marina's friend Antonia came to our house a few days ago for a dinner party. She told us that Marina was pregnant and that, according to Marina, you denied being the father of her unborn baby. I said that because I was friends with both of you, I would speak to you to try to establish the truth. Now we seem to have established the truth.'

'Well, if that is the truth, what do you expect me to do about it? I have sworn the vows of chastity and confessing to making love to Marina could wreck my career.'

'Let me tell you what I think you should do. You should confess to the bishop. You have led an unblemished career up to now. You will be forgiven. You should apply for a stipend from the church to support Marina and her child. You would have access to the child, if you wanted. You would continue as a priest so your career would not be ruined. The alternative is that the child would be brought up either by Marina on her own, or in a convent orphanage. Marina could be thrown out on the streets by her family. If so, and with no stipend, she would have to beg to support your baby. Presumably you wouldn't want that. Do you want some time to think about it?'

'Yes, I do. I'll let you know what I decide.'

'You've got a week, Christóbal. I'll be back in a week's time.'

Francisca was delighted. First, Christóbal had confessed to making love to Marina at our party. Second, that he was thinking of confessing to the bishop and seeking a stipend to support the child. 'We must tell Marina. She is almost suicidal about the whole situation.'

'Why not tell her tomorrow, Francisca?'

Francisca went to see Marina the following morning and gave her the news. She was delighted and told her mother straight away. Her mother believed her and Marina agreed that nothing would be achieved by seeing Christóbal before I had seen him again.

***

Francisca and I decided, as we had discussed before, to buy a horse each. Before we did anything, I decided to ask Lucia Nelleda, the stable maid at the palace, for advice. I told her that Francisca wanted to learn to ride and Lucia agreed to teach her. She suggested that it would be better to buy our horses from a horse auction rather than from stables. 'The auctions take place every Thursday in the Plaza Mayor. If you wish, I will come with you to help you select the horses. You don't want to buy a couple of worn out nags, fit only for the knacker's yard!'

After I had told Francisca, I went back to Lucia and said we would go ahead. So we bought two horses on the following Thursday. Francisca was in love again. Her horse was a two-year-old chestnut brown mare and mine a grey stallion a year or so older. We called them 'Chestnut' and 'Lope'. Lucia came with us as we walked them to Pedro Nieto's stables in the Calle de las Infantes where we decided to keep them. It was not long before Lucia had taught Francisca to ride. These horses became our freedom. We could ride them anywhere we wanted to go.

***

I went to see Christóbal, as I had promised, but did not tell him that I would bring Vitoria with me. We slipped into the monastery church without being seen and she sat in one of the pews, as if in prayer. Christóbal was alone in his office. 'Juan, I was expecting you. Good to see you.'

'Have you decided what you want to do about Marina and your baby?'

'Yes, Juan. I am going to do nothing. I am not convinced the child is mine. It could be anyone's as far as I know.'

'I want you to see someone who is waiting in the church.' I went to bring in Vitoria.

'Who is she?' asked Christóbal.

'You know full well,' I said.

'Just to remind you, I am the woman you almost raped at the party Juan held to celebrate moving to his new house,' she said, her head bowed, as if still ashamed.

'That was years ago,' said Christóbal.

'Ah. You admit that, too,' I said, moving in quickly.

'I'm not admitting anything,' said Christóbal, squirming and clearly on the defensive. 'Why have you brought her?'

'If you don't agree to going to the bishop to seek support for Marina then we will take the case to the bishop ourselves. And Vitoria will report you for attempted rape. We have other witnesses to the attempt. I won't name them now but we could finish your career for good.'

'So you are blackmailing me are you?'

'No. We are giving you a way out of a problem you created. I feel no loyalty to you, Christóbal. But unless you preserve the honour of Marina in the way we discussed before, you can be certain that that is what we'll do.'

'You can be totally sure of that,' said Vitoria, confidently backing me up.

'You've tricked me, you bastards. I've got no choice. I'll go to the bishop.'

'Well done,' Christóbal,' I said, shaking his hand, despite his insulting outburst. 'That's a deal. We'll tell Marina.'

He looked blank and stunned as we left him. It took him a month and further chiding from me to find the courage to go to the bishop. Marina and her family could bear the only modest dishonour of Marina's baby being fathered by a priest. At least they knew, and Christóbal by then readily acknowledged, who the father was and that was so much better than the baby being born an unequivocal bastard. Marina's monthly stipend of twelve *ducats* also helped. Christóbal's reputation improved considerably when he gave Marina 65 *ducats* from his own money to provide clothes, a cot and anything else for the baby, as well as a few comforts for Marina. Her little daughter was born nine months and two weeks after our wedding and Marina called her Damiana. Quite a number of our friends attended the christening, which was held at Christóbal's church at the monastery of San Geronimo el Real. The bishop gave Christóbal permission to officiate at the service and to christen his baby himself.

***

I was disappointed not to receive a reply to my letter to the King about my battered harps, so a year later I wrote to him again. I did not refer to my earlier missive for fear of causing him any embarrassment and he didn't mention it in his response. Within a matter of a few days, he had approved of my purchase of two new harps and instructed me to ask the harp maker to send the bill to His Majesty's Treasury. Not known for his thrift, it came as a surprise to read that he wanted me to take the old harps back in part payment.

CHAPTER 15

Having decided to allow me to buy some new harps, the King's interest in listening to the instrument was regenerated. He wanted to enjoy the harp at every chance he had, morning, noon and night. After a particularly punishing day, I staggered home feeling completely exhausted, having played solo pieces to the King almost constantly from the moment I arrived at the palace until it was time to leave for home.

'Look at your fingers, Juan,' said Francisca, shocked at what she saw. 'They are bleeding. What have you been doing?'

'Just playing my harp, Francisca. I have been playing it to the King for about ten hours today. He is obsessed with listening to it. He wants me to play to him even when he is working. I'm shattered.'

'You are going to have to do something about your fingers. The way you are going, your tips will lose their feeling and you won't be able to play at all.'

An important development in musical instruments emerged from that short, portentous exchange. I was not an inventor nor an instrument builder, but I thought deeply about how the problem of playing the harp for an excessive period of time could be overcome. Then it dawned on me. I could picture in my mind a new type of instrument which would make life for the harpist so much easier. As I saw it, the instrument would have a main body like a harp but would be played from a keyboard, in the same way that a clavichord was played. I would call the new instrument the 'clavi-harp'.

How could we turn this germinal idea into reality? I could not achieve such a development on my own. The next step was for me to discuss this possible breakthrough with Maestro Carlos. At first, he was doubtful but soon became enthusiastic because he could see other potential advantages than the one of enabling the instrument to be played without hurting the fingers. These were a greater reproducibility and purity of note, more consistent selection of keys and chords, easier tuning and an ability of the instrument to stay tuned for longer.

'How do we take this forward, Juan?' asked Carlos.

'We need to put a proposal to the King. We can explain that it may not take much money to develop the new instrument. And the palace could benefit from future sales. I can see a large market for it, especially from clavichord players who want an instrument to sound like a harp. They would automatically be able to play it. There would be markets in France, Flanders and Italy. There are plenty of instrument makers in and around Madrid and I'm sure we could get someone to build one. If it was for the King, one of them might build it for nothing. If he thought he could sell them somewhere else!'

'Put a case together and we'll put it to the King,' said Carlos, now as enthusiastic and excited as I was. 'The quicker the better. Good ideas have a habit of being stolen and developed by others.' That day, I wrote the paper, accentuating all the expected advantages. I suggested we could develop the first working model for the price of a new clavichord, about 200 *ducats*.

The reply from Private Secretary Quevedo all but killed the whole idea and provoked another row between Quevedo and the Maestro whom Quevedo called to his office to discuss my paper.

'I can't possibly put this ridiculous idea to the King. He wants proper harps, not clever imitations. If it was a good idea the Italians or the French would have invented it, not the Spanish.'

The Maestro decided that rather than to confront Quevedo there and then, he would come back to me first so we could attack him when armed with the best ammunition.

'We can't leave the project dead as a pickled pigeon,' said the Maestro. 'We need a further note to make the case stronger. What about comparing the project with a new *comedia* or a new work of art? We could give the King the credit.'

'Well, I'm not looking for credit,' I said. 'I'll go away and write something down. You can have it in the morning.'

I worked well into the early hours drafting a new note for the King. Francisca came up with some good points: we could probably make the first, test model with an existing clavichord and an old harp. Maybe one of the old ones I had traded in. Also, if the clavi-harp was as flexible an instrument as we were hoping, it might be possible to compose a larger range of music for it than could be played on a conventional harp.

Carlos put the new note to Quevedo that morning. Again he called in Carlos. I went along, too.

'No, I'm not putting this to the King. It's nonsense. An artificial harp. That's all it is. And the King has just paid out for two harps for Hidalgo here. Take the note away,' he said, coolly but forcefully.

'I'm not taking no for an answer, not from you,' said Carlos, matching Quevedo's calmness. 'You are exceeding your authority as His Majesty's Private Secretary. Your job is to put recommendations to His Majesty, not to deal with them yourself. Clever as you think you are, you have no authority to make the decision. I demand that you put the case to the King.'

Quevedo saw red. He shook so much with rage his pince-nez fell off his nose. 'Who do you think you are, talking to me like that? Get out of my office at once, the pair of you!' he shouted aloud.

'I'm going nowhere and neither is Juan. Not until you agree to put our case to the King. I don't care what recommendation you make. You can say the King should tear up our note and eat it for all I care, but you must put it forward,' said the Maestro, staying calm and making an attempt at humour.

With that the King appeared at the inner door to his office.

'What's all the noise out here? Why are you raising your voices?'

Carlos jumped in. 'Your Majesty, Juan Hidalgo and I want to put a written proposition to you but your Private Secretary refuses to put it forward. We are simply trying to persuade him to change his mind.'

'Give it to me, Private Secretary. I'll deal with it.'

Quevedo was completely undermined. We bowed our thanks to the King and left in silence. As soon as we arrived back in the Maestro's office, Carlos exploded in excitement 'We won! We won! We put paid to that pompous prune of a poet!'

'Not so quickly,' I said. 'The King will not humiliate Quevedo by leaving him out of this entirely. He is sure to seek his views. He could still wreck the whole project.'

A few days later we received a note from Quevedo. The King had given his approval. There were some conditions, however, that had Quevedo's imprimatur scrawled all over them. We would have to seek quotations from four different instrument makers. We would have to insist on the use of a used clavichord and a used harp. We would seek to have the new instrument made at no cost to the Treasury, except for the cost of materials and, finally, we could not go ahead to accept a quotation without the King's written approval. We were over the moon. We embraced and sang and danced like a pair of courting cranes.

Carlos decided that we would work together on the project and involve some of the other musicians in the Royal Chapel only when we had something to show them. He did by far the greater part of the work. He wrote out a detailed specification for the new instrument as we saw it. He said in it that the key development would be some mechanism, like a finger, for plucking the strings. It took us months to obtain the necessary four quotations. The main instrument makers in Madrid thought the idea was mad and it took the Maestro at his most persuasive to convince them that this was a worthwhile project. Even then, we could only muster two proposals, both of which were pathetically poor. In total despair and dejection, we met up one morning to work out how we would obtain the other quotations we needed.

'These people are just not interested,' said Carlos. 'They've been put off by the terms of the contract. What about Segovia? There are instrument makers there and I also know of one in Guadalajara.'

'Francisca and I have just bought some horses. I'll go to Segovia to drum up some interest. What do you think, Carlos?'

'You go to Segovia and I'll go to Guadalajara.'

'Done!'

'I'll tell Quevedo what we're doing.'

'Can I take Francisca?'

'Yes, Juan. If she wants to go.'

Francisca had taken really well to horse riding and I knew she would want to come with me to Segovia. We would take the route north out of Madrid, through the Puerta de San Joaquin and take the road to Guadarrama. We would take two days for the journey. We would sleep under the stars for a night or stay in an inn and spend one or two nights in Segovia, depending on the interest we could stimulate for the project. We would set out on a Saturday so that we would be there on the Monday to start trawling around the instrument makers.

We left at daybreak when the streets of Madrid were almost empty. There was the usual smell of the night soil but it was not strong because the air was still cool. There were a few beggars piled among their worldly goods in doorways or walking half awake in the streets and a few heavily loaded wagons lumbering towards the markets.

'This is so good,' said Francisca as we trotted northwards. 'This is going to be an adventure. We spend too much time tucked away in our house in Madrid when there is a world out there beckoning to be explored.'

She was right. For most *madrileños*, life is confined to the tiny world of work for the main breadwinner, inevitably the husband, and his home. Some of the more gregarious types go out almost daily to meet their friends at the nearest tavern. For the women, life is lived almost totally within the confines of the house and daily visits to the markets to buy essential victuals. This routine is relieved by visiting their female friends for snacks and to indulge in local gossip.

We were both hungry and parched so stopped, just after midday, in the village of Galapagar, about six *leguas* from Madrid and about a third of the way to Segovia. There were several roadside inns there and we chose one with a large water trough outside where we could tie up and leave the horses.

'Do you mind me asking where you two are going?' said the buxom landlady who wore a black patch over her left eye.

'We're off to Segovia on business,' I said, still chewing a crust of bread. 'We are hoping to find an instrument maker who will make a new type of instrument for us.'

'That's a coincidence. My brother-in-law is an instrument maker there. His name is Sebastian Alonso González del Águilla. His shop is in the Calle Centro, if you wanted to ask him. He specialises in clavichords but sells guitars, violins, basses and harps but not wind instruments. I must warn you though, he is an eccentric and his shop and workshop are chaotic. But he will do a good job.'

'Thank you,' said Francisca. 'Could you write that down for us please? He could be just the man.'

'You'll have to write it yourself, señora. I wish I could write but I can't.' She handed Francisca a piece of charcoal and a small sheet of paper. 'Make sure you tell him I sent you. He and his wife may be able to put you up for next to nothing, so go to the shop before you try a hotel. If you arrive there tomorrow, go around the back and knock on the door. They are sure to be there or at mass in the cathedral.'

'We'll definitely go there,' I said as we thanked her again and left.

We untied and mounted the horses and decided to have a siesta outside the village so that the horses did not have to be on the road in the hottest part of the day. We tied them up on a grazing area and laid down on a blanket for a snooze in the shade.

'That sounded an interesting idea, going to her brother-in-law, don't you think, Juan?'

'We have to go there,' I said. 'My appetite is whetted now. And he sounds a good possibility. An eccentric might want to try something different!'

We had our rest and set off again. By dusk we decided that we and the horses had had enough of travelling for one day so we found a sheltered area about 100 *varas* away from the road, half a *legua* or so beyond the little town of Guadarrama. We tethered the horses, fed them and gave them some of our water. They were tired and soon settled for the night. We huddled together under our blankets and made love under the stars. We fell asleep exhausted and were wakened by the sun splashing its golden beams in our eyes.

We decided to resume our journey as soon as we were ready and stop for some breakfast later in the morning. We progressed at a trot and, as usual, stopped regularly for rest. The terrain was going to be much more difficult that day because we had to cross the Sierra de Guadarrama. The views from the summit of the pass over the mountains were breathtaking.

We could see Segovia in the far distance and little villages dotted across the plains to the south west of the town.

'It can't be far now!' shouted Francisca impatiently as we had about four *leguas* to go. We soon entered the town and found Sebastian Alonso González's shop. The horses were just about ready to drop. While Francisca tied them up, I went around the back and knocked on the door. A woman answered.

'Is this the house of Sebastian Alonso González?' I asked.

'Yes, señor. He is my husband.'

'We have come on business.'

She welcomed us, almost as if she knew us, and invited us in. By then it was getting dark and we could see, by the light of the candle she was holding and oil lamps on the walls, that the woman was shabbily dressed, as if she could not afford to clothe herself properly. She took us through a large hall and upstairs into a drawing room where there was a short, thin man, sitting in a wooden armchair looking at some papers. He wore a large, dirty apron and a hat with a narrow brim. His face was dirty and his untidy beard contained what looked like wood shavings. As he stood to greet us, he stumbled a little, as if he had a damaged leg.

'Hello. I am Sebastian Alonso González del Águilla, musical instrument maker of Segovia. I am responsible for the upkeep of the organ. The one in the cathedral of Segovia. I make and repair stringed instruments. Right? May I ask why you've come to see me?'

The room was a picture of chaos and degeneration, even in the dim and flickering light of the oil lamps. There were pots, pans, jugs, plates, cups and glasses, completely covering the surface of a large table at the side of the room. There was a pile of hats on the floor: flat hats, round hats, flat sided hats, scull caps, tricorne hats, wide brimmed hats, felt hats, canvas hats and just about every other type of hat. In the poor light, they were all the same dirty grey. A heap of old news sheets reached from the floor to the table top. Dirty, ash-coloured clothing was suspended from strings that stretched from one side of the room to the other. The floor mats were the same grimy grey and badly frayed and threadbare. There were shelves around the walls which bent towards the floor under the strain of the assorted objects they bore. There were dozens of empty wine bottles, decanters, candlesticks, books, bookends, journals, an ornamental tiger, some empty picture frames, an iron, a pot of quill pens, two spare artificial legs and two chamber pots. Most of these objects looked as if they had not been moved or used for decades.

We explained why we were there. We told him about our visit to the roadside inn at Galapagar and about what his sister-in-law had said about his instrument making. We told him, in outline, about the clavi-harp project and the involvement of the King.

'I could be interested in that,' he said, showing vague signs of enthusiasm, 'but it is getting late now. Have you eaten? Would you like to stay the night? We've got lodging rooms downstairs and Marta, my wife, can easily get you something to eat. Right?'

'Let's continue this discussion tomorrow,' I said. 'Can we see the rooms before we decide?' I dreaded to see them. If this shambles of a room was anything of a guide, the guest rooms would be uninhabitable.

'Of course,' said Sebastian Alonso González. 'I'll see you tomorrow morning then, say about ten o'clock?'

We agreed and followed Marta downstairs. She showed us a bedroom on the ground floor. We could just about see, from the light of the candle she was still holding, that the room was a complete contrast to the upstairs drawing room. It was spotless and uncluttered and the sheets and pillows were crisp and clean.

'What do you think?' I asked Francisca.

'It's excellent. I'm tired. I could sleep anywhere, Juan, even on a plank. Yes, let's stay here.'

'I can bring you some food, if you wish. I have some pork chops I can grill on the fire in twenty minutes, and some potato salad.'

'All that sounds good to me,' I said. 'What about you, Francisca?'

'Yes. Me, too. I could do with something to eat.'

'Do you have stables here? We have two horses outside.'

'Yes, señor, around the back of the house. The horses will be comfortable there.'

'How much will this cost us?' I asked.

'The room with breakfast for two is three *reales*, another two *reales* for dinner tonight and seven *maravedís* to stable the horses.'

'That's fine,' I said.

As I took the horses to the stables, Francisca unpacked the saddlebags and Marta sped off to her kitchen. She soon brought us the meal and we enjoyed the succulent pork chops as well as the white wine she had also provided. We were hungrier than we thought.

'What do you think of the instrument maker?' asked Francisca, as we got ready for bed.

'I just don't know. That room upstairs was a shambles. The contrast between that room and this bedroom is staggering. And the woman, Marta. She looks as if she doesn't care a dead frog about her appearance and yet this room is perfect. I just don't know what to make of this place. I couldn't work out why everything up there was grey. Was it dust? Anyway, let's see what happens tomorrow.'

'I think the same, Juan. The good thing is that we can just walk away if we think he won't do a satisfactory job. There are plenty of other instrument makers in Segovia.'

We were up early on that bright, fresh Monday morning, had breakfast and went for a walk around the town before returning to our meeting with the instrument maker. We met him in the upstairs drawing room. Then we could see the dust. Just about everything in the room was covered in a layer of dingy greyness which had been there for tens of years. You could even smell the dust in the air. 'You have an interesting collection of objects in here,' I said.

'Yes,' said Sebastian Alonso González. 'I have a particular belief. It's similar to that of the ancient Egyptians. They believed in immortality, that death was a brief and temporary interruption to immortal life. Right? I believe that when I go to mass I am paying homage to the gods. They will ensure my immortality. When I die I will be mummified and my soul will return to occupy my body. I will be buried with all the worldly things I will need in eternity. That's why they are here.'

In the daylight, it became clear that there were many more objects that he was going to take with him to eternity than we could see the night before. There must have been fifty pairs of shoes piled on the floor. There were dozens of walking sticks, about twenty parasols, fifty or so empty picture frames, all standing against the wall. Everything was covered in acrid dust. As if he could sense that we did not enjoy being in this dirt-enveloped sarcophagus, he invited us to go back downstairs to the shop and the workshop.

'Surely, your beliefs are heretic. They are not consistent with the teachings of the Holy Catholic Church,' said Francisca.

'I am a Roman Catholic,' said Sebastian Alonso González. 'How I interpret the teachings of the church is up to me. Right? I don't proselytise what I believe, so these matters are for me and me alone,' he said, trying to conceal his anger.

We followed him. He limped slightly as he went down the stairs and walked through the hall towards the shop. It was long and narrow and packed with musical objects. There were violins, cellos, violas, guitars, a mandolin, clavichords, a harp and all sorts of accessories: cases for the instruments, music stands, batons, bows of various sizes, musical scores on shelves, tallow for the bows, strings for the instruments and seats for musicians to sit on and play. Juan de Roxas Carrión and Luis de As would love to see this Aladdin's cave of music. I could see them picking up a violin each and feeling it, then taking a bow and playing a tune on it, maybe as a duet. I sat down on one of the seats and played the harp. It was in perfect tune and had the most beautiful tone, which was as satisfying as any harp I had played.

'Did you make all these yourself?' asked Francisca.

'No,' said Sebastian Alonso González. 'I made both clavichords, all of the violins, except one, and the harp. All the other instruments were made abroad. Some were made in Italy and the others in Flanders.'

'Why do you have that one in a glass case?' I asked, pointing to the most elegant violin I had ever seen.

'That one is made by Nocoló Amati, one of the most famous of the school of Italian violin makers. It was made by Amati himself and is signed by him. It is not a piece started by one of his students that he just finished off. It is probably the most beautiful violin outside of Italy. I bought it from the master himself. If you want to buy it you will need to pay me 2000 *ducats*. Right?'

'You can forget that,' I said. 'That's more than I earn in a year!'

I picked up one of the other violins in the shop. It was a work of art, a masterpiece, which could also have been made by an Italian master. The polished wood shone like crystal. There was not the slightest gap in any of the joins and the veneer had been laid with the precision of a Swiss watchmaker.

'This is magnificent, señor. I take it that this is one you made yourself. How long does it take you to make an instrument like this?'

'I make them four at a time. Right? And it takes me six weeks to make all four.'

'That seems fairly quick to me.'

'It is. I work fast and sometimes around the clock. As long as I keep going, and have food and drink, I can work three days with no sleep. Then I sleep all day and a night to catch up. I can start the timetable again if I want to. Straightaway, right?'

Between us, Francisca and I described the clavi-harp project in greater detail. We told him that the King had asked for the first one to be made of a used clavichord and a used harp. We explained the need for a mechanism to pluck the strings, in the same way that a human finger does. We also related the terms of the project, in particular that the King would only pay for the cost of materials.

'I don't work like that, Señor Hidalgo. No, I wouldn't be interested in those terms at all.'

Francisca looked frustratedly at me. I immediately thought we had all but finished our discussions with the instrument maker.

'No, I would never work with a used harp or a used clavichord. The problem is, señor, I guarantee my instruments for five years. I could not offer a guarantee if I used second-hand instruments to make the thing. Sorry.'

'I suppose that's the end of it, then,' I said, dejectedly. 'Thank you for your time and for showing us your instruments.'

'Oh no, señor, not at all. I have a much better proposition. I want to do this work for you and the King. Right? And I want to do a first-class job. So what I'll do is to quote you for it, as if I'm using old instruments but I'll use new ones instead. That way the King will get a guaranteed instrument. Right?'

Suddenly, our disappointment was transformed into elation. We had found someone keen to make the clavi-harp. He really wanted to do the job, unlike the instrument makers in Madrid. I explained the various formalities and that he would have to send a complete, fully priced quotation, setting out timescales and the date the instrument would be delivered to the palace. I also said that we would have at least three other quotations and that he may, therefore, not get the job.

'I'll get the job, señor,' he said, laughing. 'No one else will be stupid enough to do it under the terms I will offer. Right?'

He said he would rather that we wait and take the quotation back with us to Madrid. He said it would be ready in the morning, if he could quote against our written specification so I gave him a copy.

'Can I ask you a personal question?' I asked, handing him the document.

'Yes, Señor Hidalgo, but I cannot assure you of a full and frank reply.'

'I want to ask you about your right leg. Is it artificial?'

'Yes. I had it amputated when I was a child. It became infected and it was a simple choice for my parents: amputation or death. My parents decided on the former and they got me drunk on Spanish brandy before the surgeon barber carried out the operation.'

'Who made your leg?'

'I made it myself. It has a knee joint and an ankle joint and the toes move. The joint movements are controlled by springs and wooden stops. The toes work the same way. You will have noticed that I limp slightly but not much. And I don't yet need a walking stick.'

'Thank you for explaining that. Well, señor, my wife and I have other business to transact in Segovia so we'll bid you farewell for now and see you tomorrow morning. Thank you for everything,' I said.

'It was a pleasure, Señor Hidalgo, and to meet you, señora. You may want to reserve your room for another night, before you go. Have a word with Marta.'

We arranged to extend our stay and for the horses to be stabled for the rest of our time there. We left the house discussing our visit to the instrument maker.

'Why did you ask Sebastian Alonso González about his wooden leg?' asked Francisca. 'I am puzzled.'

'Ah,' I said. 'I asked him because we need a mechanism to pluck the strings, in the way that natural fingers do. As he said, in making the artificial leg, he made some artificial toes so he has made something similar to fingers.'

'That's interesting. I hadn't thought of that, Juan. What do you think about finding some other instrument makers?'

We agreed to find just one more who would produce a quotation. It was all a little half-hearted, especially as we thought that, unless something went badly wrong, Sebastian Alonso González del Águilla would be awarded the contract. We found a musical instrument maker close to the cathedral and soon persuaded him to produce a quotation for the work. We left him a copy of our specification and he assured us that he would reply by letter within a few days. In the evening, after spending the rest of the day exploring the town, we returned to the house to stay another night. Sebastian Alonso González presented his quotation to us earlier than expected, just before we went to bed. He was smiling and seemed happy with what he had written. We were happy, too.

We set out for Madrid just on sunrise so we could get as far as we could before the heat became intolerable. We were keen to arrive back as soon as we could so that we could relate our tale to the Maestro.

***

'It seems that you have found a willing collaborator. What an incredible man. I don't think we should say much to the King about his religious beliefs: he may be arrested by the Inquisition,' joked the Maestro. 'But you are right. He is the best proposition so far. I'm just concerned about the filthy conditions he lives in. All that choking dust and chaos. On the other hand, it seems that his shop and the rooms in the inn were an example of order and cleanliness.

'My visit to Guadalajara was a disaster. I set out on the Sunday, aiming to be there by lunchtime on the Monday. As I approached Alcalá de Henares, which is about halfway, my horse kicked a stone in the road and lost a shoe. Eventually, I found a blacksmith who was prepared to help me on a Sunday. By the time he had the horse ready, it was dark so I found an inn and stayed the night in Alcalá. I overslept and didn't start out again until eleven o'clock on the Monday morning.

'I set out from the inn and turned into a main road. I was immediately confronted by a student mob. There must have been 500 of them, chanting, shouting and waving banners about. As I stopped to work out what I should do, the horse reared up in fright, threw me off and bolted. I landed awkwardly and was unable to chase after it. After about an hour of wandering around looking for the animal, I saw a constable holding it by the reins. I managed to convince him that it was mine but it had injured itself and could not be ridden. The constable directed me to a farrier and, while he treated my horse, I found two musical instrument makers in Alcalá. The first I visited showed no interest in our project but the second said he would prepare a proposal for us and send it by post.

'I thanked him and returned to the farrier who, in the meantime, had massaged the horse's injured leg. He told me that it was then able to walk and perhaps trot short distances. He advised me not to ride it for more than a quarter of an hour at a time so I paid him and started the journey back to Madrid. I hardly rode the horse at all, so walked nearly all the way back. My feet are still sore and blistered! I never made it to Guadalajara but we may get a proposal from an instrument maker in Alcalá de Henares.'

'I'm sorry it all went so badly wrong,' I said. 'You were just unlucky. At least you are all right – apart from painful feet – and you have the promise of a proposal.'

'I was fed up and frustrated, Juan, but I can laugh about it now. I far prefer your story!'

By the end of the statutory four weeks, which we were obliged to give our prospective collaborators, we had received four firm replies, just sufficient to satisfy the King – or rather Quevedo. Much to the delight of the Maestro, we received one from his man in Alcalá de Henares. We did not, however, receive one from the second instrument maker, which Francisca and I had visited in Segovia. We examined the proposals carefully. The one from Alcalá was good and came second in order of merit but it was the one by Sebastian Alonso González that was the clear and outright winner. According to what the King had instructed earlier, I wrote a submission to enable him to decide for himself who should be granted this less than lucrative contract. The Maestro produced a covering note and we sent our case to the King, as usual, via Private Secretary Quevedo.

Quevedo's reaction was predictable: he did not agree with our recommendation. This provoked another angry disagreement with the

Maestro. This time, however, the Maestro forestalled Quevedo. At a meeting Quevedo chaired, the Maestro explained calmly and with utter politeness that Quevedo was welcomed to invite the King to select our second best prescription for the work. However, if the product of the contract did not meet the King's expectations, Quevedo would have to take full responsibility for his error. With that Quevedo relented and agreed to do as we had advised.

Within two weeks, the contract for the manufacture of the world's first clavi-harp was placed with Sebastian Alonso González. He had asked for six months to make the instrument. That included two months to develop the mechanism for plucking the strings. With the encouragement of the Maestro, I spent some time during the period of the contract learning to play the clavichord. I had played a keyboard instrument before but had never developed my proficiency to a professional level of playing. I was determined to master the instrument. I even had lessons from Martín Cabezas, a virtuoso player and brilliant teacher. I even convinced the Maestro that he should pay for me to hire a clavichord and have it installed in the music room of our house in the Puerta Cerrada. I played it to Francisca virtually every night. I came to love the instrument and eventually satisfied myself that I could play it well enough to be able to play the clavi-harp for the King.

During that time, the whole of Madrid was devastated to learn of the death of the King's brother, Cardinal Infante Ferdinand, the brilliant military strategist and Governor of the Spanish Netherlands. I say the whole of Madrid, but the Cardinal Infante had his enemies, not least the Count Duke Olivares and others in the Count Duke's circle. There was even a rumour that one of the Count Duke's stooges had been sent to Brussels to poison him. The truth is that he became exhausted in battle and died of a stomach ulcer. The great sadness was that he was only thirty-two years old. Many of us thought that his loss was a bitter blow to Spain and that, without him, the Spanish Empire in Europe was even more vulnerable to a successful attack by its enemies, notably the French. Our poor King was overcome by grief. Diego told me that he could not control his weeping and for weeks on end he was hardly seen outside the Royal Apartments.

It was regrettable that the Cardinal Infante died under a cloud that was not of his own making. While the victor at Nördlingen, in later battles he had lost several key towns to the French, including the spectacularly beautiful Arras. This was due mainly to the lack of supplies for his troops. Worst still, he was unable to recapture Breda which the Dutch had regained in '37. This alone branded him a failure in the eyes of many in the government of Spain. The disposal of his body was a matter of shame. He was buried with minimal ceremony in Brussels. Two years later, and to realise his last wishes, his body was taken to Madrid and reinterred in El Escorial, the Royal Palace to the northwest of Madrid, which is the final resting place of many of the Spanish monarchy.

CHAPTER 16

Early one Wednesday morning, not long after we had heard the shocking news about the Cardinal Infante's death, there was a loud persistent knocking on our front door. I opened it to see a tearful Francisco in a state of shock and distress. 'Juan, our father has died.' I was stunned. It was unreal. It could not be true. He was so young.

'No. When? How?'

'He collapsed less than an hour ago, while having his breakfast. Mother had been talking to him and went out to use the chamber pot. While she was there she heard a noise from the kitchen. She went back in to see him lying lifeless on the floor. She screamed for me. She cradled him as I got the doctor and a constable. The doctor pronounced him dead and has issued the death certificate. The constable agrees that the death is by natural causes and has gone. The doctor is at home now with mother and Aunt Catalina. She was staying the night. Mother is in a dreadful state. She was lying on the floor crying and slapping the ground.'

I felt my heart racing into panic. It was thumping like a hammer inside my chest. The death of someone close was new to me. I wanted to cry but I couldn't. The thought of my mother on the floor stopped me. I had to be with her. I had to tell Francisca that I was going and why.

'Juan, I am so sorry.' She began to cry. 'I must come with you. Let's go now,' she said through her tears.

The three of us went quickly up to the Lower San Ginés. I was dreading seeing my mother and my father's dead body. My heart was still pounding. We entered the house and went into the kitchen. My mother was in a state of delirium, hugging father's body. A priest, the doctor and Aunt Catalina looked on, bewildered. 'Antonio, you are not dead. You cannot be. You are fooling with me. Come back. Come back. I love you. I do. Don't go away. Don't leave me. I need you. I cannot live without you. You are my life.'

I went up to my mother and hugged her awkwardly as she embraced father's body. 'Mamá, it's Juan. I am so sad and so sorry. It's terrible what has happened,' I said, trying to convince her of the stark reality of my father's death. 'Mamá, there is nothing you can do. Papá has passed away.'

Eventually, she let go of my father's body but then cried inconsolably. It was only when Francisca hugged her that she regained a modicum of composure. We had to get her away from there. Francisca eased mother gently into the drawing room. Mother was still sobbing but gradually relented. 'What am I going to do, Juan? How am I going to live without the love of my life? I am still a young woman.' She started crying again.

'I can understand that you are worried, Mamá, but we will make sure you are all right. We will look after you,' I said.

'Juan is right, Mamá,' said Francisco. 'You will have no worries.'

All five of us were overwhelmed by the suddenness of our father's passing. Francisca brought mother a drink of water to help calm her. She suggested that mother come to stay with us for a few days. Aunt Catalina thanked the priest and saw him to the door. I went back into the kitchen with the doctor. 'What do we do with my father's body?' I asked him. 'We need an undertaker.'

'I will arrange that straightaway,' said the doctor. 'Can you get a couple of sheets to cover him until the undertaker arrives? I agree with your wife. It would be a good idea to persuade your mother to stay with you for a few days. Keep her away while your father's body is still here.'

'I'll come with you to the undertaker,' I said. 'We will let Francisco know.' I called for Francisco who was with the women and explained to him what I was doing.

'No. I'll go to the undertaker. You take mother, Juan. Once the undertaker has done his job, I'll come around to your house. If Aunt Catalina will go with you, take her as well.'

'That's fine, Francisco. We'll do that,' I said and he left with the doctor.

I found some sheets to place over my dead father. I had to speak to him before I covered him over. I knelt down near to him. Much of the colour and texture had gone from his skin. His face was already looking a gloomy grey and waxen and his dark eyes were in a fixed, aimless stare. I was shaken by his total stillness. 'I've always loved you, Papá. You are a wonderful man. Thank you for everything you ever did for me and for being my friend. I will miss you.' I stood and looked at his features which were contorted by the act of death. I then closed his eyelids. They would never open again. I put the two sheets over him so that they completely covered his body. I could feel my tears welling into my eyes but swallowed to suppress them. I did not want to cry but I wanted to feel his death by being near him and by his presence in my mind. I needed to be in control to help my mother deal with this crisis. She was the one I could help. I knew that I would eventually have to save her from the plague of loneliness. As I left the kitchen, where death had struck with such brutality, I looked round at the motionless figure, hidden beneath the sheets. I choked as I said aloud, 'Goodbye, Papá.'

The three women were comforting each other in the drawing room. Francisca was holding my mother in her arms and sobbing. 'It's so sad, Mamá. It's a lightning strike. Such a tragedy.'

'I know, Francisca, I can't understand it. What have I done to deserve this? God has taken him early. I have been robbed of my darling husband. What can I do? I want to die.' Mother started crying again and Aunt Catalina put her arms around her. Aunt Catalina did not know what to say. She was still in shock.

I agreed with Francisca. If we could convince mother that she should come to our house, a change of surroundings, if only for a few hours, would help. If she would stay for a day or two that would be better still.

'Let's all go to our house,' I said. 'Mamá, I want you to come to stay with us for a few days. Go to your bedroom with Aunt Catalina. Pack some things for a short time with us. Will you come, too, Aunty? You would be more than welcomed.'

Aunt Catalina said she would but that she would not want to stay. Once mother was ready, we walked solemnly to our house. Mother had changed into a black dress. I carried her little case. It was a sombre walk. Francisca and I took one of mother's arms each to steady and console her and Aunt Catalina followed. Some of our neighbours seemed to know that we had suffered a serious loss and, as we walked past them, they stopped and said how sorry they were. I hated hearing mother saying she wanted to die but thought I should not worry too much. Surely, she would become more willing to live as time passed by.

I wondered during this deathly, almost silent walk how my mother would manage without father. He would be about fifty-six or maybe fifty-seven. So mother would be about fifty-four or five. She was an independent person to the extent that she ran the home and she still made the pigskin purses, but that only provided a small amount of cash. My father provided the bulk of the income and paid all the bills. He earned good money as a professional musician. That I did know. I didn't know whether he had arranged a pension for my mother. I was sure that they owned the house. Everything would become clearer in not many days.

At our house, we all sat in the lounge and Francisca offered everybody a drink. Mother wanted another glass of water and I suggested that

Francisca put some brandy in it. 'It's for medicinal reasons, Mamá. To steady your nerves.' At first she was reluctant to accept since she rarely drank, the last time being at our wedding and the time before at hers, thirty something years ago. Her sobbing gradually stopped and she went into a state of shock. She seemed to pick out individual objects in the room and stare at them for minutes at a time and with a total lack of expression on her face. I wondered what she was thinking but concluded that she was thinking of nothing at all in an attempt to block out or deny what had happened. Occasionally, she would take a small sip of the brandy and water. No one wanted to say much. It was hard to know what to say to break this dismal silence. We needed to do something to end it. As I could have anticipated, Francisca had the answer.

'Mamá, I need to get some food in for our dinner. Would you like to come to the market with me? You can come, too, Aunt Catalina, if you wish. In fact, I'd love you both to come. I was thinking of going to the Plazuela de Selenque. A walk to the market will help take your mind off other things, Mamá. Three heads are better than one when it comes to buying food!'

'I need to do something, Francisca. I can't sit here glaring at the walls all day.'

What progress. Francisca was so good with people in any situation. I did not mind being left at home because I was expecting Francisco to come in at any minute to say how he had got on with the undertaker. I was alone for no longer than a few minutes before he arrived. 'There are some definite issues, Juan. Father's body is in a chapel of rest. They have no idea where he wants to be interred. I told them that we want the funeral to take place in the San Ginés church but they need to know where we want father buried. This is going to be a difficult question but we need to ask our mother. They will let us know tomorrow when we can have the funeral but it must be some time tomorrow or the day after.'

The idea of being buried in a church 'so as to be close to God' was falling out of fashion in Madrid. Many, including the church authorities, regarded it as unhygienic and the churches and vaults within them were filling up with dead bodies. We needed to know whether father wanted to be interred at the church or in one of the new cemeteries near the outskirts of our town. We could find out only when mother returned from the market. We also needed to decide about an obituary notice. We agreed that mother should not be involved in this and decided to publish one in the news sheet that would issue the following day. Our father had many friends and contacts and it would be impossible to let them know any other way. Everybody read obituary notices. We would have to let our grandmother in Pedraza know, presumably by letter. We drafted an obituary that Francisco could take to the undertaker and a letter to our grandmother in Pedraza. We had to be sensitive with the wording because of the risk that the news of her son's death could kill her.

The women returned loaded with bags of food and various beverages. Francisco and I broached the subject of interment with mother. She was to our surprise much less mournful and not unhappy to tell us that father wanted to be buried in one of the new cemeteries. She also said that he had always asked that only his name be put on his gravestone, no dates of birth and death, no mention of anyone else and definitely no mention of his profession as musician. He had also said that that no women, including mother, should ever visit the grave. He did not want tears shed over his tomb.

Francisco reported back to the undertakers and took them our text of the obituary notice, which still had to give the date, time and place of the funeral service, the internment and the venue for the wake. Francisco made all the arrangements for the funeral which would be at four p.m. on the Friday. I went to the palace to explain my absence to the Maestro who hugged me in sympathy. Fortunately, I was not due to play to the King that day or for a few more days, so I was free to stay and comfort my mother and, of course, to attend the funeral.

***

The hearse stopped outside my parents' house in Lower San Ginés at exactly half past three. The elegant vehicle was drawn by two black horses with black feather plumes mounted on their bridles. Through its glass sides we could see father's plain wooden coffin. It seemed to be afloat on a sea of white flowers. As the chief mourners, mother and I travelled in the carriage behind the hearse and Francisca travelled with us. Francisco and Aunt Catalina were in the carriage behind, as were my grandparents on my mother's side who were by then quite frail. The carriage had brought them from their house just off the Calle Mayor.

My mother seemed by then to have reconciled herself to father's death and accepted the fact of her widowhood but she was still in great pain. Staying at our house for a few days definitely helped her. We had spent much of the day before the funeral reminiscing over some of the things in father's life with us. We spoke about the way he carried us on his shoulders on our way to our grandparents house; the journey to our grandparents in Pedraza and how he had shot dead the highwayman who was attempting to rape mother and badly injured his accomplice; his implacable dedication in teaching me and Francisco to play the guitar and violin; his joy when he could see we were making some progress; how nervous he was before he played in Lope's 'Punishment without Revenge'. The whole day was difficult but we were all together and talking; talking about our father. There were many tears but they were punctuated by laughter.

'I am not looking forward to this, Juan,' said mother, her eyes red with crying.

'I will be with you the whole time, Mamá, and have my arm around you during the service. You know the priest. He's the one who conducts morning mass on Sundays.'

The church was only 200 *varas* from my parents' house. The carriages stopped outside and four, stern-faced pall-bearers lifted father's coffin from the hearse and carried it into the church. By then, mother was sobbing quietly and had put a handkerchief to her face. Mother and I followed the coffin down the aisle. Francisca, Francisco and my grandparents came in behind us.

There was hardly an empty pew in the church. The obituary in the news sheet had clearly worked. Father knew more people than I had ever imagined. There were his colleagues in various groups of musicians; actors and actresses from the theatre companies: Maria de Riquelme, Bernarda Ramirez, Maria de Ceballos were there; my colleagues from the Royal Chapel: Juan de Roxas Carrión, Vitoria de Cuenca who had come with Balthasar Favales, Alonso Arias de Soria with Antonia Rodríguez, Luis de As with Angela Suarez, the Maestro; our friends: Honofre and Teresa, still going out with Simón Donoso, Beatrix de Santander, Marina de Riviera and her baby, Damiana, Diego and his wife Juana; friends of mother and father and their neighbours; and people whom I had never seen before. I would find out who they were at the wake.

I cannot remember much about the service. My mind was in a strange, stuporous state. I had my arm around mother and I could feel the warmth of her. It was a case of mutual support by each being physically close to the other but, because it was not me who had lost my spouse, the appearance must have been that it was me supporting her. I remember Francisco giving an oration about my father and thinking that I could not be so courageous. I would be fearful of being overtaken by emotion. He managed it without as much as a break in his voice. I remember the priest sprinkling holy water over the coffin and the pall-bearers carrying it out of the church. Mother and I followed with the other family members behind us.

There was confusion outside. Mother thought she was coming to the internment but I told her that she should not go. She had been so brave and did not need to witness that. I said I would represent her there and throw some dirt on the coffin both for her and for me. The rest of our little group of mourners agreed and Francisca took mother into the hall by the church for the wake. The plan was that mother, Francisca, Aunt Catalina and the grandparents on my mother's side would welcome the rest of the mourners in the hall while Francisco and I would go to the internment. That is what we did and a number of the male mourners joined our procession behind the hearse.

The new cemetery was on a large plot of consecrated ground about fifty *varas* to the south east of the Plaza de la Cevada on the Calle de Peñón. There were only three other graves in this bleak, featureless place and the grave for my father had been dug so that it was alongside the others. It was under an oak tree so at least he would benefit from some shade. There were some people whose houses overlooked the cemetery looking out of the window at our little gathering by the grave. They were strangers remotely sharing in our grief.

After we had thrown our handfuls of earth on father's coffin and as we walked slowly away from the grave, I was confronted by a tall man dressed in a long black cape and wearing a wide brimmed, black hat. He wore a beard and a moustache and had streaks of what appeared to be brown paint down his forehead and cheeks. At first I did not recognise him. He came towards me and placed his arm around my shoulder. 'I had to be with you in your moment of grief, Juan. I felt compelled to come here.' It was the King.

'Your Majesty,' I replied, in utter astonishment.

'No need for formality. I don't want anyone else to recognise me. Hence the painted lines on my face.'

'I am so grateful to you for coming.'

'I want to speak to your brother, too. You can reveal my identity to him. Just say, "Philip wants to be with us at this time."'

I did as instructed and the King said the same comforting words to Francisco, adding, 'I did not want to bring the Queen but she sends her profound condolences.' He then turned and went, merging anonymously into the group of the other mourners. I shall never forget this extremely generous act. This man was the King among kings.

We returned to the church hall to find that all the food and most of the drink had gone. The atmosphere was not good. I swear there were more people there than there were at the church. I recognised some of the hawkers and beggars that usually cluttered the area outside the church and some of the women as local, street prostitutes. Some people were passers-by, carrying shopping, who could not let pass an opportunity for free refreshment. While I could not claim to know everyone there that my father knew, it was obvious that many of these people should not have been present. Many of them were arguing about being fed properly. Others were threatening to go to an inn to get some food.

Mother was getting quite upset and some of the interlopers were shouting at her. I comforted her and assured her that everything would be fine. I managed to identify at least a dozen of the intruders and Francisco and I escorted them out. This provoked quite a reaction but we persisted in getting rid of them. Francisco, the organiser, asked the caterers to bring in more refreshments and quickly. He then confidently made an announcement. 'Ladies and gentlemen, we appear not to have provided enough food and drink. We just did not expect so many of you to come. We are delighted that you did. But please be patient: more food will arrive as soon as the caterers can bring it in. In the meantime please chat amongst yourselves.'

Francisco and I agreed to encourage Francisca, Aunt Catalina and our mother to circulate and encourage people to talk to each other. By then she was more settled and pleased to help. Like the rest of us, she was glad the funeral service and the internment were behind us and that we had ejected most of the spongers. The five of us split up and managed to stimulate a good level of conversation. I spoke to a lady dwarf, with bright, apparently dyed, red hair, who was sitting at a table, by herself. I went to sit next to her and, as I did so, she spoke. 'You have a wonderful mother, Juan,' she said, as if she had known me and my family for years.

'Thank you. You are kind. Do you know my mother well?'

'No. In fact I had not met her until today. I know your father well and he told me all about his family.'

'What is your name?' I asked.

'I am Agueda de Recalde. I have acted in some of the plays for which your father has played the guitar. Are you the harpist who plays for the King? Your father is so proud of you. He told me you compose music. That must be a wonderful skill to have.'

'Yes. I am the harpist but my brother plays the harp, too. I can't say I remember my father speaking about you. Do you live near here?'

'Yes, I live in the north of the town in the Calle de la Luna. I am not sure I should tell you this but... your father and I were lovers. That is probably why he won't have mentioned me.'

I was incredulous. 'Lovers?' I could hardly say the word.

'Yes, lovers. A number of us women here were his lovers.'

'Well you are a good-looking woman,' I said. 'Any man would find you attractive.'

'Not true,' said Agueda de Recalde. 'Not many men want to make love to dwarfs, only other dwarfs. But your father was an exception. He was one of the kindest men I have met. And I am sure you will be just as kind as he was.'

I wasn't sure I wanted to continue this conversation but didn't want to leave her on her own. 'Well, I am glad you appreciated him,' I replied, immediately realising the ambiguity in what I had said. 'I am going to have to circulate, Agueda.' So I introduced her to Vitoria and Balthasar. I then headed over to Aunt Catalina and calmly told her what Agueda de Recalde had told me.

'That cannot be true can it, Aunt Catalina?'

'I have to tell you the truth, Juan. Yes. It is true. Your father enjoyed the company of women and he regularly made love to a number of them. He could not resist. I am not that proud to admit it, but... he often made love to me, too,' she said, in a strange, quiet tone, as if this was a confession but not a request for forgiveness. Indeed, it was not for me to forgive her.

I was finding this all very difficult and I was becoming angry but it could explain several things about my father. First, it could account for his enthusiasm to ensure that Francisco and I knew sufficient for us to be good lovers – by sending us to Esmeralda Pechada – and, second, it became clear why he had had such a passionate embrace with Aunt Catalina at our wedding reception.

'Are there any more home truths I should know, Aunt?'

'Well, you will find out sooner or later, I suppose. You know that I share a house with two nurses who work at the hospital in the Calle de Atocha. They are much younger than me and share a bedroom in the house. From the squeals and groans that come from that room, I sometimes wonder if they are in love with each other. Your father used to make love to them, too. He would go into their bedroom when both of them were there and make love to the two of them.'

So within five minutes or so I had discovered that, assuming that Agueda de Recalde did not know about Aunt Catalina and those with whom she shared her home, father had at least five lovers, at least three of whom were at the wake. Whatever was going to be revealed next? I had no idea but this proved to me, if proof were needed, that it was difficult to know someone really well, however close to him or her you thought you were, especially if that someone did not want you to know about some aspect of his or her life. Did that make them a worse person? I suppose it depended on what it was they did not want you to know about. If they concealed ill treatment of another or a mortal wounding or some other serious criminal or moral act, then yes, it made them worse. If my father was cheating on my mother, that, too, was bad and would change my opinion of him. I was disappointed. It seemed totally out of character for him to be unfaithful to our mother. I wished I hadn't found out.

Eventually, the waitresses brought in more food and drink so patience was rewarded. Francisco had arranged a buffet meal so we were all able to help ourselves and continue mingling with our guests and fellow mourners. I noticed mother in a relaxed conversation with Esmeralda Pechada. I dreaded to wonder what they were talking about. Mother turned to speak to Barbola, who was with Esmeralda, and complimented her on the cleanliness of our house in the Puerta Cerrada. Barbola lit up like a star sapphire. Francisca joined the conversation and agreed that it was only because Barbola was so conscientious that the house was spotless and so fresh. Mother introduced Francisca to Esmeralda and they were soon both laughing. I heard my name mentioned and laughter again.

Deciding to ask Francisca later about this exchange and to avoid any possible embarrassment, I went over to the group from the Royal Chapel and told them about the clavi-harp project and how it was progressing. Then I chatted to Marina who was carrying Damiana in her arms. Christóbal was there somewhere but we could not see him. Likewise, everyone else seemed to be chatting to each other, sometimes about my father and also about other things, so the wake became something of a reunion. 'Why do we only get together on occasions such as these?' was a sentiment I heard expressed several times that day.

Afterwards, mother, Francisco, Aunt Catalina, Francisca and I returned to our house in the Puerta Cerrada. We all sat at the table in the kitchen and Francisca, Aunt Catalina and I complimented Francisco and my mother on how successful this sad day had been. I told the women about the extraordinary and unforgettable presence of the disguised King at the internment.

'Juan, I just cannot believe that,' said mother. 'What an incredible thing to do.'

'It shows what a great man he is,' said Francisco.

Francisco then opened a drawer in our kitchen cabinet and took out an envelope which he opened.

'This is father's will,' he said. 'Shall I read it out?'

We all looked at my mother for the necessary approval. She nodded.

'This is the last will and testament of Antonio Hidalgo, musician of Lower San Ginés in the town of Madrid.

I make the following bequests:

To my wife, Francisca de Polanco, all my possessions, except as stated below. My wife inherits my share of our house in Lower San Ginés and the sum of 5000 ducats which she will find in a box hidden underneath my bed.

To my son, Juan, my violin and my flintlock pistol.

To my son, Francisco, my guitar and all my music books.

To my wife's sister, Catalina, 200 ducats which is in the box mentioned above.

I also mention: Luisa de Alvarado, Violante de Castro, Leonor Escobar, Quiteria de la Rocha and Agueda de Recalde.

Signed,

Antonio Hidalgo,

this day, 25 June 1638'

'So you are now the sole owner of the house, Mamá. Do you know about the money?' I asked, astonished by its revelation.

'Yes. Your father told me he would leave me 5000 *ducats*. It's a fortune. He saved it over many years.'

'We'll locate it tomorrow,' said Francisca.

'Why has Papá mentioned these women?' asked Francisca, completely puzzled.

'I have to tell you something which Catalina knows about already. As you all know, your father and I were very happily married. We enjoyed the physical side of our marriage and for many years made love regularly and with mutual pleasure. Then the change came and my desire for the physical side completely vanished, like a raindrop drying in the sun. Father still needed to do it so we reached an agreement in which I released him from his marriage vow of faithfulness.

'I told him that I did not want him to father any children. Not outside our marriage and I made some devices to help him with that. As you know, I have made purses out of pigskin ever since you boys were children. From making the purses, I developed the idea for a device, also made of pigskin, which he could wear on his member. To stop his fluid from getting into the woman. These leather sheaths certainly worked. None of the women became pregnant. And believe me your father made love to them enough times.

'When I released him from the vow of faithfulness, he already knew a number of women who would service his needs. Some were actresses and others were friends of friends, shall we say. I'm sure Catalina won't mind me saying that she was one of the women who helped your father in this way. All those he mentioned were his mistresses. Three of them, Leonor Escobar, Quiteria de la Rocha and Agueda de Recalde, came to the funeral. Agueda de Recalde was the dwarf woman with the red hair. Leonor and Quiteria are actresses. The other two, Luisa de Alvarado and Violante de Castro share a house with Catalina.'

'But why have they been mentioned in the will and not been made beneficiaries?' asked Francisco.

'Well,' said mother. 'You know your father had an odd sense of humour. He promised these women that if they did various naughty things for him, they would be mentioned in his will. He tricked them because they got the mention and assumed that he meant a financial benefit when he only said "a mention"...'

'The rascal! The scallywag! I wonder what they will say when they find out,' said Francisco.

'I don't know,' said mother. 'I'm not so sure that I am worried. I have plenty of other things on my mind.'

It was a relief to me that our father had mother's permission to make love to these women. He could not therefore be said to be cheating on mother in indulging himself with them. Indeed, mother had tacitly encouraged him. Furthermore, he had specifically passed on to mother his share of the house in San Ginés. He could have left that to anyone. So my view on my father changed for the second time that day. He wasn't that bad after all.

As it was dark by then, Aunt Catalina agreed to stay at our house for the night and mother and Francisco also stayed. We all woke up early the following morning and went up to Lower San Ginés to look under the bed for the hidden money. I went to the bedroom and looked. There was nothing there. I looked in the wardrobe, in the cupboards and behind the mirror in the corner but could find nothing.

'I can't find anything, Mamá, but it must be here somewhere. Papá is tricking us somehow and we'll soon find out where the money is. We haven't been robbed, have we?'

'No, Juan, this house has never been broken into and we always lock doors at night. And when we are out. I will need that money because I only have a little in savings.'

'If we cannot find it, Mamá, we will look after you and we will find something for Aunt Catalina. But I'm sure we'll find it here somewhere,' I said, trying to sound convincing.

Francisco and I went into the bedroom and looked again. 'It's not here, Juan. There is nothing under the bed. I wonder if father is playing a game but it's a lot of money to be fooling about with and a cruel gesture to boot.'

'Just let's think, Francisco. What did the will say? I think it said the money was under "my" bed not "our" bed. Did mother and father sleep in separate beds and if so which one was his?'

'They mainly slept together but sometimes father slept in your bed, if he was out late and did not want to disturb mother when he came home.'

We looked under the bed I slept in when I was at home. The box was not there either. We did not know quite what to do. The money had to be somewhere in the house. Or could it be somewhere else? 'What exactly did he mean by "hidden underneath my bed"? If the box was under his bed, it would not exactly be hidden. It would just be there underneath the bed. So it's hidden. Where?' I said.

'We'll just have to move the bed and take the floor up. I'll get some tools. You tell mother what we are doing.'

Mother was keen for us to continue with our explorations. The floor was partly boarded with wood and partly earth, covered with large limestone slabs. The bed was on the slabs. We cleared the reed matting which was on the floor next to the bed, removed the slabs under the bed and started to dig. 'Have you posted the letter about father's death to grandmother, Francisco?' I asked, dumping a shovel full of earth on the floor by the side of the hole.

'No. I am thinking of a visit to the farm to see her,' he said. 'I could not bring myself to put my letter in the post. I will ride to Pedraza as soon as I can find a couple of days free.' By the time we had finished digging, the floor was covered in soil, broken bricks and all manner of rubble the builders of the house had concealed there, fifty or so years before. The box was nowhere to be seen. We told mother that we had found nothing up to then but not to worry because we were sure to find the money somewhere. We then refilled the hole and replaced the bedroom floor. 'Now what do we do?' asked Francisco, beginning to sound impatient.

'I don't know,' I said. 'It has to be here somewhere. We need to think again. I'm sorry, Francisco, but I am going to have to leave you here to go to the palace. I am playing for the King this morning and I have to see the Maestro.'

I felt thoroughly miserable at having to leave mother, Francisco, Francisca and Aunt Catalina at mother's house without having found the box with the money. I walked straight to the palace from the Lower San, Ginés, puzzling all the way about where the money could be.

CHAPTER 17

Maestro Carlos Patiño showed me an elaborate and unexpected letter he had received that morning from Sebastian Alonso González del Águilla. It took the form of an Egyptian parchment scroll, tied with a cerise, silk bow from which hung a purple wax seal the size of a small plate. It was the seal of Águilla. The message in the scroll was enclosed within a border of gold cherubs blowing bugle horns. In a flowing, florid, purple script, that could have been written three centuries before, it said in a single sentence that Sebastian Alonso González had finished building the clavi-harp and wanted to deliver it in person to the King.

'Hurray! The first clavi-harp in the world!' I said excitely. 'I could never have guessed he would send such an extraordinary letter. But he's an oddity, an eccentric. And he's early completing the job, with three weeks to go. I don't agree with him seeing the King, though. We'll have to test the instrument and make sure it's reliable before it can go anywhere near the King.'

'I think we toss this one in Quevedo's direction. Let him decide. We recommend that the King doesn't see him. We'll propose that the palace sends a covered, sprung wagon, with an armed escort, to bring it back here with its maker. We don't want it stolen by highway robbers. We'll pay for him to lodge in Madrid for a night or two. You are busy, Juan, so I'll draft a submission to the Private Secretary.'

For once Quevedo didn't question the Maestro's judgement. He asked the Maestro to write to the instrument maker telling him how the clavi-harp was to be delivered to the palace.

***

That night, Francisco dined with Francisca, me and our mother who was still staying with us. We stretched our brains to their limit, trying to work out where exactly father had hidden the box with the money. We did not want to excavate all the bedroom floors in mother's house for fear that the whole structure might collapse. Nor did we wish to dig up the floors in any of the other rooms. Francisco suggested that it could be hidden under the bed father used to sleep in at grandmother's farm in Pedraza. Indeed, he often referred to it as 'my bed' when he stayed there on his way back to

Madrid from musical engagements to the north. Francisco would arrange to go there as soon as he could so as to tell grandmother about father's death and he would have a look for it then. Mother had enough money to manage for several months so, while we needed to find her cash inheritance, it was not a matter of great urgency. At least, we convinced mother that that was the case. The reality was that 5000 *ducats* was a fortune. Not even a *titulo* could afford to lose that much, let alone a poor widow who without it would have to survive on the income of a street beggar.

After Francisco had left and mother went to bed, Francisca and I were alone. 'I have a question for you Francisca. I have been meaning to ask you since yesterday. What were you and Esmeralda Pechada de Burgos laughing about at father's funeral? I am so curious.'

'I am glad you didn't ask me while Francisco was still here. That would have been so embarrassing. Mind you, if he was, I would have had to adjust the story! I told her that you had mentioned her to me. And that I was grateful to her for the tuition she gave you. I told her that you had been excellent in putting it into practice. And had clearly remembered everything she told you, not to say everything she had shown you. She then mentioned Francisco, saying that he revealed to her something she had never seen the likes of before: his enormously wide member. That's what made us laugh. I didn't know Francisco was blessed with such an unusual appendage. You never told me. I could have married the wrong brother! Your mother just listened knowingly with a wry grin on her face.'

'I never knew whether father had told mother about our lessons with Esmeralda but I'm beginning to think she did,' I said. 'If she didn't, she certainly knows now!'

'Now I feel bad, Juan. Maybe your mother didn't know and I shouldn't have been so open to Esmeralda in front of her. I'm sorry.'

'Don't worry. My mother is a sophisticated lady and knows much more than she will reveal. You must have been struck by how open she was in discussing her love life with father. And her permission to release him from his vows.'

'That's true, Juan. Thank you for saying that. I feel better already.'

***

Within a week or so of father's funeral, Diego came into my office to see me. 'Juan, I was so impressed by the way you comforted your mother at the funeral. She must have felt better to have you so close to her, especially during the service. But that is not why I have come here to see you. You remember me asking you whether I could paint your portrait? Well, the King has given me his approval. When can I start?'

'You have taken me by surprise, Diego. I'm sure we can find some dates. What about in two days' time? Do you prefer to paint in the mornings or afternoons? If the King knows you are painting me, he won't expect to see so much of me and my harp!'

We spent the whole of the first session talking and he didn't put brush to canvas. There was no canvas. He was as generous as a rich patron in allowing me to influence the content of the picture. He asked whether I wanted to pose with my harp or another instrument, a violin perhaps, with a musical score on a desk or on a music stand, what other objects we might include, a pen and ink, flowers in a vase, an oil lamp or a lit candle, a picture in a frame, a small sculpture of someone, maybe of Lope de Vega.

He asked me what I wanted to wear, the maroon pantaloons and cream shirt of a Royal Chapel performer or something less formal. Did I want to wear a wig or have my hair natural? Did I want to wear a hat and if so what type of hat, a hunting hat, a tricorne hat, a wide-brimmed hat or what?

He questioned me about what should be in the background, what level of lighting we should have, whether any parts of the painting should be accentuated by illumination. How did I want to appear in the picture, contented, quizzical, serious, stern, humble, aloof or wear another expression? As for the pose: did I wish to sit, stand, lean against something, be sitting on a horse? These were my choices, my range to select from. It was my portrait and I could choose.

'I am not a complicated person, Diego. I am what I appear. I just do an honest day's work. And then go home to my lovely wife. I don't want to appear in military uniform or in something else that represents something that I am not. Nor do I want a background that portrays a place that I have never visited or something I have never done. I am a simple musician, an entertainer, a composer of music, a servant of the King. I am not rich nor am I poor. I will always be a worker, an artisan. I have my interests, in my family, in my friends, in politics and in riding and seeing new places. I am of interest only because of what I do.'

'I think we are getting close and I will make some suggestions. You are primarily a harpist and then a composer. You work in the Royal Chapel. You should, I think, wear the uniform of office, the maroon breeches and the cream shirt. You should be sitting with your harp, I think. Better still, you should be playing it. The expression on your face could then reflect the mood of the music you are playing. We could have a table with a page of music you've written. And a pen and ink so that it appears that you are composing. Something for the harp and could change it if you wished. We don't have to decide today, Juan. Just let me know what you want and then we can start. Why not talk to Francisca about it? Whatever you decide will be for eternity because your portrait will last for ever.'

***

Not many days later, I was on my way into my office when I was greeted by the Maestro, almost in panic. 'Juan, the clavi-harp has arrived. Where are we going to put it?'

'In the music practice room, just down the corridor. That was the plan,' I said, reminding him politely of what he had already agreed.

Minutes later, two muscular porters arrived and we told them exactly where the new instrument was to be placed. They brought in the keyboard part of the instrument and were followed by Sebastian Alonso González del Águilla. Then, under the protective eye of the instrument maker, the porters carried in another piece which looked like a conventional harp. 'It is going to take me an hour or so to assemble it and to get it working, Juan,' said Sebastian Alonso González. He was dressed immaculately, in a long blue coat and black breeches and wore shiny, black-buckled shoes. He was clean and his beard and moustache had been neatly trimmed. I hardly recognised this transformation as the chaotic, dishevelled individual Francisca and I had met in Segovia.

'Can I watch you build it?' I asked.

'Of course. Watch carefully and you'll be able to take it apart and re-assemble it yourself. Right? I've written a handbook for you to use when you want to change a string or a plucking finger.'

'Don't tell me. It's on a parchment scroll and written in ancient Spanish script!'

'Don't tease me, Juan. I wrote that letter as a special missive for His Majesty. I am still disappointed that he does not want to see me.'

'Maybe we will get you an audience later. When it's clear that he has fallen in love with the new instrument. It will have to satisfy him like one of his most voluptuous mistresses before he will even think of seeing you. But we'll do our best to seduce him with it.' He smiled, his bruising eased.

He produced, from a large leather bag, a roll of various tools which he used to assemble the new invention. There were pliers, small hammers, screwdrivers, spanners of various sizes, wire cutters and, not least, a set of shiny new tuning forks. He placed each of his tools in its allotted spot on the practice room floor. We moved the keyboard section to a place in front of a wall and below a window, leaving sufficient room to move behind it to attach the stringed, harp piece.

'We have to mesh the strings with the plucking fingers,' said Sebastian Alonso González. 'There is a finger for each string and each corresponds to a key on the keyboard. When you press a key, the finger comes towards you and plucks the string. There is a spring-controlled mechanism which pulls the finger back quickly so that you can play the same note again, just a fraction of a second after you have just played it. It works quite well. I bought the springs in Seville and I think they'll be reliable.'

We eased the harp section over the array of plucking fingers, which had a small leather pad attached to each. 'It took an age for me to decide what to put on the fingers,' he said. 'Plucking the strings with fingers of bare wood didn't sound right at all. I tried felt but it wore away too quickly. That's in exactly the right place, Juan. Can you see how the holes in the harp frame mesh with the lugs I've made on the keyboard section? Now I have to put the nuts on these bolts and that will secure the two main pieces together.' He tightened the bolts under my attentive eye. He then went round the front to press a key. The key went down but there was no sound.

'That's odd,' he said, looking puzzled. Then, after a few moments' hesitation, 'I know. I've forgotten to link the keyboard to the plucking fingers. Right? No problem, but we'll have to take the harp section off and start again. It's just a bit of a nuisance.'

We soon dismantled the incomplete instrument. Sebastian Alonso González then had access to the system that linked the keys to the strings. He had to clip each key to a small eye on the plucking mechanism. It was a fiddly job which took time and patience. 'My fingers are too big for this. You do the last ones so you get the feel of how the linkage works... That's it, Juan. Well done. We can attach the harp section now.'

He then spent a little time adjusting the pitch, aided by his set of tuning forks and plucking the strings by hand. He cut a few overlong strings. He then sat at the keyboard to press a key. The instrument made a sound from heaven. He pressed the same key several times. The note was exact in pitch, intensity and sound colour, every time he struck its key. He played more notes up and down the keyboard. He then stopped and looked up at me, smiling and seeking my reaction. The results stunned me. 'Congratulations, Sebastian Alonso González. You have made the perfect instrument. The sound is magnificent. I love it already!'

I could see immediately that the instrument would transform the music of the palace, like a hatchling changing into a fully fledged eagle. The change would be striking and profound. I played a few tunes myself. Playing it was almost automatic because, of course, I had learnt to play the clavichord. Our new instrument was at least as good as a harp.

'Well, that is it,' said the instrument maker of Segovia. 'I am giving you some spare parts so that you won't need my help if something goes wrong. Right? Here is a range of strings, some tuners, some spare plucking fingers and some spare leather pads for the fingers. I suggest we set up a small maintenance contract between the palace and me. I would say a yearly visit will suffice, depending how many hours a day you use it. Here is a logbook to record the number of hours you play it and the dates on which you do so. You should have it serviced every 500 hours of play or once a year, whatever comes first.'

He seemed to have thought of everything. 'We'll have to speak to Maestro Carlos Patiño about maintenance,' I said. 'I do not have the authority to make the decision myself. We'll see what he says.' The Maestro was equally impressed. He could not believe the amazing beauty and repeatability of the notes and how easy it was to play the device. We reminded the instrument maker that he should submit his bill to the Treasury and agreed to put the idea of a small maintenance contract to the King. 'I will only charge you ten *reales* a day plus the cost of parts and my expenses.' This seemed reasonable to us.

Again to our surprise, the Private Secretary agreed to our proposal for a contract. There was a slight rebuke: we should, he said, have thought of having one when we invited the original proposals. Because we hadn't, we had no real choice but to accept what Sebastian Alonso González had wanted. The Maestro was annoyed but had to admit that Quevedo was right.

'I want you to play the clavi-harp on and off for a week. Then, all being well, we will demonstrate it to the King,' said the Maestro. That was fine. I just could not wait to get my hands on it.

***

Francisco rode up to Pedraza to our grandmother's farm to tell her the news about father's death. On the way there, he tried to work out what he would say, but he just could not find a means of telling her which would not leave her in utter agony and distraught. She loved our father and, when he went to see her, always made a fuss of him. He was her only child and she treasured him infinitely more than any material riches. She always asked about his latest performances and where he had been playing his guitar, about mother and Francisco and me and our latest exploits. She cared for him and cared for us. Francisco reached the farm in Pedraza and hesitated outside before deciding to enter but grandmother had heard his horse pull up and had seen the sad look on his downcast face as she looked out of her window.

'Francisco, what is wrong? What has happened? I can see it in your unhappy eyes. What has gone wrong? Has someone died?'

'I am afraid so, Grandmamá. It's Papá. I am so sorry to tell you that he has died and I have come to see you with the terrible news.'

She immediately broke down. 'My son. My only son. The apple of my eye. First my husband and now my son. Both are dead and in such a short space of time.'

Francisco put his arm around her but was no consolation. 'We were so shocked when he died, Grandmamá. It was so unexpected. Mamá had been talking to him only minutes before and then suddenly he was dead.' With his arm around her, he took her into the drawing room and led her towards her favourite chair where she sat down, still sobbing.

'Why do these things happen to us, Francisco? What have we done to deserve the wrath of God?'

'Nothing, Grandmamá. Nothing. These things happen and there is nothing we can do to stop them. I don't think God can either.'

Eventually, Francisco was able to console her a little and offered to stay for a few days so she could have someone in the house with her. 'I have the servants, Francisco, but I'd love you to stay at least overnight. You cannot start back for Madrid now. It's nearly dark. Would you please come with me to the church? I want to say a prayer before I go to bed.'

Francisco stayed. In the morning, before our grandmother was awake, he went into the bedroom which our father used to sleep in and looked under the bed. There was nothing there. At breakfast he explained to grandmother that he wanted to search for the box that father had mentioned in his will. She encouraged him to do so. He found some tools in one of the farm buildings and lifted up some of the floorboards in the bedroom father used to sleep in. He could find nothing under them so put them all back, exactly as he had found them.

'It's no good Grandmamá. We shall have to search again in our house in the Lower San Ginés.'

Francisco hated to leave grandmother grieving for her son. It seemed so hideously cruel. But he had to leave and, before he did so, spoke to one of her servants to ask her to take special care of her. She was a middle-aged, smiling, black woman called Isabel. In asking for Isabel's help, he placed five silver *reales* in her pink hand. She initially refused the money but he persuaded her to take it, if only to make himself feel better. He bid farewell to a tearful grandmother, climbed onto his horse and made for home.

***

Diego was keen to start painting my portrait, so, having discussed some of his ideas with Francisca, we decided that I would pose as if playing my harp. We would use one of the new harps the King had recently bought me. I would wear my own hair tied into a pony tail and a light brown shirt over darker brown trousers. I would not wear the cream shirt and maroon pantaloons for playing to the King because I would not be playing to him but composing a piece for the harp. So there would be some music sheets, one of which would be partially completed, and a pen and a pot of ink.

We settled on a title: 'Juan Hidalgo, the Harpist of Madrid'. There would be three crucial areas of the picture which the lighting would have to accentuate: my face and each of my hands. These were the key elements to which everything else would be subservient and he would arrange them to be in a well placed triangle so as to show them to the best possible effect. The look on my face would be, as Diego put it, 'my thoughtful look'. This man knew everything about composing a portrait.

The day he started, I wheeled my harp to his studio. It had a south-facing window through which daylight poured in like a torrent of molten gold. He had some large silver mirrors so that, like a general commanding an army, he could direct the light to where he wanted it. He also used oil lamps to amplify the effects of the natural light.

He placed me at an angle facing the window with my harp in front of me and my hands on the strings. I asked him about the music sheets and the pen and ink but he told me he would add these later. The immediate objective was to position me so that my face and hands were precisely where he wanted them. He physically placed my hands on the harp so they were not too close together for the portrait he had in mind and I had to adjust my fingers so that I was playing realistically with each hand. He did not want to be criticised by painting something which was musically wrong. He then took a fine paintbrush and produced an outline of me in white paint on the canvas. I had to sit motionless while he did so.

While I sat there, I could not help wondering how grandmother had reacted to the devastating news of father's death and whether Francisco had found our mother's inheritance at grandmother's farm. Then an idea burst into my brain like a Chinese firecracker. If Francisco did not find the box containing the money at grandmother's, we had to ask mother a crucial question: where was father's bed on 25 June 1638, the day he signed his will?

***

Francisco rode straight to our house as soon as he returned. 'How was she? How did she take the news?' asked our mother, solemnly.

'Not very well, as we could have expected, but I took her to church while I was there and I think she took some comfort from her prayers. I left her in the hands of her black servant who seemed a kind lady and who said she would take special care of her.'

'What about the money?' I asked.

'I could not find it. I pulled up the floorboards in father's room there but could find nothing.'

'Well, I've had an idea, Mamá. Father signed his will in the June of '38. Was his bed in a different position then?'

Mother's face lit up like a full moon at midnight. 'Yes, Juan. It was on the other side of the room then. Over the floorboards. He moved it because the boards creaked and would wake me up while he was getting into bed.'

The four of us went up to our house in the San Ginés and went into the bedroom father would use when he came in late. Mother removed the matting from over the floorboards. There, right in the corner of the room, was a small, hinged door cut into the floorboards with a tiny brown tag, made of ribbon, attached to the door, on the opposite side to the hinges. Francisco pulled the tag and the little door opened with a shrill squeak. Inside was the box. Francisco and I heaved it out from under the floor. We all cheered aloud and hugged each other. In a state of barely controllable jubilation, we counted out the money. It was 5200 *ducats*, exactly. 5000 *ducats* for mother and 200 *ducats* for Aunt Catalina. Excellent.

'How could we have missed this?' asked Francisca. 'It's maddening.'

'It's because, when we searched in here before, we were fixated on the idea of something being underneath the floor where the bed was situated,' said Francisco. 'The closest we were to finding the door was when we put the earth back in the hole in the floor. I can't even remember seeing the piece of ribbon when we lifted the matting. Or when we moved the earth back and brushed the floor afterwards. The ribbon is so short and a similar colour to the floor.'

'Well, all's well that ends well,' said our mother, with a look of welcomed relief on her beaming face. 'What am I going to do with all this money?'

'We'll have to think about that, Mamá,' I said. 'We don't want to rush into anything.'

***

In my next session with Diego, he started painting my portrait in earnest. I sat with my harp.

'I am going to start by painting your face in quite a bit of detail. First, I am going to get the light just as I want it. Then I want you to look in the direction you would normally look when playing. I may need to move you around so I can get your face in position.'

He moved his mirrors to adjust the light and I shuffled around on my stool like a broody chicken settling over her eggs. 'Stop there,' Diego said, abruptly. 'That's just right! That's exactly where we left off last time and I can start with the colours now.'

We started to converse. 'There is something I have been meaning to ask you, Diego. Do you think the Council for State Security is serving a useful function? It's very much like the Inquisition, in my mind.'

'Well, we know each other well enough to know that we are both special agents. In answer to your question, though, it performs a different function from the Inquisition. The Inquisition is based on the church not the state,' he said, mixing some paints he had transferred with a knife from some small, labelled jars. The heart-shaped palette, which he held with one hand, had been used so many times it had more colours than a rainbow.

'You are right to assume that the state is run on lines parallel to the church. But there are issues that the Inquisition cannot deal with. For example, if someone decides to undermine the government by setting up a private army to fight the King, that would be treason. Treason is a matter for the state. Heresy, and, of course, other crimes against the church, is what the Inquisition deals with.

'There is something else, too,' he said, dipping a fine brush into the paint and then applying it to the canvas. 'The Council can take a proactive role in state security whereas the Inquisition is there to try individuals against a range of indictments, usually against the church and its code of morality. Let me tell you something as a fellow special agent, trusted implicitly by the King. Do you remember me telling you about my visit to Rome at the end of the '20s? General Ambrosio Spínola came with me. He was due to report to the Council on his return but, as you know, he died so couldn't.'

He stopped painting for a moment and looked me squarely in the eye, as if I was a cornered wildcat. 'You are not naïve, Juan. Far from it. You don't think it was an accident that I, a special agent for the King, travelled with Spínola. No, it was not. I went as a spy. Before I went to Italy, I was called to a meeting of a sub-committee of the Council. It was chaired by the Chief Clerk. They told me, to my astonishment, that my mission was to go as a spy and exactly, to the letter, what they expected of me. I asked them for written terms of reference but, for my own safety, they refused to give me any. They said that, if any document they produced fell into Italian hands, the Italians would kill me. I would be found drowned in the River Po.

'The purchase of the pictures by famous Italian artists was a front. An expensive one because I spent a fortune on them, a king's ransom. My main purpose was to work out the disposition of the Italian army, the strength of their navy in Genoa where we landed and the security arrangements for the Papal States, especially the Vatican. On my return, I was welcomed back by having to spend two whole days being debriefed.'

'I thought the Italians were our allies.'

'That's what they think but that is questionable,' he said, looking again at the canvas and applying more paint.

'Were you told why the Council for State Security wanted the information you harvested in Italy?'

'No. I didn't want to know and I've no idea what they did with it.'

'It's interesting that you were called to the Council and, on the spot and quite unexpectedly as far as you were concerned, they enlisted you as a spy. I suppose that could happen to me.'

'Anything could happen, Juan. Once you've agreed to be a special agent for the King, you could be instructed to do anything, legal or illegal.'

'Interesting,' I said, as Diego indicated that we should finish then and agree a date for the next session.

It was disappointing for me that there were many things that were said or that happened at the palace that I could not discuss with Francisca. I would have loved to have told her what Diego had told me about his spying activities. I was startled by his revelation and to share it would have eased the burden of my knowing something about him that seemed contrary to his character. From what he had said about being a special agent, I was beginning to worry about my own position and what the Council could ask of me. I felt they might well task me with something but, if Diego's assignment was anything of an example, it would be disguised behind my skills as a musician. I didn't see the point of worrying further: as Diego had said, I would just have to accept their instruction and implement it. Still, they had yet to approach me for anything.

***

We were all curious about how father had accumulated the vast sum of 5200 *ducats* he left in his will. Francisca and I spent many hours speculating. We wondered whether one or some of his women friends had

233

donated him cash for 'services rendered' or whether he had stumbled across hidden treasure on one of his journeys to venues where he performed. The most likely answer was that, over many years, he had simply saved this money to help mother and him in their old age. It would be their pension. The one conclusion we did reach was that he had obtained it honestly.

Aunt Catalina was delighted with her two hundred *ducats*. It was more than she earned in two years in her job as an assistant in a wine store. She even suggested having a party to celebrate this unexpected inheritance. Francisco, Francisca and I concluded that the best option for disposing of mother's 5000 *ducats* was for her to keep it. After all, the coins were gold and inflation in Spain was rampant and would exceed the interest paid by any bank. She could use it to buy Treasury bonds but the King had confiscated or devalued millions of *reales* worth of these bonds to pay for his military campaigns. We agreed that to buy some was not a sensible option.

So we divided the *ducats* into two and Francisco looked after half and Francisca and I looked after the other half. We hid the *ducats* in our respective houses for mother to draw upon and use. To avoid a problem similar to finding the original haul, we made sure we each knew where the other had hidden them away. The obvious place in Francisco's case was to put them back where we had found them. We put our half of the money in a wooden box which we hid in a stone-lined pit Francisco and I spent a weekend constructing in the cellar floor of our house in the Puerta Cerrada. We covered the pit with a trapdoor similar to the one father had used. We put Francisco in charge of accounting for the money so that mother always knew how much she had 'in the bank'.

***

The Maestro and I spent many hours playing the clavi-harp and testing it to its limits. It never failed us. Within a matter of a month or so of receiving it from the mad instrument maker of Segovia, we felt confident enough to have it taken to the King's apartments for a demonstration performance. The King was amazed at the quality of sound it produced. 'Juan you have invented a miraculous piece of musical engineering. From now on we are going to refer to you as the harpist and clavi-harpist to the Royal Chapel.'

I felt quite flattered. The King credited me with inventing the clavi-harp when it was a joint development between the Maestro and me and, of course, Alonso González del Águilla who had transformed the ideas we had dreamed of into an instrument that produced the most satisfying of sounds.

The Maestro was not the least concerned at the King giving me the credit. He said that his job was to ensure that the King was happy with the performance of the players in the Royal Chapel and we were clearly achieving that.

***

Our father's death had consequences, not only for our mother, but also for the other women he had left behind. Francisco, who was still single at the time, used to visit Aunt Catalina regularly and share himself with her. They started off again where they left off before, when Francisco gave up his virginity to our Aunt and seemed only too pleased to lose it. She even used the same little white jug for the olive oil.

While visiting our Aunt, Francisco had the good fortune of meeting Aunt Catalina's house mates, Luisa de Alvarado and Violante de Castro. Luisa was pretty, petite, and dark-haired with eyes as brown and round as pickled walnuts. Violante, on the other hand, was a larger, stronger-looking girl with a large face and big arms and hands, who could have been a successful woman wrestler. They slept together in the same bed, 'just like man and wife', as Francisco had remarked.

They told Francisco that they had so desperately missed father that they had to do some improvising. Father had left one of his pigskin sheaths at Aunt Catalina's. Luisa and Violante had filled it with pieces of cloth and pushed them in tight so that it looked like and felt like father's member. They had then managed to sew the open end to a flat piece of leather to which they attached a leather belt and leather thong to pass between the legs. One of them could strap the 'thing', as they called it, on to the other, tie the thong at the back and the wearer could pleasure the other one, just like father did. Violante said that she was the one who had preferred to wear the 'thing' and use it on Luisa who would shriek with paroxysms of delight.

'Mind you,' said Luisa to Francisco, 'if you want to help us in the way that your father did, that would be much better than relying on a wet piece of old leather.'

Francisco was willing to oblige. Luisa and Violante were as inseparable with Francisco as they were with our father. This meant that Francisco had to please one in the watchful presence of the other. They were fascinated by the size of his manhood but the first time they set eyes on it they wondered how they would accommodate it within themselves. Francisco explained the trusted effect of the olive oil which worked for each of them, especially as each gave the other a helping hand in aiming his manhood to its target.

Unlike his Aunt Catalina who was past the change and therefore could not become pregnant, these two women were still in their late thirties and could easily be put in that position. Francisco decided, on the first time he made love to them, to withdraw himself before releasing his fluid. That gave him an interesting idea: he would ask his mother to make some sheaths out of pigskin to fit him, in just the same way as she had for father.

So that was three of our father's mistresses that Francisco had adopted as his own. He wondered how he might experience the other three but did not know where they lived.

**

Our mother eventually settled well into her widowhood. No doubt this was eased by her happy realisation that, with 5000 gold *ducats* to draw upon at any time she wanted, she would never be poor. She delighted in visiting Francisca and me and we entertained her to a hearty, if rather plain meal, which is what she preferred, at least once a week. Naturally, she still missed our father and would still weep for him, when she felt a little low. She continued looking after her own parents and visiting them in the Calle Mayor nearly every day. They were, however, becoming very frail and mother began to fear the worst but nothing happened and they kept on going, like a pair of ancient tortoises.

We were delighted that she continued with her little business of making the pigskin purses, not only because of the additional income it gave her but mainly because it gave her an interest and got her up to the market to sell them. She and Francisco decided that they should continue living in the house in Lower San Ginés because it was a nice house and convenient for both of them. It was only a short walk from there to me and Francisca and that was good in itself. Francisco plucked up courage to ask mother to make him some leather sheaths, just like the ones she made for father. 'Yes, I'll make them, son, but you'll have to give me the measurements. I'm not going to measure it myself!'

Diego finished my portrait in three more sittings. He had captured my likeness with the keenness and accuracy of a falcon diving for a fieldmouse. The painting was a masterpiece.

CHAPTER 18

Even after seven years, when men are supposed to want to try new pastures, we still enjoyed a wonderful marriage. We were the greatest of friends and were each a source of help and support to the other. The physical side was a marvel to each of us and we never tired of our lovemaking. If anything, we became more adventurous and daring. We would take the horses out for a ride with the simple aim of making love outside of the town. We were always discreet and made sure we could not be seen before we tied up the horses and just did it.

Our disappointment was that, however often we made love, Francisca never in these seven years ever showed signs of becoming pregnant. We went to see a physician about it but he just said it would either happen or it would not. So that was a waste of time. Francisca said she was so happy with her life that it really did not matter whether children came along or not. She was, as she said, a very busy woman, not least with the soup kitchen, attached to the Shod Carmen Convent, and was not exactly sitting around waiting to become pregnant. I felt sure that she really wanted to become a mother, but did not want me to feel bad by knowing this.

A few years after father died, my grandparents on my mother's side also passed away. They always said that they each wanted to die at the same time as the other and they achieved that with remarkable precision. On one dreary, cold, midwinter's day they died in each other's arms. No one knew how old they were but mother reckoned that grandfather was about eighty and grandmother was about three years older. Aunt Catalina discovered them dead when she dropped in, apparently the day after they died, to see if they needed anything. She was horrified to find their stiff bodies in a seemingly permanent embrace on a wooden sofa in their drawing room. It was all very well for them to pass away as they had wished but it certainly created problems for those they left behind.

The doctor refused to issue the death certificates for fear that they had committed suicide and the attending constable suspected poisoning by a third party. Francisco thought they may have died of the cold but that was not the case. The embers of a wood fire were still glowing faintly in the hearth when Aunt Catalina discovered their simultaneous departures. A post mortem showed, to our great relief, that they had both died of old age. It was, of course, the simultaneity of their release which was so shocking.

Mother was badly affected by the deaths and would not speak to anyone for nearly three months. Try as we did to encourage her, she simply would not utter a word. Her mind seemed to disappear into the deepest reaches of her being and all she wanted to do was to sit in the kitchen on her own, looking at the walls, or spend her time in bed. There was a point, after about two weeks, when we all thought that she had gone dumb. She seemed to understand us but simply would not reply to questions about anything or anyone. She barely managed to look after herself and, had not Aunt Catalina decided to live with her for a time, we dreaded to think what would have happened.

We were all preoccupied with this sudden change in our mother's countenance. While we understood that she was in mourning, her response to her parents' deaths nearly destroyed her. We all thought of ways to try to bring her out of this state of oblivion. We would wander into her room and sit and speak to her about father, about her parents, about our work and just about anything else that came into our heads but all to no avail. It was as if she was conscious and in a coma at the same time. Then one day, Francisca took mother up to the market in the Plazuela de Selenque. They walked over to the stall which sold mother's pigskin purses.

'Hello, señora, we wondered where you were. We are completely out of purses,' said the lady mother dealt with. 'Could you make, say, two dozen more please? A dozen with the embroidery and the rest just plain.'

'That will be no trouble,' said mother. 'You can have them next week.'

That brief encounter jolted mother out of the universe she had been living in and back into the world of two-way communication. She chatted with Francisca all the way back to her house in Lower San Ginés and, when she arrived back, chatted with Aunt Catalina and Francisco, as if she had never stopped speaking in the first place. She was back to her normal self. We were all delighted and mightily relieved.

***

Francisca and I kept in close touch with many of our friends, especially those who lived in Madrid. We were not surprised to be invited to the wedding of Vitoria de Cuenca and Balthasar Favales. Francisca was right: Vitoria was the first of the unmarried women at her wedding to lose the pin which Francisca had attached to her dress so she should be the first to the altar. It was the most spectacular of events and took place in the San Sebastian Church, which is the one in which Lope was interred. Vitoria arrived in a carriage completely covered in gold gilt, except for the panels on the two doors which were scenes from the Greek myths painted by an

Italian artist who lived in Madrid. The carriage was drawn by a pair of white horses and driven by a horseman dressed completely in white from his wide-brimmed hat to his white leather shoes. Francisca was a maid of honour and managed with undeniable skill to negotiate the five *vara* train of Vitoria's dress from the carriage to her place next to Balthasar in front of the flower bedecked altar.

The reception was the party of parties. The food was prepared by the most expensive caterers in Madrid and the wine was the very best Rioja. Like our wedding, it was a reunion of friends. For most of the time, the conversation was convivial and friendly. Marina was there with her daughter Damiana who, by then, must have been four years old. Many of our other friends and colleagues were there, including Luis de As and Angela Suarez who were engaged themselves. Most of our colleagues at the Royal Chapel came, along with the groom and bride's families.

Vitoria's father gave a short speech in which he mentioned Vitoria's uncle, an old *tercio*, who had been killed only two weeks before, defending our army against the French at Rocroi. Another uncle stood up and said that the dead uncle was 'a dirty wanton bastard', who deserved a violent death because he just could not keep his hands off this uncle's wife. A minor skirmish broke out at that point, somewhat stimulated by the generous flow of wine. About a dozen of the couple's uncles engaged themselves in a brawl. Fists flew and blood splashed until Vitoria's father smashed an empty wine decanter on the table in front of him, threatening to push the jagged glass end into the face of anyone who continued fighting. Peace was thus restored but the rest of us were badly shaken by this unforgettable incident which seriously marred the occasion.

We heard, just after Balthasar and Vitoria's wedding, that Antonia Rodríguez, Francisca's friend from school, had fallen pregnant. Her boyfriend, Alonso Arias de Soria, was the father. She told her parents about her pregnancy, which was unwanted, and their angry response all but caused a miscarriage. Much to our surprise and dismay, they threw her out of the house. Her mother reminded Antonia that she had laboured hard to arrange her marriage to an extremely successful gunsmith but had abandoned these plans when she came home with Alonso, whom she did not like. Her father was a coward who, for a quiet life, went along with the views of Antonia's furious mother. Fortunately, Alonso was then renting a house in the Calle de la Paz and Antonia was able to go to live with him there. Her parents made her move everything from their house and that included all the material from her jewellery workshop. Antonia was heartbroken.

Matters became worse when, about two weeks later, there was a fire at Antonia's father's printing works in the Plazuela de la Leña. The fire was so intense that the fire warden and his intrepid band of bucket wielders could not get near it and the whole place was left a smouldering wreckage. The warden inspected the embers and was left in no doubt that it was an arson attack. Antonia's father immediately blamed Alonso, claiming that he committed the offence so as to seek revenge for the expulsion of their pregnant daughter. Alonso's house was just around the corner from the works and on the basis of this, the thinnest circumstantial evidence, the judicial office arrested him and detained him in the town prison.

Antonia knew, however, that her father owed an ink manufacturing company in Burgos about 500 *ducats*. She told the constabulary who, after Alonso had been incarcerated for two weeks, traced the arsonist, a well known criminal, whom the ink company had engaged to set fire to the print works. Apparently, Antonia's father had been threatened with such action after failing for many months to pay for the ink. Antonia's father was charged with perverting the course of justice and jailed for six months. Alonso was released and the judicial office sent him a written apology with fifteen *ducats* compensation.

***

Francisco fulfilled many of his ambitions. Totally against my advice, he successfully applied to become a *familiar* in the Holy Office of the Inquisition of Toledo. He was delighted to be sworn in when he was only twenty years of age. The Holy Office used him many times to arrest suspects. Following my recounting the incident, which led to Honofre's dismissal, Francisco avoided issuing the verbal summons to anyone who would not actually be accused. Although we were both officials of the Holy Office, not once were we asked to work together on the same assignment. Perhaps that was for reasons of security.

However, the event which gave him the greatest pleasure was his appointment as harpist to the Royal Chapel. We were, apparently, the only brothers who had worked in the Chapel at the same time. The King was much amused. He loved us playing duets to him. It was a delight and a source of great pride for me to introduce Francisco to my friends and colleagues at the palace, many of whom he had already met at functions at our house or at our father's funeral.

Francisco made an interesting pledge to me. I remember him saying, not more than a few years after the funeral, that he would settle down and find himself a wife, once he had met the three of father's mistresses to whom he had not made love. These were, Agueda de Recalde, the dwarf with her hair dyed red, and the other two who attended, Leonor Escobar and Quiteria de la Rocha. I said I thought he was joking but he assured me that this was a solemn pledge, as solemn as a cardinal's benediction. He explained that this meant only that he wanted to meet them and that the pledge did not necessarily mean he would follow the ghost of our father into bed with them.

His implacable efforts paid their dividends and he found each of them, Agueda living to the north of the town and Leonor and Quiteria to the east. Leonor was the first Francisco located and he called at her house one Saturday afternoon. She invited him in and asked him to sit down while she prepared him a drink. He thought his fortunes looked good at this point but when a tall, slim man with long hair appeared, whom Leonor introduced as her fiancé, he realised that the encounter had probably reached a dead end.

Francisco met Quiteria at a play in which she was performing and in which, unusually, Francisco was playing his guitar. She recognised him from the funeral and they talked about various things before he said, somewhat undiplomatically, that she was mentioned in father's will. At this point she spoke in the foulest terms about father, accusing him of lying and deceiving her into believing she would be a major beneficiary. Francisco thought he was to be the loser again and was about to bid her goodbye when she invited him to escort her back to her house. He imagined that this was simply to save her finding a chaperone.

His patience was rewarded. She lived on her own and invited him in for a drink. She said that she had heard about his physical attributes and wanted to experience them for herself. Once again, success was eventually achieved with the help of judicially applied lubrication. After they finished, Quiteria thanked him profusely for the experience and they put their clothes back on. She then politely showed him to the door and said, in the calmest tones, that she hoped she would never see him again.

The story of his meeting with Agueda de Recalde was altogether more touching. She arrived unexpectedly at mother's house one afternoon. Francisco answered the door and a sad little red-haired figure told him that she would like to ask our mother for her forgiveness.

Francisco showed her into the kitchen where mother was just beginning to prepare the vegetables for a meal. Agueda burst into tears when she saw our mother and went up to hug her. It was, as Francisco recalled, a very moving sight as the tiny lady put her arms around mother. Agueda's little body was so short that her arms embraced mother's bottom and her head pushed into mother's tummy. She sobbed and sobbed until mother could resist no longer and began to cry herself.

Agueda then spoke: 'I have let you down. I have betrayed your womanhood. I am so sorry. I have come to ask for your forgiveness.' They both recovered themselves and mother said that Agueda had done nothing that needed a pardon. Mother said that she was well aware that Agueda and father were lovers but that did not worry her at all. 'I was happy, you were happy and he was happy. So there was nothing to worry about,' she said, philosophically.

Agueda was surprised at mother's reaction but pleased to accept it without further prostrating herself. Not wanting to spend much more time speaking to one of father's mistresses, mother asked Francisco to take Agueda into the drawing room while mother prepared some drinks. Francisco did as mother suggested and, within the space of a few minutes, discovered that Agueda's family were from Valéncia where they worked as servants to a wealthy family of *morisco* landowners. The family lived in a separate house from the main residence and the landowner used to entertain his friends by bringing them to see the dwarfs whom he regarded as curiosities.

Agueda's father later discovered that the landowner was charging the local populace six *marvedís* a person to come to see them. Her father decided that he had had enough of this abuse and would make a new life for his family in Madrid. The whole family escaped one night and, a month later, having suffered every form of deprivation, arrived in our town where they had lived ever since. Apart from her mother, the whole family worked as actors in various theatre groups. They were much happier in Madrid where most people treated them as normal. This was no doubt, due, in large measure, to the fact that the King himself had a number of dwarfs working in his household in the Alcázar Palace. Some were immortalised in Diego's sensitive paintings of them.

After she had had a drink of grape juice with mother and Francisco, he offered to take Agueda home. They walked the whole way to her house and Francisco stayed the night there. Agueda herself took the initiative in asking Francisco to do with her as our father did. From what he said, she was the most appreciative of lovers and gave him a hearty, fried egg breakfast before he came back home. Although we saw Agueda from time to time at the markets and elsewhere in the town, the relationship between Agueda and our family never developed further. We felt that our mother was happy with that.

True to his 'pledge', Francisco had succeeded in locating all of our father's mistresses and had made love to all but one of them himself. He therefore began to look for a wife with whom he could settle down. He had plenty of time: he was only twenty-six when Agueda came to say sorry to our mother.

**

It was around that time that one of the assistant private secretary's came to my office early one morning to tell me that I had been summoned to see the King. He said he had no idea what it was about. While we loved our gentle King, he wielded great power and could use it as a weapon of destruction. Fearing trouble, I went to see the Maestro who reassured me. 'Sometimes he wants to speak to someone different. He may be bored. He may want to try out some new idea on you. No, Juan. He likes you. Don't worry. Be just a bit nervous but, if you appear terrified, he will soon notice and it will be a short conversation.'

The King was in a strange, unsettled state of mind. He had been through a period of immense difficulty and had suffered the loss of his brother the Cardinal Infante, his sister the Infanta María, his wife Queen Elisabeth and his precious son the Infante Balthasar Carlos, all within the space of the previous five years.

'Let me tell you something,' said the King, looking uncomfortable and not quite managing to smile. 'I am the King of Spain and the Empire. I have more than a hundred million subjects. Yet today I feel like the loneliest man in the Kingdom. That is why I thought I would speak to someone I frequently see but do not speak to often. There are many senior officials I can see but they would think it odd if I asked them to listen to me say what I want to tell you. I also have a request to put to you. I want you to help me with a specific matter which we will discuss later in this conversation. I don't want to ruin your day if you have other plans, so you must tell me if you can give me the time.'

I could not believe the King was asking me this question. 'Your Majesty, I am free and can spend all day with you. If I can help you in any way I can, I would be pleased and honoured to do so.'

'I want to tell you some truths about myself. I am not a good King. I have failed my country, my Empire and my family. First, I am still deeply ashamed of our catastrophic defeat by the French at Rocroi. I hold myself personally responsible for 14,000 dead or wounded men. It was the most humiliating defeat our incomparable armies have ever suffered. We were outmanoeuvred, outgunned and routed. There is a sense though in which we deserved to be beaten. We were mean, Juan. We did not provide our army with enough cavalry support. So our infantrymen faced up to the French unaided and fought to the death for their King. I still bleed for the 14,000. I can never forgive myself. It will weigh on me for the rest of my life. God will never forgive me. I believed our men would defeat the French and go on to capture Paris. But no, that did not and could not happen.

'I blame myself for the sorry state of this once great country, the desperate mess we are in today. We are almost destitute. Almost bankrupt. We have devalued the currency, endlessly. We are behind in paying our troops. Behind in paying our own staff in the palace. If you are not owed a month's salary, Juan, you are one of the lucky ones. Some days we have no money, even to pay for our own food. We cannot go on like this.

'Then I have all but ruined my own family. I sent my brother and your friend the Cardinal Infante to govern the Spanish Netherlands. He was a superb fighter, maybe no use as a Cardinal but he was a brilliant military tactician. Look what he did at Nördlingen with his cousin, Ferdinand III of Hungary. They led our armies to the defeat of the Saxons and Swedes. They smashed them into tiny pieces. While he was Governor he goes into battle against the French. Then what happens? He dies of a terrible illness, weakened in body and spirit by fighting for me, his King. Another disaster. That man had the ability to be King, a better King than I. And we drove him to the Netherlands to die in the prime of his life.'

The King was in a sad and sorry state. Several times he came near to tears and I didn't know what to say to ease his pain. I stayed silent while he purged himself. It was odd that he had referred to the Cardinal Infante as 'my friend'. I had spoken to him a number of times and there was the musical evening I spent with him, the King and the Infante Don Carlos, a good few years before, but I could hardly call the Cardinal Infante a friend.

'Then I took my son, Balthasar Carlos, to Pamplona. There he contracts a terrible illness and dies at the age of seventeen in a hospital in Zaragoza. Juan, I should never have taken him to Pamplona. It was a tortuous journey. The road was rough. The horses misbehaved. The weather was bad. I should never have gone there, let alone have taken my son.

'The worst thing, though, is that I have betrayed my loving wife, Queen Elisabeth. Others, like the disgraced Count Duke, tried to come between us but failed. It was I who drove her to illness and then to her death. She knew I was taking pleasure in other women. She knew of this weakness in my character that, try as I could, I failed to bring under control. I still keep having them. It is like a drug. I cannot resist them. Juan, I have over twenty illegitimate children. You know of Juan of Austria, son of Maria Calderón. He is one. But there are many more, the children of actresses, singers and other women to whom I took a passing fancy and who wanted to oblige their King.'

The King fell silent and I could not resist commenting. 'Your Majesty, you are blaming yourself for many things for which you cannot be solely responsible. Take Rocroi. Yes, it was a huge and humiliating defeat. But you were advised by others about taking on the French, on what terms and on the strength of the army which fought them. Yes, you are King and are ultimately responsible. But others are answerable to you, not least, the Count Duke, whom you tactfully and graciously retired. In my opinion, it would be better for Spain if you challenged some of these people about the advice they give you. You are too kind, Your Majesty. You would rather inflict pain and guilt upon yourself than bring others to account.'

'Juan, you surprise me. I did not expect you to question me.'

'I hope you do not regard me as impertinent, Your Majesty. However, I am only saying what I and many others will be thinking. You are my King, Your Majesty. I love you as my King. You are so kind to the likes of me, your humble servants. You had the grace to attend my poor father's funeral. You treat us all with the greatest of dignity, humility and respect and you are genuinely grateful for our efforts in serving you. So it hurts me to hear you flagellating yourself. You have been the victim of unimaginable misfortune. Your son, Infante Balthasar Carlos, for example. You could not have expected him to become ill and die. You could not have expected your wife, our Queen, to be taken from you by the ugly hand of fate. And likewise, your brother, the Cardinal Infante. He was a strong, healthy and self respecting man. He would not give up lightly to his death.

'As for all of these women to whom you have made love, Your Majesty, I do not see that that is such a great vice. Many kings before you have had mistresses and illegitimate children. There is hardly a French king who didn't have a mistress. Henry II's mistress, Diane de Poitiers, appointed ministers, made laws and even imposed taxes. Henry II had at least ten mistresses. Her Majesty, Queen Elisabeth, knew of your affection for women and, like the wives of the French kings, she simply turned a blind eye. After all, Her Majesty was French and was well aware that this is part of a monarch's expected behaviour.'

'Juan, have you ever had a mistress?'

'No. I can honestly say I haven't. Nor do I need to. The reason I do not need a mistress, Your Majesty, is that my wife and I keep each other totally happy in love. So I do not need to look elsewhere. I do not know how long that will last. We have been married for more than seven years now and I do not want to look elsewhere. This is not to criticise you, Your Majesty, nor your relationship with Her Majesty the Queen. It is simply a statement of my relationship with Francisca, my wife. I must tell you though that my father had mistresses. He had at least six. This was revealed to us at his funeral. Four of them were also present and my mother was well aware of his extra-marital proclivities. She released him from his vow of faithfulness and gave him the means to prevent his having illegitimate children.'

'Now I am really interested, Juan. How could she help him with that?' he asked, leaving his ruefulness behind.

I told the King about my mother's little business of manufacturing the purses and how that developed into making the pigskin leather sheaths that my father wore to prevent his mistresses from conceiving. The King listened in rapt amazement. I could divine with total certainty the way his mind was working.

'Do you think your mother would make some of these sheaths for me?'

'I can only ask her, Your Majesty, but I think she would be deeply honoured to do so. I do not think she has made any for anyone outside of our family, but she would regard you as one of our family. Yes, I think she would make some. I can let you know.'

'Juan. Please do so. Tell me, Juan, you seem to have lived an unblemished life as far as women are concerned. Have you made love to any other woman than your wife?'

I told the King about my relationship with Teresa de Espinosa and about my encounter, almost twenty years before, with Esmeralda Pechada de Burgos.

'My God, Juan, not Esmeralda. I know her so well and learnt so much from her. My father sent me to her when I was fifteen. I was already married to Queen Elisabeth but the marriage had not been consummated. What my father did not realise was that I had already lost my virginity to one of the palace stable maids. Anyway, the Count Duke took me to Esmeralda's house. I was disguised as a priest with a wide-brimmed, black hat that almost hid my face. She was wonderful as a teacher. I never made love to her but she showed me around every curve, crease and crevice of her smooth, unblemished body. Just as she did for you, she showed me how to pleasure a woman, what to touch, where to touch and how to touch to give the woman maximum satisfaction.

'I went back several times over a year or so to see her and we kept in contact for many years afterwards. She would not charge me for her services so I gave her many beautiful gifts. I paid for her portrait to be painted. It is a beautiful picture and it still hangs in her hall. I still see her and she teases me with her body. She must be seventy now and she is still an attractive woman. Do you know that, like you, she is one of my special agents? She has been brilliant in providing us with information, mainly that her foreign customers revealed to her while they were enjoying her professional services. I cannot tell you the details, but to say that she was instrumental in finding out about the strength of the French armies in Lorraine.'

The King paused. 'I think we have dealt with the personal issues and I am sorry to have burdened you with my troubles. I said earlier that I wanted your help. There are two connected matters. The first is one for which I may engage your help. The second is one for which I will certainly need your help. Juan, I and my government are about to embark on a new initiative. You are aware that the financial position of our country is desperate. We may have to declare ourselves bankrupt. That is all but unavoidable.

'We are planning a way out of this mess which will involve an attack on another country. I cannot, at this stage, tell you which one and it is a fact that we have yet to make a decision. You see, our political strategy, up to now, has been to secure new territories. My great grandfather, Charles V started this in the early fifteen hundreds. Our aim has been to control the wealth of these territories and to direct much of that wealth to Spain. Until recently, this has been incredibly successful, especially as far as the huge fortune we have gained from the Americas is concerned.

'However, these sources of wealth have all but dried up and the Council of Finance and the Council for State Security are discussing a plan which will mean breaking into and robbing an alien treasury. It could be the Dutch, the English, the Germans, the Swedes or the Italians. We have created a sub-committee which has members from each of these two councils. It has been charged with working out the best option.

'There will soon be a meeting to consider the recommendations of the sub-committee and I foresee the need for some detailed, important work for a number of our special agents. Their role will be to fill out the details of the plan. All special agents will be expected to attend this meeting. Who knows, you could be involved yourself in some way.

'Now to the second matter. Have you met the new papal nuncio, Giulio Rospigliosi? He has been in Spain for about three years now. He is very clever. He has a doctorate in philosophy from the University of Pisa. Since he came to Spain in '44, he has been extremely busy. Apart from his ambassadorial duties, he has been working with Baltasar Moscoso y Sandoval, the Archbishop of Toledo, in reviewing the functions of the papal nuncio to Spain. I should say that the initiative was theirs, not mine.

'They have concluded that there would be benefits in having a closer relationship between the nuncio and our government and that the nuncio should have the position of observer on some of our councils of state. My view is simple. It is a preposterous idea. We cannot have aliens observing our activities. The Pope would not allow our ambassador to Rome to sit on councils in the Vatican. So I will not support it. However, there are powerful forces in the Catholic Church which want to back this nonsensical intrusion into our affairs. Instead, I want Rospigliosi to be so engrossed in other pursuits that he has no time to go near our councils, let alone to sit on them.

'This is where you come in, Juan. Rospigliosi is a distinguished playwright and a dabbling composer. I do not believe he is very good at writing music. I want you to befriend him and gain his confidence. I want you to encourage him to do some composing, possibly in collaboration with you. He will still have duties to perform as papal nuncio. These are his functions as ambassador and I will continue inviting him to attend a whole range of state occasions so he will have other preoccupations besides his music.'

'Your Majesty, I have not met the new nuncio, Rospigliosi. Does he have an office in the palace?'

'Yes. I have given him an office next to the Royal Master Huntsman, Don Juan Mateos. This was a tactical move. I did not want him close to the seat of government, the offices of the councils. You have not responded to my request that you collaborate with and befriend him. What do you think?'

'Your Majesty, I would be pleased to help you. Of course, I will do it.'

'I think I have come to the end of what I wanted to tell you, Juan, There is only one other thing. That relates to handling what I have told you,' the King said anxiously. 'You must, as I mentioned earlier, say nothing about the personal matters we have discussed and nothing about the new initiative in which the Council for State Security will be engaged. I will, of course, treat with confidence the private matters you have discussed with me.

'However, I want you to let Maestro Patiño know about our plans for Rospigliosi and I want your wife to know, too. This is because I want him to become a family friend of yours, if only a fairly remote friend. I want him to develop a trust in you. Thank you, Juan. Thank you for your time.'

In return, I thanked the King and left. I needed to meet Rospigliosi as soon as possible but only after talking to the Maestro about him and the King's request. The question in my mind was why the King was so keen on my befriending Rospigliosi and gaining his confidence. This was at least one step further than collaborating with him. That was a puzzle.

CHAPTER 19

I felt elated by my conversation with the King. I thought I had improved his state of mind, particularly by telling him he was not solely responsible for what had gone wrong in our country and in his family. On my way home, I had to sort out in my head what I could tell Francisca and what I had to respect as a confidence. I could see as I walked up through the Puerta Cerrada, which was thronging with people going to and fro, that Francisca was already at the door waiting for me and I wondered if anything was wrong. When she saw me she came running towards me.

'Juan, Juan, I'm sure I'm pregnant,' she yelled, excitedly. 'I'm as good as certain. I didn't tell you last month I missed my bleed and I thought it may be just a miss. But I was due for one again yesterday. It has not come and I don't feel as if it will. I am sure I'm expecting a baby.'

I was thrilled and hugged and kissed Francisca as we stood on the busy, dusty street. 'What brilliant news. After all these years. Congratulations to us and especially to you, my love! Have you told anyone else, your father, maybe?'

'No one. You had to be the first, Juan. I'm so excited. I was beginning to think it would never happen but it has!'

'I think your father should be the next to know. Then we should tell my mother and Francisco.'

'I think we should keep it to ourselves for now. It's too early to say for certain and I think we should tell no one else until we are sure.'

'I agree. Let's not rush to tell everyone. It is wonderful news and I am looking forward to being a father. Which room will we use as the nursery? We'll have to buy a cot and all the other things a baby needs.'

'It's all too soon, Juan. We do nothing just yet. Wait until we know it's a real pregnancy and not a false one.'

By then, we were inside the house and I gave her a hug and told her I loved her and would love her forever. What a tremendous step it would be for both of us: our very own child to love and share. A new and exciting dimension of our life together.

'Well, you have given me a surprise. A wonderful surprise and I have a little, much less important surprise for you.' I told her about my meeting with the King and his request that I befriend and collaborate with Giulio Rospigliosi.

'What an honour, Juan. An incredible honour. I wonder what the King has in mind when he's asking you to befriend him.'

'I don't know, but it is vital that I gain Rospigliosi's trust. The King even asked me to tell you about him and to make him a family friend. If only a remote friend, as he put it. I'm not totally sure what he meant by a "remote friend" but I think that means someone we can bring into the circle of our family but at the same time keep at a certain distance. He would not be intimately involved in our family life in the same way as, say, Antonia and Alonso, Diego and Juana or Vitoria and Balthasar. But be nearer the fringe of our lives, perhaps in the same way as Carlos Patiño or Honofre Espinosa who seems to be more remote since his dismissal from the Holy Office.'

Francisca was keen to help. 'I have an idea, Juan. We should have another dinner party but this time inviting Rospigliosi. Has he any friends we could also invite?'

'Good idea. Let's do it. I only know of one other person who knows Rospigliosi. He is Baltasar Moscoso y Sandoval, the Archbishop of Toledo. The King told me that Rospigliosi has been working with the Archbishop here in Madrid. Do we want to invite an archbishop? I'm not sure about that. He is an immensely powerful man and would outrank me by ten pay grades, but if it made the nuncio feel at ease, then it might be a good idea. We could invite Diego and Juana... I've just had an interesting thought, myself: let's invite Pedro Calderón de la Barca, the playwright. If Rospigliosi is a playwright he will get on well with de la Barca who is an interesting character in his own right. He has been a soldier. He is the director of the Buen Retiro and he has a mistress.'

'That's it, Juan. We invite de la Barca and his mistress, the Archbishop, Rospigliosi, and Diego and his wife. You will have to get to know Rospigliosi well enough to invite him and the Archbishop. Then we invite the rest of them.'

'Perfect. I'll find Rospigliosi tomorrow. I think I should have a word with the Maestro before we invite the Archbishop and de la Barca. I'll just see what he says. By the way, the King made a strange request. I'm not sure how the subject arose but there was some talk about his illegitimate children. He did not want any more, if he could help it. So I mentioned the pigskin sheaths that my mother made for father and Francisco. He told me to ask mother to make some for him!'

'Juan, you didn't! How could you let the King into such a sensitive family secret?' asked a mildly shocked and slightly embarrassed Francisca.

'I was only trying to help him!' I said, jokingly. 'It is my public duty to help the King with his problems.'

Francisca quickly recovered and saw the amusing side of this. 'Do you think your mother will make some for him, Juan?'

'I don't see why not. It will be an honour! She'll just have to make a range of sizes and let him try them on!' We both laughed and I said I would ask mother.

***

The papal nuncio was spending a few days in Toledo but he eventually returned to Madrid and I managed to introduce myself to him. He was a very tall, thin, gentle-looking man with a long narrow face, a tidy, brown beard and a moustache to match.

'Señor Hidalgo, I don't think we have met before. May I ask why you have come to see me? I am intrigued,' he said with a puzzled but friendly smile.

'I had a meeting with the King a week or so ago and he suggested I make contact with you. I understand you are a playwright and that you write music. I am a composer for the King and write songs and musical accompaniments. The King simply thought we had these things in common and that we should get together.'

'I am very much a beginner in my writing of music but I have written several plays. It would be interesting for me to find out more about what you do for the King. I want to do some work on drama or music, or even both, while I am here in Madrid. I would be delighted if you would discuss some of your thoughts with me.'

'Why don't we arrange to meet in the next few days to take this forward? Are you free first thing tomorrow?'

'Say, eight o'clock tomorrow morning.'

We met as agreed. I was surprised and delighted that Rospigliosi understood so much about the musical and theatrical culture of Spain. He knew about Lope de Vega and his prodigious output. He also knew about some of the earlier Spanish playwrights such as Tirso de Molina and about Encina, who probably introduced theatre to Spain. Rospigliosi said he was deeply interested in the new Italian concept of opera in which all the words of a play are sung with an instrumental accompaniment and there are no spoken parts. He had written the libretti for two operas, some years ago, while still in Italy. I knew next to nothing about this art form and admitted that to him.

He said he was keen to write a play, based on a Spanish theme, and composing some music for it. He said he also had some ideas for some songs, also based on Spanish traditions, which he could take back to Italy. I had no difficulty in convincing him of my enthusiasm to help him develop these ideas and we arranged to meet again. I suggested we meet the Maestro who might well make an input himself.

**

Mother was completely taken by surprise when I told her about the King's request for some pigskin sheaths and immediately panicked. 'What do I do, Juan? You've put me in a very difficult position. It's deeply embarrassing. I would rather not do it but it is a request from the King and I really have no choice. Why did you have to tell him about them? I don't know his size or anything.'

'It was all a bit of male conversation, Mamá, and I'd rather not go into the detail, except to say that he wants to avoid any more illegitimate children. He has twenty already. All I can think, Mamá, is that you make, say, half a dozen in various sizes. I'll take them along to him with a note, maybe, inviting him to let us know which fits him best so that we can make him some more.'

'I can't think of a better approach, Juan,' she said, quickly accepting the situation, 'so I'll make a range of them. You can have them in a couple of days.'

Mother was true to her word and I took a package containing the leather devices along to the King's Private Office. Mother had written a number on each so that the King did not have the embarrassment of returning one that had, as it were, been 'worn'. She included a note asking him to let us know if one of them fitted and, if so, its corresponding number. The following day, the Assistant Private Secretary came to see me. He said the King had a message for me. He said he was totally puzzled and that he had never before had to deliver a message like it. The message was simply the number 'five'. He uttered the number, said he hoped I would understand it, turned around and returned to the Private Office. Mother then made half a dozen of size five and I delivered them to the King.

The King had not remarried by then but, having recovered to some degree from the death of Elisabeth of Bourbon, made industrious use of his new found freedom. I never did establish who took over from Olivares in keeping the King supplied with women willing to satisfy his desires. The Count Duke Olivares was expelled from the palace in '43 after his incompetent handling of the revolts in Catalonia and Portugal. Those of us who made it our business to know about such matters noticed, despite Olivares's shamefaced departure, a steady stream of at least one sweetly attired paramour a day being escorted to the King's private apartments.

Most were actresses but some were courtesans who were fortunate enough to be invited to serve at the very highest level.

Evidently, the sheaths, which mother made, worked well, as far as the King was concerned because, not many months after we had provided them for His Majesty, various other palace dignitaries and officials, who for reasons of discretion shall remain nameless, approached me to ask if I could supply them with some. Obviously, the King, or the women who had entertained him, had spoken to others about the sheaths. I spoke to Francisca about these requests and we decided that we would discuss them with Francisco before talking to my mother about them. Francisco was very excited and suggested that we set up a small manufacturing facility and go into business making them. He suggested using other materials such as muslin or silk. His plan was that we rent a room, maybe behind a shop, and engage some women to make the sheaths, or covers, as he called them, and sell them in the markets and other shops in the town.

'Where would we get the money to set up as a business?' asked Francisca.

'I would be happy to invest some of my money in it. The demand could be colossal. What about you two?' he said, turning to me and Francisca.

'I think the idea is basically good but we don't know what the demand would be. I would prefer to be more cautious and start small. I can't think of a way we could find out the level of demand. Can you imagine going up to people in the street and explaining what the "covers" were for and asking them if they would buy them. How embarrassing!'

We all burst out laughing. Francisco who had been serious up to then also saw the amusing side of it. He suggested we all ponder the idea for a time and meet up again to talk it over further before seeking our mother's opinion.

***

I told the Maestro what the King had said about collaborating with Giulio Rospigliosi. He encouraged me, suggesting that there were many things on which we could engage him. We could write some music for one of his plays or ask him to identify a Spanish play for which he might want to write some music. Or, as Rospigliosi had suggested to me, we could provide the material for some songs. The Maestro insisted that I should discuss the final range of options with him because I would be using time working with Rospigliosi which otherwise would be available for entertaining the King. The Maestro could see no reason why Francisca and I should not invite the Archbishop of Toledo or Pedro Calderón de la Barca to our party.

I hardly knew Calderón de la Barca and had a slightly prickly meeting with him. I decided to see him at his office in the Buen Retiro. I remember seeing him a number of years before at Lope's funeral. He looked stern then and seemed daunting, as if he did not particularly wish to speak to those who were not fellow playwrights. He looked remarkably like Lope, almost as if he had adopted Lope's little beard and moustache as a symbol of his reverence for the great master. If so, he must have developed his admiration after Lope's funeral, when, among others, he refused to sign the book of condolence. I told him that our principal party guest would be the papal nuncio, Giulio Rospigliosi, who was a playwright and composer. He was cool towards the nuncio, saying that he, de la Barca, had heard nothing of his talents as either a writer or composer. However, he would give him the benefit of the doubt and be delighted to accept our invitation. I asked him whether he wished to bring a lady to accompany him. He tersely said, 'No, thank you.'

'It should be an interesting occasion,' he said after I told him who the other guests would be.

The party took place one pleasant evening in the Madrid summer. We decided to start late so as to allow the heat of the day to subside sufficiently for us to enjoy a reasonable level of comfort. The whole thing started frostily with the nuncio and Archbishop seeming awkward in each other's presence, which was odd. To begin with, Calderón de la Barca did not seem to want to speak to anyone but Diego Velázquez. Francisca and I dispensed some wine and that loosened a few tongues before the meal.

The only ones of our guests who had met before, apart from the Archbishop and the nuncio, were Diego and Calderón de la Barca. So we all agreed to introduce ourselves by saying a few words about our origins and what our work was and our connection with the King. We also agreed that we would all be on Christian-name terms. First, Francisca and I talked about ourselves, then Diego and Juana spoke.

It was then the turn of Pedro Calderón de la Barca. 'I regard myself primarily as a philosopher,' he said, with a certain degree of superiority. 'I am interested in the condition of man and how he interacts with the universe which he cannot possibly master. I reveal my thoughts through my plays. I have written a large number and they have almost all been performed in our town in our theatres. I am director of the court theatre at the Buen Retiro and that is where I spend most of my time. It is a salaried post.

'Until recently, I was also a soldier. I fought against the Catalan rebels. I resigned from military service in '42 after being badly wounded in battle at Constanti, near Tarragona. I almost died of my wounds but, mercifully, fully recovered. I was born into an old-established Castilian family of aristocrats. My mother was a noblewoman who was brought up in Flanders. Just like Juan, I went to the Jesuit Imperial School in the Calle de Toledo.

'I must tell you about something that happened back in '29. My brother Diego was involved in an argument with an actor. It was about a woman whom Diego had befriended. The actor, also an acquaintance of hers, became intensely jealous. The man murdered Diego by stabbing him with a knife. It was horrific. Several of us chased the man into the Convent of the Barefoot Trinitarians. Some of the nuns, including Lope's daughter, Sor Marcela, were injured in the fracas that broke out and I was arrested for assault and breaking and entering. I spent three days in the town prison before I was released without charge. So life has not always been so easy for me. It was an error to chase the man and not leave his arrest to the authorities. We live and learn. Fortunately, this had all been forgotten when the King made me a Knight of the Order of Santiago a few years ago.'

Giulio Rospigliosi followed Pedro but was much more humble about his background, almost embarrassed. 'I, too, happen to be from an aristocratic family. Mine is from Pistóia, in the Grand Duchy of Tuscany. Also like you, Pedro, I was educated by the Jesuits and, again like you, studied philosophy. This was at the University of Pisa where I took my doctorate.

'I came to Spain under the direction of Urban VIII, a controversial Pope of the Barberini Dynasty. He and I were close friends. He died in '44, the year I was sent here, and was succeeded by Innocent X who sent the most prominent Barberinis into exile. They went to Paris. I was lucky in that I was allowed to remain here as papal nuncio while this was happening. I enjoy writing and have written a number of plays and the libretti for two operas, both of which have been performed in Italy. I have also written quite a lot of poetry. I also compose music but I regard that as a minor pastime.'

Then it was the turn of the Archbishop, Baltasar Moscoso y Sandoval, who was definitely ashamed, about one of his relatives in particular. 'Likewise, I am from a noble background. My father was Count of Altamira, Cantabria and my mother was the sister of the infamous Duke of Lerma, the First Minister to King Philip III. His corruption was boundless and, as you will know, he amassed a huge fortune much of which was confiscated after the king expelled him from this post. None of the family liked this self-promoting scoundrel.

'My education took a totally different path from yours, Juan, Giulio and Pedro. I was educated in the college of San Salvador de Oviedo in

Salamanca. I then did both a degree and a doctorate in canon law at Sigüenza, near Guadalajara. I became rector at the college of San Salvador de Oviedo before I graduated and canon in the cathedral of Toledo just before I received my doctorate. Like you, Diego, I've spent some time in Italy, Rome in particular. That was in '30 to '33 so we must both have been there at the same time, at least for some of our stay there.

'I became Archbishop fairly recently and have spent much of my time bringing the Holy See of Toledo back to a semblance of order, after its neglect by the Cardinal Infante Ferdinand. My predecessor, Gaspar de Borja and Velasco, started this work but there was still much left to be done when Gaspar died in '45.'

There was so much that had been said which was of interest to all of us that we nearly all jumped in with a question after the Archbishop had finished. Diego asked the first one. 'Tell me Baltasar, why did you visit Rome? I am intrigued.'

'I went on a diplomatic mission, instigated by the King, to see His Holiness Pope Urban VIII. The King was aware that the Pope had supported the Protestants in the War in Europe. He had discovered, for example, that Urban VIII had sided with the Swede, Gustafus Adolfus, in the fight against the Spanish and Hungarians. He wanted the Pope to change his position and support Spain and its allies. The Pope was furious when we confronted him with this and denied that he had gone beyond his position of neutrality. However, by way of compensation for this misunderstanding, as he put it, the Pope made one million *ducats* available from the Vatican Treasury to support the Spanish war effort.'

'So you must have enjoyed the confidence of the King for him to send you on such a mission,' said Pedro. 'Did you go alone?'

'No. I went with Gaspar de Borja y Velasco when he was Cardinal. We both had an audience with Urban VIII in speaking on behalf of the King. I have to say that Gaspar was not particularly diplomatic with His Holiness who was so angry with him that he refused to endorse him as Archbishop of Toledo. He had to wait until the death of Urban VIII when Pope Innocent X confirmed him as Archbishop, only shortly before poor Gaspar died.'

'I am surprised that there was so much that needed doing after the death of the Cardinal Infante,' I said. 'Why didn't the other bishops keep the See of Toledo in good order while the Cardinal Infante was Governor of the Spanish Netherlands?'

'That is a good question,' said the Archbishop. 'You know they say that "while the cat is away the mice will play". That is exactly what happened. The priests and bishops had a wonderful time while the Cardinal Infante wasn't there. They engaged themselves in all kinds of corruption and indulgence. Many of the nuns and women in Toledo became pregnant by these philanderers. This is not to say they were all bad eggs but many simply could not resist temptation. What made matters worse was that the post of Archbishop of Toledo remained vacant for four years after the death of the Cardinal Infante. It has taken a massive effort for us to get back the confidence of our people.'

'Tell me about your operas, Giulio,' Pedro said. 'When did you write them?'

'I wrote "Saint Alexis" in '32 and "Let He who Suffers Hope" in '36.'

'Come on Giulio, tell us about them. What are the plots?' said Francisca, just a bit impatiently.

'They are both very simple. Saint Alexis lived in the fifth century and went on a pilgrimage to the Holy Land. He lived a life of poverty and kept his identity a secret when he returned as a beggar to his father's house. Not even his wife recognised him. It was only when he died that his identity was revealed.'

'What about the second opera?' asked Diego.

'This is a totally different plot. It is a love story. Egisto falls in love with a widow, Alvida. She rejects his advances and he becomes so distraught he destroys his pet falcon and a tower he inherits from his father. The widow is so impressed with the strength of his love that she gives in and marries him. They find buried treasure in the ruins of the tower and a heliotrope growing there. Alvida uses the heliotrope to cure her ailing son. Another woman falls in love with Egisto. She threatens to kill herself when he rejects her in favour of Alvida. It turns out, to everyone's astonishment, that the woman, who comes to Egisto in disguise, is his own sister.'

'How good are you as a composer?' asked Pedro, looking at Giulio.

'I compose only as a pastime. I've set some of my poems to music but I keep my compositions private and only my friends know that I write music. None of it has ever been performed.'

'I ask only because I want a composer to help me with the music for a play I am writing. To be performed at Corpus Christi. Juan, might you be interested?'

'Interested? I'd be only too pleased to compose for you. What a collaboration. The King's composer and the King's playwright, working together. If you really are interested, I'll ask my boss, Maestro Patiño.'

'Juan, I want you to work with me. Yes, please ask the Maestro.' So we were on the verge of a collaboration.

'What is the subject of your Corpus Christi play, Diego?' asked Juana.

'I am still working on the plot but I am thinking of the way the lore of the New Testament has taken over from the Old. I am wondering about something allegorical that personifies this change. There is much work to do on it yet. In case this play does not work out to my satisfaction, I have a couple of other ideas. One is to have the Virgin Mary making furniture in Joseph the carpenter's shop. She becomes pregnant and he gets very upset not knowing who the father could be.'

'As soon as I see the Maestro, I'll ask him if I can work with you.'

'One point you could make is that the King has commissioned the play so, if you can write the music, you will be working for the King, as you are now,' said Pedro.

'One topic we have not dealt with is how we can help Giulio,' I said. 'He wants to do some work with us, maybe by composing something or writing a play.'

'Yes, Juan. That's right. I want to write something that has a Spanish flavour that I can take back to Italy and have performed there. I was thinking of writing a libretto, or two maybe, based on a Spanish *comedia*. If I can produce the libretto I can easily find a composer in Italy to write the score. I don't want to score it as well.'

'I am sure we can help with that,' said Pedro. 'Don't you agree, Juan? There are hundreds of *comedias* to choose from.'

'Yes, I'm certain,' I said.

'On a different subject, I painted Gaspar de Borja y Velasco, some years ago when he was Cardinal,' said Diego. 'I have painted Juan and Francisca's portraits. I wonder about painting yours, Baltasar, or Giulio's or yours, Pedro?'

'Why not all three,' said Juana, enthusiastically. 'You men have certainly made some work for each other, while we have been enjoying Francisca and Juan's hospitality.'

The party ended at about two a.m. It had, by any measure, been a success. After a shaky start, we had all got on well with each other. It seemed that a number of collaborative projects would emerge, from painting portraits through writing librettos to composing music for a Corpus Christi play. I really took to Giulio, who was a modest and likeable man. I was less sure about Pedro, who seemed haughty and remote but I was looking forward to working with him and regarded his complex character as a challenge.

***

Francisca, Francsico and I met again to discuss the possible manufacture of the 'covers'. We started by changing the name to 'tubes' which seemed a more accurate description. Francisco said he had a few ideas about testing the demand for such a device. To begin with, he thought we should ask the lady who sold mother's purses in the market in the Plazuela de Selenque. Then we could try one or two of the houses of pleasure in the Calle de Arganzuela, just off the southern end of the Calle de Toledo. Francisco said he would make the visit and I said I would see mother's customer in the market. The plans were to be followed through, only if mother agreed.

Mother was quite enthusiastic saying that, if necessary, she would invest some of her inheritance from father's estate in the project. She said that she would want to see a detailed plan before committing any of the money but thought that demand would be huge. 'After all, not everybody makes love solely for the purpose of procreation,' she said, sagely. She would be more than willing to instruct anyone we employed to manufacture the 'tubes' on how they should be made. She even offered to write a little instruction manual with diagrams. She said she did not want to be involved in managing the facility we might set up. She might be interested in the sales side of the operation but did not want to decide at that early stage.

We all agreed that we needed to know what the potential demand would be and I said that I would test out her customer at the market stall, if Francisco explained the idea at a house of pleasure. Both of us would take some of the tubes mother had made so that these potential customers could see what they would be getting. We also agreed that we would sell them for about eight *maravedis* a piece, the price of a large loaf of bread. The sellers to the public could charge a price which would reflect their profit.

Francisco had no qualms about visiting the brothel at the top of the Calle de Arganzuela. In fact he took a certain amount of vicarious pleasure from it. He went at night to minimize the risk of being recognized and took some sample tubes, including one our mother had made for him. As he approached the establishment, he felt less brazen about going in and stopped on the opposite side of the road to observe the premises. There was a dribble of men surreptitiously going in and another trickle embarrassingly coming out. He decided that he had had enough of waiting, plucked up his courage and entered.

It was dark inside and oil lamps provided the sole means of illumination. The furnishings were spartan, as if it was one of those places that served only the lower end of the market. The floors were bare stones with loose dirt filling the gaps between them. The walls in the entrance hall were bare. Inside there was a sweet smell, a mixture of rose petal oil, ambergris and cedar wood. He was greeted in the hallway by the madame, a plump, black-haired lady wearing a red skirt and a white top that exposed a huge area of the cleavage between her large, drooping breasts. She looked as if she had been one of the ladies herself in the past but had since taken to managing the place. 'What can we do for you, love? Anything you particularly fancy? Anything goes here, ya know.'

'I have come here to show you a product, which I and my business partners are thinking of making. We wondered if it may be of interest to you.'

She escorted Francisco past a number of side rooms, from which he could hear the various sounds of the business being transacted, into a shabby office which again had a bare stone floor, a desk strewn with cash and some papers, as if she had been recording the takings in her accounts, a single bed covered with a white mattress and a couple of rickety-looking, wooden chairs. The only adornments were four explicit, framed, line drawings mounted on the otherwise bare walls, each showing a young, naked woman performing a sex act with a partly dressed man. Each act was different. 'Well, spit it out, love. What's this contraption ya wan' a sell us?'

'It's a tube made of pigskin. It fits over the man's member and prevents the woman he is making love to from becoming pregnant.'

'So the bloke puts it over 'is cock does he? 'Ow does it stay on? All that shaggin' movement and the damn thing soon falls off, I bet.'

'No, madame. It's held on by a ribbon that threads through some holes around the base.'

''Ave you got any with ya? Show me what they're like.'

'Yes, here are some of various sizes.'

'Christ. Look at the size of that one. You'd need the cock of a horse to fit into that. I wan' a demonstration. Get yours out, mister, get it up and put one on.'

For nothing more than the sake of the project, Francisco dropped his pantaloons and began to stimulate himself but his member would not respond. ''Ere, 'ave a look at this,' said the woman as she lifted her skirt, sat on a chair, opened her legs wide and, totally without inhibition, showed him her parts.

'That's better,' said Francisco.

'Fuckin' 'ell,' she said, looking directly at his member. 'I pity the poor tart who 'as to put that in 'erself. That would make 'er eyes water.'

Francisco put the tube on. He had previously oiled it to make it easier. Still seated and exposed, the madame responded. 'That's blinkin' good, that is.' She then shouted out at the top of her voice, 'Mimi, come and 'ave a look at this!'

A beautiful young blonde woman appeared, dressed in nothing but a small white towel which barely covered her charms. It was as if she had just emerged from a bath, except that she was bone dry. 'Mimi is French, love.

She's got a class body and is one of me most popular girls. She can do anything for the punters. Take your towel off and show 'im yer wares.' Mimi dropped the towel to reveal her shapely young body.

'See that thing on 'is cock. It's a "tube" 'e calls it. It stops ya from becoming pregnant. I want to see it tested. D'ya think you could get that inside ya.'

'I think it will be easy,' said Mimi, in a false French accent as she went to lie down on her back. Francisco, still ready, entered her – without the use of olive oil – and in his characteristic fashion hung on for about five minutes with the madame stooping down, turning her head to and fro and up and down to get the best possible view as she watched the proceedings closely, looking in particular at what was happening to the tube. He lifted himself off after he had finished and the madame could not believe that the tube was still secured in place.

'Tell me,' she asked, ''ave you filled the thing?'

'Yes, madame, it is now full.'

'Marvelous,' she said. 'I'll buy 360 of all different sizes. When can I 'ave 'em?'

'As soon as I can get them to you,' said Francisco, smiling inwardly at his success. 'I'll take that as a definite order. They'll be about eight *maravedís* a piece.'

Meanwhile, our mother had decided to see her customer at the market stall in the Plazuela de Selenque, rather than to allow me to go. She explained the tube to the woman and put one over her finger to demonstrate its purpose. The poor woman all but collapsed in waves of uncontrolled laughter. 'You've got to be joking, señora.'

'No. I'm as serious as the Pope. They will prevent the woman becoming pregnant. Are you interested in selling some?'

'The more I think of it, the better the idea becomes. I'm just wondering if I'd be embarrassed but maybe I wouldn't. I'm married, after all, so I've seen it all before. Yes, señora, I'd sell them. How much would you charge?'

'We were thinking of about eight *maravedís* each. They are reusable. They just need washing and drying after use and they are ready for the next time.'

'Not bad value,' said the stall holder. 'I'll take three dozen, if only to give them a try.'

Francisca, Francisco, our mother and I met up after our market exploration. Mother could not wait to report her success at selling three dozen of the tubes. She was so excited by her success she was almost disappointed to hear that Francisco had virtually sold 360 to the brothel at the top of the Calle de Arganzuela. 'How are we going to make that number?' she asked.

'We need to find a room somewhere and engage someone to make them. I reckon we could sell five hundred or more a week without a huge effort,' said Francisco, confidently.

'I wonder about asking Barbola, our cleaner,' said Francisca. 'She's always talking about finding other ways of earning money. She only does a few hours a week now for Esmeralda Pechada who has all but given up her lessons. She is over seventy now.'

'Brilliant. We can ask Barbola. Can you ask her, Juan or Francisca?'

'I'll ask her,' said Francisca, chuckling. 'It might be less embarrassing for me.'

'Why can't we start by making them in my house?' said mother. 'It seems silly to hire a room somewhere when all we need is the space for one or two women to do the cutting and sewing. I'll do some of the work myself. I can still sew quickly enough for this.'

'By the way,' said Francisca. 'On a completely different subject, Juan has agreed that I should tell both of you that I am expecting a baby which is due in six months time'

'What fantastic news,' said Francisco. 'Congratulations to you both.'

Our mother was overcome by this sudden revelation and immediately burst into tears. 'If only your father could have known, Juan. He would be so pleased to have a grandson.'

'But you could have a grandson yourself, Mamá. So you have every reason to be happy.'

'I am happy, Juan. That's why I am crying,' she said, wiping her eyes with the bottom edge of her pinafore.

Barbola agreed to help make the tubes. She was delighted that she would have more money and was pleased to be part of our new business venture. The money would be useful to her because her daughter, Melchora, was then twenty years old and about to be married. Mother arranged to buy a large quantity of the pigskin leather from her supplier and we were in business. Francisco made some templates out of wood so we could standardize on the sizes. Size five would be King size but that detail would be shared only with those who worked in our little enterprise.

We calculated that a competent needlewoman could do the sewing necessary to make six tubes an hour, say about fifty a day. So within eight days of sewing we would have enough to satisfy our first two orders. Mother cut out the pigskin to Francisco's templates and did some sewing herself. So just over a week after we took the original orders, we were able to make our first two deliveries, which Francisco made in person.

A day or two later, we all met again to discuss what to do next. We wondered whether we should hold back from making any more until we had some idea of how satisfied our customers were with what we had already delivered. We agreed that we should continue to make the tubes on the assumption that they would be popular with the customers. Sure enough, they were. Within two weeks of our satisfying their first orders, both the brothel and the market stall came back for more. So we made them some more and I took some to the palace to sell them to those who had asked me for them.

The madame at the brothel wrote to Francisco to ask for a meeting. It turned out that she wanted to offer us a substantial amount of money, provided we would sell them exclusively to her brothel. Francisco discussed this offer with us and we refused to take it up. It was far too early in the development of the business to agree to such a deal. It soon became apparent why the madame had made this request. Within a week of her doing so, we had requests from five other houses of pleasure in the Calle de Arganzuela for some tubes. Within four months of starting the business, we had engaged two other women besides the redoubtable Barbola, whom we put in charge of the other two. We were making almost a thousand tubes a week. Business was booming. We wondered where it would all end.

CHAPTER 20

'Juan, Juan, I think I'm having the baby!' Francisca shrieked, on the verge of panic. 'I keep getting these bursts of pain which go and come back again.' She woke me up and broke the news to me at five o'clock in the morning of 10 January '48. We had a midwife standing by but she was not expecting a knock on her front door at ten past five in the morning. She appeared in a long nightshirt, holding a lit candle in a holder. 'I'll get dressed straight away. Come inside and wait for five minutes.'

Francisca was writhing in pain on our bed when the midwife and I returned. 'I can't stand this, Juan. The pain is unbearable. I didn't expect this.'

'My love, the midwife is here. She will make it easier for you. I will stay until the baby is born.'

'I don't want you here, so go to work as usual,' said the midwife. 'First though, you can boil up some water over a fire and find some clean towels.'

I did as I was told and then stood or sat in the drawing room as the midwife tended to Francisca in our bedroom. It all took me back to the day Francisco was born, nearly thirty years before. I just hoped Francisca had an easier birth than mother did with Francisco. Eventually, I went up to kiss her before I departed to the palace. 'There is nothing you can do here. You'll be a father when you come home from work. When will that be?' asked the midwife.

'I'll get back around siesta time, at about two o'clock this afternoon.'

I usually worked through the siesta but would ask the Maestro if I could come home early that day. I just could not concentrate while at the palace. 'Juan, you should go back home. You are no use here. I'll get your brother to play for the King this morning. Have you told him about Francisca?'

I had simply forgotten about mother and Francisco. 'I'll go and tell him now and ask him to substitute for me, if you wish.'

'Yes, Juan. Please do.'

I spoke to Francisco and then took the Maestro's advice and left but instead of going straight home I walked to mother's house. Barbola, her two assistants and mother were there, all working furiously on the next batch of love tubes. Mother was surprised to see me and I blurted out my news to her. She knew Francisca was almost ready to give birth, so the fact that she was in labour was no surprise. 'Juan, you should be at home, not here.'

'I know, Mamá, but there is a strong-willed midwife with Francisca and I've been banished from the house until the siesta.'

'You'd better stay here then. If you want something to do, get the girls here a cup of water. They will probably appreciate a drink. I would, for sure.'

I filled some cups from a large jug mother kept in a cupboard in the kitchen and supplied the women with a drink. It was odd to see Barbola working in mother's house instead of ours. 'What do you think of the work?' I asked her, looking for something to take my mind off Francisca's plight.

'We all like it, Juan. It's different and needs some skill. The seams have to be sewn properly. Otherwise the love tube won't work as it should. The money is good and we don't feel exploited, do we girls?'

The two assistants were about the same age as Barbola who was about five years older than me, I guessed. All three of them seemed happy in their work. In unison, the two assistants agreed with Barbola. One of them, a very tall girl with jet-black hair, said how nice it was to be working with a group of women. They could gossip all day and enjoy some laughter. After all, they were making objects of pleasure and if they couldn't enjoy a giggle about them there was something wrong somewhere. The other, a woman with a red face and a little more round in shape, remarked that it was good to be working with my mother who obviously cared for her workers.

Although it was pleasant to chat to the women, I could not get Francisca out of my mind. I kept looking at the clock on the wall in the kitchen and that made the time pass even more slowly. By midday, I could stand no more and decided to go home. I walked inside the house and there was not a sound from anywhere. I wondered if the midwife had admitted Francisca into a local hospital. I ran up to our bedroom and knocked gently on the door.

'Come in quietly,' said the midwife. I entered. 'You are the father of a little boy.' Francisca was asleep and had her arm around a little bundle she was holding to her chest. The baby was also asleep. 'Your son arrived about three hours after you went. Your wife had a normal birth and everything is fine. Congratulations.'

The sight of Francisca and our new baby son brought tears of joy and pride to my eyes. This was one of the best, if not the best, moment of my life. 'I am a father now. I am responsible for this little scrap of humanity as well as my lovely Francisca,' I thought as I watched over them, almost in a dream. 'I shall look after the pair of them for the rest of my life and make sure they are safe and have the very best in their lives that we can afford.'

'I'll have to go now,' said the midwife, bringing me back to a different reality. 'I will probably have another two to deliver today.'

I thanked her for all her help and saw her out of the house, only to return to my treasures in our bedroom. They were still asleep so I left them and went downstairs to prepare myself some food. I still hadn't eaten that day. I returned to the bedroom every half an hour or so and within a few hours Francisca was awake. 'God, Juan, I feel so elated but exhausted at the same time. Look at our son!'

'I saw him a few hours ago, Francisca. He is beautiful. I love him already. I love you, you clever angel. Well done!'

He was still asleep. 'It was hard work for him as well as for me,' said Francisca. 'He is exhausted, too.'

'I'll leave you here resting, Francisca. Is there anything you want?'

'A glass of water, please.'

I took her some. We sat together with the baby. 'Well,' I said. 'Here begins the next chapter of our life together.'

'I'll drink to that,' she said, sipping at the water.

***

True to his word, the King convened a meeting of all his special agents. I felt nervous. I had never attended a meeting like this before. It was chaired by his Ministerial Head of the Council for State Security. The King never chaired these meetings but always attended. We all gathered in the Council Chamber at the palace. There were fewer present than I expected: I imagined that there would be upwards of 200 special agents but in fact there were exactly sixty. That was the maximum number and this was maintained. A replacement was appointed as soon as somebody died, resigned or was expelled. I wondered who had been appointed to replace my father. The only woman there was Esmeralda Pechada de Burgos. Diego was also there.

The King said that the meeting would consider the recommendations of a sub-committee, comprising members of both the Council of Finance and the Council for State Security. He said he had declared the country bankrupt only a year ago and desperate measures were now needed to secure our country's future. We would need about ten million *ducats* to escape from the mire of bankruptcy, as he put it. One option was to steal from the treasury of another state. The sub-committee had recommended that we attack and rob the Vatican. There were other options but this was the most attractive for a number of reasons. The first was the element of surprise. No Pope would expect to be attacked by Spain, one of his principal allies.

Second, there was reason to think that the Vatican was less secure than some of the other national treasuries. Third, the King wanted to hit back at the Pope for siding with the French in the European War. However, an attack on the Vatican would not mean declaring war. We would mount a highly organised operation in which we would simply remove ten million *ducats* from the Vatican. There were some logistical problems, as he said, but this meeting had been convened with the aim of clarifying them and taking measures to overcome them.

There was no discussion of the other options. The King had decided on an attack on the Vatican. At that time, I did not know whether the decision had been taken before or after my conversation with him. The King asked the Ministerial Head of the Council to explain how the attack should take place.

'Gentlemen and lady, the exact situation is that, at present, we have insufficient information on mounting the attack. There are some practical considerations that will have to be overcome. Ten million *ducats* weigh thirty-eight *toneladas*, that is 76,000 *libras*. There is therefore the problem of transporting it. We are not certain of its exact location. We know that there is a coinage store in the Vatican but we don't know where it is. We will use men from our infantry to carry out the attack. They will be dressed as civilians. They will travel to Genoa by sea and overland to Rome. This will also be their return route. We have therefore only a sketch of a plan and there is much detail to fill in before we can carry out the attack.'

The King resumed. 'This is where we will need some of you to help us, gentlemen and lady. I want a small group of you to go to Rome, via Genoa, to collect intelligence on the problem so that we can fully develop the plan. I would prefer some of you to volunteer and I am looking for two of you. I don't want to have to compel anyone to go. I believe that whoever volunteers would be away for about three months. All expenses will be paid and the level of comfort throughout the journey will be the best available.

'The visit will take place in two months' time. Those who go will be accompanied by Giulio Rospigliosi, the papal nuncio, who will not be made aware of our intentions. Those who are not special agents will be told that the members of our small group are on a cultural visit. Giulio Rospigliosi has been instructed to attend a briefing meeting with Pope Innocent X and that is why he is going. If any of you wish to volunteer, please contact the Chief Clerk of the Council for State Security, Alvaro Gutierro de Marchena. Does anyone have any questions?'

'Your, Majesty,' said one of those attending. 'I thought that the Vatican under Urban VIII and Innocent X was in a desperate financial state and had to borrow money to pay the priests and to finish some of Urban VIII's extravagant projects. Do they have ten million *ducats*?'

'Yes. They certainly do, at least according to our limited intelligence. Taking out the loans is a cover designed to hide their wealth. They pay the interest from taxes they charge the rest of us.'

'How are we going to move thirty-eight *toneladas* of gold coins? We will need an army.'

'Not necessarily. We have yet to work out a strategy for moving the money but first we need to locate it. If it takes an army we have an army.'

From another: 'Why is the Archbishop of Toledo here? His loyalty is to the Catholic Church, not to the finances of Spain.'

'No. The Archbishop is here because he knows his way around the Vatican. He is a Spaniard and is one of our greatest allies. We need him. If you know someone else we could use instead, I would be grateful to know,' said the King.

There were no other questions so the Ministerial Head of the Council declared the meeting closed.

***

'What are we going to call our little baby, Juan?'

'What about calling him after your father, Domingo? It's a lovely name.'

'No. I don't want him to be called after my father. It will remind me of mother too much.'

'What about naming him after Diego? He would be overwhelmed with delight.'

'No, Juan. I want to call him Juan, after his father.'

'That will be so confusing, Francisca. We will have two Juans in the same house. Mind you, if you call for Juan, you should get at least one of us replying!'

'I really want to call him Juan, Juan.'

'Francisca, my angel, we will call him Juan. Maybe we call him little Juan when he is small and Juan junior when he is bigger. I agree that we should give him the name you like best. Mind you, I might want first choice if we have another child!'

So we called our baby, Juan.

***

On my way home, I wondered about volunteering for the mission to Italy. I was interested for several reasons. Because Giulio would be going, the visit would give me an opportunity to get to know him better. It would also give me a chance to hear some Italian music and that could help the future development of music in the Royal Chapel. But most importantly, I felt I owed something to the King. He had helped me in my career and I wanted to repay him. I pondered how I would put the idea to Francisca. The complications were the arrival of our new baby and, of course, that I could not reveal to Francisca that I was a special agent.

'Francisca, I have a difficult question for you.' I explained it all to her.

'Juan, you have taken me by surprise. I don't know what to think. I would miss you terribly and the baby is so young. I need time to think about this.'

'I would make sure you had some help in looking after baby Juan. I was thinking of engaging a maid for a time. She would assist you with baby Juan and help Barbola with the house. I'm sure mother and Juana would be delighted to help you, if you wanted them to do so. What do you think?'

We discussed the visit several times and Francisca eventually agreed that I should go. I was pleased because I had decided, although I had not said as much to her, that I would not volunteer unless she fully supported me. We decided that we would, if necessary, engage our full network of friends and relatives to help her and baby Juan while I was away. Exactly a week after the meeting, I informed the Chief Clerk that I was volunteering for the mission. 'The King will be delighted, Señor Hidalgo. You are the only one of the available special agents who works with the papal nuncio. So you have an excellent chance of being selected, if it is not a certainty already. If I were you, I would assume you will go.'

What the Chief Clerk said made me think. Could I influence events? I was aware that my colleague Juan de Roxas Carrión was also a special agent. He had accepted this position some five years or so before. We had never discussed the fact because there were no issues to discuss, but I had once seen him in the outer office of the Council for State Security, looking at a briefing paper. I thought he was also at the meeting which the King had convened but I was not sure. I wondered if he might be interested in volunteering, especially if he knew I had. It would be easier if those who went already knew each other in advance. A day or so later, I asked him.

'Yes, Juan, I was at the meeting the other day. But no, I cannot go to Italy. I am too busy here in the palace. I have many performances to give over the coming months. The Maestro would be most upset to lose both of us.'

'You are making decisions that others above us have to make. If the Maestro doesn't want to lose both of us, I'm sure he will say. There are other violinists in the Royal Chapel and none of us is indispensible.'

'I suppose you have a point, Juan. I must say, I was attracted to the idea when the King mentioned it at the meeting. I could not imagine then who would go with the nuncio. But if you and I went we would learn so much about the Italian style of music. It could help us in the future.'

'Exactly. You are in a better position than I. You are single and have no immediate family commitments. I'd love you to go as well as me. If you volunteer, as I already have, I think we will both have a good chance of being selected. Have you met Rospigliosi? He is a very likeable man and would make a good travelling companion. He is so interested in music and theatre. He has written several plays.'

'No. I haven't met him but I will need to, if I am selected. I'll definitely volunteer.' Once he had reached this conclusion, the exuberant Juan de Roxas could not stop telling me where we would go, what we would see and what we would learn in our visit to the Vatican. I was sure that he would be excellent company, if we were chosen for this extraordinary mission.

Within about two weeks of offering ourselves as volunteers, Juan de Roxas Carrión and I were selected. Juan bounced around with excitement. My feelings were mixed, a combination of delight, apprehension and concern about how Francisca would manage in my absence. Her reaction was positive and reassuring and she said she would help me with the necessary preparation. We told our friends about the visit and all offered to assist Francisca with baby Juan while I was away.

There was a particular piece of business to which I had to attend before I departed. I explained to Pedro Calderón de la Barca that I would not be officially available to compose the score for his Corpus Christi play until I returned from Italy but that, if he could provide the text before I left, I could probably make good headway with the work while I was on the journey. He said he would do his best to complete at least one act and give that to me before I went. I agreed to his request that, if he managed to complete the first act, we would meet so that he could explain what form he thought the music should take.

About a week after I had been informed that I was to go to Italy, that is, about a month after the meeting of the sub-committee, the Chief Clerk of the Council for State Security, Alvaro Gutierro de Marchena, called me in to see him. He told me that the King had asked him to give me some pertinent instructions. The first was that I would be responsible for the King's part of the mission. This meant that I would be Juan de Roxas's boss for the duration of the trip. Giulio Rospigliosi would be responsible for his own actions.

The crucial instruction was, however, that I should be party to compromising Giulio Rospigliosi with some women. He explained in detail how it would work. Esmeralda Pechada de Burgos would invite me and Rospigliosi to a small, private reception at her house in the Calle de Santa Clara. It would be held in a fortnight's time, two weeks before we were to depart for Italy. Several high-class women of pleasure would be at the reception. Esmeralda and I would arrange for Rospigliosi to drink an excess of alcohol and he would be forced to become involved in an intimate session with the women. He would, when he recovered, be in the company of both women who would be naked and still caressing him. He would become intensely embarrassed by these events and would not, at any cost, want the Vatican to know about them for fear of prejudicing his future career as a prelate.

That I was expected to treat my new friend Giulio in this devious way infuriated me. It was dishonourable, preposterous and totally against my standards of conducting business. I had never before felt such antipathy towards the King. He must have believed that I would, by volunteering or by compulsion, join the group to travel to Italy, otherwise, why would he ask me to befriend Giulio? I could now see why: so that I would be in a position to compromise him. And I seriously doubted that the King had told me the whole truth: the decision to rob the Vatican was surely taken before the meeting in which he asked me to help him. Giulio was going to Rome, not to London, Paris or The Hague. 'Señor Gutierro, I simply cannot do that to my friend. It's impossible. It's an outrageous thing to expect me to do. Why do you want me to do it?'

'Are you naïve, Señor Hidalgo? We want you to use the position of the papal nuncio to obtain what we presume will be confidential information about the exact location of the ten million gold *ducats*. Rospigliosi will be able to help you. Should he be disinclined to do so, you will threaten to reveal to the senior cardinals in the Vatican his activities with these women. Esmeralda Pechada de Burgos has agreed to provide you with a sworn testimony of what will have happened and give it to you to take to Rome. Obviously, if you can obtain the information we require, without having to threaten Rospigliosi, then so much the better. However, it is the King's view that we need to proceed in the way I have described. I repeat, it is the King's view.'

'If it is the King's idea to compromise the nuncio, why can he not engage the nuncio himself with some women? Why involve me?'

'Simple. You will be a witness and you will be going to Rome. If the authorities in Rome have any doubts about the authenticity of the testimony that Esmeralda Pechada will provide, they can ask you. You will be a witness to the nuncio's session with the women. He will know that you have been there and won't be able to deny it.'

'May I register in the strongest terms my objection to being party to compromising the nuncio?'

'Yes, but what do you expect me to do about it? Are you refusing to follow these instructions? If so, you could be dismissed from your position as special agent and might well prejudice your position as harpist and composer to the King.'

'Let's be clear then, for the purpose of dealing with my own conscience. I have no choice but to obey.' My anger must have been obvious.

'You have understood perfectly, Señor Hidalgo.'

'What happens next?' I asked, with deliberate bluntness.

'You will receive an invitation from Esmeralda Pechada de Burgos to attend a reception at her house in honour of those going on the King's mission to Rome. You will accept the invitation and go to the reception. We will convince the nuncio that he should attend. I would be grateful if you don't mention the forthcoming invitation to him. If, once he has received it, he asks you about it, you simply encourage him to go. After all, you will be going, too. It's simple isn't it?'

I felt trapped like a rabbit in the talons of an eagle. I had to comply. I understood fully what was happening. As the state was to rob the Vatican, someone had to obtain the necessary intelligence. That person was me. I would need every means at my disposal to secure this information, even moral blackmail. That was what I had been inveigled into doing, if it became necessary.

I opened Esmeralda's invitation in front of Francisca. I told her that I had expected such an invitation and felt it was an honour of sorts. 'But she is a retired whore. What has she got to do with the King's mission? How does she know about it?'

'I don't know, my love, but I feel I have to attend. After all, I am one of only three of us on the mission to Rome.'

Francisca was finding all of this difficult to understand and to cope with. 'Fine, Juan. You attend if you feel you have to. I trust you implicitly but I would rather it was not Esmeralda sending out the invitations.'

'Don't worry, my love. She is well over seventy now and won't be interested in offering me any further education,' I said, attempting to make jest of it.

Before I departed for the reception, I warned Francisca that I could be late home and suggested she did not wait up for me.

There were about forty people in attendance, many of whom I knew. The Maestro was there, so was Francisco de Guypúzcoa, Juan de Roxas Carrión, Diego, Pedro Calderón de la Barca, Alonso Arias de Soria and several other colleagues from the Royal Chapel and elsewhere in the palace. Other than Esmeralda and a waitress, there were no women there, at least not at the start of the reception.

After the waitress had passed around with glasses of wine, Alvaro Gutierro de Marchena made a short speech. 'Esmeralda and gentlemen, as you know, the papal nuncio and your colleagues, Juan Hidalgo and Juan Roxas de Carrión, are about to embark on a short cultural visit to Italy. Italy has made many advances in the field of sung music and has developed the concept of opera, a play in which all the words are sung. My friend Giulio Rospigliosi is going to meet the Pope but the King has asked Giulio to ensure that our two colleagues learn about and are entertained by some of the delights of the new Italian operas. I would like to propose a toast to these intrepid gentlemen who are about to embark on this journey.'

'So we will be specifically learning about the new art form,' I thought. 'Interesting.'

More drinks were served and two more waitresses appeared, serving food from large silver platters to all of those at the reception, who by then were chatting to each other in Esmeralda's upstairs drawing room. The food was delicious. Not only did we have Spanish *tapas*, of all imaginable kinds, but also samples of Italian dishes, which were mainly enclosed in pasta of various shapes and sizes. These two maids appeared with yet more food and I could swear that, while they served the previous round of delights, they were wearing blouses that fully covered their upper bodies, virtually to the neck. By the second round, they had changed their tops to something much more revealing that only just contained their firm, round breasts.

'Were these the ladies of pleasure who were to be used to compromise Giulio?' I asked myself. They were both beautiful young women of no more than twenty-five years of age. They both wore their hair long and were made up with rouge and face powder. Both were dressed in identical, patterned skirts decorated with tiny orange and red flowers printed on the fabric. They were so similar in appearance they could have been twins.

'Did you see that?' asked Juan de Roxas. 'Those women are showing their nipples in those blouses.'

'No,' I replied. 'They are revealing but I didn't see that much.'

'One of them bent over to put some food on a plate. And her breasts all but fell out of her blouse. Who are they? Do you know?'

'No, Juan,' I said. 'I've no idea.' But, of course, I had a very good idea.

The waitress who served the drinks passed around again and we took yet more. I saw the nuncio lift one from her tray as he was talking to Pedro. Then I saw him discreetly pour the contents of the glass into a pot containing a large, flowering, tropical plant. 'Good,' I thought. 'We will have trouble compromising him if he's sober.'

I could not resist renewing my acquaintance with Esmeralda, so I crossed the floor, passing little clusters of her conversing guests, to talk to her. She was wearing a stunning green-patterned dress, tied with a golden fabric bow, beneath her still ample bosom. She was proudly displaying the cleavage I remember admiring all those years ago and right in the centre was a large emerald pendant, suspended from a delicate gold neck chain. I imagined it was the one made by Francisca's friend Antonia Rodríguez. 'Do you remember me, Esmeralda? I am Juan Hidalgo, son of Antonio Hidalgo, the guitarist.'

'Of course I remember you, Juan. I remember you coming to see me when you were a young man. I worked on your education a little. Then, sadly, I came to your father's funeral. How is your mother now? I've heard of her new love tube business. They are catching on well, it seems. I hope she makes a fortune.'

'That emerald pendant, Esmeralda, was it made by Antonia Rodríguez?'

'Why do you ask, Juan?'

'I am curious. Antonia is a friend of my wife Francisca and she makes jewellery. She mentioned once that she had made a large emerald pendant in a gold clasp. She said she made it for a beautiful woman and I wondered if the lady was you.'

'You do flatter me,' she chuckled. 'I can solve your mystery. Yes, Juan, this is the pendant Antonia made. Are you looking forward to your journey to Italy?'

'I suppose I am. I shall miss Francisca and our little baby but I think it will be such an adventure.'

The reception seemed to be going well. However, no one expected the waitresses to be so blasé in exposing their charms and I am sure some of the guests wondered what might be the next surprise on the agenda. This did not discourage people from talking to each other but, naturally, the main point of the visit to Italy was not even lightly touched upon. Eventually, Pedro and Giulio came over to talk to me. 'Juan, do you know what is going on here? We don't like the atmosphere. Something isn't right. The clue is in those women who have changed their tops, as if they are trying to seduce us. Are they prostitutes?' asked Pedro.

'I don't know,' I said, keeping strictly to my script. 'I really don't. Have they changed their blouses?'

'Yes, definitely,' said Giulio. 'They are now all but revealing their breasts. Before they changed you couldn't see a thing. You look when one of them bends over.'

I knew exactly what they meant. 'I have decided to go,' said Giulio. 'First, I'll bid Esmeralda goodnight.'

'I have, too,' said Pedro. 'By the way, Juan, I have written the first half of the Corpus Christi play. I have completed the *loa* and am more than a third of the way through the main text. You can take it on your journey but only if you want to do so. I'll bring it around to your office. I expect I'll have the second half ready for when you return. I have decided to rely on your judgement about when in the play there should be accompanying music and what it should be. The play is called "The General Vacancy" but I will say no more.'

'That's magnanimous of him,' I thought. 'So I can make my own decisions.'

Giulio and Pedro made their way across the room and spoke to Esmeralda who raised her voice in disappointment. 'You can't go now, Señor Rospigliosi. Nor you, Señor de la Barca. The party has hardly begun. There is more food coming in and we want to entertain you. Our girls will sing to you soon.'

'I am sorry,' said Giulio. 'I have an important meeting tomorrow and I don't want to be too late to my bed. Goodnight and thank you for inviting us.'

Pedro followed Giulio to the front door. With Pedro and Giulio not there, the party died out like a bonfire in the rain. The Chief Clerk of the Council for State Security made his way towards me and eased me into a quiet corner. 'What have you told them? What the hell have you done?'

'I am sure you will be looking for a scapegoat, Señor Gutierro. But don't blame me. You have bungled your attempt to compromise the papal nuncio. Could you have been more unsubtle with these women? Getting them to change their blouses so their breasts just about fell out was so blatant. The guests were so suspicious that the whole atmosphere of the party was affected. I hope you have a good explanation for this tomorrow when the King asks you about what happened.' I must have hit him hard: he glared at me and said not another word.

I left with Juan de Roxas Carrión who lived in the Plazuela de los Herradores, not far from Esmeralda's house and not far off my route home. 'What did you think of all that?' asked Juan, just as we stepped into the street. Juan did not know about the plot to compromise the papal nuncio so I told him, in confidence. 'What a hopeless failure,' he said. 'I wonder if they will try again.'

'I can't imagine they will and the more I think about it, the more unnecessary I think it is. When we are in Rome, Rospigliosi will show us around the Vatican, if we ask him to do so. We will find out then exactly where the ten million *ducats* are located. At the moment, the trip is, as far as the nuncio is concerned, an innocent, cultural visit. He has no idea of our underlying intentions. If he was compromised before we went, he would sense there was something wrong and probably not be so open with us when we are there.'

'You are home early,' said Francisca, as I went into the drawing room where she was sitting in an armchair feeding baby Juan.

'Yes, my love. It fizzled out like a damp firework.'

'What happened?'

I told Francisca that Giulio and Pedro had left early, Giulio because he had meetings the following day. I mentioned the toast proposed by Señor Gutierro and what he had said about the cultural purpose of the visit. 'It will be very good for you, Juan. You will learn many new things.'

'There is something else I must tell you, Francisca. Esmeralda was wearing a beautiful emerald pendant right in the centre of her cleavage. Do you remember Antonia telling us at our party, a few months after our wedding, about a pendant she had made for a retired lady of pleasure?'

'Yes. I remember.'

'Well, I asked Esmeralda if her pendant was made by Antonia and sure enough it was.'

'That is amusing, Juan. You were right all along!'

I felt bad that I could not tell Francisca about the failed attempt at compromising Giulio.

***

The following afternoon, both Juan de Roxas Carrión and I were summoned to a meeting with the Chief Clerk of the Council for State Security. We were ushered into his office by an assistant. I failed to recognise the official sitting behind the Chief Clerk's desk. The official greeted us. 'I'm sorry,' I said. 'I expected to see Alvaro Gutierro de Marchena.'

'In which case you will be disappointed. Señor Gutierro de Marchena was dismissed from his post this morning. I am the new Chief Clerk of the Council for State Security. My name is Jorge Sanz de Aranda. I took up this position two hours ago.'

'I'm pleased to meet you, Señor Sanz,' I said.

'And I am, too,' said Juan de Roxas.

'I have asked to see you so that I can tell you about the plans for your journey to Rome. You will leave in eight days' time.'

'But the plan was that we would be leaving in about two weeks,' I said, registering my surprise and irritation that the mission had been brought forward.

'I know,' said the new Chief Clerk, shrugging his shoulders. 'I am not in a position to provide you with more detail, save to say that you will be leaving early for operational reasons. The first stage will be on horseback from Madrid to Barcelona. This is 110 *leguas* and that will take about six days at twenty *leguas* a day. You will use horses from the postal relay so will be changing mounts up to four times a day, which is nothing like as frequently as postal riders, but it will ensure you a speedy journey all the same. I trust you can both ride a horse.'

We both said we could.

'You will take the merchant ship, *El Clavel*, from Barcelona to Genoa. This will take about a week, maybe less in a strong following wind. You will then travel by carriage from Genoa to Rome. This will take a week or even more. The road is not good and there could be delays due to landfalls and subsidence. You will stay in roadside inns for all your travel overland and we will pay all of your relevant expense. You will share a cabin which will be the best available on board the ship. The nuncio will have his own.

'You will travel with minimum luggage from Madrid to Barcelona. This is because you will be riding. You must not take more than a saddlebag each and I suggest the main item is water. You will each need to pack your luggage in a trunk, which we will arrange to be transported by wagon, which will leave ahead of you, for the journey from Madrid to Barcelona. Pack your trunks in time for them to be removed from your homes in two days' time at exactly nine o'clock in the morning. For the journey from Barcelona to Rome and back, your trunks will be transported in convoy with you. We will arrange for them to be taken to and from your cabin on board the ship. We will give each of you 300 *ducats* in gold coin. You will have to account for every *maravedí* you spend. Is all that clear?'

'Yes, I think so, Señor Sanz. I have only one question. Where will we stay while in Rome?' I asked.

'You will be taken care of by the nuncio, so you may wish to ask him.'

'Will we be paid while we are away?' asked Juan de Roxas, always conscious of such practicalities.

'Of course,' said Señor Sanz. 'You may nominate anyone in your family to collect your monthly pay from the Paymaster's Office.'

'Where do we start from?' I asked.

'From the stables at the palace. All three of you will leave at the same time. By the way, I should tell you that you will have two armed officers from the cavalry escorting you from Madrid to Barcelona and the Pope's Swiss Guards escorting you to Rome.'

Francisca was annoyed and unprepared for our early departure. She was simply not reconciled to our going so soon. 'There is nothing I can do, my love. That is the decision of the King and we have to obey,' I said apologetically and sympathising with her.

Francisca and I packed almost every item of clothing I possessed. This was either for the journey to Barcelona or to fill a large, round-topped, wooden trunk we had borrowed from her father. I would need some warm clothing for the ride because we would be departing in March and the winds at that time of the year on the plains by Tarragona could be so cold that they could freeze you to an early death.

As we placed my things in the trunk, Francisca said she wanted me to write to her while I was away. I promised that, provided I had a spare moment, I would write something every day, in the form of a journey log, and post it to her in letters as often as I could find an opportunity to send them. So we packed paper, ink and envelopes as well as note sheets and music paper. The latter was to enable me to start writing the music for Pedro's play. We carried the trunk to the end of the hall and it was collected by a wagon and driver, just when the new Chief Clerk had said.

The night before we departed for Rome, Francisca put on a modest, family dinner party for me, Francisco, our mother and Francisca's father and his lady friend. It was an enjoyable if slightly sad occasion, especially for my mother who did not want me to go. 'What if something happens to you, Juan? It would kill me. I am so worried.'

'Don't worry, Mamá,' said Francisca. 'They'll be escorted all the way and stay in the safest places. This trip is important for the reputation of Spain and the King has made every effort to ensure its success. He has spared no expense, either. If anyone should be worried it's me.'

Early the following morning, on the front doorstep, I said my goodbyes to Francisca and kissed her and baby Juan. Tears came to my eyes as I told Francisca that I loved her and would miss her terribly. I slung the packed saddlebag over my shoulder and walked alone to the palace stables, contemplating the adventure ahead of me.

CHAPTER 21

I had never ridden as hard. Our two cavalry officer escorts, known to us only as Antón and Bernadino, set a breath-taking pace and, after changing horses countless times, we arrived in Barcelona totally exhausted, five days after leaving from Madrid. We stayed two nights in a shabby inn on the quayside. It was far from the quality we had expected and I never felt at ease there. I was probably being oversensitive, but I could not speak the local language and was not going to risk speaking Castilian Spanish in public for fear of being assaulted by a gang of former rebels.

On the second night, Juan de Roxas and I had a useful conversation with Giulio. 'Tell me, you two, what do you hope to accomplish in Italy?'

I had thought about our mission so had an answer at the ready. 'We have four objectives. We want to see at least two operas performed, we want to meet the Pope, I hope to play the harp at a public concert and Juan wants to play the violin, preferably in a major city, and we want to explore the Vatican in detail, including Saint Peter's Basilica. I hope that one of the operas is one you have written.' I put the stress on 'detail' in relation to the Vatican. 'Do you agree, Juan?'

'Yes, I am in total agreement. That would be the perfect programme.'

'Our people are already carrying out some of the organisational work which will help you achieve these objectives,' said Giulio. 'I am delighted... and flattered... that you want to see one of my operas. I hope we can see one in Rome.'

'What do you want out of this visit, Giulio?' I asked. 'It's only fair that we should be aware of what you are expecting.'

'My main purpose is to brief the Pope about my apostolic nunciature in Spain. It is vital for relationships between Spain and the Vatican that the Pope is up to date with developments. I write to him periodically but now he wants a meeting. I will also be using this visit as an opportunity to see my own family, who live in Tuscany, near the road we will be taking to Rome. I want you and Juan de Roxas to come with me. Lastly, I want to ensure that your visit is a success.'

'I would love to visit your family, Giulio. That would be a great honour.'

'I agree,' said Juan de Roxas.

'Excellent. You two will come then.'

This was my first real chance to write to Francisca so I assembled my account of the journey so far and, with a note saying how much I missed her and baby Juan, posted it at the customs house which was near to where we stayed.

Although I had seen many in pictures, I had never seen real ones before, so I gazed in awe at the mighty merchant and navy ships, some of which flew the French tricolour, moored along the quayside. These leviathans creaked and groaned as the waves rocked them on their moorings. Seeing the sea was also a totally new experience. I relished its smell, its sounds, its changing colours and its constant restlessness. It seemed to be alive. Our escorts, who by then had changed into civilian clothes to preserve their anonymity in this alien place, remained with us until they knew that our trunks had arrived and were safely on board *El Clavel.* They then took us to the ship where we thanked them and bid them farewell. We were greeted at the gangplank by the captain, Señor Miguel Moll. He showed us around the vessel and was clearly proud to be in charge of this beautiful ship which he treated as a schoolboy would treat a favourite toy.

'She's a square rigger, gents and is almost new. You can still smell the freshness of the wood on the decks. She displaces 248 *toneladas* and was built right here in Barcelona. Under full sail and with a following breeze, she can easily handle eight to ten knots so we should reach Genoa in about six days. I've fixed you up with a cabin each so you won't have to share. They are quite comfortable but you'll have to watch your head as you stand up.'

He was right. Six days later we were in Genoa. We were greeted at the port by our new escorts, three Vatican Swiss Guards. We duly thanked Señor Moll for getting us safely to port and, without the need for an overnight stay in this historic city, climbed into the softly furnished carriage that was to take us to Rome. This was by far the longest stage of our journey and took a full two weeks. Our luggage travelled in a covered wagon, never more than a few hundred *varas* behind us. The roads were in an appalling state and we were thrown from side to side in the carriage as our driver negotiated the ruts and potholes in the road. The regular and frequent stops made the going bearable.

Giulio's family home in Pistóia was one of the largest private houses I had ever seen. His mother greeted Juan de Roxas and me as if we were her own sons. Naturally, she made a greater fuss of Giulio and they were both virtually in tears as they hugged each other. Giulio's father had died ten years or so before but Giulio's nephew, Vincenzo Rospigliosi, a commander in the Italian navy, and his family, were staying in the house, partly as a holiday and partly to help Giulio's mother with the supervision of some maintenance work on this immense property. Giulio's mother insisted that we all stayed in her house and we stopped there for two nights. She was able to accommodate the whole of the party, including the three Swiss Guards and the carriage and wagon drivers. The stop there provided a welcomed break for all of us and we were able to rest our weary bodies from which the appalling roads had taken their toll.

***

We were exhausted when we arrived in the Vatican City. Giulio and his colleagues had made arrangements for the three of us to stay in a large apartment the Vatican used for visiting foreign dignitaries, even though Juan and I felt that we did not qualify for such treatment. We had a huge bedroom each and I even took the trouble to unpack my trunk. We slept soundly the first night after enjoying a modest but filling meal of Italian pasta, which we ate in a refectory at one of the papal colleges.

Juan de Roxas and I spent some time just admiring the architecture and getting the feel of this great city. It was quite different from Madrid. The buildings seemed to have 'more room to breathe' as Juan put it, whereas in Madrid they were more densely packed together. The public buildings were generally larger and the Basilica of Saint Peter must have been the largest church in the world. We admired the huge number of publicly displayed statues of the Popes, the Caesars, heroes from Roman mythology and, not least, local people such as painters and architects who had become famous through their work. We visited the monumental and elegant Palazzo Barberini with its stunning staircases built by Bernini, the Palazzo della Cancelleria with its cloisters by Bramante and the Villa Doria Pamphili, built on the Janiculum, with its huge symmetrical gardens.

I spent some of the free time in Rome writing letters to Francisca, whom I missed terribly. I did not realise how much I would miss her. It was painful to be so far away, both in distance and in time, from the love of my life. In many ways, I wished she and baby Juan could be with me but, of course, I knew that that would be impossible. I missed baby Juan and wondered whether Francisca needed to call on the offers our friends had made to help her with the baby while I was away. In my little missives, I told Francisca about our ship, our stay at Giulio's family house and the bruising trip from there to Rome. I told her how much I loved them, that I missed them both and that I thought about them both many times a day.

I also worked on my score for Pedro's Corpus Christi play. By the time we reached Rome, I had twice read the whole of the text that Pedro had given me and was more confident then that I understood it. There were a few lines in a soliloquy which I felt that Pedro had written especially for me. The character who represents the Church says that its centre is Madrid and that everybody goes through the Puerta Cerrada so that only one may pass through. He knew I lived in that street because he had been to our house at the party we held for him, Giulio and the Archbishop of Toledo. There was a hint of mystery here: who was the one that passed through the Puerta because others had permitted him to do so? Would that be clear when I read the rest of the play? I wondered if the presence of these lines were an, albeit indirect, indication that Pedro wanted to be more friendly towards me. In the meantime, it was a challenge to think of different tunes and moods to represent the various personifications and people in his play.

Our audience with Pope Innocent X was the first major event on our itinerary. Giulio escorted us from our apartment across the courtyard of Sixtus V to the entrance to the Papal Apartments in the Apostolic Palace. The Pope's personal area in the palace was at least as big as Philip IV's in the Alcázar. Giulio showed us around before our meeting with him. There must have been at least ten large rooms which included a reception hall, a study, which the Pope was occupying during our tour, his bedroom and a number of reception and dining rooms. Then it was the time for our audience.

'How should we address him?' asked Juan.

'Your Holiness,' replied Giulio.

We two Spanish visitors were impressed by the informality of the Pontiff who was arguably the most powerful individual on earth. People with real power keep that power hidden and undetectable. They do not mention what they have at their command and display it only on the rare occasions on which it has to be exercised. This applied to Pope Innocent X. He gave no impression, not even an aura, of his own immense authority. He had sharp, penetrating eyes as if he could see deep into the mind of those standing before him. He welcomed us to Rome, and apologised for the mess the city was in with the building work that was taking place there. Jokingly, he said that he hoped it would all be finished by the time of our arrival but that Italian builders were not renowned for their speed and there was still much work to be completed.

With a little prompting from Giulio, he acknowledged that we were all working together to promote the culture of Italy in Spain and the culture of Spain in Italy. He asked about our work for the King in the Royal Chapel. He laughed as he accused us of stealing the idea of our Royal Chapel from the Papal Chapel which performed for him in the Vatican. He asked about our arduous journey from Madrid to Rome and thanked us for making this hazardous undertaking. He wished us good fortune for the rest of our stay in

Italy and especially wished us a safe journey to Venice, a city he said he 'would love for ever'. He asked us to give his personal best wishes to the King on our return to Madrid. Finally, he gave us the Papal Blessing. Then we left with Giulio.

My analysis of our audience with Innocent X was simple. He still had affection for Spain and the Spanish that had not left him since his time as papal nuncio, which began in the '20s. This was demonstrated in what appeared to be a genuine friendliness towards us. Although he was informal, he still had a remoteness about him that I suppose one should expect of the man who was Pope. Giulio confirmed this impression. Innocent X was not and had no intention of being the people's Pope. He would not conduct a daily confessional. That was someone else's function. He would not take mass on a Sunday morning. Again, this was for somebody else. His function was to lead the church and, to that date, he had succeeded. He had removed from it those who were corrupt and those who had found their way into well-paid, key positions by the blatant nepotism of his predecessor.

***

True to his word, Giulio took us to see a performance of one of his operas. It was 'Saint Alexis'. It took place in the spectacular great hall of the Palazzo Barberini, which Juan and I had already admired in one of our walks around the city. Before the start, Giulio took us behind the stage to introduce us to the brilliant young conductor and to some of his cheerful, chatting orchestra.

'This is Leonardo Landi, nephew of Stefano Landi, the composer who wrote the score for "Saint Alexis",' said Giulio, proudly acknowledging Landi's contribution to his work. 'Leonardo is a great friend and is conducting tonight's performance.'

'I am pleased to meet our guests from Spain,' Landi said. 'You'll love this opera. Giulio has written a masterful libretto. It is the first historical opera ever written.' Landi was a short, dynamic individual who explained the range of contrasting themes in his uncle's music by gesticulating wildly as if he was conducting it there and then.

The opera house was full and bubbling with chatter as we took our excellent seats just to the right of the stage and quite near the front of the auditorium. The performance was nothing short of spectacular. The degree of opulence in the scenery and costumes, except that worn by the Saint himself, was simply unbelievable. The great hall of the palace, with its gilded finishing, ceilings by Cortona and massive silk drapes, showed an extravagance bordering on the ridiculous. I could not but wonder whether this was all a statement designed to impress the Catholic audience by brazenly mocking Protestant austerity and uniformity. If it was, then it succeeded.

The singers and orchestra performed with passion and verve. I was shocked that there were no women in the cast. This was in stark contrast to what we had in Madrid: very few, if any, men performers. These men were castrati who sang at the top end of the scale. I had never experienced the idea of the castrato before and it seemed ragingly cruel to take away a man's sexuality for the benefit of a concert show. Alexis's mother, his wife and the nurse as well as the servants were all parts sung by castrati. Once I had accepted the style of rendition and reconciled myself to the notion of the castrato soprano, I enjoyed the twists and turns of the story which I could glean only from the atmosphere produced by the music and from the action on stage. The cast sang in Italian which we could barely follow.

Both Juan and I congratulated Giulio after the applause at the end of the third and final act had died down. Leonardo Landi, from his conductor's rostrum, succeeded in persuading Giulio to take a bow to the audience. I decided there and then that I would write the music to the first Spanish opera. I had to write one. Pedro Calderón de la Barca could write the libretto.

***

The following day we explored the Vatican, the key to our visit as far as I and Juan de Roxas were concerned. I decided to take a few sheets of paper to make some notes. Giulio himself conducted the tour and met us after breakfast. We had already seen the Basilica of Saint Peter but he took us in again to see the miraculous 'Pieta' by Michelangelo. It was a statue one could never tire of viewing. Giulio, as we expected, had some unexpected gems of knowledge. 'This was the first and only work that Michelangelo signed. He signed it late one night to prevent it being copied.'

He took us from there to the Belvedere Courtyard. As we walked in, we saw a jousting tournament in full flow. Suddenly, there was a crash as a player, covered from head to toe in armour, fell from his horse. His opponent raised his arms in triumph as the audience cheered. 'This is where Pope Leo X paraded his pet elephant, Hanno,' said Giulio. 'And this is where the elephant is buried,' he said pointing to a plaque set in the floor. Another of Giulio's gems.

I felt uncomfortable, wondering how we would extract from Giulio the information we so badly needed about the location of the ten million *ducats*. I was becoming impatient to know. I might have to ask him directly if he did not say first. Then another diversion. He took us to the Sistine Chapel to show us the ceilings by Michelangelo. He opened the main door with a key from a bunch he was carrying. Even though I had the problem of the gold *ducats* firmly in my mind, I stood in awe beneath the fresco of the creation of Adam. It captured the muscular structure of the human body with sheer perfection. I was moved to be in this sacred place which was adorned by these works of genius. I had never before seen anything like it. It must have cost the fortune of King Midas to build and decorate it.

We then walked via the Piazza del Forno into the gardens of the Vatican. Wherever is all this money? Could the gold *ducats* be hidden here? I was getting even more impatient. Juan de Roxas seemed oblivious to the whereabouts of the Vatican's money and, still as enthusiastic as ever about the place, chatted to both Giulio and me about every arch, every statue and just about everything that he cast an eye upon. We strolled through the gardens and turned east towards the Viale Vaticano. The shapely flowerbeds looked delightful with the daffodils and tulips heralding in the spring. I then totally lost my forbearance and decided to start a conversation about the wealth of the Vatican. So I interrupted Juan de Roxas, 'Is it true that the Vatican is bankrupt because of the extravagances of Urban VIII?' I asked Giulio.

'No. Not at all. It is true that we are borrowing money but we have a gold reserve of about fifteen million *ducats*.' At last we were getting somewhere.

'That sounds strange,' said a puzzled Juan de Roxas. 'Why borrow when you have all that money?'

'It's a question of good financial management. We are borrowing less than the total value of our gold currency. This means that, if the banks ever foreclose on us, we cannot be declared bankrupt. We are using the money we have borrowed to fund some of the building projects in the Vatican. We are paying it back though taxes we collect.'

'Where is all this money kept?' I asked, somehow keeping composed when my mind was galloping. 'Not here in the Vatican?'

'Yes. We are now approaching the Palazzo del Belvedere. Let's go in.'

We walked through the main entrance at the end of the courtyard. 'This was built by Innocent VIII, in the early part of the last century. Let's go down this staircase.'

We descended the steps to the building's basement. Our voices echoed in the empty stairwell. Giulio selected a rusty key from his bunch and opened a large oak door. 'Come in,' he said.

Inside there were well over a hundred pyramid-shaped piles of small canvas bags on the floor. The piles were arranged neatly in rows and columns. We walked between two of the rows and Giulio lifted one of the bags and untied the string by which it was closed. He poured the contents on to the polished marble slabs upon which we were standing. There was a tinkling of metal against stone as gold coins flooded the floor. 'There are a thousand *ducats* in each of these bags,' he said.

'Good God,' said Juan, involuntarily as he glanced at me.

'Please, no blasphemy in the Vatican. It is a Holy place.'

'Sorry,' said Juan. 'That was not meant.'

'I'm just teasing you,' said Giulio, smiling. 'There are exactly one hundred bags in each pile.'

'You've made your point,' I said. 'There must be... well... a thousand times a hundred times a hundred... say ten million *ducats* here.'

'And the rest,' said Giulio. 'Fifteen million.'

My mind was racing. My heart beat faster. Well, here it was. Here was the fortune which would rescue Spain from bankruptcy. How would we take it from here to Madrid? There was so much of it. As the King had said, we have an army. We would need one to shift this fortune in gold. The main mission of Juan de Roxas Carrión and me was complete. It was to locate this mountain of money. It was someone else's job to remove it to Spain. I could not help wondering, though, how this might be achieved.

Giulio and the two of us collected up the thousand *ducats* that he had poured onto the floor and put them back into the bag. 'That's fine. We've recovered every one of them,' he said before neatly retying the string.

***

We returned to our apartment via the Swiss Guards' barracks where we saw the men who had escorted us from Genoa to Rome. They introduced us to another three who would be taking us to the venue of the second opera we wanted to see and participate in. The opera was to be in Venice and we were to go to a performance of 'The Woman Feigning Madness'.

'You will have to pack tonight,' said Giulio. 'We'll be leaving first thing in the morning.'

We travelled to Venice in a beautifully appointed carriage, similar to the one that brought us from Genoa to Rome. Once we reached Florence, where we had stopped briefly on way to Rome, the roads became better and we made excellent progress with our luggage following on our heels in the covered wagon. Even so, it took us more than a week to reach the city. We had some interesting discussions on route. I asked Giulio about the building projects which were underway in Rome.

'What's the next large project?'

'I think the next one will be the Square for the Basilica of Saint Peter. The Pope wants to have a large, ornate square in which 300,000 people can stand to see him at his balcony. Gian Lorenzo Bernini has been appointed to design it. He wants to make it in the shape of a huge ellipse with curved cloisters at the sides. The project is in the early stages yet and we will not start the building for several years, partly because of the lack of money. The stone for the building will cost a fortune. So will the granite cobbles we will need to cover such a massive area.'

'Why not use marble to cover the floor of the square?' asked Juan de Roxas.

'It's too expensive.'

'Where will the granite come from?' I asked.

'Verona. It's well known for the quality of its granite.'

'How will it be carried to Rome?' asked Juan de Roxas.

'By wagon. There is no other way.'

'Interesting,' I thought.

We arrived in Venice two days before the performance of the opera which was to be in the Teatro Novissimo, Venice's first opera house. Giulio's staff in Rome had arranged for us to stay in a comfortable lodging house in the Calle Spaderia, not far from Saint Mark's Square.

Juan de Roxas and I were unsure about performing in the orchestra when we had only two days to go before the performance but Giulio and the leader of the orchestra, a violinist, convinced us that we would have no difficulty in mastering the musical parts we would be playing. He provided a harp and violin for me and Juan de Roxas respectively. We rehearsed in the concert hall both with the orchestra and on our own, after the rest of the ensemble had gone. We returned the following morning, before the other members of the orchestra arrived, and practised again. Giulio heroically stayed with us through all our attempts to achieve a reasonable familiarity with the music. 'I think you've done it now. I'm sure you will both be fine,' said Giulio, after we had played our parts through for what seemed the hundredth time.

Once again the opera house was packed. There were people standing against the walls because every seat was taken. The Venetians were treating our presence as a major public event unless, of course it was pure coincidence that the mayor of Venice, the composer of the opera, Francesco Sacrati and the librettist, Giulio Strozzi, were all present on the night of the performance. The beautiful soprano, Anna Renzi, probably the most famous opera singer in the whole of Europe, played Achilles' mother. The use of women players contrasted strongly with what we had seen and heard in Rome. There was not one castrato in the opera.

The plot was about the devious means to which Achilles and his mother resorted to keep him out of the Trojan War. She dressed him as a woman and his beloved Deidamia, also played by Anna Renzi, feigned insanity to persuade Achilles to marry her. She fully succeeded in sounding mad. Her voice quivered, her mood changed violently, she became angry, then calm, then pensive, then free with her ample charms and then angry again, all within the space of a few tens of bars. Not only did this singer change mood, she changed from being a woman to being a man and then back again. She started as a Helen of Troy and then she became a soldier and then to being Achilles's lover. Her voice was high and enchanting. It was totally under her control. She was one of the best singers and actresses I had seen. She was as good as, if not better than, the talented Bernarda Ramirez.

Achilles was also played by a woman. So, in his case, it was a woman playing a man who was dressed as a woman. Achilles thrived on being a transvestite, even expressing the pleasure of being dressed as a woman. This renowned example of mythological manhood even expressed the wish to become a woman. Juan and I, without understanding the language, found the changes of sexuality confusing, even if they were necessary to sustain the complicated plot. The opera was erotically charged. It was no surprise that it was probably the most popular opera of its time in Europe.

After this brilliant performance, which deserved the standing ovation it received, Giulio, Juan and I discussed my idea for a Spanish opera.

'It will be popular in Madrid,' said Juan de Roxas, 'judging from what we've seen here. A Madrid audience will immediately warm to it.'

'How do you know?' said Giulio. 'They have never tried a piece that is fully sung. It is peculiarly Italian.'

'You just cannot be right, Giulio. My opera will inspire them. I'm certain they will love it.'

'I can feel it in my bones,' said Juan de Roxas, really quite excited. 'A Madrid audience will go wild. We have denied them an opera until now. You must write one, Juan,' he said, looking earnestly at me.

'We will have to convince the King,' I replied. 'We will have to persuade him.'

CHAPTER 22

Juan de Roxas Carrión and I had achieved the main, secret objective of our exhilarating and satisfying visit to Italy. We had also experienced opera, in both Rome and Venice, and that confronted me with a major challenge. I just had to write the music for one myself. And, of course, we had had an audience with Pope Innocent X.

We enjoyed our welcome home even more than our visit. They say that absence makes the heart grow fonder but I had no idea how much. We had a different pair of escorts on the way back. They called themselves Cosme and Domingo. As we left Tarragona, Domingo went ahead so as to tell the Chief Clerk of the Council for State Security that we would be arriving at the palace stables two days later and probably in the middle of the afternoon. His timing was almost exact. We arrived at three o'clock to a modest but emotional reception. Francisca was carrying baby Juan. I raced up to them, jumped off my horse and embraced both of them.

'It is so good to have you back, Juan,' said Francisca. 'Baby Juan and I have missed you so much. Please don't go away from home again.' Poor lass, she cried as she uttered these precious words.

'I promise I won't go voluntarily again, Francisca, unless I can take you with me. I will never go without you, unless I have no choice.'

We said our goodbyes to Juan de Roxas Carrión and his mother and sister and to Giulio and went home. Our trunks were at least a week behind us but I had my saddlebag and carried it back home slung over my shoulder. Francisca and I had so much to tell each other.

'Juan, thank you for your lovely letters. They made it so much easier to bear your absence and gave me something to look forward to.'

'That's good, Francisca. I did my best to keep you in touch with what we were doing.'

'A lot has happened while you have been away. The biggest piece of news is that Francisco is now engaged and is to marry in two months' time.'

'Incredible! I'm amazed! A whirlwind romance?'

'Yes. She is an enchanting girl. You will love her. Her name is Juana Vélez. She's the same age as Francisco and lives in the Calle de la Lechuga, at the end near the Calle de Toledo. She works as an assistant in the Royal Weights and Measures House.'

'Their relationship hasn't been going on since our wedding, has it?'

'No, Juan, but he met her when he went to the building before we were married. He next saw her about two months ago and, to cut the story short, they fell in love. I've helped her with her wedding plans. We are both invited, of course, and I am the maid of honour. We've chosen the wedding dress and organised the reception. Everything is well underway.'

'I am so surprised and pleased for him. Good for Francisco. Is there any other news?'

'Your mother is making a fortune from the love sleeves. Yes, we have changed the name of them yet again. We have started a new line in sleeves made of silk. These are doing so well that we may stop making the leather ones, which people complain of being uncomfortable and awkward.'

'We always thought the love tubes... sorry, sleeves... would make a lot of money. Good for mother.'

'Another piece of news, Juan, but I'm less sure about how good this is...' She hesitated.

'Tell me, Francisca. Now. What's wrong?'

'It is not so much wrong, Juan, but I feel uncomfortable and upset by it. My father has decided to marry again. He is to marry the lady who came with him to our wedding.'

'Surely that's not bad, is it, Francisca? They've been seeing each other for many years now.'

'I suppose I find it difficult that he's found a replacement for my mother. Maybe I shouldn't think like that.'

'If it makes them both happy, Francisca, should we stand in the way? What would your mother be saying, as she looks down from above?'

'I guess that is the question, Juan. I just don't know how to answer that.'

'Are there any wedding plans?'

'That's what's so strange. I've asked my father and he just says that they have no plans. But that they will marry.'

By then we were approaching our house. 'Is there anything else, my love?'

'Just that everyone wants to see you. There's a meeting at the palace tomorrow, which will be attended by the King. Diego will be there and Juan de Roxas Carrión has to go, too. His mother knows and will tell him. I've seen her several times while you have both been away. I showed her your letters and she is cross that she did not hear one word from Juan. Another thing. The King is sending Diego to Italy. They are putting together a huge programme. He will be going for two years. The main aim will be to buy selected paintings for the King's collection. Juana is furious and wants to go, too. Oh, and Pedro Calderón de la Barca wants to see you, too.'

Francisca settled baby Juan in his cot and we went into our bedroom, took off all our clothes and resumed our married life. We both exploded with the excitement of love denied. We each touched and kissed each other's bodies and did the same again before bursting once more with pent up love.

'Try this,' said Francisca, pushing one of her engorged breasts towards my mouth. Her milk tasted of nectar and I quite took to its warmth and flavour. 'That's enough. Save some for the baby!'

'You look so beautiful in your state of motherhood, Francisca. I love to just sit and admire you.'

'You just like big breasts,' she said, sitting on the bed laughing and wobbling them from side to side. 'Welcome home, Juan. It's so good to have you back again.'

***

As soon as I arrived at the office the following day, I was greeted by the Maestro. 'Welcome back, Juan. It's great to see you. I just hope everything went well. And that you've had a wonderful time. We must talk about your visit and the operas. But not now. We have to go to a meeting of the Council for State Security. It's in the Council Chamber at nine o'clock.'

Once again, the meeting was chaired by the Ministerial Head of the Council. This was a proper debriefing meeting and was attended by only eight of us: The King, the Ministerial Head, the new Chief Clerk, Diego, Juan de Roxas, the Maestro, myself and a note taker.

'I don't want a prolonged meeting,' said the chairman. 'Señor Hidalgo, can you tell us how successful you were on your mission? Did you manage to locate the gold *ducats* in the Vatican?'

'Yes. Our mission achieved its stated aims. Giulio Rospigliosi, without prompting from Juan de Roxas or me, showed us not only the location of the money but also the money itself. There are about fifteen million *ducats* in bags of a thousand, in piles of 100 bags, on the basement floor of the Belvedere Palace, in the Vatican. There are 150 of these piles, arranged in neat rows and columns, about a *pie* or two apart, that look like little pyramids on the basement floor.'

The King cheered. 'Bravo, you two! Bravo! Brilliant!' Taking their lead from the King, there was a short, muted round of applause from those who did not visit Italy. Juan de Roxas and I glowed as we nodded modestly in acknowledgement. Then the King asked the key question. 'Have you any ideas on how we can, shall we say, retrieve the money for ourselves and bring it back to Spain?'

'We have one idea but it is not fully developed. There is a large amount of building work to be done in the Vatican and, in particular, there is to be a huge square built in front of the Saint Peter's Basilica. It is to have a cobblestone floor, made of granite from Verona. We estimate that about a thousand *toneladas* of granite will be needed.'

'What has that got to do with the ten million *ducats*?' asked the King.

'Well, we thought that if we could intercept enough of the wagons which they will use to transport the cobbles from Verona, we could use our soldiers to take over from the drivers, unload the cobbles in the Vatican, drive the wagons around to the back exit of the Belvedere Palace and take the money from there. If we were really clever, we could substitute the bags of money for bags of stones or sand. So the Pope couldn't even know his money had been taken.'

'I like that,' said the King. 'That could work. What do you think, Diego? I should explain to you and Juan de Roxas that we are sending Diego Velázquez to Italy as the next phase of this project to, among other things, work out a detailed plan to obtain this money.'

'It is a good basic idea. There would be a great deal of detail to fill in,' said Diego. 'For example, we would need to know when these wagons were leaving Verona, which route they were to take, and exactly how we would intercept them without being seen. How we would enter the Belvedere without being noticed and take the money to Genoa.'

'I agree,' I said. 'There is much to work out. The square is being designed by the architect, Gian Lorenzo Bernini. He will know about the timetable for constructing the square if there is one yet. The gold *ducats* are locked in the basement of the Belvedere. There is no one guarding the money.'

'What do you mean?' said the King. '"If" there is a timetable.'

'Well, the Vatican is short of money. They will not use their gold reserves and are accumulating cash from tax income. The building will start only when they have sufficient funds.'

'We should increase our taxes to be paid to the church,' said the new Chief Clerk.

'That is not amusing,' said the King. 'The Pope won't want to waste time unnecessarily on this project. So there will be no major delay. I don't see this as a concern. I make only one constraint which any plan we put into action must follow. That is that nobody will be killed. If we are going to take this money, that is one crime the Lord may forgive me for but he won't forgive me for killing innocent people. We can kill only in self-defence.'

The King turned to Diego. 'You now have your specific terms of reference, Diego. Not only will you be buying Italian works of art for me in

Italy, you will be working out a plan to get this money from the Belvedere Palace back here. I will want a written report on your return.'

He then turned to me. 'What about your secondary mission, the cultural side of your visit. How did that go?'

'That, too, was achieved, Your Majesty,' I said. 'We saw two operas performed, Giulio Rospigliosi's "Saint Alexis" in Rome and another opera by Giulio Strozzi in Venice. Juan de Roxas and I played in the one in Venice. I was so impressed with the concept of the opera, Your Majesty, that I would like to write one for us in Spain and for a Spanish audience.'

'What do you think, Carlos?' asked the King, looking at the Maestro.

'I haven't had chance to speak to Juan Hidalgo or to Juan de Roxas Carrión so I'll have to let you know, Your Majesty. Sounds like a good idea, on the face of it.'

'Let me know in due course,' said the King.

***

Shortly after, I met with Pedro. It was the friendliest encounter I had had with him.

'How was Italy, Juan? Did you see any operas?'

I explained to him what I had reported to the King and said that I had mentioned to the King that we should create a Spanish opera.

'Why do you want to write an opera, Juan? Our *comedias* seem to be what people want to see performed in the *corrales*. Why create an opera just because that's what they like at the moment in Italy? They could be a passing fancy that soon dies out.'

'My thinking is that opera is an art form that is all embracing. There is the script, the libretto. Then the music. Then there is the scenery and to see what the Italians do for scenery is impressive. They have machines that move the players across the sky like soaring angels. They can move carriages through the air. This is no passing phase, Pedro. It is a new art form that is here to stay. I want us to work together to realise an opera. Maybe two. The audiences of Madrid will love them.'

'Neither of us can decide on this separately. We need to ask the King.'

'I know. He wants the Maestro to put a case together.'

'How would it work, Juan?'

'You would write the libretto. I would write the music. We would need someone for the scenery.'

'Let's see how the Maestro's case is received by the King. Let's say, I like the idea in principle. If it is to go ahead, I'd like to be part of its realisation,' he said, sounding quite enthusiastic. 'Can I change the subject somewhat? Did you have time to compose any music for "The General Vacancy"?'

'Yes. I have written parts for all of the characters which appear in what you have given me so far. I suppose I have written music for about half of the text.'

'Well, Juan. I've completed the rest of it now and I have a copy that you can have. Did you enjoy reading what I gave you? What did you make of it?'

I told Pedro that I did enjoy it and found that the idea of a conflict between the laws of Judaism and the Old Testament and those of Christ and the New Testament was fascinating and, as far as I knew, original. I said I thought that the idea that Judaism was a spent force matched the prejudices of the many. I said I liked the way he had made Madrid the focus of the Catholic Church.

'Is it a device to attract the attention and sympathy of the audience?'

'Yes, Juan. You have seen right through my method.'

'I was puzzled by your mentioning the Puerta Cerrada.'

'That was not a coincidence. I was struck by the name of your street. Of course, I had noticed it before but coming to your house for the party, with Rospigliosi and the Archbishop, reminded me of it. I thought it was symbolic: a closed door that everyone could go through, so I mentioned it in the play. If I had not been to your house I'm sure I would not have done so. I also thought it would be a small tribute to you, my new collaborator, to mention the street where you live.'

'Thank you for the explanation, Pedro. I think that's a wonderful gesture.'

'I'm glad you are enjoying the play, Juan. I am pleased because you are the first person to have read it. I hope you also appreciate the rest of what I've written. May I borrow your score so that I can see what you have done so far?'

'Of course, Pedro.'

I told Pedro that I would finish my work as soon as I could but he was not in a hurry because the King was still enforcing the ban on public performances following the death of his wife, Queen Elisabeth of Bourbon.

***

Francisca was still new at being a mother and, because of my absence, I was newer still in the role of father. We were so proud to be parents and our little baby gradually formed a loving bond with each of us. I just could not wait to get home from the palace after work and play with baby Juan to make that relationship between father and son even stronger. I spent many hours playing with him, talking to him and admiring this little bundle that Francisca and I had produced.

I wondered what sort of world he would inherit and what profession he would enter, whether he, too, might become a musician like his father or Uncle Francisco. I wondered where we would be sending him to school. Would he be accepted by Imperial, following my footsteps, or would he attend a different school? Would he, unlike me, complete his education at one of our universities? All this was speculation but what could be wrong with that?

We committed ourselves to giving baby Juan the maximum stimulation of his senses. We carried him out of the house on walks, spoke and laughed to him as often as we could and played with him and showed him many different things in our house, at the markets and just about anywhere else we went. We even devised a way that Francisca or I could carry him in a device that looked a bit like a hammock, slung around our necks, when we were going anywhere on our horses.

Baby Juan's response to our attention was incredibly positive. He soon learnt to laugh. He began to crawl around the floor of the house and it was not long before he could walk, say the odd word, then short sentences of a few words and then speak quite well. We idolised him and he loved to be with us. We had no problem finding other small children baby Juan could mix with. Antonia Rodríguez's second child was born only a few days before baby Juan. He was called Agustín and was a little brother to their daughter Antona, who was by then nearly five years old. It was when Antonia was pregnant with Antona that Antonia's mother threw her out of the family home. Antonia and Alonso Arias de Soria, to whom Antonia was belated betrothed by then, lived in the Calle de la Paz, not far from our house and Antonia and Francisca used to meet at each other's houses with the children who would happily play together as their mothers chatted and drank fruit juice or coffee.

Francisca temporarily stopped working at the Shod Carmen soup kitchen and decided to concentrate on bringing up Juan and generally looking after the house until he was at school. Barbola continued helping with the housework and became like an aunt to baby Juan. Barbola had developed into a woman to be respected for her mature, calm approach to any problem and for her reliability and honesty. Having a child herself, Barbola was a ready source of advice to Francisca who was still very new to the craft of motherhood.

'Don't be dictated to by the baby,' Barbola used to say. 'You can take him anywhere. He can't take you.'

My mother doted on baby Juan and would bring him little presents, such as wooden toy soldiers and a board and chalk for drawing and colouring. Francisca's father, Domingo, and his lady also loved to come to see us and baby Juan who seemed by his own existence to have brought the members of our family closer together.

'My mother would have loved him,' said Francisca, many times and with wetness in her eyes.

***

We were lucky with the timing of Francisco's wedding only because it was before Diego went to Italy. As with our wedding, it was a grand reunion. Francisco had invited our grandmother from Pedraza. She was by then over eighty-five years old and with commendable courage decided that she would come to Madrid for the wedding. As she said, she did know how many more years she would live, so to have the chance to meet with our families and friends was an opportunity she was not going to miss. She came with her black servant, Isabel, who had the whitest, most majestic teeth I had ever seen and displayed them every time she smiled.

Francisco and Juana Vélez decided to live in Juana Vélez's rented house until they could afford to buy a house of their own. From the wedding, our mother began to live on her own. She coped amazingly well and often said she only had herself to please so making decisions about what to do what to eat and where to go and when became so much simpler. Our mother paid for the wedding and the reception from the profits from the making of the love sleeves. Having the marriage ceremony in the church of San Ginés brought back the sad and complex memories of our father's funeral. Not surprisingly, we did not even mention to our mother that we would not invite our father's various girlfriends along. There was no point in creating a problem where a problem did not exist. The interesting woman who Francisco did invite was Esmeralda Pechada. She was, after all, a long standing family friend and our mother loved her.

***

Juana failed in her attempt to visit Italy with Diego. She was bitterly disappointed. The case went right up to the King who said he would not take the responsibility for her travelling there. It was a very difficult journey and there were many potential hazards, not least the risk of piracy on the high seas. Diego was lucky that Juana was such a tolerant wife who eventually accepted the King's refusal. She was helped by Francisca who

296

argued that it would be more difficult for Diego if he had to concern himself about Juana when in a strange land where she did not even speak the language. As she said, Diego would be meeting people, choosing paintings, creating paintings himself and selecting other works of art to bring back to embellish the Alcázar Palace. What she did not know, of course, was that Diego was expected to return with a detailed written plan to extract ten million *ducats* from the Vatican and I could not possibly tell her. My view was that the King did not want her there because of this part of Diego's remit. Diego left Madrid for Italy in the February, the year after Juan de Roxas, Giulio and I returned. Juana was so upset, she came to stay with Francisca, me and baby Juan for nearly two weeks.

Diego travelled to Italy with the Duke of Nájera who was sent there by the King on an important mission. The King's young son, the Infante Balthasar Carlos, and Mariana of Austria, the King's young niece, were betrothed when the Infante Balthasar Carlos died. Mariana was then a young girl of twelve and Queen Elisabeth had died two years before. There was much toing and froing between Austria and Spain after the Infante died and the Emperor agreed to the surprising proposition that Mariana should marry the King, who was just about old enough to be her grandfather.

We all thought the whole idea was mad but the King clearly thought otherwise. Anyway, the King agreed that when Mariana was fifteen he would marry her so he sent the Duke to Austria with the sole aim of bringing her to Madrid. The Duke was never a special agent so had no involvement with the plan, sketchy as it then was, to attack the Vatican. Although Diego did not go to Italy with his wife, he took his trusty manservant, Juan de Pareja who was himself a highly gifted and intelligent artist, taught by the master himself. Juan de Pareja was a special agent and was to be instrumental in helping Diego complete the detailed plan of attack.

***

Diego unfortunately missed the performances of Pedro's Corpus Christi play. Although Pedro said I need not worry too much about completing my part of the work, I'm glad I pressed on because the King relented on the prohibition of performing works of art in public and wanted a private performance in the March before Corpus Christi day. The work I had completed on it while in Italy stood me in good stead for several reasons. The first was that quite a number of the verses in the new material were repeated several times. This meant that I could use the same tunes to underline them. Second, there were only a few more new characters in

Pedro's new text, so I only had to invent a few more tunes to identify with the new individuals in it. I enjoyed writing the tunes for the songs that Pedro had written into his play. I was not born to be a songwriter so it was good not to have to go begging to Francisca again to write some verses for me.

While I had earlier told Pedro that I was impressed by his play, as indeed I was, it seemed to me a very abstract work. This was mainly because it was an allegory. I could not imagine that, when the people of Madrid saw it performed, they would take to the various personifications and characterisations in it. Judaism, the Church, Innocence, Faith, the Eucharist, Apostasy were all personified. I was totally wrong. Francisca and I saw only one performance, which was the one in the open air in the Plazuela de Santiago. We left baby Juan with my mother, went up to the Plazuela and stood at the side of the square in a crowd of at least 400 other people waiting for the celebrations, which preceded the play, to begin.

A huge stage had been set up on the northern side of the Plazuela. A large gap had been left between it and the walls of the houses on that side. The stage had two levels, the right hand side being about ten *pulgadas* higher than the left. Hanging from the edges of the stage were deep purple curtains and the space at the front of the stage had been cordoned off for the musicians. After we had taken our places in the crowd, four gigantic figures appeared from the southeast corner of the square, accompanied by a band of musicians. The figures were made of wood and *papier mâché* and each was propelled on wheels by a driver concealed within its structure.

These mobile statues stood all of four *varas* high and were the most frightening objects anyone could imagine. The one in the lead, the *tarasca,* had a long body and tail, was ten *varas* long and was covered with painted black and grey scales from top to tail. It was a hideous dragon with seven ugly heads, one of a goat, one of a fox, one of a dog, another of a snake, one of a donkey, another of a crocodile and the largest and most frightening, the head of a monster with three red tongues projecting from its scaly lips.

'I'm glad baby Juan isn't here,' said Francisca. 'He'd be terrified!'

Mounted on the back of the dragon was the effigy of a woman, the 'Whore of Babylon'. Her blond horse hair was glued to her misshapen head. Her face was wrinkled and bespattered with some kind of red make-up. She wore a maroon dress and a red bodice from which her flesh-like breasts spilt over. She carried a golden goblet containing, they say, 'the abominations of her filthiness and fornication.' Hung from her neck was a paper streamer on which was written in large letters: 'MYSTERY. BABYLON THE GREAT. THE MOTHER OF HARLOTS AND ABOMINATIONS OF THE

EARTH.' She was the personification of evil, the Antichrist of the Book of Revelation.

Behind the Whore of Babylon were three giants, the *gigantones*. Each represented a person from a different race or creed. There was a Negro with jet black hair, naked apart from a dirty loin cloth, a *morisco* in a white kaftan and a Jew, in a skull cap, who had an exaggeratedly hooked nose. Each of these figures was painted with fresh paint, as if they had been painted only the day before. Running along or walking with these four figures, a group of men, dressed as Greek soldiers, threw paper balls at the heads of these figures and, having thrown one, would run to pick up another from a basket, being carried on a mule, or simply pick one up from off the ground and throw it again. As each ball hit its target, the crowd would cheer or shout in approval. They would hiss or boo the ones which missed.

Behind the giants came men and women in fancy dress, wearing masks. The men were dressed in tricorne hats and jewel-encrusted jackets, white pantaloons down to their knees and white stockings and black shoes. The women wore white blouses and bright yellow dresses. They bowed and smiled to the crowd as they made their way across the Plazuela as the crowd cheered and applauded them. Each of the men escorted one of the women onto the raised stage near the north side of the square and a band of guitarists, violinists and drummers appeared at the front of the stage.

'Let's go,' shouted the leader of the band. The little group started playing a slow dance tune and each of the men danced with his partner. Some of the couples in the crowd also danced and, by the time the band was into its third or fourth dance, nearly all the people in the Plazuela were dancing. The dances became quicker and wilder and the band started to play a daring *chacona*. The dancers on the stage whirled around wildly to the cheers of the crowd. They kissed and touched each other erotically as they danced. Couples in the crowd began to dance with the same passionate frenzy. Francisca and I joined in and hugged and kissed each other as we did so. It was as if we were at an open air party. People were whooping and shouting and thoroughly enjoying themselves. The dance action was just too much for some people who became so excited that they adjourned to an alley off the Plazuela to indulge themselves in more intimate physical contact. Some just stood up against a wall in the Plazuela and did it to each other there and then, in full view of the crowd whose reaction was to cheer them on.

'Look, Juan,' said Francisca, staggered at what she saw. 'Can you see those young nuns over there? They seem as willing as any of these women to share their charms with any lad they fancy.'

Gradually, the excitement died down as the dancing on the stage reverted to a more demure kind which heralded the arrival of the carts for the play. Four huge, extravagantly painted wagons appeared in a slowly moving convoy, drawn by oxen with bright red and white sashes over their backs and plumes of white feathers tied to their heads. The closed sides of the carts confounded the crowd who could not see what pieces of magic they contained. Strong men dressed as sailors held the reins of the oxen and carefully drew the carts to their positions in the space behind the stage, untethered the oxen and guided them away, out of the square.

We all stood in silence for a few minutes until the play began. The prologue set the scene. Faith tells Apostasy that the play is about the need to renew the ideas of the Old Testament. Music tells him that it will be a celebration of a mystery. Apostasy tells them to let him know when to cry or groan and Faith refuses, saying that he will not have to be miserable. He then asks where the play is to be. They tell him that it is right here in the Plazuela de Santiago, in front of the town hall. People from all over Madrid, the court of the world, will come to see it. They were right. The streets were packed. The crowds were silent until the end of the prologue when they burst into spontaneous applause and cheered. Apostacy sulkily sloped off the stage while Music, Faith and Mascara, the masked one, took a deep bow.

During the musical interlude, which followed the prologue, women with refreshments sold their wares to people in the crowd, who by then appreciated a drink and something to eat. Francisca and I were parched and famished. The whole of the interlude gave way to an increasing anticipation of what this play was about. It soon became clear. It started with the character Music crossing the stage followed by John the Baptist, dressed in animal skins, carrying a banner on which was emblazoned, 'For all the prophets and the law were valid until John', the words of Mathew 11 verse 13. So John the Baptist heralds the new law, the law of Grace. John the Baptist then invites the whole of mankind to turn up at a public examination to fill the jobs that the prophets have left vacant with the arrival of the new law, as set down in the New Testament. The musicians accompany him as he sings his message.

Judaism and the Synagogue are baffled by what they have heard and do not understand why there are any vacancies to be filled. As far as they are concerned, the three posts filled by the law of Moses, the penitence of Elias and the preaching of Jonas are still pre-eminent. They do not intend to resign themselves to being displaced by any new law.

The Church then declares that there really is a new law. She says that this law displaces the written law which itself, by prophecy, anticipates the law of Grace with the arrival of Christ. She then announces that Madrid is the centre of the church. With that, and as predicted by Pedro, the audience delivered a loud burst of applause and cheering. She then cites the Puerta Cerrada through which all have passed so that one may pass, that one being Emmanuel. I could feel the hairs rising on the back of my neck as the mystery was resolved, even though I had read as much, in the text. There was another burst of applause.

'Pedro has certainly found ways of keeping the attention of these people,' I whispered to Francisca.

'You haven't done badly either,' she said. 'Your music engages the audience, too.'

Judaism and the Synagogue deny that Christ has arrived because there had been no thunder and lightning nor earthquakes as foreseen in the Old Testament. They put all this talk of a new law down to rumour. Eventually, they become seriously worried at what they have heard and wonder who could replace Moses.

Then, with a trumpet fanfare and a drum roll, the first of the carts is opened to reveal the scene inside. It is a ship in a raging storm, with Peter at the helm, Andrew at the sails and John and James at the oars. This is pure symbolism. The ship is the Church. As Moses led his people across the desert, Peter leads the ship in the tempest, and therefore succeeds Moses as a leader. Andrew, who demonstrates his skill with the sails, the arms of which are in the shape of the Saint Andrew cross, replaces the skilful Aaron. The popular David is replaced by the beloved disciple, John; and James, who has beaten the storm, substitutes for Joshua, the valiant fighter.

Judaism then asks who will displace Jonas. There is another roll of drums and a trumpet fanfare. The doors to the second cart are opened. A country landscape appears with Paul riding his horse hard with a servant alongside him. The servant tells Paul that he is at risk of falling if he does not control the horse. Paul replies proudly that he is prepared to take the risk, even if the hills would be delighted to see him fall. Jonas is also a risk taker. He is God's rebel so both Paul and Jonas have something in common and Paul takes over from Jonas.

'Then tell me,' says Judaism. 'Who will be the second Adam?' With another flourish, the third cart opens to reveal Emmanuel dressed as a pilgrim and Innocence, dressed as a villain. Innocence immediately proclaims Emmanuel as the successor to Adam. Glory sings of Emmanuel as the true Christ in his majesty.

Judaism and the Synagogue look for consolation and Saint John the Baptist appears from the fourth cart, repeating his initial proclamation, calling the whole world to present themselves at the public examination to fill the vacant posts. He sings again, this time, directing the Synagogue and Judaism to 'behold the lamb of God who takes away the sins of the world.' Judaism and the Synagogue cower at these words.

Emmanuel blesses Madrid, using its Arabic name, 'the mother of the sciences' and makes parallels between the offices and majesty of the state and the operation and function of the church. Emmanuel expresses the strength of patriotism. The response of the audience is overwhelming. People shout and cheer and even provoke a reaction from Emmanuel who pauses and holds his hands up to the audience to quieten down the noise.

Peter denies Christ three times to Judaism and the Synagogue. He is roundly booed by the audience and seeks Emmanuel's forgiveness. Peter then confirms to Emmanuel that he feels sorry to deny him but says he is confused and is having difficulty in accepting that it is Christ who is the Emmanuel.

Judaism becomes even more disturbed. He addresses the audience and asks them who is king. They shout to confirm it's Emmanuel the powerful and the strong. 'Perhaps it is you,' says Judaism to Emmanuel.

'It is I,' says Emmanuel.

'Who are you?' says Judaism.

'I am a competitor for the general vacancy which has been announced today.'

'So am I,' says Judaism. He threatens Emmanuel with a cutlass and Peter, with a renewed faith, attempts to restrain Judaism. It is only a threat and Judaism realises that he has lost the competition to fill the vacancy. He therefore concedes the post to Emmanuel and does so by presenting him with a cross, saying, 'Take it, take it. This seat is your gain and my loss.' On taking the cross there are the sounds of thunder and an earthquake. The play ends with the whole cast, except Judaism and the Synagogue, celebrating the triumph of Emmanuel and singing and exalting the Eucharist.

A huge round of applause and cheering signalled the conclusion. Francisca and I were disappointed that Pedro was not there to see how well his work was received. I could not believe I was so wrong, even to contemplate that the audience would not follow it. Most of its members had all but joined in the action. The crowd gradually dispersed and Francisca and I made our way back to my mother's house to collect baby Juan. 'What did you think of that?' I asked Francisca.

'Amazing. Pedro is so clever to think of all those characterisations. I especially enjoyed the Synagogue and Judism. I could not work out whether Christ was killed or not.'

'I think he was killed but quietly and imperceptibly. Isaiah prophesies that there will be earthquakes, thunder and storms at the coming of the Lord and, sure enough, that is what happened at the end of the play. So yes, I think Christ was killed and killed by Judaism, rather than on the cross.'

'It is an original story, Juan and your music fitted it so well. I am proud of my composer man.'

'You had to say that!'

CHAPTER 23

Diego had taken much longer on his travels than the King had anticipated and had angered the King with his delays and procrastination. The King's wrath showed itself some days after Diego's return when he rewarded Diego's dilatoriness by entreating that he would never be allowed to go to Italy again. Diego had spent a king's fortune on works of art. He brought back over twenty paintings, mainly the works of the Italian masters Veronese, Titian and Tintoretto, and some three hundred sculptures. Nearly the entire haul was eventually displayed in the Octagonal Gallery at the Alcázar Palace and transformed its drabness into a spectacular display of artistic genius.

Within days of Diego's return, the Council for State Security convened a meeting at which Diego and Juan de Pareja reported on their plan for the attack on the Vatican. The King attended as did Juan de Roxas Carrión and I, the Ministerial Head of the Council, the new Chief Clerk, Jorge Sanz de Aranda, an assistant private secretary and the Maestro. Diego was astute and confident in his reporting. The plan was a development of our outline. It was that fifty soldiers from one of our infantry divisions, dressed in civilian clothes, would establish themselves in some properties they would rent at some outlying and remote point just off the main road from Verona to Rome, the route that the wagons carrying the granite cobblestone to the Vatican would be taking. Six hundred and fifty wagons would be needed to transport all the cobblestones to Saint Peter's. The cobblestones would be delivered in convoys of twenty wagons a day. Each wagon was to have a canvas tarpaulin which would cover the whole of its contents. There would be two drivers on each wagon which would be pulled by a team of four horses. The soldiers would intercept a whole convoy of the wagons at gunpoint, tie up the drivers and hold them, under an armed guard, in one of the rented buildings. The soldiers would take over the driving of the wagons and deliver the cobblestones to Saint Peter's square.

However, before driving to the Vatican, they would load each wagon with 500 bags of sand. The bags would be made of the same type of canvas and be the same size as the money bags in the Belvedere Palace. After delivering the cobblestones, the drivers would take the wagons to the rear entrance to the palace. They would leave the wagons there until nightfall. They would then enter the Belvedere Palace and substitute the bags of sand for the gold *ducats*. One of the soldiers would be a trained locksmith who would use his skills to open the door to the palace and to the room in the basement. Pareja confirmed that the palace was unoccupied at night. The loaded wagons would be left overnight in the grounds of the Vatican while all the soldiers, except four, stayed in lodgings. These four would remain with the wagons to guard them until the morning.

The wagons would then head out of the Vatican and take the road back to Verona. When they reached Florence they would bear to the left and take the road to Genoa where each wagon would be put onto one of two of our navy ships. Ten wagons would be loaded onto each ship so as to divide the load. The ships would sail to Barcelona where the gold *ducats* would be unloaded and taken to Madrid.

'This just will not work!' said the Ministerial Head of the Council, angrily and loudly. 'It's full of flaws. How will the soldiers know which wagons to stop? How do you know that the Belvedere Palace will be unoccupied? The wagons will collapse under the weight of the sand and the cobblestones or under the weight of the gold.'

'Let me take each of those points in turn,' said Diego, maintaining his composure. 'The wagons will be labelled with a number on a post in the front left hand corner. Each convoy will be labelled separately and the numbers will be Roman numerals from one to twenty.'

'How do you know that?' asked the Chief Clerk, in the same tone as the Ministerial Head.

'While Señor Pareja and I were in Rome, we sought out the architect Gian Lorenzo Bernini,' continued Diego, remaining utterly calm. 'By lucky coincidence, the Vatican had just issued a draft public tender notice for the supply and delivery of the cobblestones. We arranged to meet him, pretending that we could be interested in quoting for the work. Bernini provided us with a copy of all the relevant documentation. In one paragraph it specified the numbering system for the delivery wagons and explained that this was for security purposes and only correctly labelled wagons would be allowed onto the site.

'We know that the palace is not occupied at night because we visited the building during a conducted tour. Apart from an exhibition area, where there are a number of religious artefacts on display, the building is used as a centre for administration and nobody lives there. That was what we understood.'

'Yes, señor,' said Pareja, in the same composed tone as his master. 'I asked the guide who showed us around. I said that the Belvedere Palace would make a wonderful home for some Vatican dignitaries. He said that that may be, but nobody lived there.'

Pareja continued. 'I can answer your question about the wagons collapsing. We will be extremely unlucky to lose a wagon. The permitted maximum load for the wagons to be used, according to the draft tender documents, is two *toneladas*. From the dimensions of the square that is to be constructed, I have calculated that they will need 1134 *toneladas* of cobbles. The specification says that no wagon should carry more than one and three quarter *toneladas*. This will require 650 wagons, that is, thirty-two convoys of twenty wagons with an additional convoy of ten. The 500 bags of sand will weigh just over a fifth of a *tonelada* so, even loaded with the sand, the maximum permitted load on the wagons will not be exceeded. The gold *ducats* weigh thirty-eight *toneladas*. Divided between twenty wagons, this comes to one and nine tenths *toneladas* per wagon. This is also within the maximum permitted load.'

'You have done your homework,' said the Ministerial Head, sarcastically.

'I've merely done my job,' said Juan de Pareja, replying with due politeness.

Then the King spoke. 'This sounds a good plan to me. What are the timescales for implementing it?'

'That is a difficult question, Your Majesty,' said Diego. 'According to Bernini, the building work is to commence in the spring of '57.'

'That's ridiculous!' said the King, suddenly exploding in anger. 'I've never heard such nonsense. We can't possibly wait around for six years to sort out the finances of Spain. We've declared ourselves bankrupt once and we are on the verge of doing it again. We need a plan we can implement in a year's time at the most.'

'Your Majesty, all building work at the Vatican has stopped because they, too, are in dire financial trouble. According to Bernini, they are at the limit of what the banks will let them borrow and need to pay off some of their massive debt before they can build the square. It's not just the cobblestones. There will be a complex of surrounding buildings and this is where most of the money will be spent.'

'We need another plan,' said the King, then a little calmer. 'Has anyone any ideas?'

There was an awkward silence which was so intense that you could hear the breathing of those at the meeting. Nobody wanted to reply so nobody answered. Then the Ministerial Head spoke. 'I suppose we could buy our own wagons and just go in and take the money.'

'You have completely missed the point,' said Diego, coolly and courageously. 'The whole point of using the wagons carrying the cobblestones is that these wagons will have legitimate access to the Vatican because they will be delivering the cobbles. If we intercept their milk delivery, which, of course, has equally legitimate access, we won't be able to take more than a handful of gold. And what would we do with the milkman?'

There was an outburst of laughter. Even the King laughed.

'Surely, we could legitimately enter with a convoy of some kind,' said the King.

'Not to my knowledge,' said Diego. 'Not before the spring of '57. We could highjack a laundry wagon or a removals van or two but we still need a convoy of vehicles to carry off the ten million *ducats*. As Pareja has already said, we are talking of around twenty heavy wagons. It is a huge undertaking.'

The Chief Clerk, Jorge Sanz de Aranda, then spoke. 'I have a question. What eventually happens to the wagon drivers you tie up and detain at the properties you rent?'

'That is why we need fifty soldiers, Señor Sanz de Aranda,' said Diego. 'We leave ten of the soldiers to take charge of and feed and water the wagon drivers. The soldiers will be armed, of course. It is important that the rented properties are on the road between Rome and Florence. The nearer to Rome the better. This is to minimise the time the wagon drivers are detained. And so the convoy can call in soon after they have left the Vatican, to pick up the ten soldiers. You will see that there is more detail, like this, in my paper for the King.'

There was some more, often heated discussion and all who attended agreed, albeit reluctantly, that this was the only credible plan. The conclusion was that we would have to muddle along, in or on the edge of bankruptcy, until we could implement it. The King made a half-hearted request that we all think of other possibilities but nobody volunteered to spend any time on them. So the meeting was closed.

***

It was only a month later that Diego was appointed Grand Chamberlain of the Palace. There were a number of equally able, if not better qualified, applicants for the post but the King decided, to the irritation of many, that Diego would be offered the job. As well as being a renowned painter, Diego was by then a well experienced courtier who had been Assistant Superintendent of the Palace for a number of years before being promoted to Supervisor of Palace works. He was delighted, as I discovered when I went to congratulate him.

'Juan, I am overjoyed. It completely vindicates my plan for the attack on the Vatican. I can handle what the other applicants think.' Little did he know that the job would kill him and leave his reputation in question.

***

Francisca and I decided to have a party at our house to celebrate baby Juan's fifth birthday. We invited all of our friends and their children, all of our relations and all of our colleagues at the palace, as well as Francisca's colleagues at the Shod Carmen soup kitchen. There was another reason for celebration. About a year after the performances of 'The General Vacancy', the Maestro had recommended to the King that I become the chief composer for the Royal Chapel. We waited several years for the King to reply but eventually he accepted. I was delighted not only with the new position but also with what seemed a colossal increase in salary, which became 1750 *ducats* a year, plus 100 *ducats* in expenses, with additional payments for individual works I composed.

Francisco came with Juana Vélez. Vitoria de Cuenca and Balthasar Favales came, too. Vitoria was three months pregnant for their first child. They were so pleased. By then they had been married six years but it seemed only days before that we were at their wedding and the reception spoilt by the unfortunate fracas over her uncle the *tercio*. Balthasar's business was expanding almost by the day and he had set up offices in Toledo and Guadalajara. He had bought a magnificent house with a huge garden in the Calle Pardo, opposite the Calle de la Santa Catalina.

By then, Luis de As was married to Angela Suarez but, as yet, there were no signs of any offspring. Angela said that she wasn't sure whether she wanted the responsibility of being a mother but would accept and love any baby that came along. It was wonderful just to see our friends and colleagues chatting away with each other, as if they had all known each other for years, as indeed they had. We were pleased that Diego and Juana could come and Pedro, as well as Giulio Rospigliosi who by then had written three more librettos, and was preparing for the end of his nunciature and his return to Rome. Everybody made a great fuss of baby Juan who spent most of the time playing with Agustín, Antonia and Alonso's little son of the same age, both under the supervision of Antona, their lovely, nine year old daughter.

Domingo, Francisca's father, had brought his new wife, Pascuala. We could never work out why they went to Toledo for what was apparently a holiday and came back to announce that they were married. For several weeks, I had to console Francisca, who was, of course, Domingo's only daughter. She just could not understand why we, at least, were not invited to the wedding. They claimed they decided to marry on the spur of the moment, when they were already in Toledo. Francisca, however, thought they were resolved to marry in Toledo, well before they went, and just did not want anyone else to know about it or to attend. It became clear, during the latter part of the evening, that Francisco knew Pascuala surprisingly well and went up to speak to her to renew their acquaintance.

'Pascuala, it's good to see you again. So we are related by marriage then, and not just business contacts and friends anymore.'

At first Pascuala denied knowing Francisco. 'I'm not sure I remember you, do I?' she said while standing next to Domingo.

Domingo was immediately suspicious and defensive. 'Do you know each other or not?'

'Of course we know each other,' said Francisco. 'I've known Pascuala for a number of years. Are you still working in reception at the house in the Arganzuela?'

The house that Francisco had in mind was one of the brothels which, since the development of the flourishing business in love sleeves, was one of the family's better customers in this street.

'What are you insinuating?' asked Domingo. 'Are you saying my wife is a whore?'

'Absolutely not,' replied Francisco, firmly. 'I remember the time when Pascuala worked at the door of one of the houses of pleasure in the Arganzuela. I still go there periodically on business, selling our patented love sleeves.'

'You never told me you worked for a brothel!' said Domingo, utterly outraged by what he had heard. 'You told me you worked at the hospital. So I've married a liar!'

Pascuala, not surprisingly, became very distressed. 'I thought you'd hate me if I told you what I did for a living,' she sheepishly said to Domingo. Then, turning to Francisco: 'Thank you, Francisco. You've caused me to have the most embarrassing day of my life. My husband now knows I worked for a whorehouse. Thank you very much.'

Domingo grabbed Pascuala's hand and stormed out of our house, virtually dragging her with him, calling her a liar, a slut and all manner of other disgusting names. By then she was in tears and howling in shame. Poor Francisco felt terrible. He wrongly imagined that Domingo would be fully aware of Pascuala's previous employment. There was one other detail that he imagined that Domingo would not know. This was that Pascuala and Francisco had become rather more than just friends and that she was the last of Francisco's fancy women before he fell in love with Juana. This noisy, heated and unfortunate argument was so loud it was noticed by everyone at the party, except, by good fortune, the children who were all in bed and sound asleep. 'What was that about?' asked Balthasar, addressing his question to Francisco.

'That's very difficult,' said Francisco, attempting to hedge around the issue. 'Someone said something and Domingo and his wife started an argument about it and they decided to go.'

'It looked as if he was dragging her to the door,' said Diego.

'Well, let's just carry on,' I said. 'Would anyone like another drink?'

Francisco was annoyed with his lack of diplomacy and judgement in speaking as he did to Pascuala, and the resulting uproar which ensued. Sadly, the argument at our party was far from the end of the story. Domingo threw Pascuala out of his house never to have her in his life again and Pascuala went back to live with her mother in the eastern side of Madrid. We never saw her again. Domingo would only ever speak to Francisco out of politeness and Francisco was devastated to realise the damage that had been done by this encounter at our house.

Fortunately, Juana Vélez took a very sensible and liberal view. Francisco felt obliged to tell her all about his relationship with Pascuala. Juana said that what happened in Francisco's life before he fell in love with Juana was nothing to do with their new lives together. 'The past is the past. I'm glad Francisco had a good time with Pascuala. He is a very gentle person and I'm sure he was with her. I am the beneficiary of his experience.' It would have been awful if she had formed a less favourable construction.

***

When you are promoted to a more senior position in an organisation, it is not for the reason of paying you more and giving you a little more status. It is, in fact, to extract from you a volume of work of a quality commensurate with your elevated position. From the time of my promotion and for many years into the future, I was constantly in demand, not as much as a harpist or clavi-harpist, but regularly as a composer. My earliest collaborator, in my new post, was a dramatist called Luis de Ulloa Pereira. He was married three times, the first time to his niece who mysteriously died a few months afterwards. When Olivares was sacked from the King's Court, he went to live with Luis de Ulloa Pereira for a time so Ulloa was known to and influential in the palace. I first met him when he came to see me in my new office. He was a short, bearded man with a large paunch that hung over his trousers.

'I have asked to see you, Señor Hidalgo because I have heard from my friends in the court of the King that you may be available to compose music. Is it possible that you can help me?' he asked with a smile.

'That depends,' I said, not knowing in any detail what he may want.

'I have written a *comedia* in three acts called "Picus and Canens" and I need a composer to write the musical accompaniment.'

'I can do that,' I said, 'but I need to have musical directions. That means I need an indication, on your script, exactly where you want the music and what verses you want set to music. Some idea of the mood you want also helps.'

'I have done all that,' replied the enthusiastic playwright. 'I have the text here.' He opened a bag and placed an untidy pile of paper on my desk.

'Is it all in page order?' I asked.

'Oh yes. It's all in order. I've written out separately the pieces I want set to music.'

'That's good,' I replied. 'That will save me time. What is the story about? I have heard of King Picus, I think.'

'Yes. The story is simple,' he said excitedly. 'It's based on a story from Roman mythology. Circe, the daughter of Helios falls in love with Picus, the King of Rome, who is already married to Canens. He rejects Circe who turns him into a woodpecker. Canens cannot find her husband after searching for him for six days and is so distraught that she kills herself.'

'God, what a tragedy,' I said.

'Yes. It is a true tragedy. I have elaborated the Roman myth with some characters I have put in and have invented subplots to interest the audience.'

'I'd like to see what you've written before making a decision. Can you come back in three days?'

I read the script which was a mess. Nearly all the pages were of different sizes and of different kinds of paper. Some had other material written on the back. His writing was almost illegible in places. This was in stark contrast to the pieces he wanted set to music which were in immaculate writing and on clean paper. I decided to see what Francisca thought, so I bundled the whole manuscript into a bag and took it home.

'What a terrible story,' she said. 'How can you read all this? It's almost indecipherable. What do you think of Luis de Ulloa Pereira?'

'I cannot help liking the man. He is so enthusiastic about me doing the job for him. He has written other plays but I've no idea who has written his music before.'

'You should do it, Juan. It will be such a challenge and you like a challenge.'

So I did it. It took me a full three months to compose the tunes and indeed it was a challenge. I first had to sort out the numerous inconsistencies between Luis de Ulloa's script of the play and what he had written out for me to use. It was necessary to have several meetings with him to clarify these issues. It was all worth it, despite the frustrations. The work was performed in the Buen Retiro to celebrate the 'good health of the new Queen, Mariana of Austria'. What an odd concept, I thought. The King attended along with many of the staff of the palace and the whole performance was a great success.

Within days, I had another request to compose, this time from Antonio de Solís, a great friend of Pedro Calderón de la Barca. De Solís, by then a well-established playwright, had recently been appointed to the position of Private Secretary to the King and had presumably discovered from his contacts in the palace that I could be available to compose the supporting music for a *comedia*. He made no arrangements for a meeting but turned up one afternoon in my office. He almost begged me to write the music for his 'Triumphs of Love and Fortune'. Once again, I decided to see the work he had completed before agreeing to take on the task. He had written a beautiful piece and his preparation was totally immaculate. The manuscript was one of the most elegant pieces of writing I had ever seen.

'Where's the script you want me to use for the music?' I asked.

'What do you mean?' he said.

'Well, I'll need the words you want set to music.'

'I see,' he said. 'I have shown that on the manuscript.' And he had, in blue ink.

'Let me take your manuscript and I'll let you know in two days whether I'll do the composing.'

'Can't you tell me now?'

'No. I need to know what my commitment will be.'

I enjoyed reading de Solís's script. It was an allegorical play featuring the characters of Love and Fortune, each of whom wanted to prove to the other that he was the more powerful. De Solís had brought characters from Greek mythology into the play with Endymion, the son of Zeus, suffering agonies over his unrequited love for Diana, the virgin goddess of the hunt. Psyche, the goddess of sensual pleasure, is treated bitterly and cruelly by Venus because Fortune has proclaimed that Psyche is more beautiful that Venus herself. Love decides to intervene and helps Psyche to thwart Venus's cruel insults. Fortune, not to be outdone by Love, decides to come to the aid of Endymion and make him lucky so that he becomes lucky in the love of Diana. Zeus, the king of the gods, resolves the conflict. He announces that Venus is no longer jealous of or angry with the beautiful

Psyche. He says that both Love and Fortune have helped bring happiness to Psyche and Endymion. He concludes that Love's rewards are true while Fortune's rewards are merely dreams.

'Do you agree to write the music?' asked de Solís when, exactly two days later, to the minute, he burst into my office.

'Yes, I'll do it,' I said.

He came around my desk and almost in tears hugged me. 'I'm so pleased. I'm so grateful,' he said.

'It's fine. That's fine,' I said, disengaging myself from him. 'There's no need to be so emotional. I have read your play and I like its theme. It will be a great success. We must get it performed in the Buen Retiro, in the Coliseo.'

I could not have been more wrong. The performance of de Solís's *comedia* was a disaster. The audience booed at some of the characters, Endymion and Fortune, in particular. They simply loathed the work and we could not work out why. De Solís was distraught and I could not console him. Despite this, I still had the overwhelming, still unfulfilled desire to write an opera.

***

There was one crucial piece of information missing from the King's plan to attack the Belvedere Palace. It was the dates for taking the cobblestones from Verona and their delivery to Rome. We could hardly put a group of our soldiers by the side of the road from Verona for them to wait through the whole of 1657 for the wagon convoys to appear over the horizon. So, at a meeting of a select group, chaired by the Chief Clerk of the Council for State Security, the King decided to send our party guest, Baltasar Moscoso y Sandoval, the Archbishop of Toledo, to Rome to find out what the vital dates were. By then, the Archbishop, who was a special agent, was in his seventies and nobody would suspect that he was going to the Vatican as a spy. The pretext was that he was to see the Pope about a nuncio to replace Giulio Repigliosi's successor, Patriarch Camillo Massimo, who was only in the post for just over a year before being recalled.

The Archbishop, accompanied by a small retinue of escorts and assistants, was away for three months. The arduous journey almost killed him and he came back totally exhausted. When he returned to the Alcázar Palace he was so worn out he had to be lifted bodily from his horse. His condition was so dire that his infantry escorts put him in a carriage and rushed him to the Casa de la Misericordia hospital. Aided by his favourite nun, Sister Maria de Albacete, it took him a full week to recover. The King was anxious to see him so, with Jorge Sanz de Aranda and an assistant private secretary as a note taker, he went to visit him in the hospital, only two days after the Archbishop's return.

'Wake up. The King has come to see you,' whispered Sister Maria. 'His Majesty has brought some colleagues with him.'

'Your Majesty, you should not see me in this state,' he said, obviously still weak. 'I haven't even shaved today, and I am still undressed.'

'Don't worry, Baltasar. I was anxious to visit you. I just wanted to make sure you were making a good recovery. From your terrible journey from Rome.'

'Oh yes, Your Majesty, they say I am recovering well but when we reached the palace I think I fainted because the next thing I knew, I was in hospital under the care of Sister Maria here.'

'I am so pleased to hear that you are improving,' said the King. 'I'd have felt awful if anything had happened to you.' Then, bluntly revealing the true reason for his visit, 'Incidentally, did you find out when the cobblestones will be leaving Verona?'

'Yes, Your Majesty. The first convoy of twenty wagons will leave on 1 May. Then there will be convoys of twenty wagons every other day, except in the last convoy which will comprise only ten.'

***

The expedition to the Vatican left at the beginning of March. It was led by an army lieutenant who, as planned, took a team of fifty soldiers. Nothing was heard of the mission until a convoy of dirty, battered wagons turned up outside the Treasury building on the east wing of the Alcázar Palace, nearly six months later. The lieutenant was summoned to report to the Ministerial Head of the Council for State Security. The King, myself, Juan de Roxas Carrión, Diego and Juan de Pareja, as well as the Chief Clerk, also attended.

'Well, tell us what happened,' said the Ministerial Head, urgently and impatiently.

'It is a long story but I'll keep it as brief as I can. I'll concentrate on the things that did not go according to plan. We decided to rent a farm and found one just off the road from Florence to Rome, just outside of a little town called San Casciano dei Bagni. We paid the landlord one month's rent in advance. When we arrived at the farm we discovered it was occupied by gypsies who refused to move out. They were armed and we fought them with our weapons. Three of our men were shot dead in the battle but we flushed out the gypsies and took over the farm. We estimated that it would take two weeks for the first group of twenty wagons to reach San Casciano so we gradually built up food supplies for the wagon drivers whom we would kidnap and detain at the farm. Eventually, the first convoy appeared. One of the drivers on each wagon was armed. That was totally unexpected.

'We decided to ambush the fifth convoy. We attempted to hold it up by discharging our guns into the air to get them to surrender. This failed miserably. The armed drivers fought back with all the daring they could muster but we eventually overcame them. Another five of our men were lost in the exchange of fire. Three of the drivers were killed.

'We tied up the remaining drivers and...'

'I'm getting impatient,' shouted the King. 'I'm really interested in how much money you recovered.'

Standing his ground, the lieutenant replied. 'I'll get to that shortly, Your Majesty, if I may...'

The King looked around the others of us, as if seeking some indication of our impatience but there was none. He relented and sat back in his chair.

'As I said, we tied up the drivers and left ten men in charge of them. We arrived at the Vatican just over a week later. We followed the plan, so unloaded the cobblestones and went to the Belvedere Palace and parked outside. We decided to wait until nightfall to go into the building. Our locksmith was able to open the rear door and two of us, holding lit candles, followed him down the stairs towards the basement. There was a cry of "Who goes there?" from near the door of the room containing the money.

'The room was under guard and, using a plan we had hatched on the road to Rome, I replied, "We are the fire-watchmen. There's smoke coming out of one of your windows."

'"Well, I can't smell anything," said one of two guards sitting by the door.

'"It's a fact," I said.

'"It's a strange time to see smoke. It's dark out there."

'"I'm just telling you what someone's reported."

'We rushed at the two guards, knocked them out cold and tied them up. The locksmith opened the door to the bullion room and there it was exactly as Juan Hidalgo had described: 150, pyramid-shaped piles, each containing one hundred bags. We then engaged our whole team and replaced the bags containing the gold with the sand bags we had brought from San Casciano. We left the gold *ducats* that were nearest the door so that nobody would detect that a crime had been committed, if they examined only those there. We loaded the wagons before daybreak. We decided to take the guards hostage and make our way out of Rome towards San Casciano. We brought some paint to camouflage the wagons, so not even the drivers of the other wagons from Verona would recognise us.

'We went back to San Casciano to pick up the ten men we had left at the farm. The place was empty. We couldn't find any of our men and the horses were gone. There were the obvious signs of a gunfight with musket-ball holes in windows and doors. We think the gypsies returned to take possession of the farm, killed the soldiers and released the hostages. We therefore left the farm with thirty-two men, our original fifty, less the three we lost taking the farm from the gypsies, the five we lost apprehending the convoy at San Casciano and the ten who we left looking after the hostages.

'After we had travelled about fifty *leguas* off the Verona road towards Genoa, we noticed that the last four wagons in the convoy were missing, along with eight men. They had simply disappeared. We do not know exactly what happened but can only surmise that the drivers of these wagons decided to steal the money they had on board and desert. So we reached Genoa with eight million *ducats* and twenty-four men. We released our two hostages from the Vatican, still tied up and blindfolded, by the side of the road, about twenty *leguas* from Genoa. They were left in the open on this moderately busy road so we presume someone must have found and released them.

'We were held up by a gang of about fifty highway robbers on the way from Barcelona to Tarragona. There was a battle on the road and we lost three more soldiers and one wagon in an almighty gunfight.

'We arrived in Madrid with fifteen wagons, seven and a half million *ducats*, twenty-one men and fifteen worn out wagons. I am sorry, Your Majesty. I have failed to bring back all ten million *ducats* and have lost twenty-nine men and fifty horses in this abortive mission. That is the end of my report,' he concluded, his head lowered dejectedly, as if he was deeply embarrassed.

Despite the series of setbacks the officer reported, the King was delighted. 'Congratulations, Lieutenant. You have had an incredibly difficult mission. And you have all but succeeded to the letter in the challenge you were given. It is extremely unfortunate that you lost so many men. It sounds like eight were deserters. The families of the others will be compensated in the usual way. Your actions may well have saved Spain from bankruptcy. Well done!' There was a short, spontaneous round of applause. We counted the mission as a success but the price paid was high, even in purely military terms. The seven and a half million *ducats* did, however, give the Council for Finance sufficient funds to declare the country solvent again. In effect, we had been bankrupt or on the verge of bankruptcy for all but ten years.

The Vatican must have at some time discovered their loss. We presumed that, if they did, they did not want to admit to their bankers that such a huge proportion of their gold currency reserves had disappeared. This audacious robbery remained, certainly to my knowledge, the largest valued robbery ever committed anywhere in the world. I was never sure whether to be proud or ashamed of my role in it. The fact is that we had used my friend Giulio Rospigliosi to cheat the Pope. My abiding fear was that Giulio would find out and work out for himself the role I played. If he did, I hoped he would realise that I had very little choice but to be a collaborator in this amazing venture. He might then forgive me.

CHAPTER 24

I had earned several increases in salary, and additional fees, in my posts of harpist, clavi-harpist and chief composer for the Royal Chapel. We had also benefitted from the handsome profits of mother's love sleeve business. So Francisca and I decided to buy our own house. We had a difficult decision to make because our new home had to be situated not too far from the palace; not far from our parents; not far from the theatre district, where I was spending more of my time; and not far from Juan junior's school which was the one I went to as a child, the San Martín Convent School in the Plazuela de las Descalzas Reales. It was the first time in our married life that Francisca and I had a serious disagreement.

'As far as I'm concerned, Juan, the most important thing is for us to be near Juan junior's school and our parents. You can always go on horseback to one of the theatres or to the palace.'

'I'm sure we will find somewhere convenient that satisfies all of our criteria.'

'No. I'm sorry but, of everything, I want somewhere near to Juan junior's school,' she said, coldly and emphatically.

It was rare for any house in the district of the Lower San Ginés to come up for sale, so I could see us waiting for years for something we could afford in that area. Francisca and I were at loggerheads over the location and the very notion of moving almost came to a halt. Then I hit on an idea. We would ask Balthasar Favales round to talk to us and maybe make some recommendations. I put the idea to Francisca.

'No. He is mainly a friend of yours and he will recommend what you want. There is a lot of property for sale on the east side of the town near the Buen Retiro and he will tell us to move there.'

'Come on Francisca. He loves us both and so does Vitoria. He won't say something, just to please me. He is a professional and will give us the best advice he can,' I said, placing an arm around her shoulders and attempting, not very subtly, to cajole her.

A few days later, we invited both of them to our house for a chat over a meal. We agreed to ensure that we were both part of any conversation about a move so that we both heard everything Balthasar had to say. The mere fact that we had agreed this course of action seemed to take the problem away and for the next week or so, before Balthasar and Vitoria came to our house, we speculated to each other, in the friendliest of terms, about what Balthasar might say. Would he recommend a house near the Calle de Toledo, a little to the south of where we were then, to the east, maybe off the Calle de Atocha or the Calle del Prado or maybe to the north, somewhere near the Calle del Desengaño? We started to work out what we wanted in the house, for example, an enclosed courtyard, at least two drawing rooms on the first floor and a large kitchen. Some stabling for the horses would also be useful but not essential. It would be good not to have to go up the Pedro Nieto's stables every time we wanted to ride them. Presuming she agreed to continue working for us, we would retain the services of Barbola who had been with us for nearly twenty years. So we became quite excited about moving, even though we had not a clue where we would be going.

By then, Juan junior was just over nine years old and had just over a year left at the convent school before moving to the senior school. He was a very intelligent child, constantly questioning the world around him.

'Papá, why is it that all animals, including human beings have the same type of eyes when their bodies all look different?' He would make comments about the things he saw in everyday life. 'Papá, why is it that they say the man who invented the wheel was a genius. Surely, the genius was the man who thought of using all four wheels together.' He turned out to be very good at mathematics and science, and, helped by my tutelage, became a talented harpist. Some clever children are quiet and lonely. Not Juan junior. He mixed with all the other children near where we lived and at school and got into just as much trouble as Francisca and I did when we were young. We idolised him and congratulated ourselves that we had produced this normal, popular child.

We had an excellent meal with Balthasar and Vitoria. They brought their four-year-old daughter, Clara, whom Juan junior entertained while we ate and chatted. Balthasar had a number of properties on his books but suggested that we could delay buying until Juan junior was at the grammar school. By then, he would be old enough to make his own way there and the closeness to the school would not be such a problem. Francisca, ever the protective mother, was less sure about that point. Balthasar suggested that, as an alternative, we could buy a house and keep the other going while we did anything that needed doing in the new house. We could then move out of the Puerta Cerrada when it suited us to do so. We decided to wait for six months and leave it to Balthasar to let us know then of any properties, not too far from our parents' houses, which could be suitable.

About four months later, slightly earlier than we had expected, Balthasar came to see us one evening. 'I've found this fantastic house that exactly fits what you want,' he said, smiling and excitedly. 'It even has its own stables for three horses, an enclosed garden, a massive kitchen and servants' quarters. You could move your mother in there if you wanted to, Juan. It's in the Calle de la Madalena, at the end of the street near La Fuente de los Relatores.'

'You are too early, Balthasar,' said Francisca frostily. 'We agreed we would wait six months. You are back within four.'

'I know, Francisca, but it is such a good property that I could not resist offering it to you, at least for you to look at. You can always leave it. And you don't even have to see it if you don't want to.'

'Let's at least go to see it, love,' I said. 'We cannot lose. If we like it we can have it. If not, we forget it.'

Balthasar was not exaggerating. Francisca absolutely loved the house. It was on the south side of the street and was built around a courtyard at the centre of which was a pretty fountain with its vertical jet of water leaping into the air and falling into a shell-shaped bowl which sat on a carved stone column. To the side of the main house there was stabling and an area for storing hay. We could even put our own carriage under cover in the yard by the side of the house and there was a carriage gate off the road. Imagine: us with a carriage!

Francisca was overwhelmed by the kitchen area which was large and light. There were two wood-burning stoves and so much storage space it was hard to see how to fill it all; but I knew Francisca would succeed. There were three bedrooms, a dining room and a lounge on the ground floor, all of which looked out onto the courtyard. The lounge and dining room also overlooked the street. There was a large, main bedroom on the first floor and three large drawing rooms, one of which was easily twelve *varas* long. The upstairs rooms could be reached from a large landing area at the top of a double curved staircase which rose majestically from the *zaguan* or from a balcony that completely encircled and overlooked the courtyard. The servants' quarters were in the southeast corner of the house and their four smallish rooms were on the ground floor or in the basement. The Calle de la Madalena was a side street and the nearest main road was Calle de Atocha, a good 200 *varas* away from the house. So the property was in a relatively quiet road in which children could safely play.

'Juan, this is our house. I do not want or need to see another. I have fallen in love with this one,' said Francisca, clearly enthralled. That was enough for me. I just loved it, too. We agreed with Balthasar to buy it, there and then.

We continued living in the rented house for about another fifteen months but moved the horses into the stables at the new house in Calle de la

Madalena, so there was something living there that was ours. We decided to sublet the house in the Puerta Cerrada. Our landlord, Juan Pardo Moncón, agreed and said it would save him finding some more tenants himself. Balthasar advertised it and eventually we rented it to a banker and his family who were moving to Madrid from Lisbon. That would make us a modest income and give us a bolthole in the Puerta Cerrada which we thought Juan junior could move into at some time in the future. In our spare time, we furnished three rooms in the house in the Madalena: the main bedroom upstairs, Juan junior's room which was off the *zaguan,* and the downstairs lounge. We moved in the day after Juan junior left the convent school.

Juan junior, by dint of his own ability and intelligence, had won a place at Imperial. His mother and father were so proud.

***

My need to write an opera became so great it burnt me inside. It possessed me like a demented demon. It became one of those terrible, almost frightening, ambitions that has to be satisfied, at all costs. I would write the first Spanish opera. But what would it be about? Would Pedro write the libretto? I did not want to ask him to write a libretto without having a clue about the subject. I urgently needed a plot. I wanted something that would capture and enthral an audience. I wanted nothing short of a complete opera with the costumes, the staging, the libretto and the music forming a totally integrated work of art. The one thing I lacked was an idea. Mine all seemed familiar or uninspiring. I agonised in frustration. Then one day, Diego asked me to come with him to look at the pictures in the Octagonal Gallery at the palace. 'Juan, it is complete now. The paintings I bought in Italy for the King are hanging there. Come and see them,' he said proudly and excitedly. I took little persuasion and we went to the gallery.

'What do you think of these?' asked Diego, pointing towards a matched pair of canvases by the Italian painter Paolo Veronese, hung one above the other. The upper picture was called 'Venus and Adonis' and the lower one 'The Death of Procris'. In the first, Adonis is asleep and lying with his head in the lap of the half-naked Venus who has her arm across his chest. She is fanning Adonis and looks sad and anxious, as if she is anticipating his imminent death. Venus looks down at a naked child hugging a dog, as if in a parody of the two lovers. The picture reminded me of the Michelangelo 'Pieta' I had seen in Saint Peter's in Rome, with the dead Christ in the lap of his mother.

In the lower picture, Cephalus is distraught and leans over his dying wife, Procris, who has his javelin stuck in her side. Cephalus had mistakenly attacked her and she looks up with a doubtfully forgiving smile. Each picture was painted in the brightest colours. Cephalus wears a gold sash with a blood-red tunic while Procris is in a gold-patterned white dress, which delicately exposes her breasts. Adonis is dressed in the brightest orange and green with Venus in blue and gold.

'These are the most moving pictures,' I said. 'They are not painted in your style, Diego but they are just as full of emotion, and mark the sad end of two great love stories.'

'I knew you would like them,' he said. As if fate had told him to say it, he then asked, 'Do they give you any ideas?'

An explosion occurred in my head as I realised what he was suggesting. His idea was to use one of these love stories for an opera. 'Diego, you are a genius,' I said. 'An opera. Yes!'

My mind began to race ahead of me. 'There are two operas here,' I thought. 'Most of Madrid knows about Venus and Adonis, a story of illicit love. We could write a short, trial opera around this one, and a more substantial work around the lesser known myth of Cephalus and Procris.'

'Have we solved a problem?' asked Diego.

'I think we have but we may have created more. There could be two operas here, one in each picture. If so, we need to convince Pedro that he should write the libretti. That will keep him occupied!'

The seeds were sown. Now I could go to Pedro with some ideas. There was, however, a little hindrance, namely that some years before he had become a priest and was the chaplain at the Chapel of the New Kings at the Cathedral in Toledo. I decided that, rather than writing to him, I would ride there and speak to him, face to face. We could then have a proper conversation rather than suffer a peremptory exchange of letters. There was sure to be some argument and I felt he would be negative about it, at least to begin with. Toledo was only fifteen *leguas* from Madrid and I left very early one morning to ensure that I arrived there within two days of travelling. I found him reading in the Chapel.

'Juan, what are you doing here? What a surprise.'

'I need to see you Pedro.'

'What's up, Juan? Something is troubling you.'

'Nothing, Pedro, but I want to discuss an idea with you. Can we go somewhere and sit down? I need a rest and a drink.'

We walked to his tiny office where he picked up a jug and poured me a cup of water. The walls were bare and the floor was cold stone. There was a small desk presided over by a large crucifix which forced anyone sitting opposite him to move to one side to see him. The high, tiny windows, bracketed by long, black curtains, barely lit the room so that he was hardly visible as his gloomy, black tunic merged him into the shadows.

'What is your idea?' he asked, relying on the darkness to conceal his facial expression.

'It is an idea for some operas,' I said.

'Go on.'

'Well, do you remember? I said I was keen on creating an opera with you when I came back from Italy. You seemed to warm to the idea?'

'Vaguely,' he replied, still not revealing his thoughts.

'The other day, Diego Velázquez showed me some pictures that he had brought back from Italy. We both thought that two of them would make good subjects for operas.'

'Oh, yes.'

I was beginning to feel as if I was pushing a boulder uphill. Had his post as chaplain here changed him that much? Was he still writing plays? Was he as friendly with me as I thought before, when we were both working on 'The General Vacancy'? I would soon find out. I described to him what I had seen in the pair of Veronese's pictures and how they had inspired me. I explained enthusiastically how we could write one opera to 'test the water', as I put it, and then create a larger, perhaps more impressive work.

'No. I am not so sure.'

I thought his reply was not a final refusal but a holding reply, which anticipated further questioning. So I saw the 'no' as mildly positive.

'Who will sponsor these works?'

'The King.'

'What makes you think that?'

'When I came back from Italy, he said he wanted Maestro Patiño to put a case together. The Maestro has since written to the King, who agrees that it is a good idea. He is keen for a Spanish opera to be written and will finance it.'

'Really?'

'Yes, Pedro. The King agreed with the Maestro,' I said, leaving him in no doubt.

'As you know, Juan, I have new responsibilities now and I am still not sure whether I can find the time. Can you leave it with me and I will let you know what I decide? I will write to you.'

I was disappointed and felt sick inside. I was not a playwright so I could not write the libretti myself. I was not a student of Greek mythology so barely knew the stories. I bade farewell to Pedro and decided to stay at an inn for the night in Toledo before making my way home. All the way back, I wondered what I could do to realise this idea. I knew several playwrights who were capable of writing a good script. Not least among them were Luis de Ulloa and Antonio de Solís, with both of whom I had already collaborated. There was also Juan Vélez de Guevara who had spoken to me before about collaboration and Juan Bautiste Diamante who was becoming more prominent then. However, the outstanding playwright, by a long way, was Pedro Calderón de la Barca and I suppose I had little choice but to wait for him to tell me what he wanted to do about this new venture.

As always, I put on a brave face as I put my horse in the stables and Francisca and Juan junior came running out of our new house to greet me.

'How did it go, Papá?' shouted Juan junior who understood my ambitions for an opera, if not their raging intensity.

'How did you get on, Juan?' said Francisca.

'Surprisingly badly,' I said. 'Pedro is not that keen. He did not refuse to write the libretti. However, he wants time to think about it.'

'How long will he take to decide?' asked Juan junior.

'I don't know, son. He didn't say and I didn't want to press him. He could have gone off the idea all together. So I just left him to think about it.'

'Didn't you stay with him or have a meal with him?' asked Francisca.

'No. I just wanted to find an inn for the night, sleep and get up early to come back home.'

'I'm so sorry,' said Francisca, embracing me tenderly.

'Don't worry, love. There is just nothing we can do. We'll just have to wait to see what Pedro wants to do.'

***

Juan junior made an uncertain start at Imperial. He was reluctant to go to school, claiming he felt ill or anxious about problems he was having there. We had to sort this out, so Francisca and I went to the school to see what was going on. We made no appointment but went straight to see his form master, a Señor García, who was clearly surprised to see us. We repeated what Juan had told us about his difficulties there. Señor Garcia said that he had noticed that Juan had become withdrawn but did not know of any particular problems he was having with any of his classmates, who seemed to involve him in games, discussions and other activities. He certainly did not feel that Juan was being ostracised in any way. In fact, he said that Juan seemed popular with the children in his own class but that he was a quiet boy. We explained that he was not quiet at home and, quite the opposite, he was energetic and boisterous. Something had to be wrong and we could not work out what it was. The teacher suggested that we ask Juan directly about the problem because, as he put it, he could not find a cure until he was aware of the symptoms.

When Juan junior came home we asked him to tell us what the problem was.

'I don't want to speak about it. I'm sure I can deal with it myself.'

'Juan, you must tell us because we are worried sick about what is going on at the school and it is clearly affecting you,' said Francisca. 'Would you like to talk to just one of us, either Papá or me, on our own?'

'Can I speak to just you, Mamá?'

We agreed with this approach and I kissed him on the cheek and left him with Francisca. He told her that one of the senior boys at the school was following him when he went to the room they used to relieve themselves and would touch him on his genital area. He said he had been repulsed by these happenings but found it difficult to fight the boy off because he was much bigger than Juan. He knew the name of the boy but said he did not want to report him because he was afraid that the boy would hit him or make life at school even more difficult for him.

Francisca's skills at dealing with anything of an extremely difficult nature came into their own in solving this problem. She explained to Juan that this boy was probably taking advantage of other young boys at the school and if Juan junior could bring himself to report the boy, and the school did something about it, Juan may be saving others from the offender as well as saving himself. Juan junior soon agreed that, as Francisca suggested, I would go with him to school the following day and he would speak to Señor García about this issue while I was with him and supporting him.

Señor García listened intently to Juan. It turned out that this boy was physically assaulting Juan nearly every day. The señor said that the school had received reports from another boy about the alleged offender but had taken no action because there was no other evidence against the boy. That day, the boy who had interfered with Juan junior was expelled and Juan's approach to school, his work there and life in general improved greatly. We told Juan junior that he was very brave in his approach to this difficulty. He promised to let us know immediately if anything vaguely similar happened again.

**

The months slowly drifted by and I heard nothing from Pedro. Nothing. Not a word. I began thinking about writing to him about finding another collaborator to draft the libretti, or at least the first one about Venus and Adonis. Seven or eight months after I went to see Pedro, one of the palace messengers brought a parcel into my office. It was wrapped in thick brown paper, tied with coarse string and sealed with a wax embossed seal of the Cathedral of Toledo. It looked as if it could be a book of some kind.

I opened it immediately and inside was a libretto entitled 'La Púrpura de la Rosa' ('The Blood of the Rose'). It was from Pedro and the story was his own version of Venus and Adonis. I could not believe my eyes. The joy of seeing it overcame me and tears rolled down my cheeks. My intense ambition could now be achieved. Once I had recovered, I noticed a letter in with the manuscript which said simply that Pedro had finished the first libretto, was working on the second one and that he would come to Madrid for the rehearsals and the first performances. I chuckled aloud at my success in dealing with him.

I spent the next few hours reading the manuscript. It was typical Calderón de la Barca. He had written a brilliant text to this beautiful, classic love story. He had exploited the eroticism of the plot to engage the audience. There was humour, subtlety and coarseness in the story so there was something for everybody, from the most literate connoisseurs to the ordinary people of Madrid. We needed to find a special royal birthday or other such occasion for which to perform the piece. At least, that is what I first thought. After reading the main text, I read the prologue where Pedro had made it clear that the work would be performed as a double celebration: to commemorate the signing of the Treaty of the Pyrenees, which set down the terms of our hard-fought peace with France, and to mark the marriage of the King's twenty-two-year-old daughter María Teresa to Louis XIV of France. 'That crafty Pedro,' I thought. 'He has already been in contact with the palace to seek their agreement for an event which we can celebrate with the premiere.'

Immediately after I had read Pedro's manuscript, I sat at my desk and wrote a reply, thanking him for his support and collaboration and saying I was looking forward to seeing him in Madrid. I also said that we in the Royal Chapel would find a theatre company to produce the work and that the first performance would either be in front of the King at the palace or at the Buen Retiro.

The arrival of Pedro's manuscript marked the beginning of a period in my life in which I worked harder than ever before. This first opera was in one fairly long act. I also had to compose for the prologue and for the little celebration at the end of the piece. This meant writing a continuous line of music to last between one and a half to two hours. The Maestro would have to let the King know that, while I was writing for this opera, my availability for any other work would be severely limited. He was superb in supporting me. Not only did he keep the King at bay while I wrote the music, he arranged for a theatre company to direct and produce the work and fixed the venue. In fact there would be two theatre companies involved, Pedro de la Rosa's and Juan de la Calle's, both of which had been operating in Madrid for upwards of twenty years. The two joined forces for the production and, between them, selected the cast, all of whom were singer actresses who worked in the town theatres. They chose the group of musicians from their regular players. The venue would be the Coliseo in the Buen Retiro Palace and the first performance, before the King and Queen Mariana of Austria, would be on 17 January 1660.

I first had to work out whether I needed to revise my methods of composing while working on a piece as demanding as an opera. I completely perplexed my colleagues at the palace by deciding to mount every page of the score, in the order in which the music was to be played, on the walls of my office. I then had to work out a style of writing the music. Many I spoke to about this, including the Maestro, thought that the opera should sound like an Italian opera, sung by top sopranos or castrati.

Initially, I agreed and started to write in this style but I soon realised that I would have to scrap what I had written and start again. It became clear to me that it was not practical to write in this way for the women who would be performing the work. These women were used to singing the popular songs, including songs to dance to, which were in the *comedias*, presented daily in the theatres of our town. They would not be happy singing in the vastly different style of the typical Italian opera. Many of our women performers could not read or write and were used to learning by rote. So in composing the music, I had to ensure the style was familiar to them, that they could easily learn the words and the music and that they would be able to manage both in the performance. The Maestro and Pedro eventually understood my thinking and agreed with my approach. I would be writing in a Spanish style for a Spanish opera.

I wrote the music as quickly as I could but realised that I would have to provide the score to the production companies in a number of completed sections. This was so that the performers did not have to wait until I had finished composing all of the music before they could start to learn and rehearse their parts. Pedro de la Rosa and Juan de la Calle agreed that I should split the text into four components of about equal size that corresponded with logical breaks in the story.

While I had nothing to do with appointing the cast, I was delighted that a number of singer actresses I had worked with previously were given lead roles in the work. It was a great thrill that Bernarda Ramirez was one of them.

'Juan, what are you doing here?' asked Bernarda, as she saw me walking to one of the rehearsals at the Buen Retiro.

'I have just come over to see you all working,' I said, planting a kiss on her cheek.

'Are you playing the harp in this opera?'

'No. I've done my bit. I wrote the music.'

'I know that but I wondered if you were playing in it as well. Do you remember what a wonderful time we had in Lope's "Punishment without Revenge"?'

'That was brilliant, Bernarda. How could I forget?'

'You couldn't forget, Juan. Do you remember Maria de Riquelme?'

'Of course I do. She also worked with us in Lope's play. Where is she now?'

'It is not a good story. Do you know she eventually married Manuel de Vallejo who was the owner of the theatre company?'

'Yes, I knew that.'

'Well, he died in about '45 and Maria was consumed in grief. She decided to give up her career on the stage and went to Barcelona to join a convent as a nun. She was there for about twelve years before she died of a stomach illness. It was sad. I kept in touch by letter. We wrote to each other about once a month. Then four months passed and I heard nothing from her. So I wrote to the convent and they replied telling me she had died.'

'I'm so sorry to hear that, Bernarda. That is awful. We were all such good friends. But I cannot say how good it is to see you again.'

It is strange how people drift out of your life and reappear again. When they do, you carry on your relationship with them almost as if you last saw them only the day before. This is exactly what happened between me and Bernarda. I was saddened to hear about the death of Maria de Riquelme. She had been a good friend and colleague.

We all completely underestimated the time it would take to rehearse the opera. 'I think we need at least one more rehearsal, maybe two,' said Pedro de la Rosa, when there was only one week left before the performance for the King. There were tears from the singers who had trouble remembering the tunes and strong words from the musicians who were getting impatient. We did two more rehearsals before we were all ready to give the final rehearsal in front of Pedro at the Salón del Palacio in the Buen Retiro Palace, with just two days to go. You could never be sure with him. He seemed incapable of showing great excitement or approval. He sat impassively through the whole work, including the prologue and the concluding refrains. He said nothing and just stroked his beard occasionally.

'Well, what do you think, Pedro?' asked Juan de la Calle, who seemed to know Pedro from previously working with him.

'Quite good,' said Pedro. He didn't ask for anything to be changed so we took that as his approval.

We did not know what to expect at the first performance of the opera. The King, Queen Mariana of Austria, more than half of the King's court and hundreds of people from our town were there. As usual, the royal party and senior members of the court were in their allotted boxes, the men stood in the main floor of the salón and the women sat in their area to the right of the theatre. Francisca and I were lucky. We had been invited to join the royal party in one of the boxes so we could sit together during the performance. The musicians were positioned at the front of the stage.

In the prologue, one of the characters, Vulgo, explains to the audience, in song, of course, that the whole work would be sung. Another, Sadness, said that the Spanish character could not possibly put up with that. Vulgo replies that the work is only a short, one act opera and not a full length, three act *comedia.* The audience laughed loudly and that alone was a good start.

The opera opens with Venus being chased by a wild boar. Adonis rescues her and she faints in his arms. She awakens and, as a reward, offers to make love to him. Mars becomes intensely jealous but is distracted by having to go into battle. Adonis explains that he is the product of an incestuous relationship and is denied physical love. He chases the boar into a village where the peasants are dancing, becomes exhausted and falls asleep. Venus calls on Amor who shoots a love arrow into Adonis who becomes overcome with desire for Venus. She and Adonis make love passionately in Venus's garden of delight. Mars returns from battle and is suspicious of Venus and Adonis. He follows Amor into a cleft in a mountain which opens to reveal Disillusion in shackles. Disillusion shows Mars a reflection in the magic mirror. It is Venus and Adonis in an embrace. Mars becomes totally enraged and commands one of the Furies to make the boar so wild that it kills Adonis. Venus rushes to the scene and faints again as she sees Adonis dying. His blood turns the white roses red. Jupiter witnesses these tragic scenes and unites the lovers on Mount Olympus, Venus as the Morning Star and Adonis as an anemone.

The love scene was the delight of the audience. The actresses playing Venus and Adonis were, but for some translucent gauze, both naked to the waist. They stopped singing as they began to kiss and caress each other to the rhythm of my music. They embraced with uninhibited passion. The audience cheered at their outrageous movements. 'They're not pretending, they're actually making love,' someone near to us shouted. But this was all an act.

The scene in which Mars goes to war stirred the house. I loved writing marches. I don't know why. Maybe, as a child, I was profoundly affected by seeing a group of soldiers marching to a band with a drum. I could not recall any march in particular but I'm sure I had the experience, probably several times as there were often soldiers to be seen in our town. I scored the march for a bass drum, a side drum and two horns, two flutes, and some guitars to provide texture. The soldiers marched across the stage to the music and the audience clapped to the rhythm.

At the end of the performance, it was as clear as a cerulean sky that the Spanish audience had fallen in love with opera, at least they had with this one. The applause seemed endless as, one by one, every actress singer in the cast took a bow at the front of the stage. Applause was loudest and the cheers and whistling were deafening for the women who had played Venus and Adonis. Pedro and I held hands at the front of the stage and bowed in unison to the audience. It was like being at a huge party. The King and Queen gave a standing ovation. The signal was obvious to both Pedro and me that we should press on with our second opera, the story of Cephalus and Procris.

'The way is now clear, Pedro.'

'I've almost finished it, Juan. It will be twice as long as this one and in three acts. I think you will like what I've written. I'll give it to you before I return to Toledo.'

CHAPTER 25

It was in the middle of one of the hottest summers we had ever had and I was struggling to finish the second opera. The oppressive weather did not help. I was tussling with some of the phrasing in the second act and remember going back home on horseback in the middle of that particular morning to retrieve some notes I had written the night before. I was annoyed at having forgotten to bring them with me. The air was almost unbreathably hot so I let the horse walk. The smell of the night filth of the town was made worse by the heat. People were walking the busy, dusty streets breathing through handkerchiefs to lessen the stench.

As I approached our stables, I was greeted by a tearful Francisca who had heard the horse coming in through the gate. 'Juan, I have terrible, terrible news. Diego has died. Juana is hysterical. She won't stop crying.'

'God. What a disaster,' I said, swinging myself off the horse. 'Where is she?'

'She is here. She came here in their carriage this morning after discovering that Diego was dead. She thought he was asleep but he didn't get out of bed and she couldn't wake him up. It's dreadful. Awful.'

We went into the house where Juana was curled up on a sofa in the downstairs lounge, sobbing uncontrollably. I went up to her. 'Juana, I am so sorry to hear about Diego. It is a terrible tragedy.' I kissed her head.

Eventually, she spoke. 'Juan. I don't know what to do. He is still lying there, in our bed. I was on my own and so upset. I had to get out of the apartment. That is why I'm here. I came straight round. I begged one of the palace coachmen to bring me here in our coach. I want to die. My life is finished.'

'Don't say that, Juana,' said Francisca. 'Life must go on. You have much to live for.'

'Not without my beloved Diego. I am finished. I must die.'

Then Francisca started to cry again, more in desperation at not being able to settle her friend. While sad and on the verge of tears, my mind turned to practical issues. The greatest painter Spain had ever produced was lying dead in his bed and only we and his wife knew that. Something had to be done.

'Where is the coach, Juana?' I asked, thinking that if I was to go to their apartment in the palace, the driver could take me there.

'The coachman took it straight back.'

'I think we should get the arrangements under way,' I said, not wanting to mention the word 'funeral'. 'What if I start at your apartment, Juana? Do you want to give me the key? Who is your doctor? We'll have to get him to see Diego.'

'He had been seeing the Royal Physician,' she said, handing me the key. 'You know he had not been well since he came back from the royal wedding and his fever just got worse. I didn't expect him to die.' She started sobbing again and Francisca went over to the sofa, sat next to her and hugged her lovingly.

'Will you be all right on your own, Juan?' asked Francisca.

'Yes, I'll be fine. You stay with Juana, Francisca, and I'll go now.'

'How are you going to get there? Take the horse.'

'Yes, I'll probably get the horse to walk. It's so hot out there. I'll plan what to do as I go.'

I lightly kissed both Francisca and Juana before making for Diego's grace and favour apartment in the Palace Treasury where he and Juana had lived since he had been promoted to Grand Chamberlain. The streets were even busier with people ambling listlessly around while they perspired in the unbearable heat. I rode slowly, thinking about my friend. I was weighed down by his death and shaken by its immediacy. I recalled our first meeting in the palace, not long after I had joined the Royal Chapel. He was a great help to me then and made me feel good about working there. However, I was not as surprised as Juana by his passing. Diego had been taken ill while on his visit to Italy with Juan de Pareja and, even after his return, was often not well.

In his new post, Diego had definitely overworked himself. He had become intimately involved in the arrangements for the signing of the Peace of the Pyrenees and in those for the marriage of the King's daughter, the Infanta María Teresa, to Louis XIV of France. The marriage was part of the terms of the peace treaty. In the April of '60, on the orders of the King, Diego had undertaken an arduous journey, ahead of the King and his entourage, to Fuenterrabía. This was to make the accommodation arrangements for the royal party to attend the wedding, which was to be held on the Isle of Pheasants, in the river Bidasoa on the newly agreed border between France and Spain. Managing the detail was a tortuous nightmare and Diego had no one but a clerk to help him. Diego appointed the contractors who built the hall for the wedding. It had to be erected exactly on the line defining the border. Louis XIV would approach the line drawn on the floor of the hall from the French side. He would be escorted by his mother, Anna of Austria, our King's sister. María Teresa would be given away by her father, the King, who would approach the line from the opposite side.

Not only did Diego have to manage this complexity of arrangements, when the day of the wedding arrived, he also had to comfort our poor King as he cried uncontrollably while giving away his beloved María Teresa, uttering between his tears that she was 'a piece of my own heart'. Diego came back to Madrid exhausted after successfully completing this almost impossible mission. The strain showed on his face when he arrived back. Within days of his return, he became quite ill and had to take to his bed. He did improve but never fully recovered.

I unlocked the door of his apartment and entered. It was hot inside and dark. The drapes to the windows were closed. Where there is death, there is a silent stillness. I went straight to the bedroom and the motionless body of Diego. I touched his forehead. He was as cold as a stone from the Manzanares in winter. I felt in my heart the passing of my close friend, which I pondered quietly for a few moments, looking at his ashen face. A picture of my dead father came into my mind. I knew that I had no time to indulge my emotions. The first thing was to report his death to the Royal Physician. I was about to leave him peacefully lying there when I heard a sound coming from outside the bedroom. It was the Royal Physician himself.

'Did you know Diego Velázquez has died?' I asked.

'Yes, his wife came to tell us about three hours ago.'

'That's strange,' I said. 'She wanted me to ask you to see him.'

'No, she came to my quarters screaming, crying and in a dreadful state. I came here immediately with her to certify death. I offered her a potion to calm her down but she refused. I then went to fetch the constable and by the time I returned she had gone, disappeared. The door to the apartment was locked and I could not get in. I heard a sound here a moment ago so I entered and here you are, Señor Hidalgo.'

'Juana asked me to come here to start making the funeral arrangements. She is still in a desperate state.'

'Where is she?'

'At our house in the Calle de la Madalena. She's with my wife, who is comforting her.'

'He will have to lie in state, here in the apartment.'

'We cannot let Juana back while his body is still here.'

'I agree,' said the doctor. 'They have a house in the Calle de la Concepción, I think. Perhaps she should go there.'

'No,' I said, firmly. 'The best place for her is in our house with Francisca and me. She can stay there until the lying in state and the funeral are over.'

Diego's body lay in state for two days in the hall of his apartment at the Treasury. The funeral directors dressed him in the robes and insignia of the Order of Santiago, which the King had awarded to him only months before he died. He was interred at the Church of San Juan Bautista which is at the junction of the Calle de San Juan and the Calle de San Nicolás. It was the funeral of a decent man. The King and Queen Mariana, along with many from the royal court attended, as did several hundred of the people of our town. The chief mourners were Juana and her eldest granddaughter, Inés del Mazo who was about twenty-five years old. She was accompanied by her father, the painter Juan Bautista Martínez del Mazo who had been a student of the master. Juana was supported on each arm by my Francisca and Diego's granddaughter. Poor Juana had hardly stopped crying since Diego died. Nor had she eaten a thing. She was doubled over in grief.

'What are we to do with your grandmother?' asked Francisca, just after the service, looking helplessly at Diego's granddaughter. 'She has been like this since your grandfather passed away. She hasn't stopped crying.' Inés was in an almost as bad a state but managed to say that her grandmother would eventually be fine. We took Juana back to the apartment in the Treasury. Inés and her father came with us. Juana still did not stop crying. Her eyes were as red as a cock's comb and her cheeks were like a waterfall running with her perpetual tears. We left the family in the apartment and made our way home.

'I am really concerned about Juana,' Francisca said. 'I wish she would stop crying, if only for a moment. She is still completely overcome, poor lass.' Juana just could not live without her beloved Diego. She was broken and continued in this sad state of disrepair for a week. Then she died, too. In the same bed as Diego.

I discovered Juana's fate before the sad news had escaped the palace. As I arrived in my office that morning, the Royal Physician was waiting to tell me. He said that Juana's maid had been worrying about her for several days after the funeral because Juana would not eat and would only have the occasional small sip of water. She had discovered her that morning when she went into her bedroom with a drink. I could not believe that Juana had died so soon after Diego. 'What did she die of?' I asked the physician.

'I have completed the death certificate and have said that she died of love.'

'I'm sorry to question you,' I said, 'but is that a medical condition?'

'It is very rare but it is acknowledged in all the textbooks.'

It took several minutes for this devastating news to sink in. 'First Diego, then Juana. Who next?' I thought.

'I'm afraid that that means another funeral,' said the Royal Physician. 'Will you tell the family?'

I spoke to the Maestro and he agreed that I should go, there and then, if only to avoid the family discovering from the news sheets or from rumour mongers. I had a doubly difficult duty to perform. I had to tell my Francisca, who was Juana's best friend, and I also had to break the awful news to Inés and her father. When we spoke to the family at Diego's funeral, an amazing coincidence emerged. Their house was in the Calle del Olivar, no more than sixty *varas* from our house in the Calle de la Madalena. Their mother Francisca, Diego's daughter, had died a few years before and her widowed husband, Juan Bautista Martínez del Mazo, lived there with their six children, Inés, José, Diego Jacinto, Baltasar, María Teresa and Jerónima.

I went home first to tell Francisca. She was heartbroken. 'It is my fault, Juan. I should never have left her in that apartment.' Her eyes filled with tears and overflowed down her cheeks.

'My love, you are not to blame. Juana died of love. That is what the physician has written on the death certificate. She could not live without Diego. She gave up. She had not eaten for a week. I must go to Inés to tell her.'

'Juan, I will come with you. Let's go now.'

Within a minute or so we were knocking on the door of Inés del Mazo's house. She came to the door in a black dress, still in mourning for her grandfather. The look on our faces betrayed a serious problem. 'What is wrong? Tell me. It's my grandmother isn't it?'

'Is Juan Bautista Martínez at home?' I asked.

'Yes,' she said. Then shouted: 'Papá! It's Juan Hidalgo and Francisca. They want to see us. Come now.'

Juan Bautista appeared on the doorstep and invited us in. He pointed towards a sofa in the downstairs drawing room and Francisca and I sat on it as they sat facing us. 'So what's wrong then?' asked Inés.

I spoke first and softly. 'It's bad news, Inés. I am afraid your grandmother has passed away. I am terribly sorry. She and your grandfather were among our best friends.'

Inés was calm and remained unflustered by the sad news. 'Oh no. Not another death. We went to see grandmother yesterday and came away very concerned. She had not eaten anything since my grandfather died. That must have been a week ago today. How do you know she has died?' Juan

Bautista Martínez put his arm around her and that was enough to make her cry a little but she quickly regained her composure.

'The Royal Physician came to my office this morning to tell me. Juana's maid went into her bedroom to take her a drink but she had passed away by then and was still in her bed. I agreed to come here to tell you the bad news. At least you know us. Maybe you do not know the physician so well.' I was struggling for the words when Francisca came to my aid.

'I am so sorry,' said Francisca. 'I think she just gave up when your grandfather died. And, of course, she lost her remaining daughter, your mother, only two years ago. She felt she didn't have anything else to live for and didn't want to carry on without Diego. She died of a broken heart.'

We did not tarry long in the house and, after having a drink of juice with them, walked back home. Juan Bautista Martínez made our departure easier when he said that they would have to go to the apartment at the palace to start sorting out the arrangements for the funeral. I could not leave Francisca in her state of sadness and shock to return to the palace, so decided that what work I felt like doing that day, I would do at home. Juan junior arrived back from school at his usual time and detected that something was wrong.

'Why are you two so sad? What is the matter? You are usually so cheerful and why are you home, Papá?'

'Mother's friend, Juana, died today. We had to go to her granddaughter's house in the Calle del Olivar to tell her and her father what had happened,' I said, placing my hand on his shoulder.

'How did you know, Papá?' I explained to Juan junior how I had discovered Juana's death and that I had volunteered to tell her granddaughter. 'The granddaughter, Inés, has a young brother called Baltasar. Do you know him?' Francisca asked.

'Is his father a painter?' asked Juan junior.

'Yes. He is Juan Bautista Martínez del Mazo,' said Francisca.

'He is one of my friends at school,' said Juan junior. 'I walk home with him nearly every day. He is two classes above me. I've been in his house. His oldest sister is a very nice lady and gives us drinks sometimes.'

It is quite incredible what you can discover from your children. They know the area in which you live better than you do. They know the people there better than you do. You can be walking past people in the street, not realising that your children know them. You can even be speaking to them without knowing your children know them. This was a classic case of just that. It was clear that Juan junior knew the family well, especially their son Baltasar. We had been living only for a short time in the Calle de la Madalena so it was not surprising that we did not know that Juana's son-in-law and his children lived close by. We had met the children's mother, Francisca, and her husband at Diego's house but had never come to know her well. I vaguely knew Juan Bautista Martínez del Mazo, the artist, but only in passing. The death of Juana changed that. We soon became friends of the Martínez del Mazo family and Francisca, in particular, became very close to the eldest daughter, Inés. It was as if Inés carried on where Juana had left off. I got to know Juan Bautista quite well through his painting. He was appointed portrait painter to the King so he took over the painting duties of his father-in-law.

We all had yet another unwelcomed surprise only a few days after Juana's funeral. It was that a Treasury official had been to tell the Martínez del Mazo family that there was a problem in releasing the items from Diego's estate. This was a tremendous shock, especially for Inés who was a major beneficiary under Diego and Juana's will. Immediately after the official had gone, Inés came up to our house to share this shattering news with Francisca.

'Something awful has happened. The Treasury has impounded the whole of my grandmother and grandfather's estate.'

'Why, Inés? How do you know?'

'An official from the court came to see me today and has just left. I don't know what to do. My father is working so I cannot tell him yet. I had to tell somebody so I came to see you.'

Francisca asked the tearful Inés inside and invited her to sit in the lounge while she brought in something for her to drink. 'But why, Inés? Why have they done this terrible thing?'

'It is all about my grandfather's job at the palace. There are some financial irregularities. In his job as Grand Chamberlain, grandfather received monies from the Treasury to pay for different types of work and goods, including works of art, for the palace. The Treasury say that he owes them a huge amount of money. It is something like six thousand *ducats*.'

'I'm confident they will find it tucked away in a drawer somewhere or in a bank account that they are not aware of,' Francisca said, trying to reassure her.

'I wish I knew the answer,' said Inés. 'Everybody will think my grandfather is a crook and I know he isn't. He was a great painter, maybe promoted beyond his ability as an administrator. Something has to be wrong. Grandfather would never embezzle money from anyone. What am I to do Francisca?'

'I'll tell you something,' said Francisca. 'The palace owes Juan nearly 2,500 *ducats* in back pay. They owe him 800 for the "Blood of the Rose" and another 800 for "Picus and Canens" which he wrote nearly six years ago. They are also two months behind in his salary payments.'

'I can't believe that.'

'Trust me. It's the absolute truth. They are hopeless. The Maestro has been three times to see the Paymaster General himself. He says he will pay up but they don't. If you want my advice, you should go to see the Paymaster. Ask them what they have to say about your grandfather's salary. I guarantee they owe him money. They won't have paid him up until the day he passed away. They will try to avoid paying if they can. Juan told me that about three weeks ago they had no money in the palace and could not even buy the King two eggs for his breakfast.'

Inés wiped her tears away and laughed. 'Now you are joking, Francisca.'

'It's true. The King had to have bread and cheese for breakfast that day. He was furious.'

Inés's tears of frustration and anger became tears of laughter. 'You are so good for me, Francisca. We'll be friends for ever.'

Inés and her father went to see the Paymaster General and eventually discovered that Diego had been owed a colossal amount in unpaid salary. It was about 10,000 *ducats*, far more than what he was alleged to owe the Exchequer. The amount they accused Diego of owing was eventually traced to some accounts that had been set up in the Treasury itself. For some inexplicable reason, these accounts had become submerged in the complexity of our government's financial system. It was therefore proved beyond doubt that Diego had been totally honest and competent in his handling of the monies charged to him by our Treasury. He was thus completely exonerated. It took six years to sort out this mess, partly because of the obscure names that Diego had used for his accounts.

Inés wanted to reward Francisca for helping her after her grandparents' estate had been frozen. She made the wonderful gesture of giving Francisca a solid gold medal. This was the one that Pope Innocent X had given Diego when he visited the Vatican. The medal was embossed with a portrait of the Pontiff himself. Somehow, the gift of the medal made the relationship between Francisca and Inés even stronger.

***

Juan junior had been at Imperial for nearly two years. He had settled well after the incidents with the boy who had been expelled. It is fair to say that he blossomed. He was so enthusiastic about going to school it was quite unbelievable. He would get up early in the morning to prepare himself and to make sure his homework was in order before he went. He would call in for Baltasar del Mazo on his way to school and they would walk all the way there, laughing and joking and often fooling about. Juan had many other friends at the school and seemed to be good at virtually all the subjects. Although he had become quite good at playing the harp, this gave way to his much greater interest in playing the guitar.

He had also given some thought to a possible career. He decided that he would like to be a lawyer. Our town was short of good legislators. How he found this out we never knew but he said that there was so much government legislation and insufficient professionals to produce it. There was a demand that needed to be satisfied. We were proud of him. You can imagine our astonishment therefore when he did so badly in the end of year exams. We were totally perplexed. What surprised us even more was that Juan himself seemed not to be as disappointed as we expected him to be.

'Juan, whatever has gone wrong?' I asked him when I read the form master's report.

'Just one of those things, Papá. I just haven't done well in the exams. I'm not sure why. I just haven't.'

'But you have big ambitions, my son. Do you still want to be a lawyer?'

'Yes, Papá. I do.'

'Well, you will have to do much better than this. You will have to go to university if you aspire to being a lawyer and results like this will slam the door in your face.'

'I'm sorry, Papá. I really am. It could be lack of concentration or I should have revised harder. I'm not sure.'

Francisca and I were so worried we decided to make an appointment to see Juan junior's form master. We went there two days after Juan had received his results. This was our last chance to see the master before the new school year began.

'Well, señor and señora, on the whole, Juan is doing extremely well. He was not the only one who did badly in the exams. Some of my other excellent pupils did just as badly, if not worse. I should say in mitigation that we decided, across all subjects, to set a very high standard this year and that is probably why the results are not as good as you might expect.'

'He doesn't seem to be doing that well to us,' I said. 'Sometimes he comes home and asks a lot of questions about his work and other times he has nothing to say about school. He shows very little interest at the moment.'

The teacher came up with an interesting reply. 'Teaching children is like observing the life of trees. Sometimes they blossom and break into leaf and grow quickly. This is when they are learning fast and well. At other times their leaves are falling, they stop growing and become dormant. The child's learning almost comes to a halt. Obviously, children do not respond to the seasons, as trees do, and these phases in their education are much less predictable than the seasons. However, the truth is that these variations do occur. Juan may be in one of these dormant times. His exam results may indicate that but, as I have said, we set very high standards and that may have affected his results. My one concern is whether he has a girlfriend or whether he has had any recent emotional upsets.'

'As far as we know, he is not involved with a girl,' Francisca said. 'But two of our family friends died recently and that may have affected him more than we realised. They were Diego Velázquez and his wife, Juana. They were like an uncle and aunt to Juan. He loved them both. They passed away just days before the exams. Juan is friends with Baltasar del Mazo. Diego and Juana were his grandparents.'

'What a tragic set of events. The country lost a great man with the death of Velázquez. I know Juan and Baltasar are good friends. It is possible that he was more affected than it appeared by the passing of your friends. My advice is not to worry. Keep encouraging Juan and see how he progresses. He will make a fine lawyer.'

***

Work on our second opera continued apace. It was certainly delayed by the untimely and tragic deaths of Juana and Diego but by the end of August, Pedro had completed the vast libretto. He had penned almost two and a half thousand lines of verse. He told me earlier that he could comfortably write fifty lines a day and a hundred if he was working to a tight schedule. By then, I had completed writing the score for the prologue and the first two acts and had made a good start on the third. There was a huge amount of effort needed before we could stage the first performance. A theatre company had once again to be appointed; the cast had to be selected as well as the orchestra; the stage directions had to be written and all the equipment needed for the production had to be supplied; new costumes had to be designed and made; and a venue was needed.

Pedro had called the opera, 'Celos Áun del Aire Matan' (Jealousy, Even of the Air, Kills). What another brilliant title. It fitted perfectly the scene of Cephalus and Procris painted by Veronese upon which, at Diego Velázquez's suggestion, the whole work was based. Procris was jealous of Aura, the goddess of the breeze – the air. Cephalus kills Procris by mistake, a death due entirely to Procris's jealousy of the air. I smiled to myself when I realised the significance of the title.

As in 'The Blood of the Rose', the Maestro was a great help in relieving me of some of the managerial work so that I could finish the composing. He arranged for the opera to be performed at the palace of the Buen Retiro and the date was set for 28 November. The presentation would be to celebrate the third birthday of the Infante Philip Prosper, the heir to the throne of Spain and beloved first son of the King and Queen Mariana of Austria. The companies of Diego Osorio and Juana de Cisneros were more than willing to cast and direct the opera and an Italian, Antonio María Antonozzi, a famous theatrical engineer who lived in Madrid, was commissioned to produce the scenery and design the special effects. If ever there was to be a work that exploited the stage machinery to the maximum, this would be it. The actors would be projected above the stage and thrown through the air, as if by some magical force. It would be the spectacular of spectaculars.

'Celos' as it became affectionately known to us who were involved in the opera, was up until then the largest compositional task I had ever undertaken. It was so useful to have completed 'The Blood of the Rose' as its precursor. Again, I stuck the music sheets to the wall of my office so I could see them in one broad vista, without having to turn over pages. My colleagues thought I was mad. Again, I used the principal of writing a Spanish opera for Spanish actress singers and not some high-flown Italian work that none of our girls would be able to sing, let alone learn by heart.

Pedro's masterpiece of a libretto inspired me. I composed the best music I had ever written. I involved Francisca and Juan junior in it. I would write down tunes and take them home to play to them. The idea was simple. Were the tunes good, catchy pieces which the singers and audience would remember? Would they remain in the audience's heads so that they would whistle them on the way home after the performance? Were they straightforward to the extent that they could easily be learned by the singer actresses? 'No. That is too complicated. It needs to be broken up,' Juan junior would say. 'That just does not fit the majesty of a goddess,' said Francisca at my first attempt to write for a long aria the goddess Diana would sing. 'The rhythms are too slow for a fast-moving scene like this,' suggested Juan junior.

Eventually, I finished the whole score. I was mentally exhausted. I vowed not to write another long piece for at least another year. The night I completed the work, I told Francisca that I felt completely burnt out and that I would never be able to write music again. 'Enough of the self-pity,' said Francisca. 'That is not the Juan Hidalgo I know. You are the King's principal composer and might have to start another work tomorrow.'

'There is something about creating a substantial work of art, Francisca. I have given this absolutely every scrap of energy in my body and mind. If I had to start again tomorrow, the work would have no quality. My creative reservoir is empty. It has to be replenished before I can start again.'

'I don't know whether you are exaggerating, Juan, but people like you don't just "burn out", as you put it. You have boundless energy and talent. You are probably the best known composer in Madrid, if not the whole of Spain. You are just tired because you have put a massive effort into Celos. If you had to start again on a new piece tomorrow you would and you would do it well. All you need is a good night's sleep!' Francisca was probably right.

In the meantime, there was much to be done before Celos could be performed. We did not want to make the same mistakes that we made on 'The Blood of the Rose'. The theatre companies selected the singer actresses very early on so that they had plenty of time to learn their lines and, of course, to rehearse them. All those to take part were offered their roles by the middle of September and this gave us ten weeks to prepare ourselves for the first performance. I was personally delighted that Bernarda Ramirez was again in the cast. This was the first time I had met another of our most famous actress singers, Manuela de Escamilla, the beautiful, talented daughter of Antonio de Escamilla. Her father was a singer-actor in his own right, as well as a highly competent theatre company manager. Antonio also played a part in Celos as the only man in a cast of women.

Similarly, we appointed the musicians well in advance. Most of the two theatre companies' musicians were engaged on other projects so the Maestro arranged for those of the Royal Chapel to perform in most of the instrumental roles. Luis de As, Juan de Roxas Carrión, Francisco de Guypúzcoa, Hernando de Eslava and my brother, Francisco, were all in the orchestra.

We worked hard on the rehearsals but were running out of time with only a little more than a week to go before the first performance which the King, the Queen and the royal household were to attend. Then we were faced with a huge problem. The palace of the Buen Retiro was so heavily booked that we could not rehearse there until 25 November.

'This is ridiculous,' shouted Pedro, straight at Diego Orsorio. 'We cannot perform this opera without more rehearsals. It is nowhere near ready. Unless someone solves this problem, I will go to the King to complain.'

'Who in hell's name do you think you are speaking to?' replied Osorio. 'Just because you wrote the accursed libretto you think you can lay down the law. Well, you can piss off and annoy someone else. Leave it to the grown-ups to sort out the problems.'

Pedro was furious but he had provoked an unnecessary row by blaming the lack of rehearsal facilities on Diego Osorio. I tried to settle the two of them but with limited success. 'Let's look at this calmly,' I said. 'It's no good squaring up for a major dispute. Let's sit around a table and work out what to do.'

After some muttering and mumbling, we decided to have a meeting. So Diego Osorio, Juana Cisneros, Pedro, the Maestro Carlos Patiño, Manuela de Escamilla and I sat in Diego Osorio's office, which was in his house, the fourth on the right in the Calle de Cantarranas, coming from the direction of the Mentidero. We immediately agreed that the Maestro should chair the meeting.

'Before we begin, I want you two to shake hands and become friends again,' he said, looking towards Diego and Pedro, who were provocatively facing each other, on opposite sides of the table. They stood, walked around towards each other, apologised, shook hands and smiled sheepishly at each other. Peace reigned once more, thanks to the ambassadorial Maestro.

'Basically, we need somewhere else, a different venue,' said Diego, urgently. 'Has anyone any ideas?'

'We could ask Sebastian de Prado,' the Maestro said. 'We've used his house before.'

'That's an option but I wonder if the room he uses is big enough,' said Juana de Cisneros.

'As a last resort, we could use it, I suppose,' said the Maestro.

'What about asking the Marquis of Heliche? He sometimes rents a house on the corner of the Calle de las Huertas and the Mentidero. I wonder if he could make it available for us,' said Manuela. The Marquis was in overall charge of the stage machinery at the Buen Retiro and was a great patron of the theatre in Madrid. He was extremely wealthy and had enormous resources at his disposal.

'Who knows Heliche?' asked the Maestro.

'I know him well,' said Diego Osorio. 'I'll ask him.'

By the noon of the following day, we were rehearsing in the house rented by Heliche. News of our problems had somehow reached the King – possibly via Pedro – so he put the palace carriages at our disposal to bring the actress singers and the musicians from their houses to the rented house in the Mentidero. The King even provided two crown constables to stand guard outside. They would prevent any passers-by from entering to watch the rehearsals.

Five days later there was another problem. The singer actresses of Diego Osorio's company had to perform a *comedia* that night before the King. It was an early work by Agustín Moreto called 'From Outside He will Come…' so they had to stop work on Celos and rehearse that work instead. 'This is a disaster,' said the Maestro. 'We will have to delay the performance. There is still so much to do. We haven't yet rehearsed it in the Buen Retiro with the stage machinery.'

'What are we going to do?' asked Pedro calmly, not wishing to provoke another unpleasant argument.

'I will go to the Private Secretary and ask him to explain to the King that we are delaying the performance. We will need an alternative date. Juan, could you go to the Buen Retiro Palace and get them to agree one?' The Maestro had asked me because I was probably the one who was least involved in the actual rehearsing. I went straight away to the Buen Retiro and spoke to the manager of programmes. He had one afternoon available: 5 December. There was nothing before and nothing after until midway through January. We were lucky. The only date on offer would suit us well.

We rehearsed and rehearsed right up to the day of the performance. We went through the whole opera twice in the palace of the Buen Retiro. We rehearsed for the last time on the morning when the work was to be played at three o'clock in the afternoon. We were as ready as we ever would be to perform before the King.

CHAPTER 26

I went home after the final rehearsal to get ready. We took Juan junior to the performance. It was the first time he had been to a theatre and was so excited to go he could hardly contain himself. 'Papá, are you playing your harp in it? Where will you be?'

'I shall be with you and Mamá, sitting in a box on the right-hand side of the auditorium. We'll have a good view from there. We'll see everything.'

We went to the theatre in our carriage. I drove with Francisca and Juan junior sitting in the passenger seats. We parked the carriage and an attendant took the horses to feed and water them. We walked into the Buen Retiro Palace and found our way to our box where there was a programme for the performance on each of our seats. The cast list was printed inside:

Diana, the goddess	*Josefa Pavía*
Procris, a nymph of Diana	*Bernarda Manuela*
Rústico, Diana's gardener	*Antonio de Escamilla*
Floreta, his wife	*Bernarda Ramirez*
Megera, a fury	*María de Anaya*
Alecto, a fury	*María de los Santos*
Tesífone, a fury	*María de Salinas*
Aura, a nymph	*Marfisa del Pozo*
Cephalus, a noble hunter	*Luisa Romero*
Eróstrato, a shepherd	*Mariana de Borja*
Clarín, Eróstrato's servant	*Manuela de Escamilla*
Chorus of nymphs	*10 women*
Chorus of men	*6 men*

All of the main characters were famous performers in their own right. Many I knew well but I had only a passing acquaintance with the others before I met them and saw them many times, of course, at the rehearsals.

Just before the performance started, the orchestra took their places. Juan de Roxas Carrión spotted me and my family and waved at us before taking his seat. The last to arrive were the King and his party who took their places in the royal box, to a muted applause from the audience. The King was beginning to look haggard, tired and worn. He did not appear well. His face was without expression and he was limping. I could not at that moment help myself from feeling sorry for this man who had been such a great ally and help to me for the length of my career. Only God could know what was in store for him. Queen Mariana of Austria was a contrastingly cheerful figure. She proudly faced the audience and, with her right hand held aloft, turned from one side to the other as she acknowledged everybody there before she took her seat.

The audience then settled and Antonio de Escamilla walked onto the stage, in front of the drawn curtains. He faced the audience and said, with authority, 'We are here today to celebrate the third birthday of the Infante Philip Prosper, the heir apparent. The work that you will experience to that end will be fully sung and not a single word will be spoken. It will be an opera, not a *comedia*. It will be Spanish from the top of its head to the tips of its toes. It will not be a clever imitation of some import from Italy. It is a great story based on a Greek myth. You will love it and it will entertain you. God save the King.' He bowed to the royal box, then to the audience and left the stage.

To a flourish from the orchestra, the curtains swept back revealing the beautiful garden of Diana's temple in the city of Lydia, Anatolia, with its fountains and lush plants, flowers and trees. A choir of scantily dressed nymphs appeared from the wings, clasping the captured Aura and pushing her, with her head covered, to the centre of the stage. From the other side, and in a yellow dress with a deep, revealing cleavage, came Diana, carrying a long spear and accompanied by other barely dressed nymphs holding bows and arrows. Procris, one of the nymphs, launches into song, protesting to Diana, the hater of love, that Procris's best friend Aura has broken her vow of faithfulness to Diana by falling in love with Eróstrato, the shepherd. Diana is furious and insists that Aura should be put to death. The nymphs tie Aura to a tree in preparation for her execution. Aura launches into a pitiful lament which demands that Procris also defies Diana by falling in love. 'Oh, unhappy is she who proved that one could truly die of love,' is Aura's repeated refrain.

'Juana died of love,' whispered Francisca into my ear.

Aura calls to the heavens, the sun, the moon, the flowers, the plants and all divinities for clemency. Aura's protests are heard only by the noble hunter, Cephalus who defies Clarín, his servant who wants him to ignore Aura's pleas, and Cephalus attempts to rescue her. Diana sees Cephalus interfering and angrily threatens him with her famous spear which is renowned for never missing its target. Cephalus puts himself between Diana and Aura so that he would act 'as a shield for her life'. Procris becomes impatient and wants to know why they are waiting. 'Why not kill her now?' The unseen Venus, Diana's arch enemy, intervenes and transforms Aura into air. In a display of pure theatre and with the first operation of the stage machines, Aura, still attached to the tree, is lifted from the stage, launched bodily into the heavens and disappears into the clouds above.

'Goodness, Papá, did you see that?' whispered Juan junior. 'The nymph who fell in love was rescued from being killed by taking her up into the air. I didn't expect to see anything like that.'

'Just watch Juan,' said Francisca. 'There's more to come!'

Diana seeks instant revenge by aiming her spear at Cephalus's heart. Venus strikes again and deflects Diana's spear in mid-air, smashing it to the ground. The angry and humiliated goddess Diana and her nymphs leave the stage. Cephalus picks up the spear and takes it but Procris sees him and in an attempt to wrestle it from him is wounded. She pleads with Cephalus not to kill her and he makes his first indication of love to her. Eróstrato appears, bemoaning the fact that he ran away when Aura needed him most. He asks Rústico what happened after he left. Rústico gives him a full account of Aura's misfortune. Eróstrato wants to hear no more and runs into the forest, swearing his revenge on Diana and her nymphs.

Diana discovers from Floreta, Rústico's wife, that it was Rústico who let Eróstrato into Diana's garden so he was behind Aura falling in love with Eróstrato. Diana, as a punishment, puts a spell on Rústico so that he would appear as some kind of animal to whoever sees him. When he tries to speak to Floreta she sees him as a lion and she calls Procris to help her. Procris sees him as a bear. They call for help and Cephalus, carrying the spear, and Clarín quickly respond. Clarín sees Rústico as a wolf; Cephalus sees a spotted tiger. Soon they chase the animal away.

In another piece of stage machine wizardry, Aura descends from heaven on the back of an eagle and encourages Cephalus and Procris to fall for each other. She breathes the breath of love over them. They sing a love duet but Procris rejects Cephalus's wooing. Clarín takes advantage of Rústico's apparent absence to make overtures to Floreta in another duet.

'Papá,' whispered Juan junior at the end of the first act. 'Is there going to be an interlude?'

'Not now son. You'll have to wait until the end of the next one. Are you enjoying it?'

'I am enjoying the singing, the clever stage effects and the music but am having trouble with the plot. So will others in the audience. Where is it all going?'

'You'll see,' I replied. 'Ssh! The next act is just starting.'

The second act began in front of the temple of Diana. It is the full moon of the vernal equinox and Cephalus, Eróstrato, Clarín and a group of peasants follow a choir of singing shepherds and shepherdesses as they approach the temple. They all come bearing gifts for Diana and her nymphs, except for Clarín who has nothing. Eróstrato is not dressed as a shepherd but is disguised as a peasant to hide the fact that he has come to avenge his loss of Aura. Cephalus tells Clarín that he has come to the temple not just out of curiosity but because he hopes to see Procris again. He tells Clarín to get some flowers as a gift. Clarín decides to steal some fruit from an orchard but perceives Rústico as a whippet and takes the friendly dog as a gift instead. To a chorus of shepherds entering from one side of the stage and a chorus of nymphs from the other, the residents of Lydia bring their offerings.

Eróstrato gives a bow and arrow to one of the nymphs, the bow signifying the love of Venus and the arrow an injured Diana, who sings, 'let love die and oblivion live.' Cephalus approaches Procris and gives her a bouquet of lilies and roses, the red of the rose signifying her wounding by the spear of Diana, the white of the lily her purity. He echoes the refrain, 'let love die and oblivion live'. Clarín gives the dog to Floreta. Rústico cannot believe he is being offered as a gift to his own wife. He sings the same refrain, 'let love die and oblivion live.'

Off stage, Aura sings the exact opposite: 'let love live and oblivion die'. She then, driven by the stage machine, descends to the stage from above, in a cart drawn by two huge chameleons and, repeating the line again, ascends from the other side of the stage. Aura is heard but not seen and infuriates Diana by repeating the message, 'Let love live against oblivion, since love does not change to hate.' Diana accuses someone's lover of treachery but fails to name him. In turn, each of Eróstrato, Cephalus, Clarín and Rústico, still appearing as a whippet, thinks he is to blame for the treachery. Each is terrified of Diana's revenge.

Diana then sings a moving, soul searching aria showing her despair at being overpowered by some invisible force and at failing to capture the hearts of the people before her. She demands that they remove their corrupted gifts from the temple.

'That was the most beautiful and expressive piece,' whispered Francisca to me. 'Your music is now exactly right for a defeated goddess.'

Eróstrato hides behind a laurel as Cephalus attempts to woo Procris. He fails again but Aura, unbeknown to Cephalus and Procris, crosses the stage in her cart and breathes the breath of love on them to avenge Procris who becomes more attracted to Cephalus but still fails to express her love for him. Floreta is baffled by the disappearance of her husband Rústico. Clarín, still with the 'dog' on its leash, attempts again to seduce Floreta and hugs her passionately. Rustico sees all this, turns into a wild boar and attacks Clarín, who recalls the wild boar which kills Adonis in 'The Purple of the

Rose'. People in the temple shout, 'Fire'. Cephalus sees a mighty conflagration coming from the temple.

'Is the theatre really alight, Papá?' whispered a frightened Juan junior, pulling himself closer to me.

'No, son. They have slid the back wall of the theatre away and the fire is outside. A model of the temple has been set on fire. It is lighting up the inside of the theatre.'

Eróstrato admits that he is the arsonist and flees to the mountains. Projected by the stage machinery, Aura appears in the air on the back of a salamander, to breathe on and fan the flames. The courageous Cephalus asks Clarín to help him rescue those trapped in the fire. But the cowardly Clarín refuses, claiming that only gentlemen do rescues, not lackeys like him. Cephalus enters the fire and, fearing that the temple may collapse upon him, rescues Procris who is suffocating and faints in Cephalus's arms. Aura continues fanning the flames with her wings and many of the people within suffer a hideous death by burning.

As the curtain fell at the end of the second act, the audience cheered and applauded. Our sullen King disappeared from his box with his Queen. Women entered the theatre, selling cups of water, jugs of wine, pots of beer, sweets, pies and all manner of other delights. 'Can we have some refreshment, Mamá?' asked Juan junior. Francisca went out of the back of the box to buy some biscuits and drinks from a woman in the adjacent corridor.

'Well, what do you think, my love?' I said to Francisca.

'It is the most spectacular production I have ever seen. I love it. You have made music that exactly fits the drama. Pedro will love it, too.'

'The actress singers are brilliant,' I said. 'Josefa Pavía as Diana and Marfisa del Pozo as Aura are just wonderful. And can they sing?'

'I just loved seeing Aura flying through the air on the eagle and the salamander,' said Juan junior. 'How do those machines work, Papá?'

The theatre wall had been reinstated and the third act began in the forest, near the ruins of the temple. As the curtains parted, a huge, flat boulder rose up from the stage with Diana and her three furies, Megera, Tesifone and Alecto, mounted on it. All were dressed in almost transparent gauze, with Diana's adorned with golden stars.

'You can see the women's breasts, Papá.'

'Sh, Juan.'

Diana explains that she is mounted on an emerald piece of the moon and will be until her throne in the ruined temple is restored. She instructs Megera, a fury, to go to the mountains to look for Eróstrato and make him feel desolate and angry. She demands that Alecto destroys Procris's love of

Cephalus by introducing the viper of jealousy. She orders Tesífone to confuse Cephalus so that Diana's spear becomes the instrument of tragedy and his downfall. Finally, and as a gesture of forgiveness, she directs that Rústico reverts to his original form. The giant boulder of emerald moon rock divides into four pieces and each of the three furies and Diana are moved aloft, on their separate segments, by the stage machines.

Procris and Cephalus are now married and in the royal saloon. She tells him that she is worried about their being apart so much, especially while he is away hunting in the mountains. He reassures her, proclaiming his undying love for her. As Cephalus and Clarín are about to go on a hunting trip, Procris asks Clarín what Cephalus does in the mountains and whom he sees. He says he calls a nymph by the name of Laura. Procris is angered and confides in Floreta. Unseen by the two of them, Alecto appears on stage and poisons Procris's mind with jealousy by placing her hand on Procris's breast. Procris tells Floreta that it is Aura who charms Cephalus on the mountain. Procris is afraid that Aura will kill her in an act of revenge. She sings, 'If the air makes jealousy, even jealousy of the air kills' and the chorus intensifies these words by repeating them.

'Someone will be killed soon, I can feel it,' said Juan junior.

'Just be patient and see what happens,' said Francisca.

The scene changes to the mountains and Eróstrato appears, disguised in skins, echoing the words of the chorus. He hears voices that drive him insane. Megera appears. Eróstrato goes blind and wanders aimlessly around the stage. Rústico appears but doesn't recognise Eróstrato who blindly hugs him. They eventually realise who each of them is and Eróstrato asks Rústico if he can hear the voices that Eróstrato can hear in his head. Rústico can hear nothing and Eróstrato goes in pursuit of whomever he can hear.

Cephalus tells Clarín that he sees Aura in the mountains and that her cool breeze prevents him from becoming drenched in perspiration. He hears Aura but cannot see her. She tempts him to call her again. Procris enters, disguised as a peasant, with Floreta at her side with her face covered. Procris hears Cephalus utter the words, 'Procris for whom I die; Aura for whom I live.' She immediately wishes she had not heard these apparently treacherous phrases, telling Floreta that Cephalus is killing her with jealousy. Rústico enters and, not realising he is speaking to Floreta, who is still covered, says he is married to a second-rate nymph. The enraged Floreta reveals herself to Rústico who is intensely embarrassed and still believes he is seen as an animal. Floreta and Clarín convince him that he is human again.

There are shouts off stage warning that a wild beast is on the loose. Cephalus, in Procris's hearing, now does call for Aura. 'Come, Aura, come.' Procris is now sure that Aura is taking revenge on her. Aura does not respond and Cephalus calls again and again, making Procris even more jealous. The 'wild beast' is Eróstrato, now preferring to die insane than to be killed by Diana. Cephalus threatens Eróstrato with his spear. Eróstrato speaks and Cephalus realises that Eróstrato is human after all. Tesífone appears and is invisible to Procris and Cephalus. Cephalus becomes confused by Tesífone and continues to threaten Eróstrato who slips from a rock and falls into the sea, denying Cephalus the chance to kill him. Aura saves Eróstrato who vanishes. Cephalus hears a rustling in the bushes and thinks it is the 'wild beast' in hiding; he throws Diana's infallible spear. Cephalus goes towards the bush to finish off the beast. Procris emerges from it with the spear piercing her breast. Cephalus realises his tragic error. In her dying breath Procris says she is jealous of Aura. Cephalus explains that Aura is merely the air, a cooling breeze. Procris cries out that if the air causes jealousy, jealousy, even of the air kills. She collapses and dies on a rock. Cephalus collapses in shame.

'I said someone would be killed,' whispered a grinning Juan junior. 'I was right.'

Diana and her three furies enter, congratulating themselves on their victory over love and proclaiming long life for the deity. Aura appears on high, on a stage machine, and descends. She calls for Diana and her nymphs to cease their celebration. She asks Venus and Jupiter to make good the tragedy that has befallen the two lovers. She bids the lovers to rise with her into the heavens and all three, Cephalus, Procris and Aura, ascend above the stage. All three celebrate, singing aloud that while vengeance can be noble, it forfeits nobility.

The final chorus echoed these words, singing that if jealousy of the air kills, favours of the air give life.

As the curtain fell, the audience erupted with wild excitement. We had captured them. We had delighted and enthralled them. The applause was deafening. The cheers and shouts were thunderous. The men who were standing jumped up and down on the floor. The women in the *cazuela* clapped frantically and screamed out loud. Even the King managed to raise a smile. The Queen was ecstatic. The opera had enchanted her.

This was one of the most satisfying moments of my life. Antonio de Escamilla appeared on stage and beckoned me and Pedro down from our boxes to accept the applause. It seemed ages before we reached the stage. Pedro waited for me and we appeared together, as we did after the performance of 'The Blood of the Rose', holding each other's hand high. There was another wave of applause as we did so. Poor Pedro was nearly in tears and so was I. Antonio then invited the actress singers to take their bow and they did so individually. They each raised a rapturous applause which was loudest for Josefa Pavía and Marfisa del Pozo. Then the orchestra stood to take their bow. The whole cast had performed to the very pinnacle of their abilities and the orchestra had played to perfection.

'We'll have to write another opera,' I said to Pedro.

'We'll see,' he said, stoically. 'We'll see.'

Going home afterwards seemed an anti-climax but by the time the tumult of applause had died down, Francisca, Juan junior and I felt we had had enough excitement for one day. It reminded me in an odd way of that day when Juan junior was born. Celos was a different kind of baby.

***

Juan junior was making good progress at school and by the time he was sixteen was determined to take a place at university. He wanted to study law and mathematics. He had never mentioned reading mathematics before but for years had been keen to be a lawyer.

'That seems an odd combination,' said Francisca when, one night, he told us his intentions.

'I know,' he said. 'I need to think of two things. First, I may not want to become a lawyer when I graduate. Second, I may have trouble finding work. So to have my second love as a possible career is a useful option.'

'But what job could you get as a mathematician?' I asked.

'There is a whole range of possibilities. I could teach. I could work in the Treasury. I could deal in shares and commercial stock. I could do difficult design calculations in engineering. I could become a natural philosopher. I could even do navigation of ships. The options are endless.'

With that he convinced us that he had at least thought out the reasons for choosing this combination. The next step was to find him a place at a university. There were a number of possibilities. The first was the university at Salamanca but Francisca did not want him to go there because it was too far away. This applied also to the universities at Barcelona and Valencia. The one we favoured most was the University of Alcalá at Henares, about seven *leguas* to the east of our town so conveniently near our home.

'What do you think, Papá? Shall I apply for more than one university or just try for the University of Alcalá? I could apply to Valencia or Salamanca.'

'Apply for all three,' I said, encouragingly. 'That way, if you don't get into Alcalá, you will probably have another option. We can deal with Mamá's worries later, if necessary.'

So Juan junior applied for a place at each of these august institutions. He did well in the end-of-year examinations at Imperial and we fully expected him to be offered places at each of the universities. Then the letters arrived. First from Salamanca. He had succeeded in gaining a place there. Then there was a letter from Valencia. Yes, he had won a place there, too. We waited and waited to hear from Alcalá. Eventually, the letter arrived. Juan opened it. No, he had failed to be offered a place there. Juan junior was not too disappointed because Salamanca and Valencia had excellent law and mathematics faculties but Francisca was unhappy. She could not cope with Juan junior being so far away from Madrid.

'I don't want to upset you, Mamá, but I have to go to university if I am to qualify as a lawyer or a mathematician. I have two offers but I would prefer to go to Salamanca. It is not very far from here, Mamá. Only about thirty *leguas*.'

'Juan, it is too far. You will be out of contact. It will take three days at least to ride there and three days to ride back. I cannot put up with you being so far away. It will kill me.'

Stalemate. Francisca just could not release him from her apron strings. I spoke to her privately about the issue and she just could not reconcile herself to Juan being so far away from Madrid. We would have to try a different tactic, if we were to keep her happy. I decided to use any influence I might have with the King to see if he could help get Juan into Alcalá. His Majesty was a patron of the university and Chancellor of the College of the King. I therefore wrote to him to explain the situation, stressing that Juan junior had been accepted by two other universities but that Alcalá had appeared to reject him, purely on the basis of the number of vacant places they were able to fill, and made the point that Juan exceeded the requirements for entry. A few days later, the King summoned me to discuss my petition.

'I'm not sure I understand this,' the King said, his look and tone showing immediately that he was not happy. 'Why is your wife so keen for your son to go to Alcalá? He has been accepted at Salamanca and Valencia both of which are excellent universities. So, he prefers Salamanca.'

'Your Majesty, my wife is very possessive about Juan. She wants him to go to Alcalá, simply so he can be near to us.'

'But he will be away from home for months at a time,' he said, impatiently. 'It is not as if he will be coming home every day for dinner, even from Alcalá.'

'It is purely a matter of proximity, Your Majesty. If he were at Alcalá, Francisca would feel that she could go there within a day and see him, to make sure he is comfortable and well and changing his clothing regularly.

You know what mothers can be like. She is overprotective and becomes anxious if she feels there are things that are happening without her knowledge. These are the reasons for my rather awkward request, Your Majesty.'

'Does your son know that you are making this request to me?'

'No, Your Majesty. He knows nothing about it.'

'Well,' said the King. 'It is an awkward request. If I grant it, it would seem that I was granting your son a special favour, above any others, who might have an equal claim for a place at Alcalá,' he said. I expected a refusal but he then showed signs of relenting. 'I am undecided. However, leave it with me, and I will consider your request further. The answer at this stage is not negative. You have been a good servant of the Royal Chapel and if I can grant your petition, I shall do so. In the meantime, I would like you to ask your son to write to Salamanca to accept his place. Furthermore, I want you to go with him to Salamanca to demonstrate some visible commitment to going there. Finally, I would expect you not to tell your son about your petition to me or about our meeting today.'

'Thank you, Your Majesty. I can ask for no more.'

I had, of course, told Francisca about my petition to the King and the meeting. She became mildly hopeful but at the same time was still disappointed. She just did not want Juan junior to visit to Salamanca, even if it was only to see the university and the student quarters where he could be staying. 'He will fall in love with the place and want to study there. Then, whatever the King does, he won't want to go to Alcalá. Why can't we wait until the King decides?'

'We have to go, my love. It is by royal command and I dare not disobey His Majesty the King.'

Juan junior and I rode to Salamanca. It was another savagely hot, Spanish summer. The horses hated the weather as much as we did. We could not ride fast. We left Madrid at four o'clock one morning, just before dawn and rode as far as we could before the sun became so hot it would fry us. We endeavoured to stop at a wayside inn or watering place before about ten o'clock so we could rest the horses and ourselves. We would start again at about four in the afternoon and ride on as far into the night as we dared. If we could find a convenient inn to stay the night we did. If not we would sleep on the ground wrapped in a blanket with the horses tied to a tree. The road to Guadarrama was vaguely familiar to me. Francisca and I had traversed it more than twenty years before when we made our amazing visit to Segovia, eventually to meet the extraordinary character, Sebastian Alonso González del Águila. That seemed so far in the past it was almost a lifetime away. We arrived in Salamanca hot, soaked in perspiration and utterly exhausted, five days after leaving Madrid. 'Now you at least know what the journey is like, son.'

'While I am studying in Salamanca, you won't see me more than once a year. I'm not doing that journey any more often than that.'

Juan junior fell in love with Salamanca. The university buildings were stunningly beautiful. The main entrance looked like the elaborate portal of a grand, ancient palace. At each side of the spectacular threshold stood a uniformed guard, stationary, clasping his pikestaff and looking like a painted statue. One of the bursars showed us to the little room in the student quarters that Juan would occupy. It was bare and basic but it was clean and the already made-up bed and a softly upholstered chair gave it the feeling of comfort. 'Do I have to go back to Madrid, Papá? It's only two months before term starts and we'll have to make this hideous journey again.'

'Yes, son. Your mother would be devastated if you did not come back with me. She would think you had been killed and I was covering up your demise. No. You must come back.'

He accepted what I said, admitting that it was selfish of him, even to think of not returning and saying that the last thing in the world he wanted was to upset his mother. Four days later we were back in Madrid, having again traversed the busy, dusty, heat-soaked road from Salamanca.

'You should see my room at the university, Mamá. It is small and bare but I am sure I'll be happy there and you won't have to worry about me.'

'I will still worry, Juan. You are my only son and I will worry about you every day. I suppose I will have to accept that. I will not stand in the way of your ambitions. No mother would do that. I just wish the university was not so far away.'

We had all but accepted that Juan would be going to Salamanca, when I was called by the Private Secretary, my old collaborator, Antonio de Solís, for an audience with the King. I was on tenterhooks not knowing what to expect. What made it worse was that there was some crisis going on in the Treasury so I had to wait two hours in the outer office before the King could see me.

'I am sorry to have kept you. These things happen and have to be dealt with. I have to say that you gave me a serious problem. I could not see a way I could deal with it. I was about to tell you I could not possibly help. Then I decided to discuss the question with one of the officials in the Council of Castile. Between us, we have worked out a solution. I have created a royal scholarship at the College of the King at the University of Alcalá, to be awarded annually to a son of a member of the staff at the palace. There is no other member of my palace staff whose son is going to university this year. This means that I am offering that scholarship for this year to your son. There is some paperwork to do but that is simply to formalise matters.'

'Your Majesty, I cannot thank you enough. I am so grateful and Francisca will be forever grateful, too.'

'Good,' said the King. 'You can go now.'

For two seconds Juan junior was disappointed because he would not be going to Salamanca. 'The good thing is that we'll all be happy with this. Mamá especially.' I was happy, too. The scholarship was worth 800 *ducats* a year. What a bonus.

***

Before Juan junior went to university, we had a party to celebrate. Once again, it was a great opportunity to catch up with relatives and friends alike. We wondered about holding it in one of the inns near the Mentidero but decided to use our own house in the Calle de la Madalena. This would give us greater freedom to do as we wanted and ensure that we did not have to cope with the possible rowdiness of an inn. All the usual culprits attended. Vitoria and Balthasar and their daughter, Clara, who was eleven years old by then, were the first to arrive. As usual, we had much to discuss. For several years after Clara's birth, Vitoria had continued singing at the palace and left the baby with her mother. However, she decided that it would be better for the child if she was at home so she resigned when the child was about five years old, just before she started in the infants' school. By then, Balthasar was so wealthy that there was just no need for Vitoria to earn an income.

'Have you heard who replaced me in the Royal Chapel?' asked Vitoria.

'No. I didn't know that you have been replaced. They have carried the vacancy for so long now.'

'Well, apparently, the Maestro became so frustrated at having to recruit temporary sopranos he decided to find someone full time for the job. Since her great performance in "Celos", Marfisa del Pozo's reputation has grown enormously. She is now in my old job.'

'What great news,' said Francisca, smiling all over her face. 'She was simply brilliant as Aura.'

Alonso Arias de Soria and Antonia Rodríguez brought their offspring, Antona, who was by then a beautiful, slim redhead of twenty-one and their son, Agustín, who was the same age as Juan junior. Agustín wanted to become a professional tenor, like his father, and had joined Juana de Cisneros's theatre company as an apprentice singer actor. Antona had become a nurse in the asylum at the Casa de la Misericordia in the Calle

Capellanes. She said that to do the job you had to be resilient in body and mind. Some of the lunatics they had to deal with were so dangerous they had to be chained to the walls. Others were sporadically violent and unpredictable so you had to watch their every move. 'You dare not turn your back on them,' she said. Some just sat all day and every day in the same spot looking at the ceiling, rocking to and fro on their haunches. One woman was kept naked in a padded cell because she would try to kill herself with anything she was given to wear or eat or sleep upon, 'anything she could force down her throat.' She was the worst case they had ever had in the Casa.

'What if one of the lunatics you chain up wants to relieve herself?' asked Juan junior.

'They do it where they are standing. The warders clean up the mess at night, when they are chained to their beds. It's bad but too dangerous to do anything else. A nurse was killed there four years ago when a lunatic smashed a full chamber pot right on top of the nurse's head. So they had to change the rules. Now, if a lunatic has to be attended to, at least two nurses have to respond.'

'I bet the place smells,' said Vitoria.

'It stinks like something vile,' said Antona. 'The stench is ten times worse than our town first thing in the morning, after the chamber pots have been emptied. But you get used to it.'

It seemed amazingly courageous that this pretty little girl had chosen a job as a nurse in a madhouse. I remember Antona saying, when she was at school, that she wanted to be a nurse. We didn't expect that ambition to be fulfilled by her working in an asylum. She seemed to cope with the job well and capable of dealing with the most troublesome of patients. If anything, she had become somewhat hardened to the circumstances of these sorrowful individuals. However, if that was the mechanism by which she was able to manage them, it was wrong to criticise her. I thought she deserved a medal.

Francisco, his wife Juana Vélez and our mother came, as did Inés del Mazo, her father, Juan Bautista Martínez del Mazo and her brother Baltasar. Baltasar was an amazingly talented artist. He could draw a charcoal portrait in a matter of a few minutes and the likeness to the subject would be striking. Like Diego, his portraits would tell something of the character and expression of his sitter. He wanted to follow his father's and grandfather Diego's path and become a professional artist. 'I'd love to be good enough to be the royal portrait painter,' he once told Juan junior. He had the ability, the personality and the intelligence. Although he was a fellow artist, in the sense that composing is an art, I found Juan Bautista Martínez remote and difficult to involve in conversation. This was the opposite of the relationship between Francisca and his daughter, Inés. They were like mother and daughter. They visited each other at least twice a week and exchanged gossip and stories with Antonia and Vitoria who also loved to chat and gossip along with them.

Mother was about seventy-six then. She had sold the 'love sleeve' business two years before to a businessman from Barcelona. We had all benefitted from this incredible enterprise. The profits had helped Francisco, me and Francisca, and Aunt Catalina to buy our own houses and to live to a high standard, at least when compared to that experienced by the majority of the people of Madrid. Mother sold the business for more than 50,000 *ducats*. Contrary to our decision over her inheritance from our father, we insisted that she put the money, which was in gold coin, into an account at one of our banks. Even after she had paid the punitive amount of tax on the sale, it was clear that she need have no money worries again, not that she had had many since we eventually found her inheritance from our father's estate. The merchant from Barcelona not only bought the business but kept on all the staff that our mother had engaged, including the redoubtable Barbola.

Francisco had become an extremely able harpist and became one of the most respected musicians in the Royal Chapel. He was always in demand at the palace and, occasionally, with the theatre companies in our town. He had settled well into married life. He and Juana never had children but they enjoyed each other's company and were always happy together. Francisco said that he had always been faithful to Juana and had resisted many temptations to do otherwise. I never asked about his married life and how the two of them coped with Francisco's magnificent manhood. It just did not seem right to pry into such things. After all, Francisca and I did not discuss our intimate life with anyone and we intended to keep it that way.

So with a great celebration of our family and friends, we successfully launched Juan junior into his life as a university student. The day before the university year began, we took him to Alcalá in our carriage, made our hasty farewells and left him there, sitting with some other students in the law school. Francisca cried as we left and I had to choke back my tears.

CHAPTER 27

After the success of 'Celos', I wanted to write the score for another opera and discussed the subject with Pedro, not long after the performance.

'I'm not so sure, Juan. The opera made a huge loss, of something like 20,000 *ducats*. I cannot imagine the palace will want to rush into doing another one, not yet, anyway. Let's leave it for a time and see if they commission us to write an opera later.'

'How could such a loss arise?' I asked.

'It was the rehearsing. Every word was sung and that alone meant that we had to spend so much time doing the rehearsals. The actress singers and the choirs all had to be paid and we had to pay Heliche for hiring the house in the Mentidero.'

I had to agree with the wise words of the master. I did not see the point in annoying the palace with a request to which they probably would not accede, especially bearing in mind the loss that Pedro was talking about. We decided to continue our programme of collaboration and Pedro said that he would write a conventional three act *comedia* for which I would write the incidental music and the music for the songs. This work was 'Not Even Love Can Free Itself from Love', a story about the love of Psyche and Cupid. The *comedia* was performed before the King and Queen who were so impressed by the work that the King ordered that it should be performed to the people of Madrid in the Buen Retiro.

Shortly after we had worked together on the *comedia*, I received a notice from the Holy Office:

'Notice is hereby given to Don Juan Hidalgo de Polanco, notario of the Holy Office of the Inquisition of Toledo, to carry out the following functions:

On a date to be notified, to act as notario and material witness at an inquiry in which a work of Pedro Calderón de la Barca y Henao is to be examined against a charge of blasphemy. The alleged blasphemy is against Jesus Christ and the work which is the subject of the allegation is, "Military Orders". A copy of the text of this work will be provided for this purpose by the Holy Office.'

How ridiculous. How could I be expected to act as an official and witness for an inquiry in which Pedro was accused of blasphemy? The answer was that I could not and no reasonable person could expect me to do so. I explained my anger to Francisca who was as annoyed as I was.

'What are you going to do about it, Juan?'

'I shall go to the Office of the Inquisition and protest that I cannot be expected to obey the notice.'

The irony of this request was that, apart from a few minor commitments to take notes in tribunal hearings, I had not been requested to perform any functions for the Inquisition for about ten years or more. Then, suddenly, just after Pedro and I had had our greatest success with Celos, this emerged, like someone clenching a dagger from behind a tree. There was no other option: I had to go to the Holy Office and ask them to withdraw the notice.

I walked to the tribunal which, at that time, was being held at the office in the Calle del Nuncio. I explained my position to the senior clerk.

'No, Señor Hidalgo. I am afraid that will not be possible. The problem is that everybody in Madrid has heard of Pedro Calderón de la Barca. We selected your good self because you are a distinguished member of the Royal Chapel. And we regard you as a reliable and fit person to carry out this duty.'

'But Pedro Calderón de la Barca is a personal friend of mine and a collaborator. We have worked together on a number of dramatic works. He had written the text and I have written the music.'

'I know,' said the clerk. 'We are aware of that.'

'Don't you understand that you will be putting me in an impossible position in testifying against my friend? I won't do it.'

'Are you refusing to carry out a function specified in a notice issued by the Holy Office of the Inquisition of Toledo, Señor Hidalgo?'

I could detect a note of a rehearsed script in what he was asking me. I imagined he had used these words before when others had objected. I was not going to fall into any trap set by this inflexible functionary.

'No. Not exactly.' I replied. 'I am merely stating an objection.'

'It sounds like a refusal to me, señor.'

'Well it isn't. But unless you relieve me from the terms of the notice, I shall have no option but to go to the Inquisitor General.' The Inquisitor I had rescued at the King's boar hunt when I was still new at the palace, Antonio de Sotomayor, had resigned from office many years before on the grounds of advanced age and ill health. The new Inquisitor was the Bishop of Ávila and Plaçensia, Diego de Arce y Reynoso, whom I had never met. So, if I was to appeal, there was a risk that a higher authority, of whom I had no knowledge, would decide against me. I would then have no choice but to take the only honourable way out, to resign from the Holy Office of the Inquisition.

'That is your prerogative, Señor Hidalgo. I have no authority to excuse you from the terms of the notice.'

I went home a disappointed man and explained the situation to Francisca who was of the same view as me. So I wrote a letter to Diego de Arce y Reynoso. I explained that I enjoyed a reasonably high level of esteem with the populace of our town and that this could be prejudiced if it became known, as it surely would, that I had testified against my friend and colleague. I added that this would be irrespective of the merits of the case against Pedro. Two days before Pedro's hearing, I received a letter from the office of the Grand Inquisitor. It said that the Inquisitor General had considered my case and agreed to release me from the terms of the notice. I was overjoyed. I would not have to resign my post as *notario*. Nor would there be any possibility that my position as a special agent to the King be prejudiced. I thought this was an issue because, rightly or wrongly, I saw a connection between the two honorary posts.

I decided to attend Pedro's inquiry hearing and watch from the public gallery. He saw me and came over to speak to me.

'What are you doing here, Juan?'

'I had to come here to see the hearing, Pedro. I will be giving you moral support.'

'I do not know what the outcome will be, Juan. We can only wait to see, but as my work is fictional, I am hoping the tribunal will take a lenient view.'

The charge against Pedro was read out by a *notario*. Presumably, that would have been me, had I not been excused from this duty by the Inquisitor General. 'Señor Pedro Calderón de la Barca, you are charged with blasphemy against Jesus Christ. You are accused of taking his name in vain in your Corpus Christi play, "Military Orders".' I had not read the text of the play so was impatient to hear the detailed charge. What ever had Pedro said to blaspheme against Christ?

The *notario* read out a summary of the offending words. 'In your play you make it clear that you believe that Jesus Christ would be incapable of passing the necessary requirements of purity of blood to qualify for a post in the Holy Office of the Inquisition. What do you have to say in your defence?'

Pedro gave a typically robust reply. 'I would have thought it self-evident that Christ would fail such an examination. He was born of Jewish parents. The Inquisition of Spain demands purity of blood in the sense that the ancestors of the applicant are of pure Spanish extraction. The play is, of course, a work of fiction. I have nothing more to say.'

I thought that, on the basis of Pedro's defence, the charges should be dropped. I was wrong. A week later, the Inquisition sent Pedro a letter telling him that they had censured the play, that all unsold copies were to be confiscated from the bookshops and that the book would be banned from publication for ten years.

The inquiry did not punish Pedro himself and he seemed totally indifferent to the outcome. 'That is just too bad, Juan. I suppose it's their prerogative but it just doesn't worry me in the least.' I thought I would be quite upset if the same thing had happened to me. I later felt that my attendance at Pedro's hearing, helped ease my relationship with him. He became more of a friend and less remote with me than he had before. This was a welcomed development.

***

Juan junior seemed to settle in well at the University of Alcalá de Henares. We hardly saw him while he was in his first year there and deliberately stayed away so he could feel that he had achieved a degree of independence from us. After he had been at the College of the King for about fifteen months, he invited us to go to there to see him and to meet some of his student friends. We went on horseback and stayed at the Inn of the King which was close to Juan junior's college. We met him at the main entrance to the college itself.

'Juan, I am missing you so much,' said Francisca, her eyes overflowing with tears of joy at seeing our beloved son.

'I have, too, Juan. It is so good to see you.' He had grown a short, pointed beard and had let his hair grow a little longer than before. He looked well and excited to see us.

'It's so good to see you, Mamá and Papá. I have missed you, too. First, you must have some refreshment. Then I will show you to my room.' He took us to the refectory area and bought us some fruit juices, water and some bread and ham.

'How are you getting on with your studies this term, Juan?' asked Francisca.

'I think I am doing well, Mamá. As I told you in the summer, I did well in the end of year exams. The work in the first year was little more than consolidating on what I had learnt at school. But it has become more specialised this year. I understand the new law work quite well and I absolutely love the mathematics. I am studying algebra and trigonometry. It is fascinating. It is amazing what you can understand in the world by applying these branches of mathematics, even the motion of the planets.'

'All that is beyond me, Juan. I am a simple harpist and composer.'

'We are lucky here because we have a mathematician from France and an astronomer from England. And we are learning about all the latest discoveries. Now we have left the school work behind us, these mathematical subjects have become really exciting and stimulating.'

'What about your law work, Juan? You say you are only doing quite well in law,' Francisca asked.

'No. I am enjoying the work in law. There is more essay work than in mathematics but I think it, too, is going well. I am enjoying law just as much as the mathematics and that must be a good indication. Come to see my room.'

We left the refectory and crossed over a cloister to the students lodgings. The rooms were tiny. Juan's had a bed, a small desk with a wooden chair, a bookshelf attached to a wall and a wardrobe with some drawers for his clothing. The room was on the fourth floor and overlooked a large courtyard with a fountain in the centre of a large circular flowerbed.

'My goodness Juan. The room is tiny. How can you manage with such a small space? It's like a prison cell,' asked Francisca, her eyebrows raised quizzically.

'Yes, but the difference is that I have the key,' said Juan. 'It's large enough for me. I can sleep here and I can study here. That is all I need. Let's go to the square and see if any of my friends are there.' The little square was just outside of the college. Surrounding its cobbled paving were other eating houses, some shops, the inn in which Francisca and I were staying, another inn on the opposite side of the square and an old theatre building.

'There is a student theatre group here, Papá, which present *comedias*. They played one of Lope de Vega's only last week. You would have loved it. It was "The Knight from Olmedo".'

'I know the story, Juan,' I said. 'It has been played many times in Madrid. I always felt sorry for the Knight's betrothed, Inés, who does not deserve the Knight being murdered by the jealous Rodrigo.'

We entered the inn across the square. It was light but noisy inside and smelt strongly as if someone had spilt an *azumbre* or so of beer on the floor. There were a several small gatherings of young people, presumably students, who were engaged in feverish discussion. 'There they are,' said Juan, moving to a group sitting in a small alcove on the far side from the door. There were three of them chatting away, a girl and two boys, all of about Juan junior's age which was just eighteen.

'Hello, Nicolas. This is my father and mother. They have come to see me. They have come from Madrid today. This is Nicolas, Mamá and Papá,' Juan proudly explained.

'My God, Juan. Why have you brought them here? This is a student college not a nursery school. You don't need your parents here do you?' said the student, a tall, thin lad, also wearing a pointed beard.

'Don't be unkind, Nicolas,' said the plainly dressed girl abruptly. Her name was Constanza.

'Why criticise Nicolas?' said the third student whose name was Salvador. He was squat, rotund with a pronounced paunch and spoke with the absence of any tone or emotion. 'Parents should be kept away from the university. They may find out things they'd rather not know.'

'If Juan wants to show his parents the university and introduce them to his friends, then that is his privilege. Señor and señora, I am pleased to meet you,' said Constanza.

'What have you got to hide?' said Francisca, obviously shocked by Salvador's comments and throwing her question directly in his face.

'There are political things going on here that you may not agree with. We are trying to convert Juan into a republican but he is too loyal to our worn out monarchy,' said Nicolas.

'You speak for yourself,' said Constanza. 'You are always stressing the freedom of the individual. So Juan can have whatever views he likes.' The three of us bade farewell to Juan's three student friends and left them arguing among themselves.

While at the university, we told Juan junior that the banker's family who had rented our house in the Puerta Cerrada were about to move to a house they had bought in the north of the town. We asked Juan if he would like to have the house as his own residence. He would then have a property he could use when he was in the town and also a place of his own when he left university and took up employment. There was an ulterior motive on our part. We did not want Juan to move out of our town when he became qualified. Living in the house would give him at least some incentive to stay and work in Madrid. Juan junior jumped at the idea.

While we were pleased to see Juan junior at the university, Francisca and I left Alcalá de Henares with some serious doubts about the type of student he was mixing with. Except for the girl Constanza, we did not like their attitude to us or their political leanings. Was this place a hotbed of republicanism? Were these students plotting against the monarchy? I thought of exercising my function as a special agent and reporting what we had heard to the Clerk of the Council for State Security but, by the time we had reached home, it seemed to me that these students also had a right to think what they wanted and if they wanted to discuss alternative types of government, that was their prerogative. We saw no evidence there of an insurrection or any other form of plan to depose the monarchy of our country.

We wondered, though, if this talk of a republic had been influenced by the recent death of the King, which was in the September before our visit to the university in the following January. Philip IV had for many months been neither well nor happy. He had never fully recovered from the tragic death at four years of age of the Infante Philip Prósper, his beloved son. Then, in the June before he died, he undertook a huge gamble. He sent an army into Portugal in an attempt finally to end their ambitions for independence. The army was led by the Marquis of Caracena, an accomplished and skilful general. The gamble failed. The Spanish army was smashed to pieces by the Portuguese who, at Montes Claros, won the most decisive victory in their history. This just about finished our war-weary monarch. He became even sadder after the army's defeat and remorseful, regretting almost everything he had done, even many of his recognisable achievements. His health began to fail and in the September he died of kidney failure. It was an especially sad death because by then, mainly because of the defeat at Montes Claros which was still fresh in the minds of many, he was regarded as a pathetic failure.

I was saddened by his death as I had come to regard him as a friend and ally. He had certainly given me colossal support both in my family life and in my career. I thought of him almost as my other brother. I loved him and was proud to have known this man whom I regarded as a hero, even if few others held him in anything like such esteem. I missed him and felt miserable for days after his passing. I kept thinking of him while writing his requiem mass, which was not one of my better works. It's hard to be inspired by the loss of a friend.

The king's death caused great anxiety in the Royal Chapel. The Maestro wondered what would happen to the Chapel and its staff under the King's successor, Charles II, who was four years old when he was proclaimed King. So as to protect the working of our country, the King had mandated that, after his death, Queen Mariana, the exuberant music lover, be Queen Regent of Spain. This was our salvation. She wanted to be entertained and the Royal Chapel continued to thrive under her enthusiastic patronage. As a mark of respect, she closed the theatres on the King's death and they remained shut for a year.

Two other notable individuals died on the same day as the King. Baltasar Moscoso y Sandoval, the Archbishop of Toledo, met his end a few hours before; and our beloved Esmeralda Pechada de Burgos expired a few hours after. The poor lady collapsed when she heard that her friend the King had passed away. We never knew how old she was but must have been into her eighties. The poor Archbishop died of nothing more interesting than old age.

**

Once we had recovered from our shock at meeting Juan junior's friends at the University of Alacalá, we quickly settled into living on our own again after sharing ourselves for so many years with our beloved son. We missed him terribly, both before and after we saw him at the College of the King, and wondered every day how he was getting on. I was fifty-two and Francisca forty-nine and while we were not that young we were healthy and still full of energy. We felt we were among the lucky ones. The King had given me so many salary increases over the years and I had been paid so handsomely for composing that we could afford to live well. I should not forget, either, that we had benefitted from my mother's love sleeve business, not only while she was running it but also from its successful sale. Not only did we eat and drink well, we enjoyed going to the theatre and would see a *comedia* at one of the theatres, usually once or twice a week. Lope's works were still amazingly popular and there were dozens of other playwrights whose work was just as entertaining, even if they did not have Lope's touch of genius.

'What shall we do today, Juan?' asked Francisca on one fresh spring morning.

'I fancy a ride out of the town. What about asking Alonso Arias de Soria and Antonia Rodríguez?'

I saddled up the horses and we called on them at their rented house in the Calle de la Paz. They were also wondering what to do that day so were delighted that we had thought of inviting them to come for a ride with us. We decided to go out of the Puerta de Lavapiés which is to the south-east of the town and take the Cuenca road. The road to the Puerta was busy with heavy carts and people going about their daily business. Some were carrying loaves of bread and others vessels of water on their shoulders. The air outside the gate was fresh and pure and we decided to let the horses gallop for a half a *legua* on the open road. We shouted and cheered our mounts, which just loved to be given the freedom of a high-speed run. We stopped at a wayside tavern, just a little further from the town, and tied the horses up before we went inside for some refreshment.

'How is Juan junior getting on at the university? He must have been there for nearly two years by now,' asked Antonia as she was sipping a glass of orange juice.

'Hm,' said Francisca. 'We are not sure. He seems to be doing brilliantly in his chosen subjects which are mathematics and law but he has made some odd friends there. They seem to be republicans. But they are young and impressionable. Juan and I think that their views have been prompted by the death of the King and the thought of having Queen Mariana as the Regent.'

'I agree,' I said. 'God alone knows what state the country will be in when the new King becomes old enough to rule. The Queen Regent is already upsetting everyone by frantically renewing her links with Austria. The next thing is that we will be taken over by the Austrian Habsburgs.'

'Perish the thought,' said Alonso. 'If the Austrians come we will be taxed to the hilt and all of our cash will end up in Vienna.'

'There would be a revolution before that happened,' I ventured to add.

'Anyway, how are Agustín and Antona?' asked Francisca.

'Antona is doing very well at the Casa de la Misericordia. She was threatened by a madman a week or so back but floored him before he could touch her. We are amazed at how well she copes with the job. Agustín is training hard to sing and he is enjoying acting more than ever we thought he would. The great thing is that he loves working for the theatre company. He loves Juana de Cisneros. She is doing so much for him and he just does not want to leave. I can see him working there for years,' said Antonia, clearly proud that both of her children were making good progress in their chosen careers.

'Are you still making the jewellery?' I asked Antonia.

'It's strange that you ask that. Since the King died, I have had numerous requests for gold medallions embossed with his portrait. I'm amazed. He was more popular than the notices give him credit for. Most of my work is with gold but I still work with gemstones and emeralds seem by far the favourite.'

We returned to Madrid recognising that we four were among the privileged of the town and that we had much to be grateful for. Alonso was earning a good salary as a tenor and we imagined that Antonia was doing well from her jewellery business. None of us was as well off as Vitoria and Balthasar but, in effect, Alonso and I were mere civil servants and could not expect the rewards that our successful friends in business enjoyed.

'How about making love?' I said to Francisca, when we were alone again, inside the house. 'Juan is not here and it will be like old times.'

'I need a bath so we will bathe each other first,' said Francisca. So that is what we did. It was pure, uninhibited joy.

***

We were all delighted to hear a few years later that our old friend Giulio Rospigliosi had been elected Pope. He took the name Clement IX. Shortly after he returned to Rome from serving as papal nuncio, he was elected cardinal and Secretary of State to the Vatican. These were positions of immense power which Giulio discharged with great humility, fitting exactly the personality of the man we had come to know so well. I wrote to congratulate him on becoming Pope and in his reply he said that he had taken the post against considerable opposition. Nevertheless, he felt that he could bring certain skills and experience to it and he hoped that his friends here in the palace and elsewhere among the people of Spain would support him and pray for him.

He said in his letter that he was writing a new libretto about a madman who was composer and harpist for the King of Spain. He said this composer goes to Italy to see some operas performed. He returns to Spain and convinces the King that he should write an opera himself. He manages to persuade his best friend to write the libretto. From the tumultuous applause it receives, the opera seems a major triumph, despite the fact that nobody can understand what it is about. Its evident success is solely due to the composer paying everyone in the audience to applaud, whistle and shout when it finishes. Giulio said he was sending me the libretto so that I could write the music. With that sense of humour alone he could be a great Pope.

***

One of the advantages of Juan having his own home in Madrid was that, unlike when he was in his first year and we hardly saw him, he came back regularly at weekends and during holidays and we saw quite a lot of him. We were sure he would have been less enthusiastic about returning, if he had no choice but to stay with us in the Calle de la Madalena. I remember having those same pangs of independence when I was about twenty. He would sometimes bring some of his friends from the college and, as I did at his age, would have the occasional party, inviting also his old school friends in the town.

The routine of Juan junior returning to our town from university continued until he was twenty-one, just before he would finally qualify as a lawyer. Then the greatest possible tragedy struck. Barbola still used to clean the house in the Puerta Cerrada, even when the banker and his family lived there. On that fateful morning, she came rushing around to our house in the Madelena.

'Juan, Francisca, something terrible has happened!' She started crying and could hardly say her words between sobs and tears.

'What, Barbola?' said Francisca. 'Say it. What has happened?'

'It's Juan junior. I think he is dying. He is very ill. He needs a doctor urgently.'

'No!' screamed Francisca. 'That cannot be true. It cannot be.'

It was as if a bolt of lightning had struck at our very hearts and souls. We had to get to the Puerta Cerrada quickly.

'Let's go now. I'll get out the horses.'

We all three rode quickly to the Puerta Cerrada. We dismounted and went in. Juan junior was lying on the sofa in the lounge. He was unconscious but still just breathing. Some brown fluid was leaking out of his mouth.

'Juan, Juan, speak to me,' said Francisca, pleading to Juan to say at least a word. But he said nothing. I tried but still he would not speak.

'I'll go to the palace and get the Royal Physician. Get a blanket to put over him and keep him warm.'

Juan looked terrible. I had never seen him as bad. I wondered about getting a priest in case we had to give the last rites. By a stroke of luck, the physician could come straight away so I sent him to the house in the Puerta Cerrada while I went to the San Ginés church to get the priest.

'How is he?' I asked the doctor as I returned and entered the lounge.

'I just do not know what is wrong. I think he is dying.'

The priest came in and gave Juan the last rites and within a few moments he let out a deep moan and was dead.

'Francisca, the love of our lives is dead. Juan is dead.' We all started crying. I put my arm round Francisca who became hysterical. She screamed and screamed, in a frenzy of shock, disbelief, loss and anger.

We stood and looked at our beloved son's lifeless body.

'I cannot look at Juan any longer. I cannot look. I must get out of here,' sobbed Francisca.

'Let me give you a potion. It will help you, señora,' said the physician, offering Francisca something to calm her. She took it with a cup of water.

What a disaster. A hammer blow. It felt as if our lives had come to a halt and that a great part of us had died with Juan. The pain for Francisca and me was unbearable. 'There will have to be a post mortem,' said the physician. 'I cannot understand the cause of death.' All three of us wanted to get out of the house at the Puerta Cerrada so I took Francisca home and

Barbola came, too. I could not stay there long as there were arrangements to be made for the removal of Juan's body to the mortuary. I settled Francisca who was herself very drowsy, having taken the physician's potion, and left her in the care of the tireless Barbola. I went to Antonia and Alonso's house to break the news to them and ask them to come around to our house to be with Francisca while I went to the house in the Puerta Cerrada to meet the undertakers. Unsurprisingly, Antonia and Alonso were totally dismayed at the news but came immediately to our house.

The post mortem on Juan junior was conducted by the Royal Physician himself. He could not give the cause of Juan's death but reported that he had suspected that it had been due to poisoning. He came to this unwelcomed conclusion after he had taken some of the lining of Juan's stomach and fed it to two mice. They both died within an hour. The physician suspected 'poisoning by arsenic, either self-administered or administered by another or others.'

This made Juan's death even more unbearable for me and Francisca. We could see no reason for Juan taking his own life and I explained this to the physician. 'He had everything to live for. He was a brilliant lawyer and mathematician. He had a great future ahead of him.'

'I am not saying he killed himself deliberately,' said the physician, neutrally. 'Arsenic is the one of the cures for syphilis and if he thought he had contracted that disease he may have decided to treat himself, so as to avoid the embarrassment of seeing a doctor. He could probably have obtained some from a laboratory at the University. Alternatively, he may have been murdered. Did he have enemies that would want him dead?'

'I am not aware of Juan having any enemies. He had some strange friends at the University, who had odd political views. But I cannot see anyone there would want to kill him.'

'I think we should ask the judicial office to investigate,' said the physician.

Before Juan's funeral, I went alone to Alcalá de Henares. There were two reasons for going there. I needed to report Juan's death to the University authorities and imagined I would have to clear his room. I urgently wanted to tell the judicial office at Henares that Juan may have been murdered and ask them to investigate the case. By then, I had the physician's post mortem report, a copy of which I gave to them. They were helpful and courteous but after six weeks wrote to me saying that they had conducted a full investigation, mainly by interviewing students at the University, and had concluded that there were no grounds to suspect that Juan had been murdered. The worst part of this sojourn was clearing Juan's room. I felt desperately sad as I removed his clothing from the little wardrobe, clothing he would never wear again. I removed his books from the shelves, books he would never open again. He had an ink sketch that Diego had made of me and Francisca. I took that, too. He would never cast his eyes on it again. Tears came to my eyes and I just let them flow.

How we survived Juan's funeral I will never know. I could not bear the thought of having it in the church of San Justo, which was the church of Juan's parish and where Francisca and I were married so I managed to persuade the priest at San Ginés, the one who had given Juan the last rites, that he should hold the service there. Poor Francisca was so distraught she clung to Juan's coffin as if she wanted to be buried with it. She probably did. I managed to hold myself together but many of the women, including my mother who was in her eighties, wept interminably. This and the day of Juan's unexpected death were the worst days of my life. Surely, nothing worse could be ahead of us.

CHAPTER 28

There is nothing worse for parents than having to bury one of their own children. The pain is unbearable but has to be borne. The death of your child racks and rages you. It burns and cuts into your heart. It never completely leaves your mind. Even in moments of happiness the scar of death is there. Such a loss destroys the concept of normality because that state is never again achievable. The pain is even more unendurable for a parent whose child is murdered, whose life is snatched from him or her by the deliberate act of another. It is even worse if justice is not delivered and the murderer escapes punishment. It is equally bad for a parent whose child deliberately takes his or her own life. Who was to blame? What was the reason? Could we have prevented the death? Francisca and I never really knew what caused Juan's death. All we knew was that when part of him was fed to some mice, they died. The death certificate did not record a cause and that reflected the Royal Physician's uncertainty. Francisca and I found it endlessly difficult just continuing to live, let alone get anything out of our lives but we had to go on. I suppose I was lucky in having my work at the palace and Francisca had started again at the Shod Carmen soup kitchen. She found it agonising to go there but she went, nearly every day.

About six weeks after Juan's funeral, I was walking home from the palace at my usual time, thinking that our lives were slowly beginning to show signs of moving forward again, when I noticed smoke coming from the windows of the San Ginés church. I deviated slightly from my normal route and ran towards the church to see whether I should raise an alarm. The fire watch had already been called and a group was forming to douse the fire. Two women were running into the church carrying leather buckets, slopping over with water. A small crowd of onlookers had gathered. I asked one of them what was happening.

'Some mad woman went into the church and set the place alight. They've taken her screaming to the madhouse.'

'The things that happen in our town,' I thought and watched for a few minutes until the smoke died down and the fire was obviously more or less under control. I then walked the rest of the way home, opened the door and let myself in. Francisca was not there. I was concerned because she would always tell me if, for some reason, she did not expect to be at home when I arrived from the palace. Her resumed work at the Shod Carmen soup kitchen was always finished by just after midday and, even if she had a meeting to attend, she was always home by the time I arrived. I had no idea where she was and wondered if she might have gone around to Inés del Mazo's house in the Calle de Olivar. So I went there.

'No we haven't seen Francisca today. But I hope to see her tomorrow. I'm sure you'll find her soon, Juan,' said Inés.

As I approached our house on my return, there were two crown constables standing by the front door. There was something seriously wrong.

'Are you Juan Hidalgo de Polanco?' said the taller one.

'Yes.'

'We have come to inform you that we have arrested your wife, Francisca.'

'Whatever has she done?' I asked. Mercifully, she was alive. I was beginning to wonder if, failing to cope with the death of Juan, she had gone somewhere and... I could not conclude the thought.

'She has committed an arson attack on the church of San Ginés,' said the shorter one.

'Has she been hurt? Is she safe? Where is she now?'

'She has been seen by a doctor and declared insane. She told the doctor that she heard a voice in her head telling her to set alight to the church. A woman saw your wife go into the church, take an altar candle and go to one of the pews. She tore some pages from a prayer book, piled them underneath the pews and set them alight. The fire really took hold and they had to call the fire watch to put it out. There is a lot of damage and the church has been closed.'

'I must see her. Where is she?'

'She is in the asylum in the Casa de la Misericordia in the Calle Capellanes. That is why we have come here. She will need some clothes and we want you to take some with you.'

'Are you going there with me?'

'No. Our job is done. Goodnight.'

The two officers disappeared into the dusk, leaving me alone and in a state of shock and dejection. My beloved Francisca had been certified as mad. Surely, she would not set alight to a church, whatever any voices had told her. San Ginés had such connections with our family. The constables would not have lied. This could be a simple case of mistaken identity. Someone else had set fire to the church. Then something in my mind compelled me to think that this report could be true. Juan's death had affected Francisca deeply. This could have been a reaction to it. I was confused. I had to go to the Misericordia with some of Francisca's clothes.

Should I go alone? No. I would pack some clothing and take Inés with me, if she would come. I put some of Francisca's things into a bag and went round to the Martínez del Mazo house. I knocked on the door and Inés opened it.

'What is the matter, Juan? You are as white as a sheet.'

'It's Francisca, Inés.' I explained to her what had happened and we then went on foot to the Casa de la Misericordia.

'I cannot understand this,' said Inés. 'Francisca was fine yesterday when we met up at your house with Vitoria and Antonia. She seemed vacant at times as if she still had Juan on her mind. But she could hardly be described as mad. Quite the opposite.'

'We will see when we get to the asylum,' I said, hoping that there had been some error, that Francisca would be able to explain everything and we would take her back home.

We went to the visitors' area in the asylum and I asked to see Francisca.

'What is her full name?' asked the attendant. I told him.

'Is she new here?' I said she had been admitted a few hours ago and that she was accused of arson.

He took us to what he called a holding room. This is where they took the new entrants for assessment before they decided what to do with them. He pulled up a bunch of keys from a chain attached to his belt and placed one of the larger ones in the door lock, turned it in the keyhole and gradually pushed the door open, as if the area contained wild beasts and he had to see where they were before he went in. It was nearly dark outside and the room was lit by oil lamps placed high up the walls. As he opened the door an invisible cloud of stench hit us. It was the smell of human excrement. The three of us entered the room. There were half a dozen people there, three men and three women. All were restrained in some way, by chains or ropes and two, both women, were tied by their wrists with their arms outstretched to rings about five feet from the floor. One of these poor souls was my Francisca. This was a living nightmare.

'Juan! Juan!' screamed Francisca, as she saw me. 'Look what they have done to me. Take me home! Take me home!'

'What has happened, my love? Tell me?' I could only just speak as I was choking back tears to see Francisca tied up like this.

'On the way back home from the Shod Carmen soup kitchen, I went to the San Ginés Church to pray and knelt down in one of the pews. I started praying to Our Father to save the soul of our Juan. I then heard this loud voice in my head. It was the voice of a woman who said her name was Aura and that she was a nymph of Diana who had been transformed into the goddess of the air. I told her I knew of her through your opera, Celos. She

374

was pleased I knew her already and said she had superhuman powers. She said that if I wanted to avenge the death of my beloved son, I would have to set fire to the church. I said I would do no such thing. She then said that she would kill me by a lightning strike if I didn't do it. She told me to get one of the lit candles from the altar, tear up a prayer book and set the paper alight. I could feel her blowing the flames, Juan, so I knew she was still there. I walked out of the church before the fire took hold. That is what I did, Juan. It was purely to defend myself. Aura would have killed me if I had not set alight to the church.'

Francisca was completely coherent and, had she been speaking about any normal event, would have sounded completely sane. But what she said and did was not normal. I realised then that something bad had happened inside Francisca's head. It had to be caused by the death of our Juan. How could we put it right? We could not do it alone. We needed medical advice and I was determined that we would get the best available. I would speak to the Royal Physician whose opinion I trusted.

'Can't you untie her?' I pleaded to the attendant.

'No, señor. That is more than I would dare do. Your lady will have to stay there until the doctor assesses her first thing tomorrow morning. Don't worry. She will be let down tonight and will sleep in a bed, even if she is tied to it. You'll have to go now, señor. Visiting is over.'

Francisca heard all this and screamed, 'Don't leave me here! Take me home! I'll go mad if I'm in here a moment longer!'

'Francisca, my love, I will always love you. They are sending me away now. I will come back tomorrow. I promise,' I said, as calmly as I could. I went up to her, still chained to the wall, and kissed her.

She immediately cried. 'Juan, I will be mad by tomorrow, or dead. Please don't leave me in this shit hole.'

'Come now, señor and señora. You must go now.'

'Juan, you must come and stay at our house tonight. I don't want you to stay alone in your house,' said Ines, as we walked away from the Casa de la Misericordia.

'I must go home,' I said. 'Just in case they examine Francisca and send her home.'

'Be realistic, Juan. They won't look at her tonight. They will assess her in the morning, at the earliest.'

I took up Inés's offer and went with her to her house to stay the night, picking up some of my things from our house on the way. Inés's father, the painter, had died of a heart attack about three years before, just after he had married his third wife. His second wife had died leaving him with four sons and Inés had taken it upon herself to look after them. All of her brothers and sisters contributed to running the family, including Juan's friend Baltasar who was by then twenty-three. It meant that her house was full of children and it had a consequential glow about it.

'I was totally dismayed at what Francisca said, Juan,' said Inés. 'What do you think about it all?'

'There is something wrong in her head,' I said. 'I don't understand it and I don't know whether it can be put right. I will see the doctor tomorrow. I cannot bear the thought of Francisca being in that awful place. It is a madhouse.' I choked a bit but managed not to cry.

I did not sleep at all that night. My mind was in utter turmoil. What was happening to Francisca? What would happen to our relationship if they would not release her? Would she forget about me or fail to recognise me? Would she be charged with the crime of arson against the church? Would she have to appear before the Inquisition? Could she be executed? The following morning, the ever helpful Inés offered to meet me at the asylum at ten o'clock, before meeting the doctor and seeing Francisca again. I was only too pleased not to have to go there alone and thanked her for her support. I then went from Inés's house straight to the palace to tell the Maestro what had happened to Francisca and to ask him for a few days off to try to sort out matters. Carlos Patiño, as I expected, was entirely sympathetic and told me to take as much time as I needed. I then went to the Casa de la Misericordia to meet Inés and to see Francisca and the doctor.

The wait to see the doctor was interminable. While in an outer room, we could hear the screams and banging of the inmates. It was horrendous, particularly as I was sure I recognised the source of one outburst as Francisca. Eventually, the doctor appeared and asked us to go into his office.

'Thank you for seeing us, doctor. Where is my wife Francisca de Abaunza?'

'First things first, Señor Hidalgo. I want to speak to you first. Who is this lady?'

'This is Inés del Mazo, a friend of our family and, in particular, of my wife.'

'I am going to get straight to the point, Señor Hidalgo. I want to be totally frank with you. Can you take that?'

'Yes. I think so. If the news is bad, I want to know. I don't want to be living under any illusions of Francisca getting better if that is not what will happen.'

'Good.' He paused momentarily. 'Your wife is a very sick lady and in her current state of mind she is dangerous. She is dangerous to herself and to the people of our town. She is suffering from a delusional illness in which she is directed by voices she can hear in her head. This is not an uncommon situation among the insane.'

'Was he calling Francisca insane?' I thought. This is just awful.

'This is why I have issued a certificate under which she will be detained in this asylum until I or other doctors believe it is safe for her to be released.'

'How long will that take?'

'Any amount of time you can name. It could be two years. It could be ten. It could be twenty. She may never get better and die here.'

I was on the verge of breaking into tears. 'But you are talking about my beloved wife, doctor. I cannot live without her.'

'You don't have to. The only form of treatment that is known to be successful for your wife's condition is contact with the outside world. She will improve only if you visit her regularly and her friends do likewise. If you just leave her here without that sort of contact she may even get worse. I understand from what she said that your son died recently. Is that true?'

'Yes, about two months ago.'

'Her condition has almost certainly been brought about by your son's death. It may get better during the mourning process but it just may not.'

'What are the chances either way?'

'One to four. One to be cured. Four to remain insane. She'll be in a room here with other women of a similar condition. She is in the room now. You can go to see her if you wish.'

'Thank you, doctor. I am grateful.'

The doctor walked us to a ward and paused outside to unlock the door. As he did so, we could hear the yells and shrieks of the women inside. Then, as he opened it, our noses were assaulted by a similar stench to the one we had experienced in the holding room the night before. As he let us in, he said he would be back to fetch us in fifteen minutes. We walked in. The room was lit by windows high in the walls so nothing could be seen of the outside, except the sky. One of the women was crouched over a chamber pot emptying her bowels and breaking wind at the same time. Another was sitting on a bed rocking to and fro. Another was beating her hands on a section of wall. Before I could take it all in, there was a shout from the far side of the room. 'Juan! Juan! You have come to see me!' It was Francisca. We started to cry and Inés, bless her soul, came to settle us.

'Don't forget Juan, you have only fifteen minutes.'

We stopped crying and wiped each other's tears away. I told Francisca that I loved her and always would and that neither I nor her friends would abandon her there. I would come to see her every day and her many friends would come, too. She took great comfort in that. I told her that it might take some little time for her to get better and she said that the doctor had already told her the same. She asked me to bring her some books and some writing paper the next time I came. She wanted to start writing poetry again. I had a complex of feelings. One was that I didn't want to leave Francisca but the other was that I hated seeing her here and wanted to go. It was clear that we could not stay. We kissed each other, we all cried and Inés and I left.

'We must put together a rota of our friends and arrange visitors,' said Inés. So that is what we did.

We included Francisca's father and Francisco but my mother just would not help. She was deeply shocked to the point of shame at what Francisca had done to 'her church'. 'What a thing to do? Disgraceful.' It took several minutes of explanation from Francisco and me to convince our mother that Francisca could not help herself and that she had to obey the voices in her head. 'I'm not going near that madhouse,' said our mother. 'Not for Francisca or anybody else.'

I saw Francisca every day and usually at least one of her friends came, too. On most occasions, she was perfectly coherent and spoke normally in every way. At other times she spoke of gods she had met and told us that she had been to Lydia to meet Diana and her nymphs. She said she was at the temple when the shepherd Eróstrato set alight to it. I often wished I had had nothing to do with that accursed opera. She spoke as if these characters and events were part of the real world. They were but only in Francisca's world. The mention of fire to her doctors did little to convince them she was improving so she remained in the Casa de la Misericordia. At least she was alive and well cared for. Sometimes Antona, who was still a nurse at the asylum, was assigned to Francisca's ward. Francisca was always happy when Antona was there and at first became quite upset when Antona had to work in another ward. She gradually became used to the other nurses, but Antona was always her favourite.

***

With the expected support of the Maestro, I was able to see Francisca as often as I wanted. For the first few weeks after she was detained in the asylum, I had great difficulty settling into my job at the palace. I could hardly bring myself to compose with Francisca constantly on my mind. However, I could not give in and had to continue my work as composer for the King, especially as some of the greatest playwrights of our time wanted me to write for them. When Pedro discovered what had happened to our Juan and its devastating effect on Francisca, he rapidly completed a magnificent *comedia* he called 'The Statue of Prometheus'. He said he had finished it quickly so that I could distract myself from my problems and devote my energies to writing the music. This was typical of the way Pedro could be expected to respond to the state in which he found me. The play turned out to be one of the most spectacular 'machine plays' ever produced at the Buen Retiro. Other dramatists wanted me to compose for them. They included Juan Vélez de Guevara who was for a time the Sergeant at Arms at the palace. Agustín de Salazar y Torres also wanted my services, as did Francisco de Avellaneda, both of whom were substantial playwrights of our age.

One of these new collaborators was Juan Bautista Diamante. Francisca had been in the asylum for three years when he first came to see me to ask for my help. He was strongly built, had long black hair, a black beard which covered most of his face and a large, overgrown moustache. I suppose he was in his mid-forties. In his youth he was so belligerent that he picked a fight with a man and killed him with a knife. The courts found him guilty of murder and sent him to prison. Juan Bautista's father paid a huge sum of money to the victim's widow, and the court freed him. The condition of release was that he joined the infantry. There he learnt all of the skills of a soldier including how to defend himself. When he was discharged from the army, he joined the priesthood and, while working as a priest, became a dramatist, writing some of the most brilliant plays of this century. What a transformation. He wrote more than seventy dramas, a number of which were performed before the King and were used for state celebrations in and around the palace. Juan Bautista wanted me to write the music for his *comedia* 'Alpheus and Arethusa'. While I wrote it, we became good friends but I always harboured a sense of uneasiness in his bulky and sinister presence. He had never threatened me but I always thought that, having killed one man in cold blood, he could be provoked into killing another.

'It will not be one of your operas, Señor Hidalgo,' he said, confidently and knowledgeably. 'However, over half of it is to be sung so it will be a *zarzuela*. I have indicated in the text what I want. There are solos and duets, choruses for four voices and some for eight. There is a group of musicians, and I want you to write parts for violins, guitars and two harps. You will see what I want when you read the play.'

I had never had such explicit instructions, not even from Pedro. 'When do you want it finished?'

'I have been commissioned to write it by the Constable of Castile. He wants it played at his wedding which had not even been arranged yet, so you have plenty of time. He won't even tell me the name of his betrothed which is a big secret.'

'It will be good to have such freedom. That means you'll get a job well done.'

'That's excellent, Señor Hidalgo. I'll pay you, of course.'

'Let me know as soon as you know the date of the Constable's wedding.'

***

I threw myself into writing the score for this play. I worked and reworked it and reworked it again. I wondered if I could somehow involve Francisca in the composing, as I had many times in the past when I would take pieces of music home and test them on her or Juan junior. I would have to choose my moment carefully. Sometimes she seemed to be the only sane one in her ward. While the other women were shouting or banging their poor bodies against the wall or running around naked, she would be quietly reading a book or writing some poetry. But there were those heartrending occasions when she seemed as mad as the others, if not worse.

I will never forget the time when Vitoria de Cuenca and I went to see her. It was our thirty-third wedding anniversary and Vitoria took in the most beautiful bouquet of flowers. As usual, the attendant unlocked the door of the ward and let us in. Francisca was stark naked and had smeared her beautiful body with her own excrement. She stank and the ward stank. I went up to kiss her but had to hold back. She had rubbed it over her face and I just could not bring myself to touch it with my lips.

'What have you done Francisca? Why have you done this? It is our wedding anniversary today and Vitoria has brought you some flowers.' I could not be angry but I was shocked and disappointed.

'It is my punishment, Juan. The voices in my head told me to cover myself in my own shit as a penance. It is for setting alight to San Ginés. There are all these contradictions, Juan. I don't understand. It was not my fault the church burnt down. Aura would have killed me if I hadn't set it alight.'

We had to clean her. As was the routine in the ward, we had to ask to be let out before we could ask for nursing assistance. We went to the door and knocked. A nurse put her head to the window to see what was wrong. It was Antona. I was so relieved. 'Juan, how can I help you? What is the matter?'

I explained to Antona that we were visiting Francisca and that she was badly in need of a wash. Antona went for some soap and water and all three of us washed the faeces off Francisca until she was totally clean. We then dried her and put some perfume on her body.

'Thank you. I feel human again now. I don't know why I did that. I feel so ashamed.' So, from being able to explain coherently, in terms of the voices in her head, why she had covered herself in her own excrement, she became totally perplexed as to why she had done it. That was one of my worst experiences in the Casa asylum.

I decided to go there to test out on Francisca some of the tunes I intended to use in 'Alpheus and Arethusa'. I went alone but took my harp, dragging it on its cart along the ground. The ward attendant at first was reluctant to let me in but spoke to Antona, who was then assigned to Francisca's ward. She thought it may be helpful to all the women in there to hear some music for the harp. It was one of those wonderful days when Francisca was completely coherent, properly dressed and seeming completely sane. I played some of the tunes and all six of the women came down to Francisca's area to listen. They started dancing with each other and humming and whistling to these new tunes. It was like a party. They all loved the music.

'You can see from the reaction of the women here that you've written some lovely music, Juan. This will be perfect for your new colleague,' she said, warmly and clearly.

I was satisfied with what I had produced for Juan Bautista Diamante and it was in good time for the wedding. The Constable of Castile was, after the King, the most powerful man in Madrid. He was the seventh Duke of Frias and the Count of Haro. He was in charge of the army when the King was absent or indisposed, was a member of the Council of War, the Council of State and was, for a time, Governor of the Spanish Netherlands, almost thirty years after the Cardinal Infante had held this post. So he was immensely influential. His bride was to be Maria Teresa de Benavides Dávila y Corella whose mother was the Countess of Consentayna and who was related to the royal family of Portugal. This was a timely marriage as it took place after the signing of the Treaty of Lisbon which, at a massive cost to Spain, granted Portugal its full independence. The marriage symbolised the change in relationship between our two countries which, while it had its times of suspicion, became one of greater mutual confidence. Almost all of the King's Court and government were present at the wedding. The Queen Regent Mariana attended as did her First Minister Nithard, who was, like the Queen, a native of Austria. The work was performed by the company of Antonio de Escamilla, who had been so closely involved in Celos. I played the harp and so did my brother Francisco. A wedding to remember.

***

After she had been detained in the asylum for nearly seven years, I was beginning to despair about Francisca ever coming home. I had never given up hope but had reconciled myself to the awful, heartrending possibility that we would never live together again. It was one of those days of harbouring these dire, negative thoughts that Inés came to see me and suggested that we go to see Francisca. Inés was quite excited and could not wait to tell me something.

'Juan, Juan! You must listen. I have had a dream.'

'We all have dreams, Inés. What was it about?'

'It was really important Juan. It was about Francisca being cured. Do you remember the medallion I gave her, that Innocent X gave my grandfather? I dreamt that you and I took the medallion to Francisca and that when she touched it, she became cured. The spirit of the dead Pope had cured her.'

I felt tired and listless that day but was still keen to try anything. 'That sounds so unreal to me. Anyway, let me find it, Inés, and we'll take it to the asylum. It must be worth a try.'

'In my dream we did not tell Francisca what we were doing with the medal but she becomes cured.'

I eventually found the medallion in Francisca's chest of drawers and we took it to the asylum. As usual, the attendant unlocked the door to let us in. Francisca was sound asleep on her bed so we stood next to her for a few minutes. She woke with a start. 'What are you two doing here? What a lovely surprise.' We started to chat to her as we always did and asked her how she was. Inés then showed her the medallion. I always said that it caught the sunlight shining through a window high up on the wall but Inés insisted that it glowed spontaneously as Francisca took it from Inés's hand.

'Good God, are you two trying to blind me or something?' she said, as the intense light shone in her eyes. From that precise moment, Francisca seemed different. We never again saw the intense stare that seemed to paralyse her. She seemed more relaxed and was always properly dressed. We never saw her parading naked again. Quite the opposite, she became quite modest and would never even use the chamber pot while we were in the ward. She spoke normally and lovingly about all of our family and friends. She often spoke of Juan junior, sadly but in a way that seemed to keep him in her life. In fact, she was cured. By the miracle of the medallion or by some strange coincidence she was cured.

Yet this was not the end of this story. The next step was to convince the doctors at the asylum in the Casa de la Misericordia. Eventually, they agreed and applied to the criminal court authorities for Francisca's release. This was because she had set alight to the church and that the doctors could therefore not, on their own authority, let her go free. The court said we could have Francisca home on two conditions. They were that I paid for the damage to San Ginés and that I would return her to the asylum if ever she said she could hear voices in her head. I duly paid the court 9,450 ducats, all of what our mother had given us for the sale of the love sleeve business and a little more in addition. I then went to fetch Francisca and brought her home.

It is impossible to express the joy and elation I felt as Francisca and I walked through the front door to our house in the Calle de la Madalena. It was wonderful to have her back home and we never seemed to stop smiling at each other. We thought of having one of our famous parties to celebrate but decided that we would introduce Francisca more gradually to her newly won freedom. She had been incarcerated for seven years and by the time of her release I was sixty-two and Francisca was fifty-nine. We were not young anymore. Still, we had not forgotten how to enjoy ourselves and we set about making up for seven years of lost time. Our friends in the town were equally overjoyed at Francisca's miraculous recovery. My mother suggested that we write to the authorities in the Vatican to suggest that Pope Innocent X should be canonised for the miracle performed on Francisca. Mainly to comply with our mother's wishes, I wrote to the Vatican but never did receive a reply.

We often spoke about our Juan who we felt must be sharing our joy at Francisca's recovery, wherever his soul was residing. We often speculated at how brilliant a lawyer or mathematician he would have been and convinced ourselves that his death was caused by some mysterious illness that the doctors of our town did not have the wherewithal to diagnose; or by an accidental overdose of a poisonous substance. We could not accept that he was the victim of a murder and there was no evidence to support that or that he had killed himself deliberately. Francisca was welcomed back to the soup kitchen of the Shod Carmen where she worked for many years more. She even served some of the unfortunate characters who were in the asylum with her and who were, by some act of mercy, also released. We frequently joined up with friends to go on horse rides and, but for the absence of our Juan, life seemed all but perfect again. We even attempted to repeat some our more youthful experiences of lovemaking which we enjoyed with varying degrees of success.

Then we were struck by another blow: the death of my beloved brother, Francisco. He complained of feeling ill when he returned from a visit to Valencia where he had been playing his harp in a theatre group. His skin became sore and broke out in black patches. He had terrible stomach cramps and could not stop vomiting. He had caught the plague, a viciously cruel disease that was sweeping across Europe in an epidemic. We were all devastated, not least his poor wife Juana Vélez. Just like Francisca and me, our mother suffered from having to bury her child. By then she was nearly ninety and somehow much more able to cope with the loss of Francisco than we were with the loss of Juan.

'By rights I shouldn't be here. I don't know how I have lived so long.'

'It's because you are so strong, Mamá, in body and in mind,' I said, just after the funeral. I remembered how bad she was after the simultaneous death of both of her own parents and thought to myself that that awful experience had hardened her to the passing of others, even of her own family.

Juana Vélez came to stay with Francisca and me for about two months after Francisco's death. It struck us as unfortunate that Francisco and Juana never had children. He would have made a great father and she a brilliant mother but that is how life worked out for them. Francisca persuaded Juana to help at the Shod Carmen's soup kitchen and this she did with great alacrity. It helped to take her mind off Francisco's passing. She was so enthusiastic about helping, she became a permanent member of the staff there.

I continued composing but felt with my advancing years it was becoming more and more difficult. The Royal Chapel asked me if I wanted to retire but I decided to carry on. I just loved composing and was flattered by the fact that even into my late sixties I was still in demand. Pedro and I continued collaborating. And I continued playing the harp, an activity which still gave me great joy.

The time came around for the second performance of 'Alpheus and Arethusa' which was to be in the palace before the King. It took place on the day I started to write this book. The shocking thing that happened was that, while playing the part of Arethusa, Marfisa del Pozo stripped off naked on the stage. Although her nudity won the approval of just about every male personage in the audience, stripping off at a public performance was a moderately serious crime. We waited for months for a summons either for Marfisa or Antonio de Escamilla to appear in court or before the Inquisition. Nothing happened, but Marfisa never stripped off naked in front of an audience again.

CHAPTER 29

Just before my beloved husband, Juan Hidalgo, died, I promised him that I would finish his book. You cannot finish something without knowing how incomplete it is, so before adding this final chapter, I read the whole of what he had written before he passed away. In the pages in which he describes the death of his father, Juan says that, however long you have loved someone and shared your life with them, you do not necessarily really know them. This applied to Juan. At least, this was the conclusion I reached, having read Juan's unfinished manuscript.

While he shared with me many of his experiences about his work and life at the palace, including his relationships with many others who worked there, many of whom became our closest friends, he did not tell me that he was a special agent for the King nor about the various functions he had to perform in that role. In particular, I did not know about the main reason for his visit to Rome, with Giulio Rospigliosi and Juan de Roxas Carrión, now some thirty-odd years ago. As I read about these things, I began to question the love that Juan always said he had for me. However, I concluded that there could be no doubt that he loved me. He did so from the very moment we met until the day he died. The intensity and selflessness of his love were amply shown to me, although I had difficulty appreciating it at the time, when I was detained in the asylum of the Casa de la Misericordia. There were also many other occasions.

I finally understood that he did not tell me about his work as a special agent for one simple reason: he had sworn under oath that he would not tell others. This made me wonder whether I might know anyone else who was a special agent. In particular, I remember waking up one morning well before dawn, in the winter after my husband Juan died, when I was struck with a question that hit me like a bolting horse. Was our son Juan killed because he was a special agent of the King? This question quickly became the most important thing in my being. It became branded into my flesh. I had to know the answer.

I decided to share this burning desire with Inés del Mazo. Before I did so, I felt I should tell her that I had read in Juan's book that her grandfather was also a special agent and that one of the reasons, if not the main one, for his second visit to Italy was to act as a spy for the King. I also told her that Juan de Pareja, her father's manservant, was a special agent. Inés was as surprised as I was and, to confirm what my husband was saying, I showed her the relevant passages in his manuscript. We talked about the issue several times.

'Francisca, if you want to know whether your son Juan was a special agent you will have to ask someone at the palace. That is the only action you can take.'

'Surely, they won't tell me,' I said. 'The very existence of these agents is almost certainly something that is secret. If so, they will tell me nothing.'

'You can but try, Francisca,' said Inés. 'You are in a strong position to ask the question. You have the evidence of Juan's manuscript which makes it clear that such a cadre existed and that many of the people we knew were special agents, including my grandfather. So you will be confronting them with the facts and they will have a job to deny them.'

Before I went to the palace, I thought a little about the possible consequences. The main one was that the palace might confiscate the manuscript of the book so I went there without it. This was still in the time when you could go to the palace and freely walk straight in and up to an inquiry desk. So I went inside and explained what I wanted. 'Never heard of such a thing,' said the official. 'Wait a minute.' The man left me standing at the desk for a full ten minutes. Eventually, he returned with another man who escorted me into an interview room and sat me down in front of him on the opposite side of a bare oak desk.

'Exactly what is it that you want to know, Señora Abaunza?'

I explained who my husband was and that up to the time of his death he was writing a book about his life and career in the Royal Chapel. I said that he had revealed in the manuscript of the book that he was a special agent for the King. He interrupted me at that point.

'Is the book a work of fact or fiction?'

'It is absolute fact. There are, of course, opinions that my husband expresses about various events and people. But the book is the true story of the life of Juan Hidalgo, harpist in the Royal Chapel and composer for the King.'

'I'm sorry, señora, but I still do not know what you want to know.'

'If you let me finish…'

'I'm sorry señora. Please continue.'

'Well, about fifteen years ago, our son died while he was a student at the University of Alcalá de Henares. He became more and more unwell over a period of three weeks or so and went home to his house in the Puerta Cerrada. His cleaning lady found him seriously ill. We called a doctor but he died within the hour. A post mortem was carried out on his body and it was apparent, although not certain, that he had been poisoned. It was probably arsenic, administered over a period of about a month. The judicial office investigated the case but no one was charged with his murder. What I have come to the palace to ask you is this. Was my son Juan Hidalgo a special agent for the King? If he was, that may in itself be a motive for someone killing him. I do not know. That is my question.'

'Señora, I shall have to look into this. I cannot comment on your question or give you a definitive answer today. You will have to return to the palace at a later date to see an official from another department. I can, however, make an appointment for you. Shall we say in two weeks' time to the day, and at the same time?'

I agreed to return to the palace at the time the man suggested and went straight back to Inés's house to tell her what the official had said.

'I am still shocked to find out that my grandfather was a special agent. I remember his visit to Italy. He went for two years and came back with a number of paintings and statues by various famous Italian artists and sculptors. I find it hard to believe that he had any other reason to go. But you have shown me what Juan has written in his book and it all fits in with what happened at the time.'

***

My husband loved composing and was flattered by the fact that even into his late sixties was still given plenty of work. He said he was not as good as he was when he was younger, but he also continued playing his harp, at the palace and even at public performances. He and Pedro continued collaborating right up to the time when Pedro passed away. Pedro succumbed to old age while writing a Corpus Christi play. Antonio de Solís, who was the playwright who nearly kissed Juan when Juan agreed to composing a score for him, was with his friend, Pedro, when Pedro died. 'He didn't say his last words, he sang them,' said de Solís. 'He was singing like a swan.' There were over three thousand of us in Pedro's funeral procession which was more of a celebration than a burial. Pedro insisted on being interred in an open coffin, so as to show the temporary nature of the human frame.

Maestro Carlos Patiño died before Juan and was succeeded at the Royal Chapel by Christóbal Gálan, also a composer, who was only a few years younger than Juan. As far as Juan was concerned, he and Juan had a good working relationship: he left Juan to do his composing and did not interfere. Both Juan and I were grateful to Maestro Patiño. He had supported Juan for over forty years and you cannot ask for more than that.

Many of our older friends and colleagues in the theatre and music also passed away along the road. As we became older we found ourselves attending more funerals than we cared to remember. But some of our colleagues survived well into old age. The two violinists, Juan de Roxas Carrión and Francisco de Guypúzcoa, who shared an office with Juan at the palace, were still working there into their seventies. 'We are so poor we just cannot afford to retire,' Juan de Roxas Carrión told me. 'It's just as well that we can continue working here.' Luis de As was taken ill and died two weeks after the second performance of 'Alpheus and Arethusa', so he never did discover whether there were any consequences to Marfisa del Pozo appearing naked on the stage. His poor widow, Angela, outlived him by many years.

The strangest of the funerals was that of Sebastian Alonso González del Águilla, who made the clavi-harp for the King. I remember that he told Juan and me that he wanted to be buried in the manner of an Egyptian pharaoh. His wish was granted. His relatives and friends built a small scale 'pyramid' on a piece of land he bought on the outskirts of Segovia and put all the possessions he had accumulated over the years in a chamber, deep below the ground. They then embalmed him and transformed his corpse into something akin to an Egyptian mummy. They buried him, with the full ceremony granted to a pharaoh, in another chamber in the pyramid which they closed up and sealed for posterity. Posterity arrived about two weeks later when the authorities heard of this extraordinary burial which, of course, was illegal. His body was exhumed and was given a proper burial in his parish church.

Several members of our family also survived into old age. Juan's mother not only lived longer than Francisco, she also survived Juan and lived to the incredible age of one hundred and eight. She was credited with being the oldest person in Madrid. We all said that it was her interest in the love sleeve business that gave her a new reason to live after Juan's father died. Aunt Catalina lived until she was well into her nineties and Juan and I often used to visit her or invited her to come to see us at our house in the Calle de la Madelena. She would always bring a bottle of wine around when she came for a meal. As she came in she would always say, 'I bought you this wine, Juan. This was the last bottle they had in the shop.' Yes, she uttered these exact words every time she came through the door. Aunt Catalina came to look quite ancient with a face so lined it looked like the bark of a lime tree but she was always positive, cheerful and grateful to me and Juan for giving her a meal. My father, too, lived a long life. After he threw out his second wife, he became friendly with Juan's mother. They could often be seen together in the markets or theatres of the town and clearly enjoyed each other's company.

The offspring of our friends are also well worthy of note. Baltasar del Mazo became a famous painter. He did not succeed in getting a job in the palace, which was his childhood wish, but became well known all over Europe for painting portraits of minor royalty and the nobility. He made a fortune from his many commissions. He did so well that he was able to pay cash for the house that Inés, his sister, rented for the family in the Calle de Olivar and gave it to her as a gesture of thanks for looking after him and his brothers and sisters after their mother, Francisca de Silva y Velázquez, died. Baltasar bought a beautiful house in the Calle de Santa Isabel, in the eastern part of Madrid. For reasons which were never entirely clear, he continued renting the house Juan junior lived in, in the Puerta Cerrada, which he moved into shortly after Juan junior died.

Agustín Arias de Soria became an outstanding tenor and he did succeed where Baltasar had failed in obtaining a job in the palace. He became one of the Queen Regent Mariana's favourite singers and worked with the Royal Chapel until he was offered a job in the opera in Milan. Antona, the nurse in the Casa de la Misericordia, was badly injured when one of the woman inmates in the asylum bit her neck. She almost bled to death. One of her male colleagues was able to staunch the flow and, probably as a result, she fell in love with the man and married him. Sadly, she died in childbirth five years later while giving birth to her second child who by good fortune survived the trauma.

Clara, Balthasar and Vitoria's daughter, had an altogether different future. She became one of the very few women playwrights in Madrid. She impressed the Duke of Anteayer so much that he gave her a huge stipend, quite sufficient to support her extravagant but productive lifestyle. When the Duke's wife died, prematurely at the age of about thirty, the Duke fell in love with Clara and married her. They emigrated to Mexico where he bought a huge banana plantation, tended by over 200 slaves. She became even more productive there and within five years had produced six children, including two pairs of twins, and had written four *comedias,* two of which were later performed in our town.

***

I kept my appointment at the palace and was escorted to the same room in which my previous meeting was held. I sat at the desk to await the arrival of an official who came in and sat opposite me.

'Thank you for coming to this meeting, Señora Abaunza,' he said, coldly and formally. 'I have the authority of one of our councils to tell you the following. We understand that your husband, who was employed at the palace until the time of his death and in the name of whom you receive a pension, has written a book which refers to the existence of a group of servants which he calls "special agents". He indicates that he was such an agent, as were others to whom he refers in his book. He gives a number of details of the work and functions of these special agents. Is that correct?'

'Yes,' I said, equally coolly. 'All of that is correct.'

'The question you are addressing to the palace is whether or not your son, Juan, was also such an agent. You wish to know that because you believe it may help you to understand the circumstances and possible cause of your son's death.'

'That is correct,' I said.

'Well, señora. I am sorry but I am going to disappoint you. The head of the relevant council has decreed that I cannot confirm or deny the existence of this group of officials to which you refer. He has, furthermore, instructed me to inform you that it would be an offence against the state to publish your husband's book. This is because it would inevitably create unnecessary speculation about the existence of these "special agents".'

'Do you mean that the book cannot be printed?'

'Just that. It would be an offence to do so.'

I could not wait to share my disappointment with Inés.

'That is preposterous,' she said. 'Can you appeal?'

'I'm not sure I want to,' I said. 'In many ways I wish Juan to be known as a harpist and composer, not as an author.'

'What are you going to do?' asked Inés.

'I am going to give the manuscript to your young brother Baltasar in the hope that it may be published sometime. I suggest he hides it in the basement of the house in the Puerta Cerrada. There is a secret place there which we used many years ago to hide Juan's mother's inheritance. I will show him where it is.'

Baltasar hid Juan's manuscript in the secret place. The book was never published, at least, not in my lifetime.

***

My husband, Juan Hidalgo, died on 30 March 1685. He told me not to dwell on his death in these paragraphs, but I can say that he was buried the following day in the church of San Ginés, next to our son. I love them both.